THE
HEART
BROKE
IN

THE HEART BROKE IN

JAMES MEEK

CANONGATE
Edinburgh · London

Published in Great Britain in 2012 by
Canongate Books Ltd, 14 High Street, Edinburgh EH1 1TE

www.canongate.tv

1

British Library Cataloguing-in-Publication Data
A catalogue record for this book is available on
request from the British Library

ISBN 978 0 85786 290 7
Export ISBN 978 0 85786 291 4

Typeset in Perpetua by Palimpsest Book Production Ltd,
Falkirk, Stirlingshire

Printed and bound in Great Britain by CPI Group (UK) Ltd, Croydon CR0 4YY

To marry, to start a family, to accept all the children that come, and to help them in this insecure world, is the best that a man can do.

Franz Kafka (who never got around to it)

PART ONE

1

The story doing the rounds at Ritchie Shepherd's production company was accurate when it appeared inside the staff's heads, when they hardly sensed it, let alone spoke it. It was like a faint stink, clear enough to notice, too trivial to mention. All through *Teen Makeover*'s autumn and spring seasons, when they clustered round Ritchie, asking him questions they already knew the answers to, cadging compliments and begging him to give their enemies a telling-off, they watched him. They saw he wasn't as funny as before. Was he keeping his jokes for someone else? He moved in a weird way now, they thought. He walked with an awkward bounce, too eager, as if he reckoned something had given him extra energy, or made him younger.

As long as the rumour was unspoken, the hearts of the staff ached. The rumour was this: that after a long peace Ritchie was, once again, cheating on his wife Karin, this time with an under-age girl. They felt sorry for Ritchie's family, but what if the damage went further, to the men and women on the company payroll? They sensed a personal threat. Scandal spread from the first carrier. Everybody liked Ritchie, but they were confident that he was selfish enough to infect them all. The production company offices were intoxicated by nervousness and suspicion. When twin fourteen-year-old girls showed up one day without an accompanying parent and asked for Ritchie, his PA Paula got up too suddenly from behind her desk, caught the trailing edge of a printed email with her thigh and upended a cup of coffee across her skirt. The chief lighting technician wrote off a fresnel worth two thousand pounds. He dropped it from the bridge when he saw Ritchie smile and touch the elbow of a lanky year ten in a short dress. 'She had womanly curves earlier than most,' is what the gaffer would have said in his defence, if he hadn't been afraid to hex them all, and he only yelled 'Butterfingers!' while the people down below were jumping clear of chips of lens skittering across the floor. When the script editor saw Ritchie talking to a group of pert-bottomed schoolgirls in leotards she strode over and inter-rupted him in mid-sentence. She realised, as soon as she did it, that she was making a fool of herself. The girls' teachers were there. The ache of fear in her heart had made her do it.

The ache could only be soothed by being put into words. The production team needed an utterance to lift the dread from their chests, and when the rumour eventually found its spoken form, it relieved them so completely that they believed it. Much better that Ritchie's ten-year marriage to Karin should break up and that he should lose custody of his son and daughter over the pretty but older-than-twenty-one new presenter Lina Riggs than that the boss should be doing something illegal and shameful, something that would stain them all with the indelible dye of an unspeakable word. Without anyone noticing the shift, 'I wonder if' and 'I bet' and 'You don't suppose' changed to 'I heard' and 'I've got a juicy one' and 'I know who Ritchie's shagging.' Believing soothed them all.

Ritchie found that whenever he went near Riggsy a stupid smile appeared on his employees' faces. He didn't know how happy he was making them by encouraging them to believe he was betraying his family with a legal adult. They didn't know that their rumour had become wrong as soon as it was said out loud, and that the original rumour, the ache of fear in their hearts, was true. They didn't know that Ritchie was seeing a not-quite-sixteen-year-old girl he'd met when she appeared on *Teen Makeover* the previous season. He saw Nicole once a week. It was his intention to enjoy it for as long as he felt like it, then end it tenderly. Nicole would, he imagined, be moved that he should voluntarily give her up. It would be soon, and nobody would have found out. How could they? The two of them were careful, and London was a wild forest of red brick and roof tiles, where maps only reminded you how little you knew.

2

Ritchie woke in a soft chair in a wide, bright space. An old vinyl record spun and crackled and he heard the sound of Ruby, Dan and Karin in the orchard, three storeys below. Far away something clunked against the sides of a wooden box.

A bib of hot sunlight from the south-facing window lay on his frayed yellow t-shirt, spreading delicious warmth across his chest. The nap left him refreshed and content. His wife and children were close enough for him to hear that they were happy, far enough away to not disturb him.

Facing him, here on the mansard floor, was a ladder on a dolly and a wall lined to the rafters with shelves of records. Ritchie's study had space to ride a bicycle in, but he didn't have a bicycle up here; he had an adult tricycle. The tyres would hum on the waxed oak floorboards as he built up speed, dodging the stairwell that pierced the centre of the room, past the cabinets with his collection of British war comics, past the desk and the chill cabinet where he kept his beer and puddings, past the washstand that had been a Victorian church font and the toilet cubicle in an old red phone box with blacked out windows, to the guitar case. Inside the guitar case was one of two steel-stringed acoustic guitars Karin had commissioned for his fortieth birthday out of spruce and walnut, inlaid with their names in mother-of-pearl (the other was hers); and inside the guitar a secret thing was hidden, the mobile phone he used to call Nicole.

He got up and looked down through the window. Karin and the children were gathering fruit in the orchard. Their shining hair and foreshortened limbs bobbed in and out of the shade. He could hear that they were talking but the glass muffled the words into fuzzy, friendly unsignificances. He walked to his desk, opened the chill cabinet and took an individual chocolate pudding serving from the stacks inside. He favoured a brand called ChocPot, which came with its own wooden spoon attached, so he didn't have to hunt for one. He flipped off the lid, put down the pot and picked up his BlackBerry. He shovelled chocolate goo into his mouth with his right hand and scrolled through his emails with his left thumb. A dollop of pudding fell and landed on the shelf of his belly. He put the BlackBerry down, scraped most of the spill off with his index finger, raised the quivering dod to his lips, slurped the finger clean and walked to the font. Without taking the t-shirt off he held it under the running tap with both hands and rubbed till the brown stain almost disappeared. He wrung the wet patch out.

A desire to call Nicole, to catch her alone at home, danced in the pit of his stomach. He strode to the guitar case, flipped the catches and opened it. The guitar wasn't there.

Ritchie's palm and fingers pressed against the blue plush lining of the case. His mouth hung open.

He turned and ran to the stairs, clenching his toes to stop his old flip-flops flying off. He had six flights of stairs to go down without breaking his neck before the orchard was in reach: three storeys, five changes of direction. His hands clawed for purchase on the football-sized oak globes, varnished and polished to a high gloss, capping the banister on each landing. He lost his grip, slid off the step, hurtled into the wall, landed on his backside, got up and ran on, panting. *I get out of breath when I make love to Nicole*, he thought; *might it bother her?* Amid the clatter of his feet and the pounding of his heart he replayed the sound he'd heard when he woke up, the object knocking against the sides of a wooden box. If curious hands groped inside the guitar, why was a mobile phone there? He'd failed to prepare an important lie.

He reached the foot of the stairs, loped along the hall towards the kitchen and thanked God that the garden door was open. He got to within two strides of the threshold and felt something slither over his thighs. His shorts fell down around his shins. He fell and hit his knee against the kitchen flagstones. The cold slate pressed rudely against his bare hams. He got up, hoisted the shorts around his waist, tightened and knotted the drawstring and limped on into the garden.

A gentle English heat rolled over him and he squinted in the brightness. A wood pigeon cooed from the yew tree. Karin, her back to Ritchie, stretched towards a high branch, making the tree snap and rustle as she pulled yellow plums off it. The hem of her muslin skirt climbed up her brown calves and one of the straps of her top fell off her shoulder. There was a scent of grass where the sun heated the juice from the stems his family had crushed with their bare feet. Ritchie was sorry he was meeting his teenage girlfriend later. He wished he could stay at home with his wife and children. Dan ran from trunk to trunk holding Ritchie's guitar like a weapon, dropping to a crouch, aiming the guitar neck, lining up the sights. Ruby was heaping fruit. She saw her father and stood up.

'Look at Daddy!' she said. She twisted her little torso round to Karin and back and laughed.

Dan stood up, afraid. 'Give me the guitar,' said Ritchie. Dan dropped it on the grass and ran over to stand by his mother. Ritchie picked the guitar up by the neck, letting it swing as he raised it. There was nothing inside. He glanced down at the long grass. The phone could have fallen out, or one of his family could have removed it. The phone contained dozens of messages from Nicole so obscene that he hadn't been able to bring himself to delete them.

'I don't remember you asking if you could come into Daddy's study,' said Ritchie.

'You were asleep,' said Dan. He grabbed a fold of Karin's skirt and looked up at her.

'Mummy, Daddy's bleeding!' said Ruby. 'And he's breathing funny.'

Karin looked down at Dan and caressed his head. 'I don't see why you shouldn't borrow Daddy's guitar,' she said to her son. 'He never plays it.'

'Don't do that,' said Ritchie. Karin looked at him, and Dan looked, too. They shared a cool, expectant expression, like two doctors he'd interrupted while they discussed his case. 'Don't talk about me with Dan as if I'm not here. You're wrong, by the way. I play it all the time.' He raised the guitar and saw *Ritchie* in bright mirror writing race across Karin and Dan, reflected off the mother-of-pearl inlay, and each lift up their hands to cover their eyes as his name passed over their faces.

'Look at it,' said Karin. 'The two top strings are broken and the others are miles out of tune.'

'Mum, Daddy's bleeding!' shouted Ruby again, running over

and tugging the other side of her skirt. Ruby was the one who cared for him without hesitation, not out of duty, just because she did, Ritchie was sure. She was six, and he knew she would always feel this way towards him, whatever her age. He'd made a dangerous mistake in being angry with Dan, he saw, since he didn't know where the phone was, yet Dan or Karin – or both! – might know, and were choosing their moment to confront him. He needed to regain control. He didn't think of it as control, because his way of controlling seemed so benign: kindness, generosity. It hadn't occurred to him that striving for a monopoly on generosity was the chief characteristic of a despot.

'What happened to your leg?' said Karin.

'I slipped on the tiles. Dan, come on, show me what you can play.' He held the guitar out towards his son.

'I don't want to play anything,' said Dan, and quick as a trout shot away through the orchard, disappearing beyond the yew tree on the far side.

'Mum, can I put some leaves on Daddy's leg to stop it bleeding?' said Ruby.

'If Daddy lets you, darling.' She studied Ritchie. Her eyes ran over the blood, the frayed clothes, the stained paunch and the bristly chin.

He was afraid Karin didn't love him, which would be a catastrophe, because he loved her, and he loved his children, and if she didn't love him, it would destroy the pleasure he took in cheating on her, and feeling virtuous when he returned to her, full of love.

'Help us pick the plums now you're here,' said Karin. She turned her back to him and went on gathering fruit.

Ritchie put the guitar down, folded his arms and walked

in careful circles, stroking the grass with his toes, humming a song. He bent his head and watched for a hint of silver, glancing up every few seconds to make sure Karin wasn't looking.

Ruby came to him with a bunch of greenery. 'Mum, Dad's been eating chocolate pudding,' she said. 'Why can't we have some?'

'It's bad for you, darling,' said Karin, without turning round. 'It's only for a treat.'

'Why does Daddy get to have treats and we can't?'

'Daddy knows how to treat himself.'

Ritchie saw an opportunity. 'Let's all have chocolate pudding,' he said. 'Once we've harvested the plums.' He thought Karin would like the word 'harvested'. It sounded as if the family were doing something real together, bound to the countryside and the seasons.

Ruby kneeled in the grass next to her father and began to stick leaves onto the congealing blood on his leg. She frowned with concentration. It reminded Ritchie of the expression on Nicole's face when she performed a certain act. He winced. 'Ruby sweetheart, that's much better,' he said. 'Go and find Daddy a nice plum to eat.'

'I've got one,' said Ruby. She reached into the front pocket of her denim dress and handed him a hard little green plum. He took it and rolled it around on his palm.

'Thanks, darling, but it's not ripe yet,' he said.

'Eat it!' said Ruby. She laughed. 'Go on! You have to eat it!'

'I thought you liked the unripe ones,' said Karin. She walked towards him. The muscles on her right forearm stood out under her brown, grained skin from the weight of the bucket full of fruit she was carrying.

Ritchie stood up. He bit into the taut skin of the plum, gnawed off a sliver of astringent flesh and chewed it.

'Perfect,' he said. He forced himself not to stretch his mouth wide and spit the fruit out.

3

Ritchie found his son lying by the yew. He was on his front, propped up on his elbows, his bare lower legs kicking into the cool blades of unmown grass in the shadow of the tree's thick branches and his head and body in the sunlight. He had a device in his hands. Ritchie began to run.

When he got closer he saw Dan wasn't reading Nicole's filthy provocations. He was playing a game on his Nintendo. Ritchie sat cross-legged on the ground a few feet away. Dan wasn't going to look up until Ritchie spoke. His red lips were held in a plump wet pout. He'd been lying there, waiting to be looked for. Ritchie wondered if he'd had such chubby arms at Dan's age. Did the boy need a trainer?

'You don't like people going into your room without asking,' Ritchie said.

'It's not the same. I've got secret projects,' said Dan.

'Well, maybe I've got secret projects too.' As soon as Ritchie said this he knew it was the wrong thing to say.

'What secret projects?' said Dan, looking at Ritchie with such a Karin-like expression of curiosity that Ritchie glanced round to see if his wife had crept up on them.

Ritchie leaned closer to Dan and lowered his voice so that Dan looked up anxiously when Ritchie started to speak.

'You don't want anyone bursting into your room and seeing you without your clothes on,' he said.

Dan's shoulders jumped up in a spasm of embarrassed laughter and he hid his face behind his Nintendo. 'I don't mind!' he said. His blue eyes looked over the top of the gadget and his grinning cheeks bulged out on either side.

'Well, I do!' said Ritchie, giving Dan a soft punch on the shoulder. 'I don't want you coming in and seeing me without my clothes on!' Dan rolled over on his back, laughing, making sounds of disgust and sticking out his tongue. *He's a good boy*, Ritchie thought. *He's going to be fine.* He had wondered whether Dan was being bullied at school, but there was a man in him, even if it was going to cost a packet to bring it out. Ritchie asked Dan if there was anything he wanted. Dan stopped laughing and lay quietly on the grass, with his face turned away from Ritchie, listening and blinking.

'Would you like a guitar of your own?' asked Ritchie.

'I've already got one,' said Dan.

Ritchie remembered the child-sized electric guitar Dan never played and the drum kit he didn't touch.

'Why did you want Daddy's guitar, Danny love?' said Ritchie. 'What's wrong with yours?'

Dan turned his face further away and sniffed and Ritchie saw tears on his cheeks. Ritchie didn't understand. He laid his hand on Dan's shoulder and asked him what the matter was.

'Nothing,' said Dan. 'You don't care. You don't care about me and Ruby.'

'How can you say that?' said Ritchie. 'Don't you know how important it is to me to be a good father to you? Have you any idea what it was like for me growing up without . . .'

'I know,' said Dan.

'You just made an augmented fourth there. I *knoooow*. La *laaaaa*.'

Dan was sitting up, watching him and listening without crying or smiling, a half-familiar expression of slyness on his face. *Perhaps that's who he really is, perhaps he is the school bully, the boss of the playground, the one the other children fear*, Ritchie thought with sudden hope.

'If you made so much money without a father,' said Dan, 'why is it better for me to have one?'

'What a terrible thing to say!' said Ritchie slowly, trying to decide how he felt about it. Different paths forked out from what his son had just told him, and he could follow any fork, and still be Ritchie. On one path, he yelled at his son that he was a heartless, ungrateful little brat. On another, he said nothing, stared coldly at Dan, turned round, walked back to the house – ignoring any appeals for forgiveness – and shunned his family for the rest of the day. The third fork would see him shaking his head, laughing softly, running his hand through Dan's thick fair hair and telling him he was a clever chap.

This was the way he chose. He reached out his hand for the top of his son's head, but at that moment Karin called Dan's name from the far side of the orchard. Dan got up so quickly that Ritchie's hand brushed his ear instead. Dan glanced at his father, confused by the awkward touch, and a little frightened, as if he thought he'd accidentally avoided a blow, not a caress.

'Shall we go on the swing?' said Ritchie.

'Mum's calling me,' said Dan. 'I'm too old for the swing.'

Ruby came galloping towards them, laughing, and Ritchie caught her under her arms and lifted her up, holding her high so that her head blocked out the sun. He weighed her precious squirming density. Chaotic strands of hair fell over her face and Ritchie savoured the wholeness of her attention. 'Shall we go on the swing?' he said, and she nodded, and without looking at Dan Ritchie put Ruby down, took her hand and walked with her to where the rope swing hung from the branch of an old chestnut tree.

He pushed Ruby on the swing and decided he would have a shot. Ruby told him he couldn't, he was too fat, and while he told her not to be rude, he wondered whether it would take his weight. He sat down carefully on the length of wood and heard the branch creak. Dan and Karin were coming towards them. He shoved off with his heels, let go of the ground and swung to and fro. The creaking of the branch became louder. It wasn't so much the fear of the branch breaking as his sense that the tree was in pain that made him stop and step off the swing when Dan and Karin came up.

The moment his feet were safely on the turf, as if some goblin up in the branches had slipped the knot, the swing tumbled onto the grass and the rope fell on top of it with an angry slap. Ruby yelped and the others drew in breath and began to laugh. Ritchie caught Karin's eye and smiled. It seemed to him that this chance moment of small fear had snapped the family neatly together. He almost heard the click.

4

In the bathroom Ritchie took off his filthy t-shirt and shorts and showered. He washed, conditioned and dried his hair and fixed it with oil. He shaved, applied moisturiser and scented lotion from a bottle marked *après-rasage*, plucked wild hairs from his nostrils, ears and eyebrows, cleaned his teeth, flossed and rinsed his mouth with Listerine and spent half an hour choosing a shirt.

Karin had already caught him cheating twice, once just before the children were born, and once just after. 'If you do it again,' she told him, 'I'll divorce you, see you don't get custody, and take you for every penny.'

The idea of being stripped of what he had was frightening, but it was hard for him to imagine. The moment of being exposed seemed worse than the consequences. He'd discovered that he felt no shame about cheating on Karin until she found out. It was the great discovery of his adult life, greater than the discovery that he was a good businessman, or that he was making more money than contemporaries who were more talented musicians. His conscience only troubled him when somebody pointed out that he had one, and that it was bound to trouble him. As long as this didn't happen, he was a man doing his best to be good to two women who had nothing in common and never needed to meet. He loved his wife; he would never leave her. Apart from Ruby and Dan, Karin's happiness was more important to him than anything. That was why he would do whatever he could to protect her from the knowledge that he was having sex with someone else.

Ritchie took the clothes and went to dress in the room where Karin kept her wardrobe. It had better mirrors, and it was closer to the main staircase. If Karin came looking for a row, and the door was left open, it would force her to keep her voice down to prevent the children hearing. The disadvantage was that he had to be in the room with the big photograph of young Karin covering the whole of one wall. It had been taken when she was nineteen and he was twenty-one and the band's hit had charted in London, New York and Tokyo. One night that year in North Shields, from the window of a limousine stopped at red, Ritchie had watched a chain of girls marching arm-in-arm down the centre of a wet street, singing his and Karin's song, their coats open and the wind driving the rain onto their faces and low-cut frocks till their cheeks and throats shone.

In the photograph Karin was on a park bench at night. She was wearing short boots, a white chiffon scarf and a white bra and knickers. She sprawled on the bench with her elbows hooked on the back and her forearms hanging down, a cigarette in one hand, her legs open. A half-empty litre of vodka stood on the bench beside her. Her skin was bone-white in the flash although the resolution was so good that it was possible to make out the goose pimples and fine hairs on her limbs. Those were the days she was filling her body with poisons, not, as the newspapers said, because she hated herself, but because she loved herself, and her body's resistance to all those poisons was the exact measure of how indestructibly young and beautiful she felt she was.

The illusion of spontaneity was spoiled by the lacquered golden waves of Karin's hair and the artful black outline of her eyes, but Ritchie knew it wasn't an illusion. He'd been there in the park for the shoot. Karin had pulled off her dress and left it lying on the frosty leaves on the edge of the park road because she wanted to. The stylist had raised her hand to stop her and realised it was pointless. Ritchie knew that the missing half of vodka had gone into Karin. Halfway through she swigged from the bottle, wiped her mouth with the back of her hand, and as the make-up girl was moving in to rescue her face, let her head loll down into her chest, coughed, laughed, said 'I'm taking this off,' stood up and unzipped the dress. Ritchie saw then that his future wife was wilder than he was.

It seemed to Ritchie now that his wife had deceived him. She'd allowed him to think that no matter how bad he was she was bound to be worse. He'd designed his future as the straight one to her wild woman of rock-ness. But while he was jerking his hips to the crowd and spitting lyrics into a mike, wondering about rates of return on offshore deposits, it turned out she was thinking about children; she was thinking about it even as she gouged lumps out of the air with a hard pick on the guitar strings, singing in deadly harmony with him and making the speaker stacks tremble. Ritchie hadn't changed; she had. Years ago the virtue began to peep out from behind her hellraising disguise, and in a short time, Ritchie found himself watching helplessly as his wife's moral platform rose from the depths, shot past his own, and continued rising until she stood high above him. She didn't so much give up coke, cocktails, sleeping with boys and girls she liked and cigarettes as kick them off easily, like loose old shoes. 'Let's move to the country,' she said, and they bought a house in Hampshire. She stood by him, beautiful, talented, funny, loving, his alone, the mother of his children, and he was dismayed.

Karin came into the room and smiled at him in a way that Ritchie took to mean 'Let's not talk, shall we?' She opened one of the wardrobes and began to leaf through her old dresses. The hangers clicked on the clothes rail and Ritchie felt the wordlessness inflating until it pressed against the sides of the room. Karin took a short dress sewn with cobalt-blue sequins and another covered in black beads and threw them on the bed. She hauled out a cardboard box, dug in it and emptied it on the floor. Dyed feathers, sequinned gloves and hats of metallicised raffia slid out and spilled across the varnished floorboards. She knelt down and hunted among her old treasures.

'Are you going out?' said Ritchie. Karin shook her head without looking up. She unwound a fake jade necklace from a gold plastic tiara set with blue plastic stones and tossed the tiara onto the bed.

'I promised to find dressing-up clothes for Ruby. Her friend Deni's coming for a play date,' she said. 'I have to make supper for them. I might have time to make a few calls afterwards before Deni's mother comes to pick her up and I have to listen to her troubles. Once that's done Dan and Ruby'll need putting to bed and reading to sleep. I don't think I'll be going out.'

It came into Ritchie's mind, as it always did when his wife reminded him how her life was given over to Dan and Ruby, to ask Karin why she needed to spend so much time looking after the children when they paid Milena to do it. He didn't ask the question any more, because he couldn't argue with Karin's answer, that she cared too much about Dan and Ruby to want them to be brought up by somebody else. When Karin said this, Ritchie believed it; why not? He loved them too. But even as he was thinking *Yes, of course, because she loves them*, a parallel thought came to him: that it was part of Karin's long game of superiority and reproach. It was ingenious. She made herself look like the better parent, while depriving him of his great strength in the family, his generosity, his power to see his family's needs and wants and open his wallet to satisfy them. In the beginning, these two ideas of Karin — as a loving mother, and as a devious partner — floated in Ritchie's head together, with the first having more substance. But the idea of Karin as a loving mother was so obvious and simple that it was not very interesting, whereas the idea of devious Karin was contentious and intriguing and called for Ritchie's intelligence to be brought to bear. So he left the idea of the loving mother Karin alone, and kept turning the idea of the devious Karin over, examining and testing it, until it seemed a natural part of his thinking. He took comfort from the notion of a cunning, calculating Karin. To Ritchie it signified that her wild old self wasn't lost.

Karin put the rest of the props and finery back in the box and stowed it in the wardrobe. Ritchie's eyes flicked to the arrogant smile of young Karin spread across the wall. The Karin of twenty years later followed his eyes. She twisted her head and neck round and up and looked at the flat expanse of her immortal Then.

'She gets less like me every day,' she said.

'Do you mind that?' said Ritchie.

'You do.' Karin pinched the back of her hand and let it go. A ridge lingered for a moment before it smoothed itself. 'It's only skin,' she said. 'It's not a deviation from the essential me. If there was an afterlife I wouldn't want to hang out with the twenty-year-old you, I'm afraid.'

'It didn't seem like the real you then, either.' Ritchie went over to the wall and stroked the little pouch between young Karin's thighs with his index finger. He hadn't been able to help imagining a fantastical secret in there that he couldn't reach, no matter how he touched.

'Even then you had a porn mind. You can be so cold,' said Karin.

'What is it? What's the matter? I don't understand.'

'You never do.'

'Everybody in this family says I don't understand, but nobody in this family knows how to explain anything. Like Dan today. What does he need to take my guitar for when we already bought him one?'

'Because it's your guitar. He doesn't want a guitar of his own, he wants your guitar. He wants to be on the show. He wants to be part of that world. The kids at school are always saying to him, if it's your Dad's show, why doesn't he put you on it?'

'He hasn't asked for a long time,' said Ritchie.

'You told him he was too young.'

'He is.'

'And told him what the word "nepotism" meant.'

'Well!'

'And kept telling him how your dad wasn't around to help you.'

'Why is it so uninteresting for Dan to have a grandfather who was murdered? If I had a grandfather who was murdered I'd think it was cool. I'd go on about it all the time.'

'You do go on about it all the time. And your father wasn't murdered. He was executed. It was a war. He was a soldier.'

'If that was a war,' said Ritchie, 'everything's a war.'

Two hours later, when he was leaving for London, Karin asked why work so often cut into his weekend. 'You're not fucking some girl, I hope?' she said.

Ritchie smiled. 'You know if I don't sit in on these Sunday night meetings nobody cracks the whip. There's no girl,' he said. 'I promised not to do that any more, and I won't. You have to trust me.'

It bothered Ritchie that people lied to protect themselves. He only lied to protect his family. He loved the way a handful of false words could insulate his wife, his children and his peaceful, prosperous future with them in this house from the things he did in London with Nicole.

'I can hardly see you any more,' said Karin.

'You see me all the time,' said Ritchie. He knew that she had meant something different but he hoped that deliberately misunderstanding her would prevent her telling him what it was. He smiled timidly and his face took on a yearning look.

'Be careful,' said Karin. 'If I find out you've been lying, the lawyers will be all over this place like . . .' the left corner of her mouth turned up in a way that was dear to Ritchie '. . . Vikings in a monastery.'

'There's nothing to worry about,' said Ritchie. 'I'm not cheating on you.' *Delicate*, he thought, *economical*: fewer than a hundred false words in the day, and he kept his family safe.

5

For his liaisons with Nicole, Ritchie had bought a flat in a cul-de-sac in Limehouse, on the fifth floor of a new block. He found a parking space nearby and when he pressed the lock button on the fob and the car lights flashed out it struck him as coarse, like an invitation to passers-by to join him for dirty games upstairs. But there never were passers-by. At night, windows were lit, and there were signs of habitation. Once he saw a cactus on a windowsill where there hadn't been a cactus the previous week. But he hadn't seen another human being on foot since the estate agent who showed it to him.

He'd told Karin he needed a crash pad for late working nights and early starts. It'd cost him. Yet the ceilings of the flats were low, the rooms cramped and the windows small. A metal grille jutted out a few inches from the largest window. The estate agent called it a *Juliet balcony*. It looked like bars designed to defend the block against the mob.

He'd been grinding coffee beans and making espressos on a stove-top coffee maker in the flat for months, but the smell refused to take, and the place still stank of newness when he opened the door. He saw Nicole's bare foot and ankle, with its gold chain, disappear around the corner at the end of the hall. She liked to play when he arrived. She would scurry through the flat like a kitten, her feet pattering fast, then going quiet. He'd hear her singing, or the faint jingle of her bangles. Sometimes he walked through the motion of a chase, would find her on the bed or in the kitchen, leaning on the counter with her hands behind her back, one bare knee raised to his hand, looking into his eyes while he pushed her skirt up.

He stood in the hall, listening to Nicole banging doors and drawers. The TV was on, quietly, though he recognised the show from the bleating vowels of the Irish host, cutting through the audience laughter.

I should end it now, thought Ritchie. The alien quality of her presence inside his property thrilled, scared and irritated him as it had in the first place. He remembered the moment when his mind swung from the thought that he couldn't have her to the thought that she was his to have.

Nicole's eyes reminded Ritchie of a scholarship boy at his school called Barney Parks. Ritchie and Jules and Randeep couldn't let Barney Parks go past when they saw him in a hand-me-down blazer God knows how many sizes too big. Kudos to Barney Parks for getting into a school his parents couldn't afford but he had to be shown what it meant to look ridiculous in public. The teachers gave their lessons and the boys gave theirs. They stopped him and Ritchie and Randeep held him while Jules got behind him, lifted up his blazer and began pushing his own arms into the sleeves to show that there was room in there for two boys. The trouble with doing that sort of thing was, if the victim didn't laugh it off, it made Ritchie feel bad, and he was sure he was good, so it couldn't be his fault; it seemed to him that world was full of selfish victims who deserved a little bullying in order to teach them to take their punishment more gracefully.

Barney Parks didn't laugh it off. Barney Parks struggled. He was wiry, and Ritchie had to grip tightly. The defiance in Barney Parks' steady, dark eyes, wet with tears held back, made the blood in Ritchie surge and his face burn. It wasn't really defiance. Barney Parks wanted them to do this to him. Barney Parks never spoke, just locked his eyes on Ritchie's; his gaze declared that he wanted to be attacked, because the more urgently they wrestled him, the stronger they would see he was; that they could make him bend, and twist, even cry out in the end, but that there was a core of resistance and self in him they were seeking without knowing it, and he would never let them get there. This would make them keep coming back, and this was what Barney Parks wanted. Ritchie had begun breathing heavily, let go of Barney Parks, drawn back his right fist, punched Barney Parks in the face and run away. Ritchie was twelve. Barney Parks would have been nine. With Nicole, Ritchie felt the same fake struggle, the same fake defiance, but he didn't have to punch her. He knew what to do, and how to look at her.

Ritchie moved forward. He called Nicole's name. His stomach hurt. *I shouldn't have eaten the plum*, he thought. Nicole came out and walked towards him. Her eyes were distant. She looked at him as if she didn't know him, as girls her age who didn't know who he was would look at him when they caught him staring. Over her jeans and t-shirt she was wearing the light linen coat he'd bought her. He lifted his hands towards her and she walked past him, put her hand on the knob of the door latch, twisted it, opened the door an inch and turned her head back to him. Now he wanted her. Why should he wonder that the newness of her skin tempted him as it did? The idea of breaking up with her seemed to have been planted in his head by a traitor.

'Do you need something from the shop?' he said. He was astounded by his banality yet couldn't help repeating: 'Are you going to the shop?'

Nicole raised a hand to move her perfectly straight, precisely cut hair, which had dark streaks among the blonde, off her face and neck. The gold watchband was heavy on her hardly full-formed wrist, with the delicate tendons Ritchie loved to stroke. She had depleted, with speed and efficiency, the account he'd set up to service her wants: she didn't like cheap things.

'You've got to speak to my mum. She's in the lounge.' Nicole nodded down the hall.

A needle of terror pierced Ritchie. 'How did she find out?'

Nicole slumped her shoulders and cocked her head. 'Because I told her!' She shook her face at him. 'Don't you talk to your kids? She's known about you and me from the start. Anyway she's in there now and she needs to speak to you.'

'Where are you going?'

'Home.' She blinked and waited.

'I lost the phone,' said Ritchie. 'That's why I didn't call.'

'Oh yeah,' said Nicole. She opened the red crocodile-skin bag she was carrying and stabbed the contents with her finger-tips. She found a mobile, the twin of the one he'd lost, and gave it to Ritchie.

'Don't you need it?' said Ritchie.

'I only used it to call you,' said Nicole. She stepped across the threshold and considered him for an instant. 'I saw us in the mirror,' she said. 'We don't look right together.' She left, slamming the door. Her scent lingered.

Ritchie stood staring at the peephole, turned round in the direction of the TV noise, closed his open mouth, turned back, shouted Nicole's name, opened the door, saw the lift closing and shouted her name again. It seemed to him that events were taking place in the wrong order.

6

Nicole's mother was on the sofa, watching television. She had her back to Ritchie when he came into the room. Her bleached, shoulder-length blonde hair was piled up on the headrest. She'd taken off her shoes and her bare feet were up on the glass top of the coffee table. She was drinking red wine and feeding from a bowl of salted almonds. The chat show host delivered a gag – Ritchie didn't notice what, because he was watching Nicole's mother's scarlet toenails move as she flexed her feet – and she laughed along with the audience.

'Hello?' said Ritchie.

Nicole's mother looked round, gulped the nuts she was chewing, put down the glass and stood up, smoothing her red skirt and, Ritchie thought, getting salt and nut grease on the fabric.

'I'm sorry,' she said, grinning, leaving her hands on her hips. 'Louise. Nicole said I should make myself at home. Where is she?' She looked over Ritchie's shoulder. She didn't seem surprised when Ritchie told her that her daughter had left.

'God!' she said. She stepped back, clenched her fists and tapped them together under her chin. 'Ritchie Shepherd! I can't believe I'm this close to you. I was such a fan of yours in the old days.' She blinked several times. She was excited and her breaths came quickly.

Ritchie invited her to sit down again and went to sit in another chair opposite but she called him back and patted the place next to her. Ritchie laughed, fetched a fresh glass and the bottle and sat down with her, keeping a foot of space between them.

'I went to see you at Hammersmith Palais when I was twelve,' she said. 'You and your wife.'

'She wasn't my wife then.'

'God, I fancied you!' Louise laughed. 'If you hadn't been there with Karin, I would have tried to get backstage. I was a bit of a groupie in my time.'

'You would have been too young for me.'

Louise smiled and looked off into a corner. 'Yeah?' she said, and twisted strands of hair round her finger. Ritchie swallowed and laughed carefully. Louise pretended to look stern. She hunched her shoulders and pressed her hands between her thighs.

'You've been naughty, Ritchie,' she said.

Ritchie could smell propositions before they arrived. He asked Louise why she'd come.

'Oh, Ritchie,' she said. 'Nicole can't see you any more.'

It seemed that Nicole had begun going out with a footballer from QPR's youth squad. Bruce was eighteen. Everyone knew he was going to break into the first team when the season started. He was a lovely lad, Louise said, very gentle and polite, with a great sense of humour. She knew Ritchie would be upset; but he'd known it couldn't last for ever, hadn't he, not when he wasn't going to leave Karin.

Ritchie, who disliked hearing his wife called Karin by people who'd only met her in the pages of celebrity magazines, agreed that he had known this.

'Since Nicole's dad left, and she was only five then, it's just been the two of us,' said Louise. 'We're like girls together, you know. We're like sisters, best friends. We tell each other everything. And when she said she was going out with you I felt a bit funny. I couldn't help thinking well, he is married, and she's not really supposed to, you know, when she's fifteen, and she didn't go on the show so the producer could pick her out and say "She's the one I want, she's the best-looking, I'll have her."' Louise put out her hand and cupped Ritchie's cheek. 'Oh, I'm sorry, Ritchie. You've been sweet to her, you really have, all the things you've bought for us and everything. I was no angel when I was her age. I slept with men who had rings in all sorts of places.'

This released a parp of laughter from Ritchie. He grinned and swallowed. His upper lip stuck fast to his teeth and he prised it loose with his tongue. He didn't believe he wouldn't see Nicole again. Everything Louise was saying, it seemed to Ritchie, only concerned Louise; all he had to do was lower his head and plough through Louise's wants and get to the other side, when Louise wouldn't be there any more.

The rise and fall of Louise's chest as she breathed became more pronounced and her eyes darkened and shone. 'I was a bit jealous of Nicole for a while,' she said. 'I thought: I'm a fan of his. I'm his age, a good deal younger, in fact. I'm single, I'm not bad-looking. If he needs a bit on the side, why not me?'

'That's flattering,' said Ritchie.

'D'you want to see how big a fan I was?' said Louise. She undid two buttons of her blouse, turned round so that her back was to Ritchie and peeled the blouse down over her shoulders.

Ritchie found himself staring at his own face and his wife's, etched together by a tattooist's needle on a stranger's clear white skin, between her right shoulder blade and the horizontal white strap of her bra. He thought of the child Nicole watching Louise undress in a bedroom in a stuffy flat in Acton and asking about these indelible faces. As Louise's skin aged, would his and Karin's image age too, he wondered, or would Louise die in fifty years' time, an old woman with two immortals on her back?

Ritchie put his hands on Louise's waist and moved closer. The tattoo artist had taken the image from the cover of their first album. When Ritchie squinted he could see that the words were there, in miniature. *The Lazygods: Fountain.*

'That cover was my idea, you know,' he said, and kissed the tattoo. Louise laughed. Ritchie moved his tongue over the inked image of his own face, plunged his hands inside Louise's bra and squeezed her breasts.

The phone in his pocket, the one Nicole had given him, started to vibrate. Ritchie stood up, pushed Louise away and took several steps back from the sofa while he took the phone out. He looked at the screen in terror. *Ritchie calling*, it said.

Louise turned herself round and watched him with eyes that had hardened. When he snatched his hands away from her he'd almost shoved her. Ritchie could see she wasn't sure whether to be angry or to pretend to be angry as part of their game. She straightened her skirt and crossed her legs primly but didn't close her blouse or pull her bra up to cover her breasts. She watched Ritchie sceptically with her head tilted to one side. The phone was still ringing. It seemed to Ritchie to have been ringing for minutes. He had an urge to ask Louise what he should do. He despised himself for being weak enough to consider it. He stood still, licking his lips, gripping the phone while it buzzed in his sweaty fist, staring at the woman he'd been on the verge of having. He felt his status diminishing with each moment of speechlessness. The hardness in Louise's eyes was turning to mockery.

'You look like you're expecting bad news, Ritchie,' she said. 'Are you going to answer it?'

'Not in front of you,' said Ritchie. He hadn't meant to sound curt, but it was too late.

'Sorry!' said Louise, and began buttoning up her blouse. The phone stopped ringing.

'This isn't the best time,' said Ritchie, holding his hands out, still gripping the phone tightly, not moving towards Louise. 'I have to deal with this.' Louise got up, animated by all sorts of nervous, jerky actions, hooking her bag over her shoulder, fixing her hair, touching her earrings, checking her phone, biting her lip.

'You're a busy man,' she said. 'I don't know how you found time for Nicole but I can see you don't have time for me.' Her mouth flexed in a joyless smile and she blinked. 'Cheerio, then.'

'Goodbye,' said Ritchie. He gave Louise the full, wide, I'm-all-yours grin he gave people he'd met once when he was sure he wouldn't see them again, and she left.

Ritchie sat down, took out Nicole's phone, called his lost mobile and closed his eyes. It rang twice before somebody picked up. He could hear them breathing strangely.

'Hello?' he said.

'Is that Daddy?' said Ruby.

'Oh,' said Ritchie. He opened his eyes. 'Hello, my little angel. Yes, I'm Daddy. It's your Daddy. Where are you?'

'I'm in bed,' said Ruby. 'Where are you?'

'In London.'

'Your voice sounds funny.'

'Does it? Listen, Ruby darling, where did you find the phone?'

'In the garden.'

'In the garden!'

'In the grass.'

'Mmm.' Ritchie stood up. 'What do Mummy and Dan think about that?'

'They don't know,' said Ruby. 'It's a secret. I'm hiding it under my pillow.'

'What a clever girl you are,' said Ritchie. 'It's not easy to hide things from Mummy, is it?'

'I'm going to call the pizza place.'

'It's too late for pizza, darling. You should be sleeping. Where's Mummy?'

'Gone to play music.'

'And where's Milena?'

'In her room.'

'Has she read you your story and said night-night?'

'Yes.'

'So she thinks you're sleeping?'

'Yes.'

Ritchie was walking out of the flat towards the lift. He felt light and strong and aware, as he did before a difficult meeting with channel executives.

'Ruby darling,' he said, 'that's Daddy's phone. I dropped it by accident in the garden.' The lift was descending. The doors opened and he walked towards the street door. 'Hello?' he said. 'Are you there, love?'

'It's not yours!' said Ruby. 'It says "Nicole" in the little screen.'

Of course, they taught her to read! thought Ritchie. *They took her innocence!* His throat tightened. He was overcome with tenderness towards his little daughter, tucked in bed with her feet halfway down the pony quilt, not understanding the evil forces of disclosure that the poisoned silver box held to her ear were summoning. Only Ritchie could save her from these cruel powers. The top of his nose tingled with sadness and affection as he got into the car.

'Aren't you sleepy?' he said. He began to drive home, clamping the phone between his shoulder and his ear when he shifted gears.

'No.'

Ritchie's strength was not in foreseeing emergencies, but dealing with them when they came up. He could get her to open the window and throw the phone out; but what if she fell? He could ask her to take a heavy object and smash the phone to pieces. But did Ruby have heavy objects in her room, and if so, could she lift them? He could direct her to take out the SIM card but it was likely that her tiny soft fingers would fail to find purchase on the tricky catch over the battery compartment, she would become frustrated, there would be crying, and Karin would be alerted.

'Ruby, you do know you're Daddy's absolutely favourite girl, don't you?' he said. 'I want you to be super-brave and clever and do what Daddy asks you. Will you do that for me?'

'OK.'

'Because the phone you found is really very important and special and secret. And if you're super brave and clever I'll give you whatever you want. What do you want most in the world?'

'I want to be on television.'

'I can put you on television, darling, of course I can. And if you want that to happen, all you have to do is put the phone to sleep and hide it under your pillow and in the morning it'll be gone. And – this is very important, the most important thing, darling – you must keep it a secret, and not tell anyone you found the phone, not even Mummy or Dan or anyone at school or Granny or Auntie Bec or anyone. Do you understand?'

'Yes.'

'So just put the phone to sleep, darling, and hide it under your pillow, and then you go to sleep.'

'I want a story.'

Along the dual carriageway to the M25 Ritchie told Ruby the story of the lion and the mouse, how the lion didn't eat the mouse when it was woken up, and how later the mouse saved the lion by chewing through a hunter's net. When he finished he asked Ruby quietly if she was still awake. He asked three times, more gently each time, and when there was no answer he hung up and increased his speed.

Coming up the driveway of the house he saw the lights on in the studio, which was in an old stable block set away from the main building. He parked the car well short, trotted up to the front door of the house and went to Milena's room, down the hall from Ruby's room and Dan's. He found Milena sitting in a tracksuit on her sofa with her knees up, drinking tea and watching TV.

'Karin's in the studio,' she said. 'She wasn't expecting you.'

Ritchie grinned. 'I felt like not staying away,' he said. 'Are the kids in bed?'

'Oh, ages ago. They're asleep.'

'How were they?'

'Fine. Dan wouldn't eat his pasta. He said the shape of macaroni made it taste bad.'

'I'll just look in on them.'

Ritchie closed Milena's door behind him – it had been open – and went to Ruby's room. It was lit by a dim yellow night light. Milena had cleared everything off the floor, dolls, books and costumes together, and heaped them in a crate by the chest of drawers. Under the window the front of the doll's house stood ajar and some of the miniature furniture it contained was stacked higgledy-piggledy in the back of Dan's old Tonka dumptruck. Ruby had the quilt pushed down to her waist. Her mouth was slightly open. Ritchie could hear her breathing. It seemed to him that the penguins on her pyjamas were staring at him in a tough way. The phone had fallen on the floor. Ritchie went over to pick it up. A floorboard creaked loudly under his foot. He heard Karin's voice. She was talking to Milena. He grabbed the phone, shoved it in his pocket, leaned down, stroked his daughter's head and kissed her. The door opened and Karin whispered to him.

Karin was wary, but glad to see him. They went to bed early and made love before they went to sleep. The thought that he was cheating Nicole by loving his wife gave Ritchie strength. The thought that he had narrowly managed to save his family from terrible danger made him tender. It did not seem to Ritchie that he loved Karin any less because while he was thrusting into her he was imagining Louise and Nicole sitting next to the bed watching him with their skirts pushed up round their waists and their hands moving between their thighs.

Ritchie and Karin fell asleep wrapped in each other, which they didn't usually do, because her hair tickled him and his body heat kept her awake.

7

Ritchie was at the Rika Films studios before eight next day. By mid-morning shivers of panic were rippling through the building. One of the acts, a band of fourteen-year-olds from Rotherham called The What, had shown such rapid improvement from the original audition that the team was convinced it had been swindled. As it stood the kids sounded too professional to be put on the show and they'd been brought into the studio early to get them to recapture their previous, possibly fake, hopelessness.

At the same time Lazz, Riggsy's co-presenter, was refusing to come to work. Lazz had discovered that the blooper reel for the Christmas special, which was already in the can, didn't include any funny on-camera mistakes by him, because he hadn't made any. His agent Midge agreed that this showed a high level of professionalism on Lazz's part, but said that his client felt the absence of footage of him giggling, stumbling over words or getting into trouble with props and animals might alienate him from his fan base by suggesting a lack of personal warmth; and that, if scripted blunders were not provided, his client intended to begin making mistakes at precise ten-minute intervals, with the cold, striving determination for which he was renowned in the business.

As these crises ripened a group of BBC executives turned up at the studio without warning – just for a chat and a look around, they said.

The more anxious and pale the faces that appeared in doorways when Ritchie passed, the better he felt. This was his work. This was where he was strong, respected and necessary, and his people were right to look to him for leadership, because he'd lead them through these vexing daily difficulties, as he'd done before. He was the producer. Here in the studio he felt capable and happy in a way he hadn't for months. Was there need for anything except work and family?

For Ritchie, almost having sex with Nicole's mother had made Nicole lose her freshness. He felt the right thing to do would be to treat the eight months of the affair as something that had happened to the girl. It was true, he thought, that he'd been present, but he shouldn't be selfish. The memories were properly hers and, being young, she needed them more than he did. He tended to divide his memories into two categories: things that had happened to him, and things that had happened to other people while he was there. He felt it was part of the generosity he cherished in himself. If he no longer wanted part of the past, why shouldn't somebody else have it?

Ritchie went down the ramp towards the main stage, where the pinch-faced boys of The What, their hair swinging over their eyes, were walking stiffly to and fro with guitars, picking their way over leads. Paula grabbed his elbow from behind, looked at him with wide eyes and said that there was still no sign of Lazz, but Midge had turned up, breathing fire. Ritchie laughed, rested his hand on her shoulder, said she shouldn't worry and told her to send Midge in.

Midge made a performance of being angry. Ritchie called the gaffer over and told him that during the next two shows he'd have to drop three small bits of kit from the lighting rig over the stage while Lazz was in shot, as if by accident. 'We'll get Lazz to do a big double take the first time, not so big the second, the third kind of a —' Ritchie boggled his eyes, opened his mouth and flapped his upturned palms in the air. 'It'll be planned spontaneity. Running gag in the out-takes. Great laughs.'

'Planned spontaneity,' repeated Midge, and smiled. 'That's funny.'

Ritchie turned to the gaffer.

'Just pick some safe widgets to drop,' he said. 'We mustn't hurt him.'

The gaffer stood with his hands on his hips, facing the ground with his lower jaw jutting out. He looked up at Ritchie. His voice wavered. 'I've been doing this all my life,' he said. 'I'm proud of getting it right. D'you want to see my record? One accident in forty-five years.'

'Come on, Jeff,' said Ritchie. 'It's light entertainment. It's not life and death.'

'I've lit the real entertainers,' said the gaffer. 'The professionals. Now what it is, it's kids, amateurs and who's the biggest fuck-up, that's what gets the attention.' He walked off cursing.

'Stay and listen to the band,' said Ritchie to Midge. He called to the boys on stage and they looked up through their hair. They swung their low-slung guitars to face the little group standing in front of the empty tiers of seats. There was a squawk of feedback, the singer counted them in, and they began to play.

The bass player plucked at an ominous note. The guitarist laid a rasping chord over it, sustained it, chopped it off and repeated it. After a few bars the drummer lashed the skins of his tom-toms and locked himself into a rhythm of bass and snare. The monotony of pitch, the increasing volume and the cumulative beat of the instruments ground the listeners down, making them long for the release and their hearts kick as they anticipated it. The singer grasped the mike stand, flexed his fingers, leaned forward, opened his mouth and closed his eyes.

The hairs at the back of Ritchie's neck rose as the singer's voice filled the studio. How could a fourteen-year-old have the confidence to set out on those steady, drawn-out notes? Where did he get the power? Where did a young boy in England find the pain in that voice, then find the bravery to put a band together?

The chord shift, when it came, seemed to lift him off the ground as the guitar and bass and the singer's voice stepped up the scale.

'They're good,' said Midge in Ritchie's ear.

'They're the real thing,' said Ritchie. 'I can handle it, though.'

Clapping hard, he walked to the stage and climbed up to stand among the boys. He was a foot taller than the tallest of them. They weren't full grown, he supposed, but even so they looked malnourished, their elbow joints grotesquely large on their spindly white arms. Here and there he saw a prominent feature within the hair – an enormous Roman nose, wide red lips, dark eyes. He asked their names and they told him in turn. As they spoke they began to utter short, hissing laughs, and when the drummer gave his name, they found it hilarious.

Ritchie pointed at the guitarist's Fender copy and held out his hands. 'Do you mind?' he said. The guitarist lifted the strap off his shoulders and gave the instrument to Ritchie, who played a Lazygods riff with his thumb and index finger. At the end he closed his eyes, leaned back and quivered his middle finger on the fretboard for tremolo. He opened his eyes, nodding, and looked at the drummer, inviting him to come in. The drummer stared at him without moving.

'That was probably before your time,' said Ritchie, handing the guitar back. 'How many hours a day do you practise?'

The guitarist looked at the singer. They shrugged and said at the same time: 'Don't know.'

Ritchie folded his arms and looked from face to face. 'What were you trying to do when you signed up for this?' he said.

The word 'win' passed in a murmur from mouth to mouth.

'This is a tough business,' said Ritchie. 'I've been where you are now. And I'm telling you, you've got talent.' He waited and went on. 'That's our problem. What our audience is looking for is a story about kids who don't have talent, who get some nice clothes and a bit of coaching from professionals and go from being bad at what they do to being adequate. Our message is that we can make anyone look special. Ordinary people aren't as bad as they seem. This isn't a talent show. It's a lack of talent show. So I'm going to tell you now, we can't let you win. You're too good. Is that clear?'

The hair murmured and shook. *It's like talking to bushes in the wind*, thought Ritchie.

'You've shown that you're good enough to pretend to be crap,' said Ritchie gravely. He beat his fist in the air to stress the seriousness of his points. 'Now my question to you is, can you do that again? Have you got what it takes to show a TV audience of millions that you're a shit band, and then make out that you've got slightly better?'

The boys looked at each other. 'We've got to pretend to be losers, like,' said the singer.

'Pretend to be losers, and then show that a makeover can turn you into guys who are definitely not losers, without any hint that you could ever have been winners.'

'Losers, not-losers, not winners,' said the singer slowly. Something happened to the bass player; he doubled up, as if stabbed in the stomach, swivelled round so his back was turned to Ritchie, and fell to his knees. Ritchie asked if he was all right.

'Don't worry about him, Mr Shepherd,' said the singer. 'He gets attacks. We can play shite for you.'

'And then get slightly better.'

'Aye.' The singer glanced at the guitarist, who nodded as if to encourage him to take a bold step. 'We like some Lazygods stuff.'

Ritchie laughed. 'I haven't played for years,' he said. A vision of a revival charged into his head: he, Ritchie, older, wiser, powerful. He, the dead rock god resurrected at Glastonbury. Worshipped from a plain sown with waving arms, a field of limbs rippling out to the horizon.

'We want to play with Karin,' said the singer.

Ritchie's grin melted like plastic shrivelling in a bonfire.

'She's a mother of two young children now,' he said.

'She can still sing,' said the bass player.

'We saw her do an acoustic gig last year,' said the guitarist.

Ritchie turned away, waving his hand at them. 'You do it the way we agreed and I'll talk to her,' he said. He made for the steps and chose to jump off the stage instead. He hesitated at the edge. It looked all of a sudden like an ankle-breaker, but he couldn't back out in front of the kids and Midge. He bent his knees, raised his arms, closed his eyes and jumped. He landed, staggered and straightened up quickly. Over his shoulder he saw the bass player having another attack.

It was only noon, Ritchie saw, and with firmness and guile he'd solved the problems that had made his staff tremble. He offered Midge a lift to the West End on his way to pick up his mother and sister.

'The lovely Bec,' said Midge.

'You've got a lot of testosterone in you for a small man. Keep your dirty paws off her.'

'She's not my type. I only like the skinny ones. Is she free, then?'

'She's still seeing Val Oatman.'

'Do you think Val Oatman was crazy and made his newspaper crazy, or did it make him crazy when he started editing a crazy newspaper?'

'He's not right for her,' said Ritchie. 'She doesn't know about him.'

'I know what Val Oatman does. I can't say the same about Bec. Can you?' said Midge.

'She's my sister.'

'But she moved into a world you don't know anything about.'

'I know what she does.'

'Really? Tiny creatures swimming in her blood, birds of paradise? Could you explain it to me right now?'

Ritchie laughed and changed the subject.

8

Two days earlier the newspaper editor Val Oatman had proposed to Bec and she, taken by surprise, said yes. He gave her a gold ring with a diamond surrounded by smaller rubies and she took it between the thumb and much-pricked fingertips of her left hand and stared at it as if she were admiring it before giving it back. He had to tell her to put it on, and she did. It was a horrible feeling as the gold band slid over the skin of her knuckle. He told her fondly that it had been his dead wife's engagement ring.

They didn't stay together that night. They agreed to meet the next day. When she got home to her flat in Kentish Town Bec took the ring off, put it in an envelope and after much dithering over safe places stowed the envelope in the freezer compartment of her fridge. She didn't tell anyone she was engaged. She felt no happiness, only a jangled feeling, as if she'd been in an accident.

Missing his wife, Val had been asking Bec for kindness, and she'd been giving it. He asked her to sleep with him and she did. It probably made him think she was in love with him, she supposed. I didn't say that, she thought. I did what he asked me to do.

It seemed to her that scientists ought to be able to keep

track of numbers such as how many times they'd slept with someone, yet she'd lost count like a small child. After three, all numbers were 'lots'. As long as she kept the number in her head, she'd been able to hold Val at a distance; she'd forgotten it, and the man she'd slept with a few times was now her fiancé.

In a series of papers in scientific journals, Bec had proposed a new way to ward off malaria. Her peers said it was unsafe. One called it 'baroque'. The version she was being allowed to trial in Tanzania was a remnant of what she'd wanted to do. Val said he wanted to visit her while she was there and she'd been able to let it pass without them deciding. When he reminded her a few days later she had to say 'Of course.' She didn't want him to come but she didn't have the courage to tell him not to. They were supposed to meet in London the Sunday before she left and there was no need for Bec to put in extra hours but when Val called to arrange it she suddenly craved to be with chicken blood and microscopes in the clinical alcohol smell of the lab. She yearned to toil until she fell unconscious. The thought made her stomach flutter.

'I can't meet up,' she told Val. 'We haven't made enough haemoproteus.'

'I know what that is,' said Val. He said he could see her on Monday.

'I'm having dinner with Ritchie and my mother.'

'I could join you.'

'It's a family thing.'

'I'm going to be part of your family.'

'About the man who killed Dad.'

'What did your mother say when you told her we were getting married?'

'I haven't told anyone yet.'

She heard Val breathing. He said: 'Tuesday night, then. Before you go.'

'I'll be happier once I've cultured a few billion parasites.'

'You work too hard,' said Val, and when she didn't answer, he said: 'As long as it's that. I'll call you. On your landline at work.'

Bec didn't feel she'd been unlucky in men. She was thirty-three; her heart had been broken properly once, so that though it was mended it would always show the crack, but that was the only time. It'd been back in her twenties. She'd lived with Joel for three years while she got her doctorate in Sacramento. He followed her to the post she won in London, looked around, didn't like the set-up and went back to the States.

In the year after he left it seemed to her that she'd been reassigned, against her will, to serve as a container for misery. There was a cold corrosive goo that sloshed around in her and stung when she tried to move towards the light.

That was her first year at the Centre for Parasite Control. She was a zombie technician, able to move and communicate mechanically, but not to use her senses for much more than counting, measuring and inputting data. This turned out to be exactly what the centre wanted. After twelve months, when the colour and warmth came back, she found her stock was high and her ideas were listened to. When Bec's principal investigator Meena went on maternity leave Bec stood in for her, mentoring the post-grads, teaching and trying to break away from Meena's obsession with parasitic worms. One day, soon after her twenty-seventh birthday, she had told her mother she was going to Papua New Guinea.

'You know who else dots around the world the way

scientists do?' said her mother. 'Catholic priests. Three years here, two years there. You won't find a man willing to trail around the world after you.'

'I'm not looking for one of them,' said Bec. 'You've got grandchildren.'

'Why do you always think I'm selfish? It's about you.' Her mother drew on a cigarette and took another sip of Ayurvedic tea. The packaging spoke of its potential for karmic enhancement. 'You have to learn to accept constraints in life.'

9

A pair of married Stanford professors, an ornithologist and an entomologist, had recruited Bec for Papua New Guinea on the strength of her paper on sexual conflict among parasites, which Ruth Nickell called *ballsy*. 'It's Nick*ell*,' she told Bec on the phone. 'I'm insects, he's birds.'

Her husband Franz had come across a translated paper written by a long-dead parasitologist attached to the Japanese army that invaded PNG in the Second World War. It described how a unit of military engineers building a camp in the interior remained almost immune to malaria while troops further down the valley succumbed in their hundreds. The Japanese scientist found a biting fly that fed indiscriminately on the blood of men and birds of paradise. He speculated that an unknown parasite was being transferred from the birds to the men, and that this parasite gave immunity from the parasite that caused malaria. Before he could continue his research the Japanese were attacked and driven from the island. The scientist lost his photographs, drawings and the wooden slide case carrying the soldiers' blood samples in the chaos of retreat.

Bec flew to Australia and from there to Lae. Ruth picked her up and drove her to the bungalow in the little town where they'd set up a research base. She drove fast, over-taking buses and trucks, bashing the horn, pumping the lights with her scrawny hands. She questioned Bec about life and family in an amiable, new-roommates way, and when Bec mentioned the death of her father, Ruth nodded and responded with the story of their grown-up son and how he was in trouble with the authorities, as if to say *Oh yes, we have one of those.* Ruth turned from the road to Bec and back, and her ponytail, her breasts, untethered under a baggy t-shirt, and the ankh on a cord round her neck swung to and fro.

'My husband can be kind of cranky, but don't underestimate the depth of his intellect,' said Ruth. 'He's also great in bed.' She gave a squeaky laugh.

On the edge of their destination they passed a huddle of shacks made of bamboo and tin and old fertiliser bags, sunk in mud and woodsmoke, swarming with potbellied children and moulting, pestilential chickens whose heads sprouted bedraggled feather crowns.

'It looks like the outskirts of a bigger place,' said Bec.

'Oh my God, isn't it depressing?' said Ruth. 'These poor guys come down from the hills and try to set up shop in nowheresville. From the forest straight to the grid. No sanitation, no schools, no hunting.'

Franz was a stocky, paunchy, bearded man exposing melon calves between the hems of baggy khaki shorts and the tops of his Timberland boots. Bec prepared herself not to under-estimate his intellect but after shaking her hand he turned away without saying anything to her, took his wife to his laptop and began murmuring quietly with her as if Bec wasn't there.

Blushing, she went out on foot to explore, ending up in front of one of the shacks in the shanty town, learning pidgin words from a crowd of children and fending off the settlement's punk chickens, which tried to perch on her head. After an hour Ruth found her and pulled her into the car, telling her she was crazy.

'I'm crazy too,' Ruth assured her, laughing her squeaky laugh for credentials. 'But you don't want to hang out there. There are rascals about. They'd kill you for your shoes.'

Hefting a microbiology kit of field microscope, slides and powdered solutions on her back Bec trekked with the Nickells and their local guides up the trails to the cloudy mountain tops. They spent their first night in the hills in a broad green meadow sloping gently down from the trees to a fast-running river. The guides pitched the tents close together; one for themselves, one for Bec and one for Franz and Ruth.

At sunset Ruth took Bec aside. 'I hope Franz and I won't keep you awake with our lovemaking tonight,' she said. 'When he's inside me I can't hold back. I'm kind of loud.'

Bec looked across the meadow, which stretched for several hundred yards to the tree line. 'It seems a shame the tents have to be pitched so close together,' she said.

'Rebecca, we've got to keep you safe,' said Ruth.

Bec lay awake that night, unable to sleep, waiting, but she heard only insects and birds. She dozed off. At around midnight she was woken by a woman's cry. She heard Ruth shriek 'Holy shit!' Bec opened her eyes and waited for more. After a minute, the darkness was ripped by a tumultuous male snore.

Franz snored intermittently through the night, falling silent long enough for Bec to believe he'd stopped and get to the threshold of sleep only for him to start up again.

'I hope we didn't keep you awake,' said Ruth next morning.

'After last night, I know you must really love him,' said Bec.

'It's always tough being the single girl around a couple of lovebirds,' said Ruth, putting her hand on Bec's arm. 'He's hot, but don't get tempted.' She winked.

'I'll take cold showers,' said Bec.

'I think we're going to be buddies,' said Ruth. 'Today we're going to get you a shitload of blood.'

Franz behaved as if Bec didn't exist. He treated her as permanently temporary, as if she'd always just arrived and was always just about to leave, like someone delivering a package, to whom there was no point forming the slightest attachment. He planned their programme and decided their route and he controlled Pete, the chief guide and interpreter. He led them through the list of villages and bird species he'd worked out in advance, and Ruth and Bec followed in his wake, identifying insects, taking blood samples and questioning the locals as best they could. At breakfast and supper Franz spoke to Ruth or Pete, looked down at his food and scratched himself. When Bec spoke he didn't respond. When she asked him a question or spoke about their work he would wince and look at Ruth, who would answer for him.

'Did you notice those strange birds they keep in the shanty town?' said Bec one evening.

Franz widened his eyes and nodded at his wife.

'We don't want to hurt your feelings, honey,' said Ruth to Bec. 'There's not a bird species on this planet Franz doesn't know. We're not trying to teach you what a plasmodium looks like.'

It seemed to Bec that whenever Franz made one of his long, late-night satellite phone calls to his son's lawyers, parole officers or psychotherapists in the States, he would position himself in such a way that she couldn't help overhearing everything he said, and hearing how patient he was, and how concerned about his son. Each night, she heard the same sounds from their tent, a cry of ecstasy from Ruth, followed by Franz's snoring. One time she left her tent in the small hours, pulled out the dozen pegs fixing it to the ground and manhandled it a hundred yards away. In the morning, when she unzipped her flap and came out into the sunshine, she tripped over the guy of the Nickell tent, which had somehow followed hers in the darkness and nuzzled up against it.

'Franz,' said Bec at breakfast, biting off a piece of muesli bar, 'did you notice how your tent moved in the night?'

Franz shook his head and looked at Ruth. 'Got to stay safe, Rebecca,' said Ruth. 'Bet you we're going to find that fever bird today.'

In the mountains Bec was soaked, steamed and bitten. She told herself her father had been through worse. At night she stuffed her ears with cotton wool and in the morning, when it was cool and she watched the rising sun pick its way between the tree trunks like a hunter, when the air scratched and creaked and hooted with song, she was grateful and glad to be alive. Sometimes, when the rain beat on the canvas, she remembered a far-off episode with her brother's friend

Alex, who had, it seemed, fallen for her once, then gone away.

They scaled ridges and descended into isolated valleys and jabbed prickers into the necks of scores of jungle fowl, their gaudy feathers marred by whatever avian plague afflicted them, and delved into their blood without finding anything new. Bec took blood from hundreds of Papuans and found no strange parasites living there. None of the locals reported immunity to malaria other than what they'd built up from childhood episodes. There was no trace of the Japanese base, neither in the forest nor in the memories of the hill people. Franz crossed off candidate bird species and areas on his map and Ruth ruled out this or that bloodsucker. 'We're closing in,' she said.

After six weeks they took their first break from the field. Bec took Pete to the shanty town and asked the squatters where they'd come from and why they kept sick birds as pets. It seemed that most of them had chronic episodes of blurred vision. She visited the town clinic and talked to the doctor. She was trying to find the courage to ask Ruth to come with her to take samples from the squatters and their birds when Ruth told her she'd have to go back to the States for a while. Their son was up for parole violation, she said, some DUI bullshit.

'You and Franz will have to fill in,' she said. 'You're OK with bugs, right?' She cupped Bec's cheek in her hand and stroked it with her thumb. A tear fell from her eye. 'So bright, so pretty.'

'Who will I talk to without you?' said Bec, on the brink of tears herself.

'Oh, I know it's going to be hard,' said Ruth. 'My

husband's got so much charisma and so much charm. Try to resist, yeah? For me? Whenever you're tempted to give yourself to him, just say to yourself, "He's Ruth's guy, Ruth's guy."'

Next day Ruth drove Franz and Bec to the foot of the trail they would take into the mountains. Pete and the porters were supposed to come in another car but it broke down. Ruth embraced Bec and her husband and drove away. She'd be gone for at least a month. As soon as she was out of sight Franz turned to Bec and grinned. His eyes shone.

'Let's not wait for the others,' he said. 'What a great day for a hike.'

'Where's Franz?' said Bec. 'What have you done with his body?'

Franz laughed and began to walk up the trail. 'You don't know what jealousy is until you've seen Ruth when another female steps into the mung.'

'I'm not another female,' said Bec, panting as she lugged her heavy pack after him.

'All women are rivals,' said Franz.

They picked their way up the muddy path, studded with stones and broken up by mossy tree roots. Bec kept her anger sullenly alight, ignoring the new Franz's cheerful comments and compliments about her work, with which he was, she learned, well acquainted. But when they stopped for lunch in the meadow where they'd camped on Bec's first night in the hills, she told him he was the rudest man she'd ever met. He laughed and said he was glad she thought he was exceptional.

'Why are you taking off your shirt?' she said.

'It's ninety degrees plus. I need vitamin D. You should take yours off.' The hairs on Franz's back lay in flat waves, like barley in the wind.

'So what are those birds in the squatter camp?' she said, sitting cross-legged on the grass. 'Did you know that the squatters never go to the clinic?'

'That's cause they're broke.' Franz reclined on his side, propping himself up on his elbow, his big belly, half taut, half dead weight, not quite reaching the ground. Some of his chest hairs were pure white. 'Jesus, I don't want to talk about fucking squatters. I want to hear about your malaria work. Sex among the parasites. How do the female gametocytes pick out the males they want?'

'The females discourage the ones they don't want,' said Bec.

'Keeping themselves free for Mr Right.'

'Mr Fit.'

'It sounds kind of uptight. I like the way the girl birds do it. They check out the guy birds, see who's got the biggest thing, you know, and that's who they go for.'

'Don't you think birds might be able to look past the size of their boyfriends' tail feathers?'

'You're thinking of the cute little cock bird with the big personality, aren't you, the cute little cock bird who's never going to make you even a liiiiitle bit frightened. And maybe what you really want's the big bad cock bird, the big guy who owns the lek.'

'Birds don't make promises to be faithful, and break them.'

'What do you know about birds?'

'Enough to know that's not what we're talking about.' She shaded her eyes with her hand and looked up at the sky. 'I hope Ruth helps your son out.'

'You're so fucking demure,' said Franz. 'It's a turn-on.' He stood up and brushed grass seeds and insects off his shorts. 'If the system decides to take him down, it'll take him down,' he said. 'Let's get the tents up.'

Peter and the other guides wouldn't arrive until the evening. Saying she was tired, Bec went into her tent and lay down, wondering how she might endure a month of Franz coming on to her. Before long she heard a rustling of grass outside, a shadow fell across the tent door and the zip was torn downwards. Bec propped herself up on her elbows and saw a long, girthy penis enter the orange tent-light and hang there for an instant, bobbing gently, before its owner began preparations to follow his member inside.

'Oh,' said Bec.

Pushing herself into a sitting position, she glanced at the two books she'd brought with her – *Zelda: A Biography* and Volume 2 of the *World Class Parasites* series (the Geohelminths). She picked up the first, raised it high above her head and whacked Franz Nickell's squinting Cyclops with half a pound of Zelda. There was a sound such as a film extra makes when, playing a sentry, he is unexpectedly stabbed in the back, and the beaten organ withdrew.

Bec waited and when she could no longer stand the silence she went outside. Franz stood ten yards away with his back to her, up to his knees in flowering weeds, watching the sun go down over the forest. In different circumstances Bec would have taken a photograph. Franz appeared natural and humble there, naked before the sun. It was a scene of beauty, apart from a single detail.

'Franz,' she said, not going closer. He didn't answer. 'Franz,' she repeated. 'Are you OK? Professor Nickle?'

'Nick*ell*,' he said, without turning round.

'Professor Nick*ell*, a leech is sucking the blood from your right but*tock*.'

Some weeks later, after Bec had left the Nickell project and begged a little charity money for ad hoc research in the shanty town, Ruth came by to see her. Bec had moved out of the Nickell villa and was rooming with a geologist a few streets away. Ruth was friendlier than ever. She couldn't touch Bec enough, stroking her elbows, shoulders, waist, head. Her son was still at liberty.

'Well done,' said Bec.

'Oh, we do what we can. I had to let them medicate him. That's supposed to stop him getting messed up and self-medicating with narcotics. Everyone knows that, right? It's drug against drug in America. Everyone knows it, and when everyone knows something, nobody does anything. So now Mom's back in the jungle, trying to find something to help kids in Mozambique live long enough to contract marketable mood disorders. I'm sorry you left us.'

'I am too,' said Bec. 'Personalities, you know.' She wasn't sure what Franz had told Ruth about what happened.

'And now you're working with the squatters,' said Ruth.

'Those birds they keep are sick birds of paradise,' said Bec, joyful to have someone to tell. 'The squatters say having them around protects them from malaria. They came from the hills where the Japanese were. I think this is it. I wish you could help me.'

Bec had the impression Ruth wasn't listening.

'Good luck, honey,' said Ruth, fiddling with her car keys. 'I gave you such a chance. I can't believe you turned him down. I'm so in love with that man. I hate to see him disappointed.'

'I told myself, "He's Ruth's guy." There's a rule that says you shouldn't fool around with other women's husbands.'

'Are you saying there's something wrong with me?' said Ruth, and her voice was a little louder and higher, like a bad-tempered child's. 'How could you fail to break that rule? How could you resist him?'

10

The sick fowl of the shanty town, Bec discovered, were a species called von Hausemann's bird-of-paradise. The immunity to malaria of the squatter tribe that kept them had remained secret; health workers didn't visit much, and they didn't lack diseases, including the chronic vision problems of the adults. Bec found the Japanese scientist's biting fly in the camp in abundance. All she was missing was the parasite. She'd drawn up a plan to take blood samples from the squatters when she got infected.

One day her head began to ache and though it was hot and humid in town she shivered with cold. She took some paracetamol and went to bed. A lurid, feverish dream chased its tail in a night that had the weight of weeks. In the morning she peeled off the damp sheets and got up. The dizziness made it hard to stand. She drank two glasses of water, meaning to call the hospital, but the water made her feel better, and by the time she sat down at the microscope, she was left with a blocked nose and a sore throat.

She examined hundreds of fields of her blood. She found nothing non-human. That night the fever returned. She went to bed with a temperature of forty.

She woke up at dawn with her head swimming. She slipped

out of bed onto the floor and crawled on her hands and knees to the part of the house she used as a lab. While she was making a blood slide her body shook with fever and she pressed her wrists against the table to keep them still. A drop of sweat ran down onto the top of her lip and she licked it off. She got the slide ready, put it on the microscope stage and passed out. When she woke up, hours had gone by. Her head had cleared and she was hungry and thirsty. She made a jug of coffee and sat down at the microscope.

On the third field, she saw that one of her red blood cells had been invaded by an alien creature. The parasite was smaller than the plasmodium that caused the local version of malaria. It looked like a species of haemoproteus, but not one she could identify.

The fever didn't come back. Bec flew to Australia for tests and consultations with other scientists and between them they worked out that she'd been infected with an unknown species of haemoproteus; that the parasite seemed to have entered a dormant stage and become a hypnozoite. The doctors suggested drugs to flush the parasite from her system. She declined.

Bec sent details of her find out to committees and one evening she got an email with the last approval she'd been looking for. She called her mother and told her that she'd discovered a new species.

'That's wonderful, darling,' said her mother. 'What does it look like?'

'You can't see it with the naked eye,' said Bec.

'Oh.'

'You have to have a microscope.'

'I saw a documentary about PNG last week. They found a new kind of tree kangaroo. It was adorable. It had fruit in its paws and it was eating it, like a little boy with an apple. Perhaps you'll find something like that.'

'I named it after Dad,' said Bec. 'It's going to be called *Haemoproteus gregi*.'

'What?'

'*Haemoproteus gregi*. As in Greg. As in Dad.'

'Your father was only really interested in dogs and horses. And fish, I suppose.'

Bec bit her lip. 'They don't find a new species of invasive parasite every day,' she said.

'You named a parasite after your father?' said her mother. 'How could you do such a horrible thing?'

Bec had stopped taking malaria pills, and let her wrists, ankles and neck lie bare in the evening. The mosquitoes feasted on her, and she didn't get malaria.

When Bec came back to London, the centre wasn't sure what to do with her. They obtained money for her, an important-sounding title and a lab of her own, but told her they couldn't support her infecting healthy people – young children! – with one live parasite in order to ward off another. To show how effective *gregi* was, Bec sat in the centre's secure, windowless insectarium and let herself be bitten and infected with the more vicious African version of malaria. It caused her nothing more than a runny nose, but she only made the director angry.

'You're lucky not to be in permanent quarantine,' Maddie, the director, told Bec. 'You have no idea what that thing's capable of.'

'Stopping malaria,' said Bec.

'Look what it's doing to your eyes.'

'They go a bit blurry once in a while. It's nothing.'

Maddie told her it was ethically, politically and medically unacceptable, and Bec was obliged to take a different route, to create a vaccine out of parasites that had been carefully killed. It was this, six years later, her group was testing in Africa. It half-worked, but then so did many things.

Bec had met Val after the newspaper he edited interviewed her about her malaria work. She was flattered by the article the reporter wrote about her and her group; the journalist got it more or less right, even if he exaggerated what they might achieve and the number of lives they might save. She liked herself in the photo they took. The smiling Bec in the picture seemed like a smarter, prettier twin, the one Bec could never be as good as but who'd do her best to help her sister along.

She bought the paper edition and as she turned its pages, looking for the story, she skimmed the other articles. They made her feel she was in a room full of bitter, frightened people who reckoned the world had been going to hell for ever and it was somebody else's fault.

When she got an invitation to Val's Best of Britain party she went along. She liked parties; they were like little lives. And when Val asked her there if they could have dinner, the contrast between his nervousness towards her and the nervousness his journalists felt towards him made her skin tingle. Saying yes seemed to be another woman's risk, like something the Bec in the picture would do, and not regret. It'd been easy for her to start seeing him and sleeping with him without thinking it would turn permanent, imagining that it could be rewound in some mutually painless backward version of the way they'd got together.

Val took her to grand places – a hotel on an island on a

lake in Italy, with rose petals floating in the stone bath set in the floor of their rooms; a country house in Scotland, owned by a lord Val was friends with; the British Museum after hours, when some gazillionaire hired it for a ball and decked it out with gold and red silk organza. She liked lifting her hand out of the bath and seeing it covered with soft scarlet petals; the gold and red made her open her mouth in wonder; and the lord's house was full of touchable, gnarly artefacts made of walnut, oak and brass. But she never met the tycoon, didn't like the lord and was made uneasy by the rich guests at the island hotel, who seemed sad that they couldn't meter the goodness of the time they were having, to the decimal point of a smile. Val arranged these displays for her too close together, one showy weekend after another. She felt hurried through a process. When friends used words like 'glamorous' and 'romantic' to describe the experiences Val contrived for her, she resented him.

Since she'd begun going out with Val she'd found herself dressing up more, as she'd played in childhood, posing in her father's beret or an old miniskirt of her mother's. When she turned herself out one morning at the lord's house in green wellies, a white Aran sweater, a tweed skirt, a waxed green jacket with corduroy collar and a small string of fake pearls, her hosts hadn't looked surprised, and didn't laugh at her, even though the lord's niece was dressed almost identically, except that her pearls hadn't, presumably, cost £9.99 from a chain.

Bec wished that Val had complimented her on the success of her disguise instead of telling her she looked wonderful. At a garden party Bec thought she'd gone too far with elbow gloves, a broad-brimmed hat, a gauzy shawl looped round her waist and forearms and a ridiculous little satin-effect clutch. The extreme whiteness of her dress, the pleats, the A-line! But Val, and the other guests, had told her she looked, whatever it had been, one of those words, and she hadn't been the only woman with garden-party gauntlets on. And Val was good at it, too, exactly the part in a white linen suit. He dressed in the perfect imitation of an imaginary past archetype. Once, delighted by his mimicry of a wealthy middle-aged American being smart-casual in London – the dark blue blazer, the light blue shirt, the khaki slacks, the loafers – she'd told him that she liked his costume, and he hadn't seemed to understand. 'What costume?' he said.

After she'd taken his ring, she remembered him looking her up and down before an elaborate dinner and saying 'Celia would be proud.' She wondered now whether he'd been looking not so much to replace his wife by marrying Bec as to pay the dead woman tribute. How strange, Bec thought, that she and Val could have been moving in such different directions, so close together; that she'd enjoyed his company as a rolling holiday from the lab, and liked the feeling she was helping him recover from Celia's death, while he'd been pursuing a suitable acquisition, someone who looked fresh in a party frock, came with a sort of patriotic stamp inherited from her father and seemed to be doing good in the world.

She really had not been paying attention. He wasn't a churchgoer but she'd never known what kind of conversations he'd been having with God when, each night, he knelt by the bed, clasped his hands together, touched his forehead to the knuckle of his thumb, and was silent for a minute or two. She'd asked him. 'Just praying,' he said. It never seemed to hold him back when he got into bed with her.

The death of her father, when she was nine, and the death of the love of Joel, when she was twenty-six, were still present to her now at thirty-three in the alterations they'd made to the fabric of her peace of mind. She'd got used to the monumental remains of those disasters looming up in her moodscape. They overshadowed her and she didn't understand how the people she had dealings with didn't seem likewise overshadowed by the ridges and craters of their own encounters with fate. She wasn't the only one to have known the early death of a parent or the death of love, and she couldn't work out whether other people had come up with a system for rationalising catastrophe that she wasn't being let in on, or whether they'd learned how to fool themselves into thinking there would be no more catastrophes.

She was on the hunt for secret systems. Her behaviour outside science seemed quite random to her and she hoped that in her randomness she might stumble across some pattern that others had concocted to show them how to behave. It left her vulnerable to confident men, although she found that the moment their plans and their confidence fell apart was when she liked them most.

The post-docs would invite her to parties and she'd often drift straight from the lab late at night into the music and drunken talk of somebody's living room. One morning not long after her thirtieth birthday she got up from the bed where she'd spent the night with a man she'd just met. Karl, or it could have been Carl, she never found out, had a desk under the window in his room. Bec found her shirt on the desk, crumpled and inside out, covering a pile of folders and books. When she picked up the shirt she saw there was a sheet of paper at the top of the pile partly covered with grid-like doodles, a column of figures and a list of girls' names. Bec counted. There were twenty-five names. Bec turned and asked C/Karl if this was all the women he'd gone out with.

'All the girls I've slept with,' said C/Karl. 'Since I left university.'

'Are you going to add my name?'

C/Karl smiled, propped himself up on one elbow, and rubbed his eyes with the heel of his hand. 'I was bored. I wondered how many.'

'But why did you write the names down like that?'

'Don't you ever do it?' said C/Karl, as if this were an answer.

'No,' said Bec, sitting down on the edge of the bed with her back to him, pulling the sleeves out of the shirt. 'What do these symbols mean?'

C/Karl wriggled over and looked with reluctance at the sheet. 'Which ones?' he said.

'Here, where there's a lightning flash.'

'Those are the crazy ones.'

'There are a lot of those.'

Now that his system had been exposed he was excited to be explaining it. 'A star means they're good-looking, an M means marriage material, and the F means the sex was amazing. The smiley face is them being fun to be with.'

'What about the pound sign? That means they've got money? That's the one that embarrasses you, isn't it? Why?'

C/Karl shrugged, smiled, scratched his thigh and searched for the makings of a smoke.

'Did you propose to any of the marriageable ones?'

C/Karl shook his head, shook the match out and wrinkled

his eyes against the white strands curling up from the cigarette. 'Too young to settle down.'

Bec frowned. 'What about this one?' she said. 'Dora. Star star star, M, F F F, smiley face, pound sign. She sounds too good to let her get away. Were you in love with her?'

C/Karl laughed a soft, hoarse laugh. 'Lightning flash, lightning flash, lightning flash . . .'

'Do you have a target? Are you competing with your friends?'

'No questions before breakfast,' said C/Karl, holding her shoulders from behind. His hands slipped over her breasts and she reached up and fondled his shaven head, warm like some just-baked thing. She plucked the cigarette from his mouth and took a drag.

'I have to go,' said Bec.

'Do you really not know how many men you've slept with?'

Bec looked at him, breathed out a cloud and said she'd been with three men already that week.

C/Karl snatched his hands off her as if contact would burn them and moved crabwise back in the bedclothes. His eyes became remote and tough. She couldn't tell, when he clasped his hands over his knees, looked down and shook his head with something like a laugh, if he was disapproving or envious or just surprised.

She told a friend. 'Four in one week is quite a lot,' said the friend. 'I never had four in one week. I never had two in one week.'

'That was the only time,' said Bec. 'I was feeling unvalued. But still, who says it's a lot?'

The friend wriggled. 'It sort of kills the idea there's any intimacy there.'

71

'Is that obvious? Is there a law? Is there a rule? You wouldn't say it was a lot if I said I made four new friends in one week.'

'That would be shocking,' said the friend.

'So you're shocked.'

'You're a scientist. You're looking for the kind of certainties in life that you find in the lab.'

'You talk as if there are certainties, as if it's an obvious rule that having sex with four men in one week is excessive, and I don't see that it is obvious.' She'd raised her voice and became aware that the mothers with toddlers in the café were looking at them. She and the friend leaned in closer to each other.

'And what about his list?' said Bec. 'He wasn't a scientist, he worked in a chichi coffee shop and made dance tracks, and he was imposing his grid on the world like a system to live by.'

'It wasn't a theory, was it,' said the friend. 'He was just trying to keep a handle on matters. Look.' She woke her iPhone and flicked to an app called ManRater. She showed Bec how it assigned points; plus two for being funny, plus one for every £20,000 a man earned over the minimum wage, plus two for wanting children, minus one for every previous marriage after the first, plus two for being tall, plus two for being big, plus three for being very big.

'It syncs with your contacts,' she said.

'How much is love worth?' asked Bec.

'You get plus two if he loves you, and plus one if you love him.'

'That's rather sad.'

'It does seem to set the bar low.'

'It's just a game, though, isn't it?' said Bec. 'It's just scratching the surface.'

'Surface is all most of us have,' said the friend, her eyes widening and fixing on Bec. 'Surface is a lot to be getting on with.'

'Did you pay for it?' said Bec.

'Fifty-nine pence,' said the friend, and that made them laugh.

11

Early on Sunday Bec took the Tube to her lab at the Centre for Parasite Control. Through the grubby metal-framed windows of the old concrete block the slats of Venetian blinds could be seen, pushed up slantwise by pot plants, faded sheaves of printed matter and old plastic cutaway models of the workings of parasites, painted in Atomic Age colours of teal, cream, tongue-pink and kidney-brown.

On the third floor she hauled on a buttonless lab coat over her white linen shirt and jeans. In a secure airlocked room five incubators, grey and new and taller than she was, hummed sweetly and their lights shone steadily. They were the reward for her discovery.

'Why not put them in Dar es Salaam instead of making the stuff here and taking it there?' she once asked.

Maddie told her the Africans wouldn't look after them properly. They couldn't afford the running costs, she said.

'We can afford them,' said Bec.

'They haven't got the infrastructure,' said the director. 'I suppose you'd like to move the whole centre to Tanzania.'

'That's where the malaria is,' said Bec.

Maddie looked at her, seemed about to smile, then leaned

forward and whispered in Bec's ear: 'One day they'll take our jobs. But not while I'm alive.'

Bec put on latex gloves and a mask, took the cover off the hood and switched on the flow of air. She unlocked the first incubator, pulled out a drawer, took the nearest flask and closed the door. The machine gasped as it flushed itself free of oxygen. Bec carried the flask to the hood, sprayed ethanol over the gloves, opened the flask, drew chicken blood out with a pipette, dropped it in an Eppendorf and gave it a turn in the centrifuge. Dotting a clean glass slide with specks of blood, she smeared the blood into a film and dried it with a hairdryer, then fixed the film with ethanol, made up a flask of Giemsa solution, dropped the stain onto the blood and set it aside to take. She pulled off the gloves, tossed them in a pedal bin, took a sterile pricker and examined her left hand. She'd been pricking herself every week for years and the pads of her fingertips were speckled with tiny holes, black with dried blood. Sometimes they hurt a little.

She put on another pair of gloves, held the pricker between her lips, took a fresh slide in her left hand and a piece of cotton wool dipped in alcohol in her right, slipped off her shoes, sat on the linoleum floor with her back against a cupboard and tucked in her left leg. She swabbed her little toe, jabbed the pricker into it, touched the slide against the bright bead of blood, got up, made a film and hopped over to fill a dropper with water. She hopped back to the slides, counted to two hundred, flushed the stain off with water and put the slides on a rack to dry.

When she'd heard that her father had been killed, it seemed obvious to her that he'd died from the intervention of a not-human force. She knew he was a soldier; they told her he'd been captured, tortured and executed by someone from the other side. It didn't sound to her as if it could be of the human world. *The other side* was the place where the terrors waited. As a small child Bec had been prone to daylight fears; that the tractor driver, for instance, was trapped inside the cab of his machine because the crows swirling round the plough were attacking him. That the wind making the curtains swing when it blew through the window of their house in Dorset would keep getting stronger until it smashed the family and their furniture against the walls. That when the tap was turned off, and its mouth was open and dry and seemingly empty, something terrible was about to flow out of it, something that was not water and had no human name.

It was in the way of going up against *the other side* that Bec went to the interview room where she persuaded an admissions panel that they had to let her study tropical medicine. 'What if poor countries were infested with some huge predator, hundreds of thousands of invisible monsters six feet tall who were charging round, tearing the heads off babies?' the eighteen-year-old Bec asked the panel accusingly, her cheeks red and her forehead damp from the heat of the heavy suit and buttoned-up blouse she was wearing. 'I think we would have done something about it by now.'

'What if rich countries were infested with a predator that was tearing the heads off old people?' said one of the professors. 'Shouldn't we do something about that?'

'Old people aren't as important,' said Bec. 'Everyone has to die in the end.'

The three professors on the panel laughed in a knowing way as if in that moment she'd become one of them, as if they assumed she didn't mean it, that she was only shocking them to make them remember her.

Bec put the chicken blood slide onto the stage of a microscope, put a couple of drops of immersion oil on the thick film, turned the nosepiece to the x100 objective and looked through the binocular lenses at the indigo field of stained serum. It was full of her parasite, *H. gregi*, dark blue dots in the chicken's blood cells, growing to be killed and made into vaccine. She counted the number of parasites and leukocytes she could see, moved the slide a few microns to the left and counted again. She did this a hundred times.

When she finished with the slide from the incubator, she turned to her own blood. It wasn't part of the programme, but she liked to keep an eye on what *gregi* was up to in there. She studied hundreds of fields; at field 405 she saw a blurry darkness inside the walls of one of her cells and whistled a fanfare to herself. 'There you are,' she said. 'My dear little hypnozoite.'

Bec dallied at the lab, eating crisps from the vending machine. The incubators were full and the data was written up. In the early evening Val called and said that it wasn't too late, they could still meet. It was essential to Bec that she didn't lie to Val, yet she had no reason to stay at work. As he talked he steadily lowered a slab of obligation onto her. She felt its weight, and she would either have to come up with a way to make more haemoproteus, or see him.

She saw the face of the security guard on his rounds peeping at her through the view panel in the door and remembered that there were boxes of anaerobic flasks and candle jars in the basement.

'I still have more to do,' she told Val.

'It's Sunday. You've been there all day,' said Val. 'If there's extra work get your minions to do it.'

Bec got the guard to open up the store room and help her carry the boxes upstairs. She cut them open carelessly, ignoring the instructions not to use knives. She pulled the anaerobic flasks out of their sterile packaging and set up an assembly line with flasks, petri dishes, cultures and pipette. One by one she filled the flasks with primed dishes, popped the catalyst in and closed the seal. She emptied her mind of everything but the work. Once she'd finished with the flasks she set about another round of parasite production with the centre's old stock of candle jars. The flame drifted from point to point as Bec lit candles and placed the jars over them and they gulped down their oxygen and went out until every free horizontal space in the lab was covered in glass or flasks. The lab smelled of burned wax. Bec turned up the extractor fan and put out all the lights except a single reading lamp on the desk in her office.

It was midnight. The lamp shone a sharp yellow disc of light onto the pale varnished pine of the desk and the copy of *Parasitology Today* Bec intended to read, and a wider sphere of dimmer illumination, floating in the darkness, that Bec clambered into with a mug of mint tea. She sat in the padded chair, let down her hair, took off her lab coat, wrapped it over her front like a blanket, tucked her feet up under her, read the first sentence of the first article, yawned, laid her cheek on her folded arms and went to sleep.

12

Next day at seven in the evening Ritchie drew up outside his sister's bleak workplace, saw her standing at the gate and tooted. She opened the car door. He could tell she'd spent the night in the lab. Unwashed women, even his own flesh and blood, aroused a primitive fear. Instinctively he put out his hand to stop her sitting down on the new leather next to him, uttered a panicky bleat and faked a reason.

'Don't you want to put your bag in the back?' he said.

'It doesn't matter,' said Bec. She dropped herself carelessly into the passenger seat, kicking her bag into the corner. It rattled with small things. Ritchie supposed he would find some of these things in the car's far crannies over the months to come; and who knew what she carried with her when she left that house of disease at the end of the day?

'New car,' said Bec, pleased to notice it. The seats, she saw, were a different colour.

'BMW,' said Ritchie. 'I indulged.'

'That's OK,' said Bec.

'Your Africans could spend years living high on the hog for the price of this.'

'Sell it, then,' said Bec.

They drove south. The car smothered outside noise so that

the mass of other cars and trucks around them in the dusk receded and they seemed to pad softly from traffic light to traffic light. It was a good moment, Bec thought, to introduce the secret she wanted his advice on. All she had to do was report to her brother on a certain segment of her real and recent life. And yet introducing this truth to Ritchie in the muffled peace of his car was a great labour, as if she were having to construct a complicated lie.

When Ritchie and Karin's marriage had been a more volatile thing it had excited Bec to see her famous, beautiful brother and sister-in-law fighting in front of her like heroes of ancient legend, the accumulated layers of tiny indentations left on their bodies by millions of eyes and cameras scintillating as they moved. Ritchie hadn't begun to pile on weight then, his hair and eyebrows were sleek and black, his cheekbones stood out and the dark patches under his eyes were still smooth, making him look as if otherworldly suffering, rather than crying babies, stopped him sleeping. Now his paunch was fuller and his eyes had sunk more deeply between the lids and into the folds below them. He charmed people by seeming to fight off an agonising tiredness to speak to them.

'How are the young entertainers?' she said. She didn't like *Teen Makeover* and still her brother's creation and production of the show was a feat she marvelled at. Her imagination approached the complexity of it, the technicians, the presenters, the egotistical teenagers, the demented parents, the journal-ists, the deadlines, the advertisers, and recoiled. She didn't understand how Ritchie had time for anything else; she didn't know how he stopped himself going mad.

'There was a band from up north,' said Ritchie. 'They were good.'

'Did you pick up a guitar and play along?'

'What makes you think that?' said Ritchie. Bec liked to think of her brother jamming with a group of teenagers, but to Ritchie, her smile off into the distance seemed to mock him, addressed, as he had thought when they were young, to an invisible circle of friends, high up and out of his reach, who found him pitiable.

'You like hanging out with your teenagers,' said Bec.

'I don't hang out with them.'

'You should. Are we going to talk about Dad now?'

'Let's wait till we see Mum.'

Bec looked down and picked at the edge of the seat. They traversed the splicing and braiding of the M23 and M25, the concrete of the flyovers greenly organic in the waning light. On the tall blue motorway signs the white spears of turning off or going on were fat and orderly, like England. In shadow now, with her mass of half-combed hair, Bec seemed to Ritchie to be the resentful teenager who barely lifted her head for years after their father was buried.

'I wonder why I feel I can tell you absolutely anything,' said Bec.

'I'm your brother. You know . . . *and then there were three.*'

'I think it's because you've spanned the whole range. Selfish brat to good son, kind brother. Cokey screwing-around rock star to loyal husband and father.'

She meant to praise him. Ritchie bit the inside of his cheek, tasted blood, mixed it with saliva, swallowed it and gently cleared his throat.

'Val proposed to me,' said Bec. 'I said I'd marry him and I don't want to.'

Ritchie liked the idea of dynasty. He liked the sound of

news and entertainment joined by blood, as the foundry and the manor house in days of yore, whenever that had been. Then he thought of sly, knowing, sceptical Val Oatman opposite him at the table on Christmas Day, challenging his power in front of his family. Never!

'What would you rather do?' he said.

'Tell him I've changed my mind.'

'Do it.'

'It's horrible. It seems wrong.'

'It's normal,' said Ritchie. 'It's not as if you didn't sleep with him. He won't be happy, but that's the game. He hasn't booked Westminster Abbey. You're a free woman.'

Bec was silent for a while. 'Don't tell Mum,' she said. 'Am I that free? How can I be? I spend my time watching single-celled organisms breeding, feeding and dying and wonder how free I'd look on a slide, eighty years in a one-minute animation.'

'You don't see parasites driving these babies,' said Ritchie, patting the dashboard. He pulled over onto the hard shoulder to show his sister the nought to sixty.

13

Through the dying of engines, the tinkling of unlocked seatbelt buckles and the scrape of cases yanked out of bins, through the overamped thank-yous of the crew and the prickling silence of passengers waiting in the aisle for doors to be opened, Stephanie Shepherd stayed in her seat, filling in her food diary. She would not hurry for her children and she resented being made to fly to London to mediate between her son's schemes, her daughter's sense of propriety and her husband's absence. Ritchie and Bec had permanent lodgings in her heart, but more and more her son and daughter seemed like the interruption of something ungraspably fine of which her grandchildren were the smooth continuing.

Stephanie felt a kick of nerves when the plane nuzzled the ramp at Gatwick that the gatekeepers would find something wrong with her passport. That they'd ask her *the reason for your visit*. 'I'm British. It's my home,' she'd say, sounding unconfident. The people who checked her passport had never been her kind of people, it seemed to her, but they were even less her kind of people now. They were so mixed. She hadn't known what to say to the wives of the NCOs when Greg was alive. She'd been a bad captain's wife in that regard. But she was sure that if only she'd known *then* she might have to be patient *now* with somebody whose parents were born in Karachi, who had the power to test her passport in the glow of a mysterious machine, she would have found a corporal's wife from a council estate in Plymouth easier to talk to.

She had a guide to the humours open on her lap and the food diary overlapping. Her humourist had instructed her to use the guide and the tables in it in conjunction with the diary to keep her blood, phlegm and bile in balance. He'd made it sound simple, and it was clear that the pasta they'd been served on the plane was 'warm and moist'. But had it been a 100g serving, or 200g? Why did the table describe orange juice as 'dry' and chocolate ice cream as 'warm'? If cabbage was 'warm and dry' and mayonnaise was 'cold and moist' did that make coleslaw perfectly balanced, so you could eat as much as you liked?

Stephanie was sure that she understood her own body, and that now, only now, after tremendous effort and exhaustive research in monthly magazines and on the Internet, was she close to the point where she could say she was in perfect health. For the first time in her life, at the age of sixty-four, she could begin to live.

She badly wanted to know her daughter's views on the humourist diet, but wasn't sure how to bring it up. She knew the contours of her daughter's disapproval. How, Stephanie wondered, did scientists get anywhere if they were closed to new ideas?

Stephanie had lived in Spain since her son acquired glamour and fame in the eyes of the world. When he was twenty-two Ritchie had been socked with a series of dizzying lump sums and bought Stephanie a house in Spain without asking her. Bec was at Cambridge already; Stephanie took the gift gladly and moved. Ever since Greg's murder she'd wanted to leave Dorset. She hated the coomb at the bottom of the garden and the distant sound of rushing water that could be attenuated by music but never silenced. She hated the way crows rose up out of the trees in the cleft, looking from the windows of the house as if they were boiling up out of the earth.

Her friends now were expatriate Brits. Over time, without her noticing it, she'd come to resemble them in her way of thinking. She forgot that she'd moved to Spain because she was bored, lonely and liked sunshine. Now she believed that she hadn't left Britain of her own accord but had been forced to flee because it was rotten and decaying. Immigrants, grasping bureaucrats, socialists, workshy spongers, amoral celebrities, trashy nouveau riche types, sexual perverts and traitors squabbled over the residue. Val's newspaper – she had the printed version delivered – was her source. The discovery that the editor of her favourite rag was courting her daughter filled her with foreboding, as if the paper's astrologer had appeared on the doorstep, clutching a horoscope and asking for her second-born by name.

14

The border guard who glanced at Stephanie's passport was Asian of some sort, she supposed, and when he smiled at her, gave the passport back and wished her a good evening she thought sadly of her Moroccan housekeeper Shada sitting by herself in the hills above Malaga, when the two of them could be having supper together. Stephanie stepped gamely through customs and saw Bec and Ritchie at the rail on the far side. At the sight of her waving Ritchie raised his head over an imaginary crowd. Bec grinned the grin that bound her to the girl Stephanie reared; perhaps the only thing that did. Ritchie hugged his mother first. Stephanie glanced at the other greeters to see if they were watching. She wanted them to know that these were her children.

With Bec's arms around her, she smelled a staleness in her daughter's clothes. Bec's hair was ratty and she was wearing ugly glasses with thick lenses.

'You could have dressed up a bit for your mother,' she said, stepping back, still holding on to Bec's shoulders, feeling her daughter's body clench. Bec pulled away, pulled the glasses off her face, pushed them into her bag and dug her fingers through her hair.

'She won't come with us to Petersmere,' said Ritchie.

'I've got too much to do before Africa,' said Bec. 'I didn't have time to change.'

'I didn't mean to make you take off your glasses, darling,' said Stephanie. 'You should wear them if you need to.'

'My eyes are fine,' said Bec. 'I had a blurry spell when we came off the motorway, that's all. How was your flight?' She smiled and Stephanie thought *Oh, I do matter to her*.

'It was absolutely all right,' said Stephanie. She took Bec's hand and looked at Ritchie. She wanted to get away from the glare of arrivals and the boiled eyes of the chauffeurs holding clients' names to their bellies.

'We'll have dinner at the Carter's Arms,' pitched Ritchie, stopping to put his head level with his sister and mother. He looked from face to face. 'We'll go home afterwards. Everyone's looking forward to seeing you.'

'Why aren't Karin and the children coming to dinner?'

'Because we have to talk about Ritchie's film,' said Bec.

'Oh yes.'

'We don't *have* to,' said Ritchie earnestly.

'But that's why she came,' said Bec.

'Don't call me "she", darling,' said Stephanie, and she raised her voice over Bec saying 'Sorry, Mum,' and asked Ritchie if they were going to a pub.

'They do excellent food. Not as good as you're used to, of course,' said Ritchie.

'As long as they have plenty of different things,' said Stephanie.

'Oh, you're on a new diet!' said Bec. Her cheerfulness about it made Stephanie hope and then she thought *She doesn't care what I do any more*.

'Humourism,' said Stephanie, so nervously that Bec didn't hear.

Ritchie set off with Stephanie's case and the women followed. They processioned out of the terminal and walked raggedly, none abreast, towards the car. In the stretched-thin evening light of northern summer Stephanie detected paleness around her, pale faces, pale leaves and pale concrete, and a cold breeze jostled her through her thin blouse. She wanted to tell her children that she would be having her evening swim at this time, that Shada would have a gin and tonic ready for her under the pergola, but talking up the splendour of her Spanish life would make it hard then to lament the cruelty of her forced exile.

'I haven't been to a pub for years,' said Stephanie at the bar of the Carter's Arms, confused by the conjunction of white tablecloths and ruddy boys drinking pints, and by fantastical references to marrow bone and samphire on the densely chalked blackboard menu. 'I don't go to the English pubs in Spain, of course.'

When Stephanie asked Bec about Val the question was answered, not in the sense that her daughter spoke, with words including 'fine' and 'seeing him tomorrow' but in a space opening up between them and a gloom Bec seemed to want to keep for herself. Stephanie had a rush of panic that she was losing her daughter and said: 'Humourism is working for me. It's the first time in my life I've felt completely well. Have you heard of it?'

Bec looked over her mother's hair, artificially brown and glossy, her depilated upper lip, her plucked eyebrows, the soft wrinkles at the corners of her mouth and eyes, the silk scarf wrapped round her neck, the yearning in her blue eyes. 'You look great,' she said. 'You're never ill.'

'The headaches, the insomnia, the being tired all the time? Aching limbs? Terrible digestion.' She looked off to the side. 'The lines.' She fluttered her fingertips vaguely over her cheek.

'You are sixty-five,' said Bec.

'Sixty-four, if you don't mind.'

'And you feel healthier now than you did when you were seventeen?'

'I don't know that I care for the contrast you're making,' said Stephanie. 'It can take a long time to find a healthy way of living.'

'They're always coming up with new things to try.'

'It's as if you don't want me to be happy,' said Stephanie. 'You see what you do? Look.' She ran her index finger across her forehead. 'Lines.'

'If you were more accepting now, it wouldn't be so hard later,' said Bec.

Her mother stared at her, her head trembling, daring Bec to spell out what she meant by 'later', and Bec went red. 'What's humourism?' she said. 'Does it mean you're supposed to laugh all the time? Look, Ritchie's found us a place.'

They walked over to a wood-panelled booth. Beyond the bar fat flames flushed the kitchen space with orange light. Stephanie told Bec about the book she was using as her lifestyle guide, about the four humours, blood, phlegm, black and yellow bile, and about the four qualities, sanguine, choleric, melancholic and phlegmatic.

'That's medieval medicine,' said Bec.

'It's older than that. It goes back to the Greeks,' said Stephanie approvingly. 'They had a lot of wisdom, the ancients.'

'They didn't know the heart pumped blood. They thought

worms caused toothache. They died of infectious diseases before they were thirty.'

'My humourist is allowed to have an opinion on what's best for my health.'

'Why not take away electricity while you're about it?'

'Nobody's talking about taking anything away, darling. You mustn't take it personally when someone disagrees with you. Just because my black bile levels are elevated doesn't mean I can't go on the Internet. That's where I found out about humourism, as a matter of fact.' She smiled and squeezed her daughter's hand. 'I'm so proud of you.'

'We all are,' said Ritchie. He sat next to Stephanie, draping his arm along the back of the booth. The two of them faced Bec. When Stephanie leaned forward to speak, Ritchie leaned with her. Stephanie said, with a shake in her voice: 'We're proud of you, but I don't see why I have to die young because there's only one kind of science allowed.'

'Mum,' said Bec. 'It's too late for you to die young.'

'Bec!' said Ritchie, putting his arm round their mother.

'You're strong. You'll outlive us all.'

'A lot of scientists have a difference of opinion with *you* about your infection,' said Stephanie, lowering her eyes.

'It's not an infection. I'm hosting a benign parasite that gives protection against malaria.'

'I don't like the idea of that thing inside you and I don't like it that you named it after your father. I don't know whether to be worried or revolted.'

Wine came, and Ritchie proposed a toast to Bec's success in Africa. He was trying not to speak, to look as if he was listening and to keep his mother and sister happy. Yet it was important to him to feel he was leading them. Bec and

Stephanie no longer noticed. He'd accumulated authority as if he'd eaten a little part of the soul of each of the people who worked for him. Bec had power in her lab now too but this authority hadn't accrued to her. She was the boss of a dozen people and yet it shamed her to give them orders or rebuke them, even to praise them. She rejected her subordinates' submission to her will. She could tell they were offering some part of themselves to her and was afraid to take it.

Ritchie waited till he had his pudding bowl of rhubarb fool in front of him to tell them what he wanted to do and ask for their blessing. Four months ago he'd written to Colum O'Donabháin, executioner of Greg Shepherd, his and Bec's father, Stephanie's husband. He wanted to make a documentary about the killing, and film interviews with him. O'Donabháin was a few years out of jail, living in Dublin, and wrote back saying he had no objection. As the leader of a faction of a faction of Marxist Republicans, O'Donabháin caught Captain Shepherd on his way to meet a traitor in their ranks, beat the Englishman up to make him identify the traitor, and when he wouldn't tell them, shot him dead. Bec was nine; Ritchie fifteen.

He watched his sister. The glisten of her eyes and the colour in her cheeks made him feel sluggish and earthbound. *She's pretending to be interested*, he thought.

'O'Donabháin's an old man now,' he said. 'He spent a long time in prison. He lives in a council house with his mother and writes poetry. I never got over what happened to Dad and making a film about meeting O'Donabháin would be a chance for us to get closure and for him to atone to the family.' He beat the air with his fist as he had that morning, persuading The What to play music badly. 'I don't want to do this without your support. Tell me what you think.' He saw his mother, who'd been rocking back and forward, head bent, hands clasped, look up at Bec, who started to open her mouth. 'You first, Mum,' said Ritchie.

'Oh,' said Stephanie, who'd wanted to hear what Bec thought before committing herself. Her daughter had such strong convictions that there were right and wrong things to do that Stephanie could yield to her. She was surprised to hear Ritchie say he'd never got over Greg's death. As she remembered, it was only true in the sense that the death of his father turned him from a sullen, rebellious tyke into a precociously warm, generous man who looked after his family. It'd been Bec, surely, who hadn't been able to bear the loss, burning lines into her wrist with the edge of a hot spoon, screaming at everyone, disappearing into the coomb for hours in the rain.

Stephanie couldn't see any harm in Ritchie making his film. She'd lost a second husband to heart disease since the first. She didn't so much miss Greg as resent the sense of unfairness his departure had left her with. Twenty-five years had passed; a new generation had grown up. Long before Greg was killed she'd imagined him dying, and he'd been away so much, off smiling to his life of guns and sleeping rough, that he'd already died a little in advance.

'As long as *I* don't have to meet the murderer,' she said. 'As long as I don't have to watch the film. I don't see . . .' she looked at Bec again '. . . why I should mind. What do you think?' she asked her daughter.

'Maybe Dad would be writing poetry now, if he were alive,' said Bec. 'I don't understand what closure means. What gets closed when you do this? If this man wants to atone to the family, he should atone to the family, not to millions of strangers on TV. That's not atonement. It's entertainment.'

'It's not entertainment,' said Ritchie patiently, 'it's cathartic.'

'It's a show, isn't it? It's doing whatever you have that's intimate and private and turning it into a show. It's wrong. Go and see him, talk to him, be his friend, take his confession, whatever, I don't care, but you mustn't make a film about it.'

'You didn't ask us when you named your infection after Dad.'

'It's not an infection,' said Bec. '*Haemoproteus gregi* is a benign parasite.'

'They're not going to thank you in Africa if you cure malaria and all the kids are wearing bottle-bottom glasses and bumping into trees.'

Stephanie laughed and put her hand over her mouth.

'If you do this,' said Bec, 'it's as if the most important thing Dad did in his life was to die.'

15

At home after work the next day, dressing to meet Val, Bec put on some of the light casual clothes she was taking to Africa: a long cheesecloth skirt, a black spaghetti-strap top, a light black blouse and black sandals. Before leaving she opened the freezer compartment of the fridge, took out the envelope with the ring and put it in her bag.

The plane trees near the restaurant were full of starlings and their song was louder than the traffic in the warm evening air. Bec waited in the street, delaying the moment when she would have to step out of the light. She squinted up at the apricot-coloured sky and listened to the rub and squeak of the flock turn all the crooked spaces of the street's mismatched façade into instruments, its rusting gutters and cracked pediments and the dark chinks between bricks. She took a deep breath and walked down a flight of stairs into a windowless, air-conditioned basement.

Val was late. Bec sat on a high stool at the bar, rolling up and smoothing out the white tissue mat her glass of wine had been served on. Her heart beat hard. The bar top was made of heavy black stone, flecked with mica, cold to the touch, and the walls were black. Tiny lights illuminated red-painted recesses. Young waiters, all in black, with lacquered hair and patent leather shoes, placed a bowl of wasabi-flavoured snacks in front of her and opened for her the tall card carrying a short menu in an expanse of space. Bec wanted Val to get there quickly but when he touched her shoulder and greeted her it was too soon.

Short, dark and slim, with grey eyes that bulged slightly, Val looked as if he might be a bullfighter in middle years. He was still and alert, wary, handsome, rationing his passions, careful what he ate, jealous of his time, straight-backed. Bec told him he looked nice and when she spoke the words her mouth went dry and the blood rushed in and out of her face as if she'd been caught tipping poison in his drink.

Val glanced down at Bec's cheesecloth skirt and sandals, at the bra strap under the strap of her top. 'Didn't you have time to go home and change?' he said.

He sat on the stool next to hers and saw her naked left hand.

'Where's the ring?' he said.

Bec reached into her bag, took out the envelope and gave it to Val. It was a plain white office envelope, the kind they sell in stationery shops in packets of fifty. It was crumpled at the edges and damp where ice from the freezer had melted on the paper. Val took it, opened the flap, looked inside, stuck out his lower lip, closed the envelope, folded it in two and tucked it in his inside jacket pocket. He leaned one elbow on the bar and linked the fingers of his hands together. His shoulders quivered. He couldn't meet Bec's eyes.

'I've behaved badly,' said Bec. 'I'm sorry.'

Val looked up and swallowed. For a moment, he seemed unsure of himself. It became him.

'When I met you, there were so many people around you

wanting your attention, and all the same you seemed lonely,' said Bec. 'They looked up to you, or they were jealous of you, or they were afraid of you, and you were still lonely. You were carrying a loss, and I admired how you tried to hide it. You were . . .' She groped for a word to describe a man hollowed out by grief who doesn't become addicted to it, or to the pity of others, and who remains loyal to life. '. . . dignified,' she said.

'Go on,' said Val. Bec could see his uncertainty skinning over. She remembered how he liked to talk about his young teenage children. He found more about them to say than was worth telling, as if fending off the temptation to impress her with anecdotes about famous people he knew. She realised Val had been prepping her for a life of shared responsibility all along; a life of cohabitation with the quiet, evasive kids, for whom Val's determination not to spoil them had been, with its intermittent blasts of overwhelming attention, a kind of spoiling. He'd assumed from the start that they were moving towards marriage, and the children, perhaps, had assumed the same thing, which was why they were so quiet and evasive.

Her eyes slipped to the knot of Val's tie. She'd taken pleasure in moving his ties to one side, unfastening the second button of his shirt and sliding her hand over his chest. The memory seemed like a story she'd been told rather than something she'd done.

It was as if just by staring at her and keeping perfectly still he was forcing her mouth shut and making it hard for her to breathe. The knowledge that death had broken into Val's house and slowly killed his wife, and that he hadn't crumbled and had guarded his children, had made her interested in him and given her a feeling of kinship. It didn't seem to her that she'd dealt well with death when it came early to her family. His grief had hooked her and his assumption of power had turned her on. It satisfied a need for abasement. Several months earlier, when she'd kneeled in front of him in a half-lit room and taken him in her mouth, she felt power, mercy and humiliation running through her and mixing in a single delicious stream.

A waitress came over to tell them that their table was ready.

'We won't be needing it,' said Val. 'I'll have a bottle of mineral water, still, no ice, no lemon.' He turned to Bec. She saw herself reflected in his face: a cold, hard, trivial woman.

'It was wrong of you to take my wife's ring if you didn't want to marry me,' said Val.

'It was wrong,' said Bec gratefully. 'I should have said no. I was a coward. I didn't want to hurt your feelings. I didn't think.'

Val pinched the creases of his trousers and pulled them straight. 'Do you remember telling me about your father?' he said. 'Do you remember telling me how he died when he could have stayed alive by betraying some shit, and how his children had to try harder than most people to do the right thing? Here.' He gave Bec a napkin and she wiped the tears from her face. 'I'm making this too easy for you by letting you hate me.' He got up, seemed about to walk away, sat down again and pulled his chair closer to Bec.

'You've been saying "yes" to everything I asked for six months,' he said. 'You've met somebody else and you don't have the guts to admit it.'

'I haven't met anybody. I said yes before because you asked me and I liked making you happy. I said yes to marriage because

97

I panicked when you brought out your ring with all the weight of it.'

'You pitied me.'

'You make pity sound like a punch in the face.'

'That would have been better,' said Val.

'Yes, I see that,' said Bec. 'You never talked about love. I liked it that you weren't throwing that word around the way people do. But perhaps because you didn't tell me you loved me, it made me think it was all right that I didn't love you.'

A change came over Val's face. The muscles of his face tightened, his eyes seemed to harden and his mouth twisted into an expression of hatred.

'You really are a modern Englishwoman, aren't you?' he said in a harsh, alien voice. 'An atheist prattling about love, a hedonist bragging about her good works among the poor, an arrogant intellectual who thinks science has all the answers and who knows nothing about the lives of ordinary, decent, hard-working people. You move from party to party, from man to man, without a thought for family, loyalty, commitment. How many men have you been with? Twenty? Fifty? How many still to come? One day you'll wake up dry and alone and wonder why your house is so quiet, why there aren't any children in it.' He gulped water and the glass hiding his mouth emphasised his bulging eyes and the rage that had taken possession of him.

The shock of his words pushed Bec's spirits into a crouch, as if she were suddenly fighting for her life, and amid the roar of blood and the battering of her heart her mind was clear. 'You could have asked me to marry you before you put your hand between my legs,' she said. 'You could have asked me to marry you before you kissed me. You talk as if there are rules

I should be living by but if there are, you don't know them any better than I do. I wish there was some kind of moral foundation I could stand on or try to blow up if I didn't like it but there isn't one.'

Val's eyes softened and he relaxed, as if a demon that had possessed him had left his body, taking with it all consciousness of what it had just made its host say. 'There can be, darling,' he said. 'Be my wife, be the mother to my children, and you can stand on that moral foundation: tradition, common law and the ten commandments.'

Bec was already getting up before he finished speaking. 'I'm not the one,' she said. She put out her hand for him to shake. He didn't move. She said: 'Goodbye. I'm sorry I made such a bad mistake.'

16

A month later Val invited Ritchie to lunch in his office. In the lift going up Ritchie regretted not having brought someone with him. He stuck the clip-on visitor badge in the pocket of his jacket. You chose your team according to who you were up against, he thought. Sometimes it was better to be alone; you projected trust and confidence. But there were times when you wanted a sidekick. What they did wasn't important. Sometimes, when he was on his way to meet a cunning man he didn't like, and he wasn't sure what they were going to talk about, Ritchie wanted another body on his side of the table, just for the extra mass.

The lift doors opened and a woman was there to meet him. She smiled and he followed her sprightly march along the corridor. Their footsteps made no sound in the thick carpet of this, the executive floor. The building was a steel, concrete and glass tower from the 1980s but on this level the walls were panelled with old oak and hung with paintings of – who? Past editors? As long as it wasn't about trying to get Bec to change her mind, thought Ritchie, it would go well; there was always advantage to be gained.

'Here you are,' said his guide, opening one of a set of double doors.

Ritchie went in and the door closed behind him. Most of the room was taken up by a long, narrow walnut table, polished to a deep lustre. Val sat at the far end, talking on a mobile. Two places had been set for a meal there, with bottles of water, glasses, a bowl of fruit and a basket of bread rolls. As Ritchie walked towards him Val stood up, lifting the chair back with his free hand, and began to end the call, signalling a welcome to Ritchie by widening his eyes. The long walls of the room were panelled with the same dark oak as the corridor. Instead of paintings of editors there were framed pages from the newspaper. The room's short walls, incongruously, were windows – clear glass from floor to ceiling, framed with anodised metal. Through the glass at Val's end of the table Ritchie could see Tower Bridge, the choppy broth of the Thames and the grey and yellow clouds driven low over London by the gusting September wind.

Val put the phone away, shook Ritchie's hand and said that he hoped he didn't mind if the two of them had lunch in the boardroom. Val seemed in such a good mood, more chatty and funny than Ritchie had seen him, and seemed so interested in the O'Donabháin film, that Ritchie relaxed. Val was tactful and open about his sister. He said early on, tucking in his chin while he looked at Ritchie, as if there was something he was having trouble swallowing, that Ritchie probably knew he and Bec had broken up; and Ritchie said yes, his sister had emailed him from Tanzania, and he was sorry. Val said he hoped Bec was doing well in Africa, that she was a remarkable woman, and that whatever had happened between the two of them, he wasn't going to let it spoil his lunch with Ritchie Shepherd.

A young man in a white tunic and apron came in with a trolley and carved a chicken for them and a waitress offered wine. They were left alone. Val bent his head over his plate and cut a small slice of chicken breast in half with a sawing motion that Ritchie found finicky.

'Is this going to be the last season of your show?' Val asked, looking up and putting the chicken in his mouth.

Ritchie felt a hollowing, but laughed. 'I haven't checked my messages in the last sixty seconds,' he said. 'The ratings don't lie. They'd be insane to cancel.'

Val nodded, finished chewing and took a drink of water. Ritchie put his knife and fork down, leaned back in his chair and watched him.

'I haven't heard anything,' said Val. 'I'm sure you have your enemies. Don't you?'

'I have a strategy,' said Ritchie, taking up his cutlery again and setting to work folding a leaf of crispy chicken skin onto the tines of his fork. 'Don't give anyone a reason to hate you.'

'Enemies inside the BBC, I mean. Those who might think making a market in setting children against each other wasn't a good use of the licence fee.'

'That's not really what *Teen Makeover*'s about,' said Ritchie cheerfully. 'Is that what you think?'

'You're way ahead of them,' said Val. 'This film project of yours is a bold thing. Perhaps it's the start of a new career. You've done that before. Changed course. Kept them guessing. And made it work, which is more than can be said for most.'

What does he want? thought Ritchie, enjoying the praise. He'd only abandoned The Lazygods after three albums flopped in a row, but he remembered it differently. It seemed to him that he'd put music aside when his creativity pulled him in another direction, when producers and critics were still urging him to keep recording.

'Your father was the kind of genuine British hero we should be celebrating more often,' said Val.

'It's about honouring his memory,' said Ritchie, wondering if the girl was coming back with pudding.

'Honour. That's exactly the word. Just because the guy he refused to give up seems to have been a nasty shit doesn't change that. He was loyal. Didn't crack.'

'Yes,' said Ritchie, frowning out of respect for his father's suffering. 'It's going to be hard for me to look O'Donabháin in the eyes, knowing what he did, but—'

'Is he a Catholic?' said Val.

'Who? O'Donabháin?' Ritchie grappled with the strangeness of the question. 'I don't know. I suppose so.'

'One of these socialist Catholics, I suppose,' said Val, smiling.

'Yes,' laughed Ritchie, not sure what Val was talking about. 'He writes poetry.'

'You're not going to let him read it out on camera?'

It hadn't occurred to Ritchie that this was a possibility. 'Of course not,' he said.

In the silence that followed Ritchie watched Val use his knife to drive and scrape everything left on the plate, each tiny scrap, into one compressed lump on his fork, as if nothing further could be done until the plate was clear.

'Catholic Marxist nationalists. What a lot of bloody nonsense,' said Val. 'He's a thug who should never have been let out.' Val looked up. His eyes were gentle and inquisitive. 'What about you, Ritchie? What do you believe in?'

Ritchie laughed, realised this wasn't an appropriate response, glanced out of the window and said: 'Fair play.' He remembered what he didn't like about Val Oatman. The editor was always likely to go off on one about morality. He would bore the pants off you if you let him.

'If only there was some great umpire in the sky to raise a finger when your leg came between the ball and the wicket, eh, Ritchie?' said Val. He closed his knife and fork like scissors and left them lying on his plate with the points towards Ritchie. He rested his fists on either side of the plate. 'Maybe you think there is.'

'I'm agnostic,' said Ritchie gruffly. 'I don't suppose there's any chance of a coffee?'

'Of course,' said Val.

He got up, went to the door and called through. While he was gone from the table Ritchie ran his eye over the framed newspaper pages on the wall opposite. He saw now that at the far end of the room from where he was sitting there was no frame, just a printout or a photocopy of a newspaper page stuck to the wall with a bit of sticky tape. It looked familiar. It was hard to make out; it looked like a feature Val's paper had run on Ritchie and Karin in the days of the band. Ritchie was no longer surprised by fame, but it seemed unlikely Val had put the article there to make him feel welcome.

Val came back with the waitress. Ritchie saw that there was no sweet course. Val didn't sit but stood looking down at Ritchie and the administration of the coffee. He had his hands in his pockets. He was blocking the light from the window.

'I suppose it must be pretty comfortable being an agnostic,' he said.

Ritchie stirred his coffee glumly as the waitress left. Not even a biscuit!

'But who's there to remind you if you do something wrong? How do you even know what's wrong?'

'Those pages,' said Ritchie, nodding at the wall. 'What's the criterion?'

'Come and have a look,' said Val. Ritchie got up and followed Val to a front-page story with a headline about a long-past Olympic Games. An athlete stood joyfully in front of the camera with a gold medal in her hand.

'Now turn it over,' said Val.

Ritchie lifted the framed page cautiously from the wall. It had been hung from the corners in such a way that it could easily be turned round and put back with the reverse side showing. The reverse carried another page. It was another story about the same athlete, but from a few years later. This time, instead of the words OLYMPIC GLORY the headline included the words CHEAT and DRUG SHAME. Ritchie was going to turn the second page back to face the wall but Val said 'Leave it. Look at the next one.'

The next page showed a famous model on a red carpet, her broad smile accentuating her cheekbones as she turned to the cameras, not quite unlinking her arms with the Hollywood star who was her consort. He was pushed to the background, and looked at the model with yearning, as if realising that neither sleeping with her nor marrying her nor loving her would give him the quality she possessed that he wanted. Ritchie turned the frame over. On the reverse side was an even larger picture of the model, a grainy, blown-up shot that nonetheless revealed unexpectedly deep lines in her face as she hunched over a mirror sprinkled with white powder, a tube stuck up her nose.

The third frame, which was only one away from the page with the story about Ritchie and Karin, held a story about an elderly English rock star famous for his Christian beliefs. When Ritchie turned it over, his hands shook.

'Too much caffeine, Ritchie,' said Val.

The reverse of the Christian rock star story was blank, a smooth expanse of dark wood. Ritchie ran his palm over it.

'Some people just go on doing the right thing all their lives,' said Val. 'I can't see that space ever being filled.' He smiled at Ritchie and turned the frame again so that the blank side was hidden. 'Why don't you go on looking? I have to make a call.'

Ritchie watched Val walk to the far end of the room, take his mobile, dial and begin talking too quietly for Ritchie to hear. He kept his back to Ritchie. Ritchie went straight to the printout of the story about him and Karin. On the floor underneath it, Ritchie saw, was a framed front page about a politician, as if the printout had only just been taped up in place of the article usually hung there. Ritchie skimmed through the printout but he knew it by heart from when it had come out twenty years earlier. He glanced over at Val, who was still talking. Licking his lips, Ritchie lifted the paper a fraction away from the wall and, turning up the corner, bent his head to see if there was anything printed on the other side.

'Oh, just pull that off the wall, I only put it up this morning,' Val called, and went back to his phone conversation.

Ritchie's heart hammered. He tugged the sheet of paper and it came away from the wall. He turned it over.

Ritchie had been a passenger once in the back seat of a car whose driver had lost control at speed on a dual carriageway in Scotland. The car had spun off the road, across the central reservation, across two lanes of oncoming traffic and down the embankment on the far side. In the end no one was hurt, but Ritchie had been aware, in the seconds of spinning, that he might be about to die. He didn't scream, shout or swear. It seemed to him that his heart rate barely went up. What he remembered from those moments was an intense curiosity about the exact way he would suffer. He wanted to experience everything, to see all there was to see of the landscape he would be smashed into and the movements of the various high-speed metal boxes that would intersect in collision. He was aware that there was another Ritchie slumped inside him, boggle-eyed and slack-bowelled with terror, but this Ritchie was the captive of this unworldly other Ritchie, this shy, fascinated, inquisitive little boy trotting forward in the worship of his new hero, his own fate. Yet the fear, in the end, was stronger, since despite his curiosity, Ritchie never understood what was happening. He was never able to put all the elements together, the speed of the oncoming trucks, the sound of their horns, the shriek of the tyres, the words of the driver and the other passengers, the number of spins, the moment of tipping when the car dived over the edge towards the trees. Now, Ritchie couldn't sort the words on the front page in front of him. He saw his own name in the headline.

SHEPHERD

Then in the same headline

CHILD SEX

His eyes ran to the first paragraph of the story and he saw 'arrested' and 'allegations'. He read the word 'allegations' several times. He went back to the beginning.

PROBE

Top TV producer and former
Lazygods lead singer Ritchie
Shepherd

Accurate, he thought.

Shepherd, 40, was visited by detectives

Was he forty? How old it looked, printed. How strange
that they called them detectives, such a quaint word.

At the £2.5 million Hampshire
mansion

Three million, he'd paid, money down, and a bargain it
had been. Tasteless people lived in mansions. He was not
tasteless.

SHEPHERD
HELD IN
CHILD SEX
PROBE

Yes, he thought. *It really does say that! How extraordinary!*

where he lives with his wife, former
Lazygods co-star Karin Olsson, and
their two children.

Who was this man, this monster, who had children and had
sex with a child? He must never be allowed, thought Ritchie.

Shepherd, son of murdered special
forces hero Captain Greg Shepherd,
was taken to Paddington Green
police station in London and held
overnight.

How ashamed that man's father would be. That man
Shepherd was him. But it was not him yet.

'I'm not sure about the headline,' said Val, who had come
up beside him. 'People might think it was about somebody
who looked after sheep. Of course that would bring in the
perverts, which would mean extra readers. What do you think?'

Ritchie looked round. Val lifted his chin, smiled and raised
his eyebrows.

'Are you publishing this?' said Ritchie.

'Look,' said Val, pointing to a space just below the paper's
masthead. 'There's no date.' He frowned at Ritchie. 'I'm
surprised to hear you ask that. You haven't been arrested on
child sex charges. Or have you? Did we miss a story?'

'This is *in very bad taste*,' said Ritchie.

'*I don't understand*,' said Val. 'Is that what you want to say?
You don't understand why we've done this?'

'I can think of a couple of reasons, both unacceptable.'

'Go on.' Val was still smiling and his voice was soft and pleasant.

'One reason would be illegal.'

'Oh, interesting. Let's come back to that, shall we? And the other?'

'A joke.'

'A joke!' Val nodded and looked to one side. He took a step back and turned to stare into Ritchie's eyes.

Val raised his voice suddenly to a shout, almost a scream, so loud that Ritchie could hardly believe it came from a man's mouth. 'Do you have any idea what right and wrong is, Ritchie?' Ritchie looked at him. 'I asked you a fucking question, you weaselly cunt! Do you know the difference between right and wrong?'

Ritchie's mouth dropped open of its own accord.

'Of course I do,' said Ritchie. 'You don't need to –'

'Don't you dare tell me what I need to do, you fucking cunting piece of dogshit. You fat cunt. You sad, talentless fuck. You know what you should be doing when you're talking to me, cunt? You should be on your knees. Did you make her go down on you, you fucking exploitative abusive cunt? Did you make her go down on you with your great fucking belly hanging over her? What kind of fucking apology for a man has to get a child to suck him off?'

'Wait a minute,' croaked Ritchie, and the astonishing thing was that the loudness of Val's voice, the terrible fixity of his eyes and the violence of his language were weakening him, literally weakening him, making his limbs feel weightless and his body shudder instead of tensing for defence. When the most astonishing and silly thing of all happened, and Val came up to him and whacked him hard across the jaw with the back of his hand, it didn't seem astonishing or silly, and nor did it that Ritchie slumped onto the floor and stayed there, half lying, half sitting.

'Ask yourself why I've got this power over you. Go on, ask yourself, you cunt,' said Val, looking down at him. 'How is it that I can hit you and you don't fight back, apart from the fact you're a nasty coward who bullies little girls into having sex with him? It's because you've done *wrong*. Now you know the difference. I can see you feel sorry for yourself. You're imagining other people feeling sorry for you too, aren't you? Look at poor little Ritchie, getting a hiding from that *evil* tabloid editor. Look at him hounded and his privacy invaded. It was you, Ritchie. You did this.' Val's voice became softer. 'When you don't believe, when you don't have faith in powers beyond this world to judge you, this is what happens. You don't believe in God, so when you cheat, and lie, and bully little girls, there's nobody to punish you. There's just me.' He tightened his tie and smoothed it down. 'That's right, get up. Be brave. That must have been a dreadful experience for you. Mr Oatman can get carried away.'

The sting in Ritchie's jaw was clearing his mind. The sudden softness of Val's speech, and a new gentleness in his eyes, was so welcome that he was grateful. He almost felt like crying. He filled with self-pity.

'Why do you have to be such a sanctimonious cunt?' he said.

Val laughed. 'That's the spirit. Come and sit down. I haven't got much time but let's have a chat about things.' He crumpled the page in his hands, walked over to the table and emptied the bowl of fruit. Oranges and nectarines rumbled across the varnish and dropped onto the floor. 'Let's see how good the smoke detectors are,' he said. He took a lighter out of his pocket, put the crumpled ball of paper in the bowl and set light to it. It burned well and quickly, with a bright fierce flame. After a few seconds only black flakes were left in the bowl.

Val looked up at the ceiling. 'No sprinklers. If there was a fire here, we'd all perish,' he said brightly.

'Are you going to run it?' said Ritchie.

'As I think I said, we can't publish a story that isn't true. You haven't been arrested.'

'You know what I mean.'

'I've only got five minutes, Ritchie. Let's imagine I know that you've been fucking some fifteen-year-old. Let's imagine I run the story. You're arrested, you're put on trial, you're publicly humiliated, you get put in the chokey, your marriage breaks up, you have to fight your wife for access to your children, you lose the mansion, the BBC repudiates you, you become TV poison; you've made your career on teenagers, but you're not allowed near them any more, and nobody takes you seriously on grown-up TV; your film falls through because the man who killed your father is a good family man and doesn't want to be interviewed by a child molester; and . . . well, I don't know what happens after that, Ritchie. Were you going to say something?'

'I'm not a child molester. Don't you dare call me that.'

'As I said, time is short. What happens after that, I suppose, is that you try to earn a living touring. But you were never that talented as a musician, isn't that right? Karin was the songwriter, the one they came to see. Now let's imagine another way. That I know you've been fucking a fifteen-year-old, and I don't publish it, and I don't tell the police. That'd be concealing a crime. We'd be breaking the law, Ritchie.' He stopped and gazed at Ritchie as if he wished he weren't there.

'I'm wondering,' said Ritchie, 'what you know about any of the things that may or may not have happened.'

'It's good that you're not sure,' said Val. 'I like that. This is where I feel I'm doing the right thing. Setting clear boundaries. Helping you identify the point where you'll get in trouble. But you know what you've done, of course.'

'You invited me here.'

'These are hard times for newspapers,' said Val. 'We're fighting to survive. We can't afford to let a good story go when we have one. Unless we have another story to take its place.'

'About what, for instance?'

'About your sister.'

Ritchie's fingertips squeezed the edge of the table. He couldn't look at Val.

'This is about you and Bec,' he said.

'I'm not sure what you mean.'

'Leave her alone,' said Ritchie. 'She hasn't done anything wrong. She's never hurt anybody. She's a good woman.'

'I'm glad to hear it,' said Val. 'She was a prize bitch to me. Did she tell you we were engaged?'

'No.' The return of his power to lie made Ritchie feel stronger. 'You can't afford this kind of pettiness,' he said.

'It's nice to hear you're loyal,' said Val. He leaned forward, folded his arms on the table and lowered his voice. 'If Bec is as good as you say she is, she has nothing to worry about from either of us.'

'Either of us?' Ritchie wrinkled his face. 'Are you –'

'Stop!' said Val sharply. 'Stop.' He smiled. 'I'm not sure what you were going to say, of course, but I couldn't do it, I don't suppose, unless I knew something about you that you wanted kept hidden from the public. Are you saying there is something?'

'I'm not saying that.'

'Good. That's good. Well, I can't be sure, but I expect that in the next year we're going to be one good story short. Just one. So if we don't get one, we'll have to use one we've been keeping in reserve.'

'And if you do get one, the reserve goes in the bin.'

'I suppose it will. If we get one in the next twelve months.'

'For God's sake,' said Ritchie.

'Whose sake?' said Val, cupping his ear.

'For God's sake, my *sister*! She's my own flesh and blood!' As he spoke the words, certain they were true, a sense of horror and shame shifted in him, like a chick about to hatch, squirming in its egg. 'She's not a celebrity. She's not . . . newsworthy.'

'Not yet,' said Val.

'For God's sake!'

'Bring me what you can, Ritchie. You're not in a strong position.' He got to his feet. 'I looked up the names of your children. I was surprised to see that your daughter was called Ruby. I was sure your little girl's name was Nicole.'

'Do what you like,' said Ritchie. 'I'm not going to be your snitch and spy inside my own family.'

He went back to the studios and worked till seven, swamping the staff with excessive kindness and bursts of rage. They noticed that whatever anyone said to him, he didn't listen. On the drive to Petersmere rain thickened the wind. He caressed his last words to Val like a gift he was bringing home.

The trees were roaring in a storm when Ritchie got out of the car. The lights were on in the house, bright and steady inside each strong white window frame. He'd forgotten his keys and as he sheltered in the doorway, waiting to be let in, a gust splashed his back with rain. Karin opened the door with Ruby in her pyjamas close behind, barefoot, naughtily staying up late, and he walked inside to warmth and the savour of supper. He picked Ruby up and carried her to the table, her soft wrists cool on his neck. Later, away from his wife and children for the shortest possible time, he sent Val a message. *Do nothing precipitate*, he wrote.

PART TWO

17

The word on Alex Comrie, the drummer in Ritchie's first band, had been that he possessed some kind of genius, and not for drumming. But Alex kept good time and Ritchie wondered how he'd picked up a nice sense of rhythm on the drummer's seat without getting the ability to dance as part of the package. On the dancefloor Alex squeezed his lanky body into a narrow tube, clamping his arms to his side and his legs together, and when he should have been moving his body to the music he only waggled his hands, bobbed his beak of a nose and waddled rapidly across the room like a penguin hurrying to the sea.

He came to London, to King's College, aged seventeen, from a stern monoethnic comprehensive in Scotland where the teachers wore pleated black gowns and punished children for small misdemeanours by beating them on the hand with specially made leather belts. Alex's mother Maureen, a middle-class English immigrant, wasn't sure whether to be appalled by the savagery or pleased her sons were being exposed to a pain-based native initiation rite like the Satere Mawe of the Amazon, where, she read, boys had their manhood tested by gloves lined with stinging ants. But only the younger of her two children, Dougie, the more popular, was belted. Alex

longed to feel the bite of leather on his palm and the acceptance that came with it, but was too beloved of the teachers
to earn the grace of cruelty. He was well enough liked, and
had a peculiar intensity that attracted the shy, Gothic end of
girlhood, but he sat out school dances, and never learned to
kick a ball.

The band, Gorse, only lasted a few months. It was called
Gauze but when Ritchie first met Karin, buying guitar strings
on Charing Cross Road, she misheard him and told him how
she loved the yellow flowers. From that moment Ritchie said
it'd always been Gorse, and believed it. They gigged in pubs
and student venues before Ritchie dropped out of university
and formed The Lazygods with Karin. Alex, who of all the
ex-Gorsies seemed to Ritchie the least like a musician, was
the only one he kept in touch with.

Alex could handle the sticks as well as any multidextrous
boy with tolerant parents, a room of his own and energy to
burn who'd been given a drum kit on his twelfth birthday and
watched *Top of the Pops* and *Whistle Test*. When he went to King's
to study molecular cell biology he'd taken the drums with
him, wary of the role of gauche autist he was expected to act
out by choosing science. Might his vocation, poking into the
atomic codes of life, breaking people's molecules and putting
them back together again, make him unfit to live it? He saw
his peers turning into blinkered fetishists of pinhole-narrow
specialisations, and wondered if it would happen to him. He
turned himself into the pulse of a rock band to show fate
hadn't put data points where his passions should be.

By day the monkey of curiosity on his back drove him to
journals, equations and algorithms. He learned. He outpaced
his coursemates and teachers. In his head the human cell

became a place whose workings he could wander through like a world. At night, with the band, he staked his claim to a rebel heart and a gypsy spirit, the attributes he supposed artists were born with. He punished the drums till the sweat ran down his back and his wrists ached.

At the dozen small gigs Gorse played, the crowd moshed to Alex's falcon silhouette tyrannising the skins and cymbals at the back of the stage, his pinked mop of straight black hair bouncing off his forehead in 4/4 time, but he couldn't lose himself in music as Ritchie did. It seemed he surrendered to the beat, that the life measured by the count of his heart and the life made by the music became, for the duration of a set, one and the same, but it wasn't so. He couldn't drown his intellect. He couldn't just *be*. He doubted and feared like any eighteen-year-old, but examined his doubts and fears as if they belonged to someone he didn't care about. The student haunts burned incandescent with *want* and *need*, and so did he, but in him *why* and *how* dropped through, cooling the embers of the pile.

He misunderstood. The divide in him wasn't between scientist and artist but between focused and distracted. When he drew together all the scattered lights of his attention and turned them on a woman, she was gripped. Later she'd find how easily his mind strayed. Over the years successive girlfriends, walking and talking to Alex with his arm around them, felt their affection suddenly rendered equal in status to such momentary fascinations as the ubiquity of legless pigeons, the meaning of letters on drain covers, the social significance of corduroy or a change in car number-plate design. If the menage survived she would find how naturally, when it suited him, Alex stripped their togetherness down to the functional so as to concentrate on the teetering arc of biomathematical bricks he was assembling in his head. He did his best work when a small part of his mind was engaged in a steady, practised physical activity, like cycling along a familiar route or snapping his fingers. Drumming never gave Alex the temporary personality of the unselfconscious artist he hoped for, but as an elaborate form of fidgeting, it helped him think.

Gorse lived on for a few weeks after Ritchie left. Study ate into Alex's time and he gave up practising, then quit the band. Ritchie's ascent to fame was steep. The two men would have lost touch if Ritchie hadn't kept the connection going, and if Alex hadn't met Bec.

Alex was twenty-five, his PhD freshly inked and rolled in a cardboard tube; Bec was seven years younger, just started at Cambridge. Ritchie introduced them casually, without a thought of attraction, assuming generic scientific babble would flow easily between them, like current through a joined-up cable. He forgot his sister wasn't a schoolgirl any more. He could sense arousal in others yet was blind to the interest of men in his eighteen-year-old sister. His sense of her lagged several years behind the actual Bec. Unconsciously he thought of the fullness of her breasts and curve of her hips as if they were a kind of late childhood illness that had swollen around the fourteen-year-old girl and would eventually subside, returning her to fourteen again. He projected his lack of sexual interest in her freely over the rest of the male population.

Once, when she was seventeen, he'd seen her about to go out in a t-shirt and mentioned that Karin had bangles she could borrow and she'd seemed so uncomprehending that he babbled: 'Nobody goes out with bare arms any more.' *The scars on her wrist will make people nervous*, he thought. People would think she was a cutter and wonder if it ran in the family.

The bitter smell of her own skin burning, accompanied by an intense, clear and unambiguous pain, had eased Bec's heart when she was a small girl, angry with her father for dying and for leaving her to pity the loneliness of his last hour. She twigged early that there might be something sarcastic about young skin: how pleasurable to spoil it! But the scars weren't big or ragged when she started university, or as noticeable as they seemed to Ritchie. Bec hardly remembered they were there, more embarrassed by their neatness than by having made them.

Alex had been surprised to be invited to the launch party for The Lazygods' second album, *Windfallen*. In seven years his mind refashioned the memory of the teenage Ritchie according to the star his friend became. Alex felt he should have noticed Ritchie's talent at the beginning. He remembered Ritchie as confident, energetic and generous. If he also remembered his ordinary voice, crude guitar style and plodding way with songwriting he thought it was he, Alex, who must have been wrong, not the millions of people who'd bought *Fountain*. When Alex abandoned regular drumming to be a biomathematical traveller in the unmapped human cell, and Ritchie dropped out of university and got a recording deal, it seemed they'd moved into worlds whose spheres couldn't intersect. No matter how many times Ritchie called him, contrived to mention him in interviews or invited him to mix with musicians at events like the launch, Alex expected it to end.

The party was in a new luxury hotel opposite Hyde Park. Alex walked into the lobby in a pair of jeans ripped at the knee,

Converse trainers, a t-shirt and a black suit jacket, the way he'd dressed as a teenage drummer and a style he reckoned drew the undergraduates' eyes now he was Dr Comrie, cell biologist, junior researcher, with a desk of his own at King's and students to teach. The t-shirt was a relic of Primal Scream merchandise, the black of the *Screamadelica* mask's eyes faded to grey, the red to pink. The jacket was new. He'd been walking around campus for a few months with a badge on his lapel reading *Isn't life RNA-ic?* but just before heading out he'd swapped it for the old badge from the days of Gorse, stating *I Am Nico.*

Hope lurched upright in him when the pretty girl on the door found his name on the list of invited guests and waved him into the bar of the Metropolitan, glittering with guests and booming with talk. His was one name in hundreds on a printout yet he felt recognised as belonging to the people of music. He'd thrown in his lot with the caste of cell biologists, and they wanted him, but he was disenchanted by his peers. If only, he thought with his heart jumping, the musicians could see the savage beauty of the sub-microscopic seas. If only they could understand their songs of love, death and sorrow weren't debased by being embodied in adenosine triphosphatase.

His thumb and fingertips smeared the fog on a glass and he registered the surfaces in the room as if dumbly reading through the list of ingredients in a packet of breakfast cereal: fuzzed jaws, gelled curls, heel-stressed calves, dark glasses, tattooed calligraphy, bare shoulders, big rings. In the room he knew only Karin and Ritchie, who were talking to the guitarist-songwriter of a band that'd had hit after hit, the last number one a couple of months earlier; it'd taken the death of a princess to knock them off the front pages. Alex went over to them, determined not to care what his famous friends' famous friend thought of him, and Ritchie and Karin greeted him and introduced him to famous Noel.

'Why are you always talking about how much you love the Beatles?' was the first thing Alex said to Noel, with unintended aggression. 'You're asking to be judged according to how good someone else was.'

Noel's shaggy eyebrows ratcheted up a micron.

'Alex says what he thinks,' said Ritchie.

Noel laughed. 'What is it you do again?' he said.

Alex's mouth grew dry and he took gulps from the champagne glass, angry with himself for being familiar with a celebrity, for wanting to impress him, failing to impress him, not getting a hearing, bothering to come.

A man and a woman Alex didn't know joined the group. Alex wasn't introduced and found himself looking down at the floor. The feet of the six of them formed a circle that reminded him of the cell membrane. He watched the other ten feet creeping away from his, millimetre by millimetre, the circle opening to eject him, like a vesicle packed with waste molecules being popped from the phospholipid layer, and closing again with his feet outside. Shoulders were in front of his shoulders, blocking him out.

He stepped back, ruminating on the ballet of the proteins, forgetting he'd been angry. He wanted to sit and think. Close to a curving bench that ran along the far wall a young woman's face caught his eye and he remembered the greedy hope he'd felt when he came into the bar. The woman inclined her rosy cheeks and mass of wavy black shoulder-length hair towards a man in a suit and tie. Alex resented not being the one who was being listened to and smiled at and looked at with wide dark eyes. It seemed to Alex that the man, though better dressed, looked much like him, and she'd obviously just met him. He felt a punch of jealousy that he hadn't seen her earlier.

Then Ritchie was next to him, saying: 'Come and meet my sister. She's a science type.' He took Alex over to the woman he'd been looking at, introduced her as Bec, and steered the other man off.

Bec smiled at Alex, too, in a way that seemed trusting and for a moment, as if he'd stepped out onto the high ledge of a tall building and found the expected barrier between him and the view wasn't there, he felt dizzy.

'Brilliant,' he said.

'What's brilliant?' said Bec, tilting her head to one side.

'I have a theory of conversation that when you meet someone you should say the first thing that comes into your head and open it up for discussion. If the other person doesn't want to talk about it, it's their problem.'

'I don't think I've ever met anyone with a theory of conversation. So the first thing that came into your head was *brilliant?*'

'The first thing that came into my head was, how could we quantify the things about us that tell people here we're not rock stars? And then I had this insight that I should try getting the other person to say what *they're* thinking. I thought it was a good idea and I couldn't help saying so out loud.'

Bec considered this. 'We might be stars,' she said. 'I used to be able to play Just Can't Get Enough on the recorder.'

Alex took the message from her eyes on his that he couldn't exhaust her attention. *She's prepared to take anything seriously,* he thought, and demonstrated the attractiveness of his personality by talking to her for half an hour without stopping. He summarised his career, bullet-pointed his family and shared his ideas about the evolution of multicelled organisms. It was going well, he felt; her raised eyebrows showed interest, the way she folded her arms signified concentration. She interrupted to ask if he knew where the drink was. Alex promised to get her a glass of wine and when he returned from the bar he couldn't find her. It seemed she'd been called away.

In the days that followed he brooded over what he'd done to make her evade him and wondered how he could reach her. She was young, but he was only seven years older. He obtained her postal address from Ritchie, saying he'd promised to send her an article, and wrote her a five-page letter with a point by point dismissal of everything he remembered telling her. 'As for my family,' he concluded with what he considered a nicely humble flourish, 'they are, of course, of no interest.'

She didn't reply. He felt he'd learned of the existence of a new form of space — an extra dimension or an additional continent or a kind of human cell governed by different laws — that he had to explore, but it was contained uniquely, bafflingly, within one person, and he couldn't get to her. And she had seemed so *open* to him. She didn't have a phone, said Ritchie; he was giving her a mobile for Christmas. Alex guessed that Cambridge would have given her an email address, and sent messages to r.shepherd and b.shepherd and becshepherd and shepherd.r and a dozen others @cam.ac.uk asking if they could meet. He got a testy refusal from a random Professor Shepherd of classics and a week later Bec wrote to say he was the first person who had ever emailed her. She was sorry not to have replied to his letter, she was very busy, and she hoped he was well.

The essence of what society demanded in practical romance, it seemed to Alex, was to do something surprising that was at the same time derivative. Music would be the lever of her seduction. He would show Bec that he could play in the theatre of the passions as well as any poet.

He had his mother's old car, a little white Peugeot with a dent on one corner where she'd backed into a low bollard ferrying Amazonians to the One Earth Festival in Stonehaven. He bought a Cambridge street map and drove there to case Bec's digs. Chance had given her a room in a house with a large front garden, well covered by trees, bushes and other serenade-friendly foliage.

He did an Excite search and identified the next full moon, on a Thursday in mid-October. At ten that night he packed his gear into the car and drove out of London, reaching Bec's house just before midnight. The clouds were thick over the city and there wasn't the ghost of a moon. Autumn had banished the nightingales and slain the roses. The leaves had fallen and those that remained were thinly spread and yellow.

One by one Alex took the pieces of kit out of the car and laid them on the pavement against the low wall that marked the edge of the garden. The street was quiet, with little traffic, but dense with student lodgings. Alex whistled, hummed, clicked his tongue, snapped his fingers and rounded up his stray thoughts, racing in all directions, with the Asda jingle, *All the prices are low / Whenever you go / That's Asda price.* He slapped the change in his pockets. *Cha-ching-ching.* Students passed by on foot and on bicycles, chattering drunkenly. They looked down at the drums, glanced at him and moved on. Each time the street cleared he hoisted a piece over the wall. Gradually he transferred the stripped-down kit, snare, bass, ride, stands, pedal and throne, gave a last look round and vaulted into the garden.

He found a dark spot under a chestnut tree, partly screened by shrubs from the road and the path to the front door but with a clear line of sight to the upper windows. He set up the kit, pushing the base of the pedal into the wet leaves to find solid ground, his fingers numb with cold. He was almost ready, and was dragging the throne into place, when he heard voices and feet on the path. He saw two women walking towards the front door. One of them was Bec, wearing an old overcoat and a peaked cap. Alex stood still, feeling his juddering heart about to come loose.

Bec stopped, turned towards him and peered into the darkness. 'Who's there?' she said.

'What is it?' said her friend, skinny with short blonde hair and her hands in the pockets of a belted raincoat.

'There's somebody in the bushes.'

'We should go inside,' said Bec's friend, grabbing her elbow.

'Who's there?' said Bec again.

Alex wondered if he could stay perfectly still for hours and not be seen.

'We should go inside,' said the friend. 'We don't want to get raped.'

'You won't,' said Alex. The women yelped and tottered back. Alex stepped forward a few paces so that they could see him, the toes of his shoes parting the wet leaves with a slithering sound. 'You won't,' he said again.

'What are you doing here?' said Bec.

'She knows me,' said Alex to the friend.

'You brought drums,' said Bec.

'I'm going inside. Will you be all right?' said her friend.

'He knows my brother,' said Bec, and the friend went into the house. Bec folded her arms and came to where Alex had set up.

'This must have taken you ages,' she said.

Alex shrugged and swallowed. His mind contained magnificent thoughts Bec would like but he couldn't make them fit through the narrow opening of his mouth.

'Drumming by itself isn't my favourite kind of music,' said Bec.

'I can't play any other instrument,' said Alex. A drop of rain fell on his cheek.

'But my room's on the other side of the house,' said Bec. She put her hands in her pockets and looked over her shoulder at the door as if she hoped somebody would come out to fetch her. It was raining heavily, pattering in the leaves above and around them.

'Listen,' said Alex. He stopped back and crouched down beside the drums. He beckoned to Bec. 'Listen.'

She came over and squatted a few feet away.

'Can you hear it?' said Alex. The rain was tapping on the skin of the snare drum.

'It sounds like rain on a tent,' said Bec.

'Can you hear the cymbal? Put your ear close to it.'

Bec put her ear to the rim of the cymbal and listened. The raindrops rang faintly on the gleaming metal.

Alex took out a single drumstick and with the blunt end began softly to tap the bass drum. Bec listened to the rain's rattle on the snare, the cymbal ringing and the faint deep boom of the big drum. Streams of water ran down Alex's forehead. Bec's hat was soaked. She stood up. Alex got to his feet after her.

Bec kissed him on the mouth. A chink of warmth and softness opened and closed. 'Goodnight,' she said, and turned and walked away.

Alex called after her to wait. Bec ran the last few steps to the door and went inside, closing it behind her. Alex rang the bell, hammered on the door with his fist and called her name through the letterbox. No one came.

Soon afterwards Alex was recruited by a research lab in Baltimore. When he came back to London to work at Imperial College, four years and several girlfriends later, Bec was in Sacramento, living with Joel. By the time Bec returned to London and Joel left her, Alex had moved in with a health administrator called Maria. He was sure Maria, dark and patient, was the right partner, with her detective pursuit of his obscure lines of thought and her mission to improve him. He imagined them growing old together and seldom thought about Ritchie's sister. His drum kit sat for years in a spare bedroom, ready for action at first under a dust sheet and then, when the room was redecorated, packed away.

Alex put the drums on eBay and the buyer came round in a van one evening to pick them up. He was a short, eager, muscled young Australian with a ponytail, rolling on his heels as he swaggered into the house. He had the envelope with the cash sticking out of the pocket of his jeans. Alex let him in, a ride cymbal shimmering where it hung from his free hand. He looked over the buyer's shoulder at the blue sky and children's TV clouds and said he didn't suppose it'd rain.

'It's a beautiful day, mate,' said the buyer, winking and clicking his tongue. 'Can I take a look?'

Alex showed him where he'd set up the kit and surrendered the cymbal. The buyer lolloped through a few minutes' worth of breaks. He stood up, clenched the sticks in his fist and handed Alex the money. 'Sold, sir,' he said.

'I want to see them off,' said Alex, moving to the throne.

'Be my guest,' said the buyer.

Five minutes later Maria came to tell them to stop the noise and saw Alex soaked in sweat, hammering away at the snare and tom-toms as if trying to break through to something on the other side. The buyer shouted in her ear 'This guy's a beast!' Alex gave Maria a terrible look and she clasped her hands to her jaw. He looked at her as if someone had died, and they were both to blame.

18

When he was focused on Maria, Alex's intensity promised an extraordinary programme for which the length of their lives was hardly enough, even as the world of medicine was clamouring for his brains. He gave himself to her at a time convenient to him, between three and five in the morning quite often, or a Wednesday to Wednesday trip far away the moment he finished a project. *Why not now? You said you wanted to do things together.*

Talking to her about what interested him, his work, for instance, or whether humankind was still evolving, or his conviction that he could get anywhere in central London faster by bike than by Tube, his eyes shone with the fervour of a prophet. He couldn't bring the same passion to other people's preoccupations, or hers. In company he was a partisan for her excellence but his praise was generic. He was interested in her up to the point where he had to take, or fake, an interest in her interests.

The deeps of the cytoplasmic world he explored alone inside his head were inaccessible to her beneath layers of technical terms, where she could get to the definitions of the definitions and only find more words to look up. Yet she liked to be in the house with him when he was working. He was vulnerable and trusting when he was below the surface. She felt she, and only she, had her hand on his air supply.

She tried to change him, and discovered that in small ways she could. She couldn't stop him punctuating the gaps in his thoughts with snatches of bygone TV show themes and old advertising jingles — '*Up in the valley of the Jolly Green Giant . . . now you sing Ho, ho, ho!*' — but she got him not to do it in public, not when she was with him. She told him he drummed too much with his hands and pens and cutlery on other people's tables, and that he should suppress the compulsion to methodically empty any plate of snacks that was put in his reach, and he stopped doing these things with an eerie meekness that pleased her. Made bold, she moved into the sexual jurisdiction. He was rather good, she thought, with his long, strong hands and chubby cock. The hook-nosed face opposite hers had a crooked grandeur to it, like the picture of a great old man in his youth before he was famous. But she told Alex he should talk to her while they were making love. He took it as an accusation of sexual incompetence and grieved silently for two days, then told her she should find somebody else, someone who could fuck and dance properly. Maria didn't see the connection and soothed and seduced him and after that he talked while he played with her and while he was inside her, shyly and repetitively at first, then brimming over. It seemed to Maria that the two of them had the kind of thing she imagined parents were supposed to have before they were parents. Five years after they'd begun living together, she raised the matter of having children, not as an abstract idea for the indefinite future, but as a project it was time to start, now they were in their mid-thirties.

'D'you think?' said Alex. 'Maybe.' He frowned, scratched

his nose, raised his finger and smiled. 'Clathrin! That's the protein I was looking for. Give me five minutes.' She heard the stairs groan as he bounded up to the study, singing. *It's Marvel-ous — less fat too! Bom-bom-bom.*

One winter's night they were walking towards Farringdon station after dinner at a restaurant in Clerkenwell and passed a line of pale young people queuing to get into a club. A few had vintage fur hats and ground-trailing secondhand greatcoats but most were protected from the cold by single layers of leather, fishnet, velvet, polyester or tartan clinging tightly to their sticklike bodies. They seemed to dissolve the rest of the world; there was only the club, the queue and each other.

'Let's go in,' said Alex.

'It's not my kind of place,' said Maria. 'I'm not dressed for it. It's not for anyone over thirty.'

'I want to see what it's like in there.'

'Full of cute young trendies dancing, trying to get served in the bar, trying to get off with each other, posing and screaming in each other's ears to make themselves heard.'

'Let's take a look. We're people too.'

'I want to go home,' said Maria, linking her arm in his. 'We don't belong in there. They won't let us in.'

'Who says we don't belong? Why?' Alex pulled his arm free and walked off to stand at the end of the line. Maria stood still, watching him for a minute; he didn't look in her direction. She left him there and was woken a couple of hours later by the sound of the taxi bringing him home.

'Did they let you in?' she asked when he got into bed beside her.

'Eventually,' he said, and sulked, refusing to talk about it.

Over the years Alex registered the expansion of his tribe with detached interest. When his brother Dougie had his first child, it was bound up in Alex's mind with Dougie's financial and emotional recklessness. When his cousin Matthew and his wife Lettie started producing offspring at a steady rate, Alex talked about it with scientific curiosity: what was it about religious families that made them have more children? Did this mean that religious people had an evolutionary advantage over non-believers like him and Maria?

'Let's start the infidels' comeback,' said Maria hopefully. Alex only laughed and jiggled his knee.

Alex grew up breathing the air of success around his uncle Harry. Harry was a medical geneticist who'd discovered that most people had a few immune cells with a recurring set of benign mutations that turned the mutant lymphocytes into cancer-hunting aces. The same mutations made them vulnerable; the mutant cells, named *expert cells* by Harry, would pop up naturally every so often in the human metabolism and be ruthlessly destroyed by their peers, like lone geniuses smothered by mediocre rivals. Harry's brilliance – he liked to think of it as brilliance, as a series of perfect rapier strokes, although it was fifteen years' stubborn labour by him and his research group – was to find a way of finding the expert cells before they were destroyed, removing them from the body, tweaking them genetically to toughen them, culturing them up by the million and putting them back. He all but cured one rare form of cancer, then rested, and without realising it, never stopped resting.

Harry hoped and didn't expect his bright nephew would follow him into the life sciences, yet Alex did follow him, and excelled. He turned out to have the mind Harry longed to have had for himself: a mathematical acrobat who could run molecule-folding formulae in his head, a controlled yet outré dreamer.

Alex made it his work to discover what Harry had never been able to explain, why the expert cells worked as they did. With pen and mouse and brain he journeyed deep into the body, into the cells that make it up, into the organelles inside the cells – the fuming mitochondrion, the pancake-stack assembly lines of the endoplasmic reticulum and the Golgi apparatus, the cryptic fasces of the centrioles – into the molecules inside them, and into the atoms that make up the molecules. He spent hours Internet chatting and then, when it came along, Skyping, with a Bulgarian-American colleague in Switzerland, Thomas, who made computer animations of the choreography of the proteins. One day, Skyping from home, they were arguing over a fancy bonding sequence when a small dark shape flitted across the scene behind Thomas, the murky scrim of old pizza boxes, cliffs of paper and unwashed coffee mugs Alex avoided looking at.

'What was that?' said Alex.

'Define,' said Thomas.

'A creature crossed the room behind you, about the size of a large flightless bird.'

Thomas looked over his shoulder. 'Margarita!' he called. A waxen-skinned girl of about six, with coal-black hair and eyebrows and a smear of chocolate coming off her mouth, stepped into the picture, clasping a stuffed unicorn.

'This is Margarita,' said Thomas. 'My daughter.'

'Hello, Margarita,' said Alex. 'I'm Alex.' His eyes moved from Thomas, paunchy, incompetently shaven, with long, unwashed strands of grey hair and a baggy t-shirt of indefinable colour, to the new and normative person he had seemingly co-produced.

'Say hello, Margarita.'

Margarita twisted and turned her face away.

'I'd like to shake your hand, Margarita,' said Alex. 'But I'm in London and my arm isn't long enough to stretch to Switzerland. And I don't want to break your daddy's screen by putting my hand through it.'

Margarita looked round, tempted by the promise of broken glass, and realised the man with the big nose was bullshitting. She ran away.

'My mother's watching her in the kitchen,' said Thomas.

'I didn't know you had children,' said Alex.

'Only Margarita.'

'I didn't know you were seeing anyone.'

'I was married for a few months once. I see Margarita on Wednesdays.'

'You never mentioned you had a daughter in all the times I was in Geneva.'

'It's because children, they're not your thing,' said Thomas.

Alex clicked on the red button to end the call, yanked the computer power plug out of the wall and stood up, cracking his fingers. In that moment it seemed incredible to him that he'd spent fifteen years pondering the cell, making himself a master of life's cogs and wheels, fretting that he didn't belong in the procession of human life, an alien observer taking notes on the gypsies, fiddlers and balladeers jigging past, and had missed this insight: that men and women could have children. A child, Alex reasoned, trumped dancing, music and door policies. You were in. With a family you were the very substance of life; you were the traveller and the road together.

It was one thing to talk about evolution but having children was the way to be part of it. If life was the party, children were the after-party, and only thing that stood between you and it was nature: the big bouncer. It staggered Alex that Ritchie didn't know one ion from another, and thought evolution meant if you spent too long hunched over a laptop in your twenties you'd evolve a humped back, yet he'd instinctively understood all this, and already had a son.

You were right about kids, he texted Maria. *Come home ASAP and let's get started.*

19

When Alex was a boy his uncle Harry would read to him from a manuscript he'd written for children called *Tales of Life*. He talked about getting it published. The hero of the work was a single-celled organism born billions of years ago who evolved, through many adventures and strange encounters, into a human being. One of the stories was about how the mitochondrion first entered this hero, the sole ancestor of all men and women. The ten-year-old Alex didn't understand what the mitochondrion was when he first heard his uncle say it, but he loved the word, and the idea of having an ancestor billions of years old made him feel colossal. At school he would advise anyone who fell over in the playground and bled not to let the mitochondrion spill out.

A long time ago, read Harry, *forty million grandfathers ago, your ancestor the single cell was big and weak and slow, but his neighbour the little mitochondrion was full of energy. And the mitochondrion said to the cell, 'Let me come inside you and live in you, and I shall make you powerful, and your descendants will be too many to count,' and the cell said, 'What's the catch?' And the mitochondrion said, 'I shall give you energy, but when I make energy, I shall put a little poison into you, and it will make you old, and you will die.' And the cell said, 'What's old? What's die?' And the mitochondrion said, 'It is the end of you. But not yet, and you will have so many children that you will not mourn your end.' And the cell agreed to let the mitochondrion in, and they multiplied together in the fertile seas of the young Earth, under the young sun.*

Once, a set of sixty trillion of that first cell's descendants, a set called Alex Comrie, went to California, where a scientist in a laboratory explained to him that it was the mitochondria in human cells, and the toxins they produced as they did their work, that made people old.

He showed Alex a compound, a black powder, which, he said, bonded with those toxins and made them harmless. Not immortality; but, the scientist reckoned from their work in worms and mice, pretty close. The scientist looked round to see if anyone was watching and said to Alex, 'Try some, go on. Put a little bit on your finger. But don't tell anyone.' Alex sucked a dab of the astringent powder and left. And apart from finding, that one evening only, that he was able to drink five beers without needing to pee, the powder had no effect. The beginnings of lines appeared, his skin coarsened and his torso sagged as he approached forty, no faster or slower than anyone else's. But he did notice, the first time he ate pomegranate seeds after eating the powder, that they had the same tannic astringency, and he mentioned this to Maria.

Soon afterwards she began eating fresh pomegranate for breakfast. 'Maybe it'll work,' she said. It was when 'Maybe it'll work' was their catchphrase, when the doctors who tested them exhaustively couldn't find anything wrong with either of them and the third IVF cycle failed. 'Maybe it'll work' was anything, swallowing a fly, sex in a hotel garden, accidentally salted tea. Pomegranates. And Alex had wondered whether 'maybe it'll work', for pomegranates, meant conception, or not getting old; and once he'd asked Maria if she would rather have a child, or live for ever, and Maria said 'either'.

After the IVF debacle Maria suggested adoption. Or, since it was so important to him to have a child, she said, they could use another woman's eggs or another man's sperm.

'It has to be ours,' said Alex.

'It would be ours,' said Maria.

'Not in nature.'

'But you're a scientist, a medical scientist,' said Maria, turning red with frustration and struggling to speak through tears. 'Everything you do is not in nature. How can you inter-fere with nature to stop people dying and not interfere to let people be born?'

'Why do I always have to be the rational one?' said Alex. 'Because I'm a scientist? You're profiling. It's bigotry.'

He knew he might be the infertile one, but what, he thought, if the problem was on Maria's side? In the secrecy of his heart he compared her to his former girlfriends and imagined how it might have been if he'd stayed with one of them instead, with a little boy or girl by now.

He followed Bec's work in the journals. He found pictures of her on the Internet and staring at the bright pixels it seemed to him that he felt as he had fifteen years before, without the comforting illusion of those days that he was bound to meet others, like her, who let their true self and their surface coincide.

He turned forty as he approached the end of his research, his explanation for why Harry's expert cells worked, which other, more practical scientists could use to lengthen lives. His colleagues, and Harry, told him that if he pulled it off it would make him famous and change medicine. Alex laughed and said that he hoped the beauty of the answer would be worth more than its use, and they thought he was being pretentious, or joking.

He'd read about Bec infecting herself to test her hypothesis, and wanted to have a woman like her beside him. He tried to understand what it was about her, in their short acquaintance, that had left such a mark, and came to the certainty he'd picked up – he had no idea how – that she had a spacious mind. Once this notion lodged in him he found himself noticing how people he met, even young people, seemed able to let a handful of ideas crowd their consciousness. They seemed glad of it, as if the aim had been to fill the cupboards and block the windows of their minds as quickly as possible with the minimum of material. *Finished!* Bec, he was sure, didn't want to be finished.

In the herding of his theories to their end he summarised the architecture of the human cell and was distracted by the crisp prose of Bec's description, in a paper in *The New England Journal of Medicine*, of how her parasite got inside a human blood cell. It was as if his cell coasted along, serene in the microscopic cosmos, only to be struck by Bec's haemoproteus, tearing into the membrane like a runaway asteroid and throwing it out of kilter.

20

Through the shop window, between the red and white strokes of the letters making up the words UNISEX HAIRDRESSER, Harry Comrie saw Erkin standing alone with his hands clasped in front of him and his shoulders bowed, staring at the point where the wall joined the floor. Harry pushed the door open, tripping the bell and bringing Erkin back to the there and then. The barber smiled, shook a towel and gestured Harry towards the chair.

Erkin was a dainty, short-legged man in a blue surcoat, with deep eyes and a sharply lined face that gave him the appearance of having lived through shocking events, though he had been a barber in north London all his life. His shop was a shrine to neatness. Fingerworn utensils of antique plastic and scratched stainless steel were laid out around the Barbicide like a memory game. There was a warm smell of shampooed roots and, though it was early, sheaves of hair already lay on the worn linoleum tiles under the footrest.

Erkin draped Harry in a dark cape and stood back, meeting Harry's eyes in the mirror. It seemed to Harry that his head had been severed and laid carefully on a cloth-covered stump. An American friend had told him once that he looked like David Hume. The eighteenth century had been a time of fairness, Harry thought, when any philosopher, egg-smooth, balding or shaggy, wore a wig. Harry considered how his fleshy, thick-lipped, sixty-four-year-old face would look commemorated in marble. The trustees were too small-minded to come up with the notion of a bust by themselves. He would have to plant it.

'I want it all off,' he told Erkin.

Erkin took Harry's head between his fingertips and tilted it from side to side so that the light danced on the broad bald track of his client's scalp. Twists of white hair poked out from above Harry's ears and, Harry supposed, ran crazily down the back of his neck, over his collar.

'Would you like a number one, sir, or shall I shave it?'

'Get your razor out. I'm making a fresh start.'

'A lot of gentlemen like yourself do the same thing, sir. When you get to a certain age it looks better. I've seen men come in with half their hair gone and walk out with no hair at all, looking ten years younger.' He lifted Harry's gold-rimmed glasses off his face and placed them by the basin. He took the clipper off its hook, fitted a guard, held the clipper up and revved it. He asked Harry if he was sure.

'Go ahead,' said Harry. With a few strokes Erkin sliced off the white locks on either side of Harry's head. *That's better*, thought Harry, fighting the instinct to go down on his knees to rescue his fallen hairs from the dark mass below.

'On holiday today, sir?' said Erkin, raising his voice over the buzz of the clippers. Harry felt hairs being torn off the back of his neck. Half the morning had already gone.

'I'm the boss,' said Harry. 'I go to work when I like. My job's to think, and I'm thinking now, so I'm working. Cogito ergo laboro.'

'I didn't mean to offend you, sir.'

'The fact is I had a skinful last night.'

'Celebration, sir?'

'There was a lot of laughing and singing.'

'Nice to have a get-together, sir.'

'I was alone.'

Physically alone, thought Harry. He'd told Alex about his diagnosis, and then everyone had been on the phone, his son and daughter-in-law, his eldest granddaughter, his brother, his sister-in-law. He'd been solidly drunk by the time Maureen came on the line. He couldn't remember what he'd said to her. She hadn't been able to talk for long. She didn't cry, he remembered that; she was stoical. Or perhaps she'd cried for him later. He liked to think so.

Erkin swivelled the chair, kicked a catch and lowered Harry's head back till his neck fitted into the groove of the basin. He ran hot water over Harry's scalp, shampooed the remnant fuzz, rinsed it, wrapped Harry's head in a towel, brought him back round and lathered him up. He took a cutthroat razor and began to shave.

'Do you mind me asking what your line of work is, sir?' he said.

'I run a medical research institute. The Belford Institute. Up in St John's Wood.'

Erkin stepped back from his work and regarded his client, foamy razor held at attention. 'Is it Harry?' he said.

'That's right.'

'I don't know why I didn't recognise you.' Erkin smiled as he went back to work. 'You've been here a few times.'

'I have. I know your name.'

'Harry, yes, Professor. I don't know why I forgot.' He

bumped his forehead with the side of his razor hand. 'My memory. And you know me.'

'Erkin.'

'That's right.' He shook his head. 'I should remember because we had a conversation about my aunt.'

'Oesophagus, wasn't it?'

'Oh Professor!' Erkin wagged the razor at Harry's reflection in the mirror. 'You make me look bad. You remember everything. And now I think of it, I told you I was going to make a donation to your institute, and I never did.'

'We don't work on the oesophagal side.'

'No, but . . .' Erkin frowned. 'It's all part of the what's, the battle, isn't it.'

'Yes!' said Harry. 'Yes! Exactly!' Under the cape he clenched his fists in excitement.

'My aunt, she passed away. Terrible, terrible.' Erkin drew in breath between his teeth, shook his head and gave out a pattering of tut-tuts. 'It's harder on the ladies when their hair falls out. And then she couldn't swallow properly, you know? Before she got ill she used to love aubergine, roasted and mashed up with a bit of garlic and olive oil, but she couldn't look at it in the end. The family all made their aubergine and brought it over and she'd have to say thank you and eat some. She was a kind lady, but she was on so many drugs at the end. My mother held the bowl while she throwing up and said "Oh, these doctors with their terrible medicine," and my aunt said "It's not the doctors, it's your bloody aubergines!"'

Harry began to sweat.

'I remember, you made a cure,' said Erkin. 'It was why I mentioned my aunt, I think. You're a famous scientist, right?' He laughed as if the word 'scientist' embarrassed him.

'There are no famous scientists any more,' said Harry. 'Thirty years ago I found something out about cells and ten years later we had one of the cancers on the run. It was almost a cure. But it was just one little cancer.'

'Careful, sir. If you wouldn't mind keeping your head still.'

'One measly little cancer. A few hundred cases a year. And all the big cancers still laughing at us. Do you know what I mean?'

'You want to cure all the cancers, and you only cured one.'

'Yes,' said Harry curtly. Erkin had grasped exactly the point he'd been trying to make, yet in the barber's words he sounded like a failure.

'When it's your time, it's your time, isn't it,' said Erkin. 'It's in God's hands.' Harry hissed. Erkin didn't notice as he pressed Harry's head forward to shave between the fold at the back of his neck. 'I'm not much of a Muslim. I like my beer and cigarettes and I only go to the mosque on holidays. And my aunt, she used to say it was all rubbish. But in the end, you can't hide, isn't it. God makes his move and there's nothing you can do.'

'Bullshit!' said Harry. He felt a sting in his neck.

'Aa,' said Erkin. He put the razor down, soaked a pad of cotton wool in alcohol and pressed it against the cut. 'Just a nick, sir. You moved your head and when you spoke like that you startled me.'

'You're too fatalistic,' said Harry mildly. He couldn't bring the same sceptical zeal to Muslims that he could to Christians, which made him, he realised with sadness, a bigot.

Erkin rinsed and dried his shorn pate. 'My nephew Alex understands my work better than I do,' said Harry. 'He'll take up the torch. One day we'll understand it, the whole human machine, and work out how to make an old body good as new. Don't lose faith. There are wonders to come. I spoke to Alex yesterday and he told me such a marvellous thing about his work. He's really found the simplicity in the heart of things.' In his face in the mirror Harry saw the boastfulness of a child lying about the wealth of his parents.

Erkin took the cape from Harry's shoulders and gave him a tissue. He handed Harry his glasses and held up the hand mirror for Harry to inspect the back of his head. With his glasses on Harry didn't need to see the back. The front was enough. Whatever he asked Erkin to do to him, the barber would not contradict him, and would explain how it was a good choice, and how a lot of gentlemen did the same, and how well it looked. Now that it was done and Harry's head was shaven he did not look clean, streamlined and younger. Nor did he look, with his bumps and veins exposed, like bust material. He looked like an old conscript, the kind of old man who gets called up for the army when a war is almost lost. He looked like a convict, an experimental subject, one of a batch: a half-processed human, ready for the last stage.

Harry was out of the chair and Erkin was at the till with his back to him. Harry squatted down, plucked one of his white curls out from the mess on the floor, slipped it in the pocket of his jacket and stood up. Erkin was looking at him. Harry had moved quickly and he wasn't sure whether Erkin had seen what he'd done.

'How's business?' he asked the barber.

'Good,' said Erkin suspiciously. 'It will grow back, you know.'

21

It was after midday when Harry reached the institute. The receptionist in the lobby bulged eyes at him, picked up the phone and said into it: 'He's arrived,' as if Harry wouldn't hear. His assistant Carol was waiting for him outside the door to his office, one hand resting on the doorknob, the other free to cover her mouth when she saw him.

The room smelled of whisky. The bottle of Macallan was open on the desk where he'd left it the night before. He'd only drunk half. The letter he'd brought from the hospital was still there. He hadn't explained to the staff why he'd locked himself in his office and begun boozing but before leaving he'd made a copy of the letter, scrawled *Please close diary after March, might be late tmw* and dropped it on Carol's keyboard.

'You could've rinsed the glass,' he said.

'We didn't know where you were,' said Carol. 'You didn't come to the ten-year survival do.'

'Oh, him,' said Harry.

'Your phone was switched off. You weren't at home this morning.'

'I went out for breakfast. I went to the barber's.'

'We didn't know. We thought we should leave everything as it was in case the police came.'

'Has the survivor gone?'

'He's having lunch with everybody in meeting room one. He was disappointed not to see you at the presentation. He said he understood.'

'You told the survivor? Is there anyone who doesn't know? Has my tumour got more friends on Facebook than me?'

'Oh, Harry.'

'We need to reorganise,' said Harry with an appearance of determination. 'The institute's drifting. We've got too many research groups. We're supposed to be curing cancer here and all we do is screw around seeing who can create the most fucked-up mouse. I want all the PIs in here for a meeting this afternoon.'

'Amir called,' said Carol. 'He said you should start your treatment tomorrow.'

'Once my nephew's paper comes out it's going to shake things up. We need to be ready.'

'Amir said the sooner you start the better. He said it was the difference between six months and eight.'

Harry ran his hand over the alien smoothness where the remnant of his hair had been, skin that hadn't been exposed since he was a baby. His mother had kept a lock of his infant hair in an envelope, still blond after half a century. Where had it gone when she died? In with her old letters? Or gone to landfill in the clearout of the old house?

'It smells like a distillery in here,' he said. 'What's the survivor's name?'

'Shane.'

Downstairs, Harry stopped and listened at the door marked *Meeting in Progress*. He pressed his ear to the wood, heard the earnest hubbub and strained to hear his name. He went in.

The room stopped talking and stared at him. It had paper plates in its hands loaded with triangular sandwiches that looked glued together with some kind of brown paste. A flotsam of grey faces bobbed with wineglasses containing orange juice and still or sparkling water. In the midst of the round-shouldered, baggy-jacketed, joke-starved crew of scientists Harry saw a stranger, tall, slim, tanned, with glossy black hair, in an elegant purple shirt; he was in his late thirties.

'Shane, I presume,' said Harry. He shook the survivor's hand. Shane smiled, looking Harry in the eye. He had a gold stud in one ear and his well-shaped nails reflected the light. He had fine features and an intelligent expression. *This one I don't mind saving*, thought Harry.

'We had to press on in your absence,' said Robert, Harry's deputy, raising and lowering a half-eaten sandwich as if he were playing a fish with it. He ran his tongue over his teeth and frowned at Harry's hairlessness. 'Glad to see you. We sent out search parties.'

Two dozen medical researchers laughed in nervous sympathy and Harry's eyes skimmed their faces. He looked at Shane curiously and took Robert by the elbow. 'Come and see me this afternoon, Bob,' he said. 'I've had some ideas. We need to take the institute in a new direction.'

Robert pushed up his lips encouragingly. 'That sounds great,' he said. 'Why don't we wait until your first round of treatment? You only found out yesterday.'

'I'll decide when I have treatment.'

'Your son's on his way to London. He'll be here soon. Now's not the time to be thinking about work. You need to spend time with your family, with your friends.'

Robert said more like this and Harry stopped listening. He

looked at Shane and asked if he would like to see the institute's gardens. Shane picked up a leather sports bag and followed Harry outside.

One year Harry had chiselled money out of the trustees to make a miniature park behind the building. A scruffy lawn and hedge had been dug up and replaced by a radiating pattern of columns, trellises and arbours. He'd consulted Maureen about the plants. Vines had woven their tendrils through the interstices and, at intervals along the avenues, enamelled pots sprouted rosemary and lavender. Robert had told him it was a waste of public money.

'You should see it in spring,' Harry told the survivor. 'When the vines flower it's really quite pretty. Look.' He lifted a cluster of nearly ripe grapes in his hand. 'The money we spent could have paid a researcher's salary, but saving people isn't enough. You have to make the world you're saving them for worth it.' He gave Shane a sidelong look. The survivor had a muscular feline swagger, an aura of ease and potency. Harry's head was strewn with old hopes. What if the expert cells could do more than quench cancer? What if they made their recipients young and strong?

'It is you, isn't it?' he said. 'You're the survivor? Sometimes the survivor can't make it and they send a relative.'

Shane smiled his white-toothed smile. 'It's me. Diagnosed ten years ago, treated with expert cells, complete remission, no recurrence. A miracle.'

'I don't care for that word.'

'I'd be long gone otherwise.'

Harry sat down on a bench. Shane sat next to him. They watched a blackbird strike chips of gravel from the path with its beak.

'You look in good shape,' said Harry. 'How old are you?'

'Forty-one next birthday. I work out. I kind of feel I have an obligation to look after myself.' He fidgeted with the handle of the bag. 'I probably would anyway.'

'Wife and kids?'

'I live with my boyfriend.'

'Aha!' barked Harry.

Their eyes were caught by movement on the third floor of the institute and they watched a white-coated figure shuffle across a window, holding a flask.

'My deputy's mistress,' said Harry conversationally, pointing at the window. 'She spies on us to make sure we don't steal the public's lavender.'

'They told me,' said Shane. 'About your diagnosis. To explain why you didn't come.'

'Mmm.'

'I'm sorry. I hope they come up with something for you, like you did for me.'

'My nephew Alex . . .' Harry's mind raced and he forgot what he was going to say. He asked Shane what line he was in.

'Fashion,' said Shane.

'Excellent,' said Harry, who fancied he knew something about clothes.

'I went straight back to work after my treatment.'

'Splendid.'

'I design luxury coats for dogs.' Shane opened the bag and took out a handful of leather and metal. 'I made this for your Jack Russell. It's a present for the two of you.'

'For my Jack Russell?'

'I guessed the size, but if it doesn't fit, I'll alter it.' He unfolded the garment on the bench between them. 'The back piece, we call it the saddle, it's made of kid, and the star emblems are made of brass. The side pieces are hand-stitched and it buckles on underneath with these Lycra straps.'

'That's incredible,' said Harry.

'It was the least I could do.'

'Let me be sure I understand,' said Harry. 'All over the country there are dozens of dogs who'd be walking around without luxury hand-made coats if we hadn't saved your life?'

'All over the *world*.'

Harry turned the coat over in his hands, rubbing the different textures with his thumb. He heard the voices of a man and a woman, and feet on the gravel. Through the columns and vine leaves he saw Carol leading his son towards him. He sensed Matthew's pity from thirty yards away.

His son had learned how to aggravate him as a boy by feeling sorry for him because he couldn't believe. Matthew would look at his father with sad eyes and pity him and Harry would shout that he was happy without Jesus, and Matthew would grieve and shake his head and tell him that he couldn't be happy if he was shouting, and Harry would ask his son how he learned to be an expert manipulator of emotions. Were his Hebrew prophets psychoanalysts in waiting, marking time till they could start charging by the hour? And Matthew pitied him more. Now that Harry was ill, the old man was stepping into the vessel of filial lamentation Matthew had been preparing for him since he was fourteen.

Harry hadn't seen his son for the best part of a year. He put a sinister interpretation on Matthew's patience. It seemed to him that Matthew was quietly and humbly waiting for him to be damned, and this altered Matthew's substance in his memory to an ominous shadow. Yet the anxious man in the crumpled suit coming towards him now, the two ends of his tie at twenty-five past seven and care lines around his eyes, was his son. Harry didn't resist when Matthew leaned down and put his arms round him. His son's strength surprised him. Years seemed to have passed since he'd been held and felt the warmth of another body on his own. They began to speak, the four of them; introductions, medical matters, English awkwardnesses. While he talked Harry wondered why he hadn't treated Christianity as an affliction beyond his son's control, like a stammer or a limp. When he, Harry, was so sure that Matthew's religion was a lie, how could he allow himself to feel enveloped in his son's pity? He should have swamped Matthew's delusions with compassion.

It came to his mind to tell his son that it was good to see him, but he thought: *Later, I'll work up to it. Let him earn it.*

'You look tired,' he said.

'I got up at six to get here,' said Matthew. 'What happened to your hair? Have you started your treatment?'

Harry stroked his scalp. 'Shedding some ballast. How are my grandchildren?' It seemed to him that the question made Matthew's eyes narrow a fraction. *How can my son be my enemy when he is still a child?* he thought. They'd exchanged bitter words, and yet he was glad Matthew had come. His son was familiar. He thought again of saying to Matthew that it was good to see him. But why say it out loud, if he knew that it was true? He slipped his hand into his jacket pocket and fingered the lock of hair.

'Lettie and the children send their love,' said Matthew.

Shane said that it was time to go, shook everyone's hands,

thanked Harry again, wished him luck and left. Harry, Carol and Matthew watched him walk away, a stranger to all of them, yet leaving them with the sense that they'd lost the kindest and gentlest member of their party. Carol said she would *leave you two to catch up.*

'Why did you tell him I had a dog?' Harry asked her.

'I think you should have a dog,' said Carol. 'You shouldn't be alone in that big house.'

'I have a housekeeper,' said Harry. 'I'll have a nurse. Then there'll just be the house.'

'You should get a nice dog,' said Carol. 'A Jack Russell. I know one, already housetrained. I liked Shane. He wanted to give you a coat. I knew he'd be disappointed if I said you couldn't use one.'

'And now I have this.' Harry held up his gift, which clinked softly.

'He seemed to be a good man,' said Matthew.

'He's alive because of Harry,' said Carol. She shivered; she was wearing a thin blouse and it was a grey September day.

'Go, go,' said Harry.

'It comes with a basket,' said Carol over her shoulder as she walked away.

Matthew sat down next to his father.

'You're glad he's still alive?' said Harry. 'Shane the dog couturier?'

'Of course.'

'According to your people, when he does die, he's going to rot in hell for ever, damned for sodomy.'

'Don't talk about that now, Dad,' said Matthew.

'I thought it was interesting.'

'You spend so much time talking about what other people believe when you could be asking yourself if you live a good life,' said Matthew. 'We don't argue about religion all the time like atheists do. We don't think about it. We just live.'

I gave him a chance, thought Harry. *He's so touchy.* 'I don't want you to stop my grandchildren thinking.' He raised his voice. His anger and the joy he'd felt on seeing his son seemed part of the same flow. It was all nostalgia now. He wanted Matthew to stay and submit to being ridiculed, and then for him to hug his father again. But the boy was proud.

'I could come north at the weekend,' Harry said.

'You shouldn't travel in your condition.'

'The doctor didn't say I couldn't travel.'

'We've got so much on, so many things coming up. It's incredible how busy the children are.'

'Give me a date.'

'I'll have to talk to Lettie about it.'

'Why did you come here?'

'You're my father, and I care about you, in spite of everything.'

'Magnanimous of you.'

'On the phone you sounded frightened.'

'I wasn't frightened. I was drunk. Are you sure you know what you care about? You and Lettie care about getting the house. If you cared about me you'd let me see my grandchildren.'

'That's a question of trust.'

'You don't trust your father?'

'You said you'd take Chris and Leah to the zoo and you took them to a two-hour film about the Inquisition.'

'I didn't know it would be *realistic*.'

'You offered Peter a pound for every inconsistency he found in the Bible.'

'If you're going to attack me all over again for trying to help open your children's minds you might as well go home.'

'On my way here I thought, *He can use this for love, or he can use it for leverage.* Everything would be all right if you'd accept the way we are. Even if you don't, I want you to let me look after you.'

'Do you honestly think that after Shane dies he's going to be tortured for an infinite amount of time because he lifts another chap's shirt to get his kicks?'

'That's the path he chose,' said Matthew. 'I'm not saying I understand it. If it was up to me, I'd save everyone.'

'I already saved him!' said Harry, jingling the coat of his non-existent dog in his son's face. 'I saved that man. Not God. Me!'

22

Alex flew over the nucleus of a human cell, looking up along the shafts of microtubules that vaulted towards the distant, quivering sphere enclosing the cytoplasmic ocean, turning back to see the curving ridges of the Golgi apparatus release flocks of glittering proteins, each closing in on itself, like millions of open hands curling into fists. He delved inside them and each protein revealed itself as a form on the cusp of life and chemistry, a device of exquisite intricacy and precision, and he counted the revolutions of the atoms as they twisted and aggregated, key biting key biting key. He saw it partly as a vision, as through murky water lit by shafts of sunlight, partly as biomathematical values and partly by the physical mnemonics under his fingertips. It took him great effort to get there and he could never hold it for long – for less time now, when there was so much change in the world outside his head.

On the threshold of Alex's study, Maria watched him. He sat hunched with his back to her, a pen in his left hand, making sharp, short strokes that didn't look like writing. With his right hand he lifted, turned and rearranged a set of objects on the desk: a child's watering can, a toy rooster, a pair of interlocking wooden rings, an egg timer, a clockwork dolphin.

Scattered in front of him, around and on top of his computer keyboard, were the brightly coloured spheres and metal rods of a molecular modelling kit.

He came to the surface, singing a transition jingle he didn't know he sang.

Imagine for a moment
Real fruit as chewy as Fruitella

He realised Maria was in the room.

She said: 'I've got an idea. We could separate and look for other partners while we're young enough.'

Alex's forehead creased and he smiled and leaned towards her. 'I can see the advantages of that, and I can see three things against it,' he said. 'First, I'd miss you. Second —'

'I wish you'd stop making cases when I try to talk to you,' said Maria. 'And I don't like that expression. Can't you pay attention to me without putting on that hawk face? You smile and frown at the same time.'

'You don't want to separate?' said Alex.

'You obviously do.'

'You brought it up.'

'I wanted to see what you thought. Now I know.'

The realisation that he'd wounded his lover there and then seemed more painful to Alex than the possibility of future regret. He agreed easily to Maria's idea that they should stay together, living in Maria's house in Mile End as they had for eight years, sleeping in the same bed, having sex as before, until one of them found somebody else. It would be easier that way, said Maria. They wouldn't be lonely, and it was well known that people with partners were more attractive to others than people who were by themselves.

A month of peace and serenity went by on these terms, as

if they'd solved something, and Alex lost his way, then found it, in the shoals and narrows of the cell. But when he finished the draft of his paper and sent it to his colleagues at Imperial and to Harry to see what they made of it, it seemed to him that he and Maria were worse off than before. They still had no child and no prospect of having one. The theory of togetherness, tenderness and solidarity while they waited for one of them to be struck by love's thunderbolt was good, but what did it mean in practice? He suspected Maria wasn't really looking. Since he and Maria had been together, he'd met women he liked, but did he want to live with them for the rest of his life? Most women he met and liked were in the possibly-love category, but how, he wondered, could he bring possibly-love home to Maria? *I've met someone I might fall in love with. Let me have a week in France with her and if it works out I won't come back; if it doesn't, see you Sunday.*

He wondered if Maria had given him a licence to cheat and lie, or if she'd challenged him to have the guts to leave her, and concluded she'd done neither of these things. If before he could have made friends with women without her being suspicious, any new woman friend he mentioned now would be assumed to be a candidate lover, a threat. She'd given him the illusion of freedom and by doing so clutched him closer.

He'd been unwise about money, too, he realised. Maria had told him so from the start. He spent and gave and didn't invest. It seemed to him he was paid too much. His salary came in each month and it felt like plenty. He hadn't thought it meant anything to her until he told her he'd lent his entire savings to his brother, a hundred and twenty thousand pounds, to pay off a gambling debt. How furious she'd been, as if he'd robbed them. She was right, Alex supposed. She was right to think about the future, to be ruthless towards brothers-of-lovers who got themselves in trouble, to protect what they had so that their children would grow up safe, well fed, knowledgeable, in light and greenness. The look in her eyes when he told her, just as the IVF was starting, that had been something: savage as an animal whose mate had just eaten her young. And yet, it seemed to Alex, it was only money. He paid Maria rent each month, and had never asked for a share of the house; she'd never offered one.

One of the trustees from the Belford Institute asked Alex to help draw up the guest list for Harry's valedictory pre-Christmas party. When he'd almost filled his quota Alex called Ritchie and asked for Bec's email address.

'She's in Africa,' said Ritchie.

Alex thought back over what he'd said, working out if he'd been rude. He thought he must have caught Ritchie at a bad moment.

'I want to invite her to a party in December,' he said. 'It'll be mainly science people there.'

There was silence on the end of the line before Ritchie said warily that his sister returned from Tanzania on the tenth.

'Perfect,' said Alex.

'Scientists have parties, do they?' said Ritchie.

'Yes, we do.'

After another long silence Ritchie gave up the information.

'How is she?' said Alex.

'Busy.'

'Is everything all right?'

'Bec's very dear to me.'

'Have you two fallen out?'

'As a matter of fact we're closer than ever. She's a special girl. She's doing important work. I don't want her to be . . .' He didn't say what he didn't want her to be.

'Should I invite her boyfriend?'

'She hasn't got a boyfriend. No time.'

Alex's heart speeded up. 'She was going out with a newspaper editor,' he said.

'Oh no. That's finished, ages ago, all over, nothing to do with him any more. Didn't work out. It's just the vaccine for her now. Back to London for a few days, then Africa for the long haul. I doubt she'll have time for parties. Don't bother her. Really, Alex, best not. Listen, I've got to go, but let's catch up soon, yeah?'

23

Harry had come at the boy Alex with the confident glow of the big city, an impatient, sceptical Londoner trampling through the thistly intellects of a small Scottish town on his way to the rare orchid of his nephew's mind. He wore pink shirts with white collars, took phone calls from America in the middle of the night and brought a rich gush of aftershave, cognac and tobacco to Alex's underheated home, with its thick stone walls and condensation on the inside of the windows. Alex's parents had an out of tune piano in the living room that only Harry played. When he came to stay Harry would sit there in the evenings playing jazz, letting the ash from his cheroot fall on the keys, singing in a cracked voice and looking over his shoulder at Alex's mother. Alex despised jazz. At that time there was only The Smiths for him. But sometimes the sound of Harry singing It's The Rhythm In Me would sneak into Alex's room from downstairs, Harry's squat fingers hammering the low keys, and Alex wouldn't be able to resist riding along with it, picking up his sticks and joining in.

Harry told Alex that there was no mystery science wouldn't penetrate. Wonder in the face of natural marvels was all very well, he said, but it was no substitute for understanding. He would turn up on Saturday mornings off the sleeper from Euston and take Alex and Dougie on walks in the Grampians or along the Angus coast, lecturing them, according to what they came across, on the genetics of heather flowers, the prismatic quality of the rainbow and why natural selection made the hare's coat turn white in winter. He disparaged the local churches as monuments to ignorance and, with rhetoric so loud and abrasive that sheep looked up from their grazing in alarm and moved closer together, demolished a series of silent, invisible opponents attempting to prove the existence of God. The walks ended with a search for Dougie, who would wander away by himself while Harry answered Alex's close questions and would be found fishing for sticklebacks with his fingers, pelting rocks with rowan berries or skimming stones off the waves.

In Alex's fifth year at the high school Harry invited him to stay with his family in London for a week. On the eve of his journey south Alex saw his uncle on TV talking jauntily about his work, about taking cells from cancer patients' bodies, altering their genes and putting them back. He wasn't like the scientists Alex was used to seeing on television, stiff, nervous and suspicious. Harry laughed, leaned back in his chair and silenced the interviewer with a clever riposte. He seemed to Alex to be a master of life, shaping other people's will as lightly as he shuffled the molecules determining how long they lived. And yet when Alex sat at the supper table with Harry's wife Jenny and his son Matthew, his uncle was tense and curt. Aunt Jenny was a massive, gloomy woman who barely spoke and never smiled, her face half-covered by long black hair interspersed with crinkled strands of white. On the first night Matthew, who was Alex's age, wore a t-shirt with the words JESUS DIED FOR OUR SINS printed on it in fat red letters. He had a chunky Celtic cross on a thong around his neck and was trying to grow a beard. Before the meal he asked Alex if he wanted to say grace and Harry told his son sharply: 'I told you, your cousin's an atheist.'

'Are you?' Matthew asked Alex.

'I think so,' said Alex.

'You must let Jesus into your life,' said Matthew, dropping his eyes to the table and picking up a piece of bread.

'Why should he?' said Harry, and said to Alex: 'Don't pay attention to Matt, he's been brainwashed.'

Jenny looked from face to face and a whimper came from her, like an animal in pain.

Matthew clasped his hands together, bowed his head, closed his eyes and said: 'Dear Lord, we thank you –'

'Some wine, Alex?' said Harry, getting up and lifting the wine bottle towards his nephew, making it clink noisily against his fork and plate.

'– for the food and drink you have given us to eat today. Amen.'

'Abracadabra,' muttered Harry.

'I will have some wine,' said Alex.

Jenny sighed, sniffed and in a tiny squeaky voice said, 'Oh God.'

Harry mentored Alex far into his career, through his masters, his doctorate and beyond, swallowing his feelings each time his nephew surpassed Harry's understanding of his work. Harry thought his nephew had no politics. He thought Alex's contemplative self, which seemed dreamy and aloof, and his enthusiasms, which came so unpredictably, made him a bad collaborator and a useless leader. But when Alex came back to London from America in his late twenties, preceded by whispers out of Johns Hopkins that post-grads had started calling him *the sage of cell function*, other scientists in his field sought him out and listened to what he had to say. They were mired in grant applications, slide-show presentations, meetings, panels, conferences, committees and the gnawing, competitive hedonism of London, and the appearance of a man who seemed to do nothing except think, write and teach, with occasional outbursts of quaint philoso-phising, was like the coming of a visionary, even before they paid attention to his theories. His Scottishness gave him a touch of otherness to which the London scientists, clumped together from big cities around the world, were susceptible, as if he had drunk some special water up there. A rumour spread that Alex had taught himself maths and cell chemistry as a child.

In the ten years following his nephew's return, Harry had misinterpreted Alex's reputation as power, and confused his authority over scientific theory with authority over people. Now that his diagnosis only gave him a short time to live he became preoccupied with passing his job on to his nephew. He began a campaign at the institute to be sure the trustees' wariness of nepotism wouldn't stop Alex being head-hunted to succeed him. He didn't meet much resistance. The trustees agreed that Alex was the obvious candidate.

The trustees told Harry that they thought his illness was terribly unfair.

'Not getting cancer is just as unfair,' said Harry. 'But nobody complains about that.'

24

Outside Whitechapel Tube station, under the striped awning of a vegetable stall, a woman in full-on niqab ran her fingers, sheathed for modesty in black gauntlets, over the puckered skin of a bitter gourd. The stallholder watched. He'd zipped his leather jacket to the neck and pushed his hands deep into his pockets, pawing the ground with frozen feet. The awning flapped in the wind and the air ambulance clattered overhead towards the roof of the Royal London. The stallholder didn't suppose the woman would buy his vegetables. She was a gourd-stroker, a melon-tapper; she wanted to draw his attention to her fingers, knowing that the more she hid her skin, the more it turned him on.

His eye wandered to the Tube entrance, where a little dog appeared, dressed like a gladiator. Close to his ear a ripped young preacher of the Qur'anic word in a black army-surplus jacket, combat trousers and laced boots, fronting up in his first full beard, kept calling out, 'No running away from death!' A cluster of teenage seminarians loitered by the edge of the pavement, thin, nervy and big-eyed like deer, in ankle-length tunics, parkas and white filigree skullcaps. The preacher, who'd positioned himself so that anyone trying to cross Whitechapel Road to get to the hospital would have to pass him, was handing out one-page tracts printed on the madrasah inkjet.

'No running away from death!' he yelled. An old kafir slaphead in a mohair coat with a fleshy, pear-shaped face strode importantly towards him. The preacher looked down at the animal the kafir had on a lead, a small white and brown dog, dressed in a studded leather jacket.

'I am not running away,' said the kafir, who had stepped to within six inches of his face while the preacher was distracted by the dog. 'D'you think I'd set foot in that charnel house if I was afraid of death?' He nodded at the grimy yellow brick of the hospital, and set off towards it.

'Listen to what we've got to say, then, bruv!' called the preacher, thinking how boldly the kafir had come to him, and how forlorn he looked now from behind, walking alone with his dog trotting all pimped out beside him.

The preacher turned back to the crowd pouring out of the mouth of the Tube. 'No running away from death!' he shouted, and a tall kafir looked intensely at him and took one of his tracts as he passed. In his eyes the preacher saw something of the old slaphead who'd just gone by. Were they all beginning to look the same? 'Lot of distressed kafirs today,' he said, and the seminarians giggled, repeated the word 'distressed' and danced on and off the edge of the pavement.

Alex folded the sheet of paper the preacher had given him, crossed the road, passed through the portico of the hospital and asked at reception for Harry, who'd been due for an appointment that morning. They said they couldn't help: *patient confidentiality.*

Alex looked around the almost empty waiting room and went through the swing doors on the far side to a small public garden with a bench, a handful of scrubby trees and a bronze statue on a high plinth. The garden was overlooked by brown-brick hospital buildings covered in netting. He was clumsy and half-blind with anger.

Deep in a cranny in the human cell, Alex's Swiss collaborators had discovered a set of enzymes whose purpose he had, after a decade of work, understood: they were time counters, measuring the speed of change on the microscopic level. In the paper *Nature* was about to publish he called it the chronase complex. The reason Harry's expert cells worked, Alex found, wasn't that they sensed the different appearance of cancer cells; they spotted that cancer cells were working at the wrong speed, and marked them for death. It opened up new worlds for medicine, but it was the intricacy of the chemical mechanism that delighted Alex, and the notion that every human being contained sixty trillion clocks, counting units of time too small for any man-made machine to measure. He ended the paper by speculating that the system wasn't necessarily reset to zero at conception; that the count might have continued, unbroken, from the moment evolution set it in motion, a billion or two years ago. This was already going out on a limb. Now Harry, who'd seen an early draft, was trying to make him go further. It seemed to him that Harry had violated his inner world.

Maria told Alex he spent too much time in that world. He had no ordinary adulthood, she said; he only came out of himself as a child, distracted by a trivial novelty, some bright colour or pattern or catchy tune, or as a worried old man, shaken to his heart by an emotion that seemed to him like the end of the world – love, anger, jealousy, the longing for an heir. 'I don't know who you'll shack up with after me,' she said, 'but if she wants your attention I'd advise her to have a kazoo and a shotgun handy.'

'It's work,' said Alex. 'I'm exploring. I'm paid for my mind to be elsewhere.'

Alex sat down on the bench and unfolded the piece of paper the preacher had given him. A man doesn't die of diabetes, he read, or from drowning; he dies because the lifespan allocated to him by Allah has come to an end. The tract quoted the Qur'an: *When their time (Ajal) comes they will not be an hour late or an hour early . . . Wherever you may be, death will find you, even if you are in fortified towers.*

Alex looked up. A young man in a satin-effect bomber jacket was squatting down under the trees, trying to use the flame of a lighter to burn off loose threads wisping out from the hem of his jeans, but the gas wouldn't catch. He straightened up and walked over to the plinth, asking if he could borrow the lighter of someone Alex couldn't see. A small dog yapped and a Jack Russell dressed like a Roman soldier came out from behind the plinth and skipped towards Alex.

'Gerasim!' shouted a voice, and Harry appeared, a lit cigar and a lead in one hand, a lighter in the other. He gave the lighter to the young man and the garden filled with the smell of cigar smoke and burning cotton. The dog trotted towards Harry, who put the cigar between his lips and held the lead out to his nephew.

'Put the lead on him, will you, Alex? I can't bend down.' He looked around as if he were seeing his surroundings for the first time. 'They sent me to the wrong hospital. I should be in Barts.' He'd lost weight.

'I've been looking for you,' said Alex.

'It's not the smoking that's habit-forming, it's the going into hospitals. Once you start you can't stop.'

'I got a phone call this morning,' said Alex.

'Look at this,' said Harry. He led Alex to the plinth and showed him a bronze relief. 'There's Queen Alexandra,' he said, pointing to the image of a corseted, bonneted woman with her hands in a muff, bending over a patient. 'Do you know what that is?' He tapped his finger against the representation of a barrel-shaped object with telescopic tubes projecting from it. Edwardian nurses were applying the ends of the tubes to patients' heads. 'That's a Finsen lamp. They used it to treat lupus. Alexandra gave them one in 1900, first in Britain. This Finsen, you know, he got a Nobel prize for that, and he was only forty-two. Not much older than you. You look peeved. What were you saying about a phone call?'

'I got a phone call this morning from the editor of *Nature*.'

'He's a friend of mine.'

'He said you told him I was being coy. That I was hiding the meaning of my paper, that I didn't want to spell it out.'

'The Columbus of the human cell,' said Harry. 'He set out to find India, and he discovered a new world. But he still insisted it was India.'

'He talked as if I was trying to cheat him out of a scoop. He said you told him I'd discovered a way to stop ageing and was too embarrassed to say so. I wish you hadn't done that. I wrote what I meant to write and I didn't show it to you so you could go behind my back to get it changed.'

'Your paper explains why cells die. People are made of cells. Ergo, you explain why people get old and die.'

'I do no such thing.'

Fear glittered in Harry's eyes. 'You're not making the connection between what you've discovered and extending human lifespan. It's all there! You've written it! You're not joining the dots.'

'I'm not trying to extend human lifespan,' said Alex. 'It's long enough already.'

'Mine isn't,' said Harry.

'I want to understand how it all works,' said Alex. 'That was what you always told me I should do.'

Harry pointed at his midriff, where his tumour lay. 'I'm sick of understanding,' he said. 'It's time to interfere.'

'There was never going to be anything in my work that would help your condition, not until they've slogged away in the lab for another ten years.'

'What's the matter with you? Don't you want to heal the sick? Why shouldn't we live to be two hundred?'

'Our lives can't be long enough to make us happy,' said Alex. 'We can only live for ever by replacing ourselves.'

'Can we all replace ourselves?'

Alex's cheeks burned. 'I'm working on it,' he said.

'You told me you'd found the key to immortality.'

'I got carried away. I said I'd *seen* the key to immortality, not *found* it.'

'Even a weasel would have trouble getting through that semantic hole. You thought you'd say something nice to me because I told you I was about to kick the bucket. You thought I'd snuff it before I read your bloody paper.' Harry smiled a sugary smile and cocked his head. 'Why don't you add a final phrase to your paper, just a signpost: " . . . and has potential to delay or suspend human ageing". Isn't that where your findings take you?'

'Maybe, if the whole planet worked on nothing else for a generation.'

'You act as if fame doesn't matter to you, but I know you're proud,' said Harry.

'Don't you ever stop manoeuvring?' said Alex.

'I can't help it,' said Harry. 'The need to be strong, to want advantage and fame, these are natural instincts. Men are born with them. They make men men. That's how they know they belong in the world.'

'I'm not like you.'

'I'm only thinking out loud,' said Harry mildly. 'Whatever happens, you still have your mind. As for the human instincts, you either have them or you don't. I'd always thought you wanted to be in the great rhythm of things and not be a man set apart. It's up to you. But why not take the fame? Why not be a king?'

Gerasim barked, a high, piercing yelp, and Harry shushed him.

'He always wants to be the centre of attention,' said Harry. 'Come on, a last favour. "And has potential to delay or suspend human ageing."'

'If *Nature* publishes that the headlines will say "Scientists find fountain of youth." And I haven't found it, and I don't want to live forever.'

'Forever is a long time to draw a pension,' said Harry, tugging on Gerasim's lead. 'But I'm not even sixty-five. I'm too young to die.'

25

That night in a village in the forest south of Iringa, half a day's walk from asphalt roads, the three-year-old son of Batini, Bec's housekeeper in Tanzania, was ill. Huru lay on a blanket on a wood and reed bedstead, panting and shaking and making a sound like a bird. His skin was clammy and hot to the touch and his eyes were glassy. Batini wasn't there; she was far away with Bec on the other side of the country.

Huru's father had left Batini in the city soon after the boy was born and gone back to his home village, taking their baby son with him. He married another woman. Batini sent money and visited her son when she could, knowing the stepmother, Eshe, was wary of Huru. Eshe had children of her own. She wasn't wicked, Batini told Bec, just an ignorant country woman who believed Huru was cursed with coldness by the demons of the city. Huru's father took the money Batini sent for the boy and spent it on drink and bar girls when he was supposed to be looking for work in Mbeya.

'Why doesn't your ex let Huru stay with you?' asked Bec when Batini first told her the story.

'He would rather have his son hungry in his house than well fed with me,' said Batini. 'His grandmother Akila, my former husband's mother, loves Huru. She helps him.'

The village wasn't in Bec's original group of vaccine trial locations but it was close to others that were and she added it to the list. She'd gone there six months earlier with Batini and the vaccination team and met her housekeeper's son. Huru didn't cry when the needle pricked him. A momentary expression of betrayal appeared on his face and he squeezed his mother's thumb. Bec met the stepmother. Eshe turned out to be a petite, pretty young woman, barely twenty-one, with two small children of her own to look after besides Huru. With Bec, she was smiling and obsequious; with Batini she was defensive.

'The vaccine won't protect the children completely,' Bec told Eshe through Batini, who translated. 'They must sleep under nets and you must keep treating the nets.'

The village had no mobile signal. The nearest coverage was on a ridge a couple of hours' walk along the forest road. After Huru fell ill the family didn't contact Batini until his convulsions were so severe that his grandmother took him from the traditional healer and carried him on foot to the nearest clinic. Batini got the call in the middle of the night when Akila had carried him a third of the way and the first bar appeared on the phone she'd borrowed. Bec, who was preparing to fly to London, was woken at two in the morning by her housekeeper wailing. Bec roused one of the drivers and she and Batini set off for the clinic together.

It was a seven-hour drive. The women talked in the darkness, bending their heads towards each other to be heard over the roar of the car on the rough blacktop.

In her messages Akila told Batini that Huru's father was away in the north. Huru had degedege, Akila texted, not malaria, but the healer hadn't made him better, so she'd taken him to the clinic.

'She says it is degedege, not malaria,' said Batini to Bec in the car, gesturing vaguely with the phone.

'They took him to the healer?' said Bec.

'Yes, but he did not get better.'

'The healer burned elephant dung, that sort of thing? Herbs?'

'I do not know.' Batini sniffed and leaned her temple against the window. 'Is degedege and malaria the same disease?'

Bec didn't reply, and Batini looked at her and said: 'Is degedege malaria?'

'Yes,' said Bec.

Batini wrapped her arms around herself with a soft whimper and folded herself in two. Bec put her hand on her house-keeper's back.

'Akila did the right thing, taking him to the clinic,' she said.

'It is too far,' said Batini, her face muffled in her lap.

Later Bec fell asleep against Batini, her cheek on her ribs, and dreamed that she was carrying a boy through a forest at night. The moon lit her way, making the potholes and loose stones on the track stand out. Lightning flickered on the horizon and the bird sound coming from the child's mouth became fainter, till she could hardly hear it over the slap of her flip-flops on the dirt. In her dream Bec panicked, dipped her hand in a stream and tried to make the boy suck the moist tips of her fingers. He wouldn't suck and she moistened his dry, sticky lips. He moved his head and began to cough and open his mouth and Bec saw a beak emerging from his throat and after it the glistening eyes, the head and neck of a heron. She woke up with her heart hammering.

It was day. The sun wasn't long up and the soft gold light on farmers' solid concrete walls and tin roofs and banana trees made it impossible for Bec to imagine that anyone who'd been alive in the darkness when she fell asleep could have died since.

She congratulated the driver for staying awake and he said that it was nothing and that they were nearly at the clinic. There was a strange high-pitched humming. Bec looked around and saw that it came from Batini, who'd hunched herself up in the corner, her face hidden in her clothes. Bec touched her shoulder and Batini lifted her head and looked at her. Her mouth was open, her face wet, and a high, steady moan came from it. She spoke some words in Swahili and beat her thigh with the phone. She threw the phone onto the floor of the car and screamed and twisted violently from side to side, banging the back of the driver's seat with her fists and trying to tear the tough cotton of her dress with her hands and teeth.

26

When Bec had cleaned her funeral plate of ugali and stew in the village, it was dark. She went to find the driver. By the kerosene lamplight spilling from windows she traced the trodden way between the houses. Over the noise of frogs and insects was a murmur of evening voices and from doorways came shouts, laughter, wails, the crash of pans, radio music. She saw the whiteness of the big car and the driver squatting on the ground beside the front wheel, talking to two local men cross-legged beside him. A hand gripped hers. It was Batini.

'We must clean ourselves,' she said.

'I have to go,' said Bec. 'Will you come with me, or will you stay longer?'

'We must clean ourselves,' said Batini, tugging gently on Bec's hand.

'Now?'

'After a burial we are not clean.'

Batini led Bec along a path under the trees, between tall grasses and into a stand of reeds higher than they were. The ground yielded underfoot, mud oozed up between their toes and water came up over their ankles. They came out through the reeds to a pool fed by a stream, lit by an orange half-moon. They took off their clothes and arranged them on the reeds.

Bec launched herself into the water and swam, feet trailing along the muddy bottom, until she reached the middle of the pool. Batini stood with the water up over her hips and splashed her belly and breasts. She waded back to the shore, leaving a wake that broke up the moonlight on the water. Bec followed her to a fallen tree trunk close to the edge of the pool. Naked and dripping they sat side by side. The wood had been worn smooth by sitting.

'You are so white,' said Batini, looking down at Bec's thighs next to her own.

'I'm sorry about your son.'

'They are ignorant,' said Batini. 'You told them the vaccine would only protect them halfway. You told them to keep using nets. It is not your fault.'

It hadn't occurred to Bec that anyone might think it was her fault. She felt her heart take a jump off the edge, into darkness.

'Perhaps it is my fault,' she said. 'What use is a vaccine that only half-works?'

She listened to the frogs. There were so many of them, like a brass band: hundreds of shrill peeping ones, like piccolos and flutes, a host of tenor frogs, like clarinets and trumpets, and a handful of bassoons and tubas. *Those frogs must be huge,* she thought. *Gorilla-sized.*

Batini said: 'Where are your children?'

'I don't have children,' Bec said. *You know that,* she thought.

'Where is your husband?'

'I don't have one, as you know.'

'Why not? You are beautiful and healthy and educated.'

'Do I have to have children?' asked Bec.

'Of course,' said Batini.

'Tell me why, one more time?'

'It is joy.' Batini looked down and made little movements with her fingers on her lap as if fidgeting with the folds of an imaginary skirt.

'Will you marry again?' said Bec.

'Yes,' said Batini. 'I will marry next month.'

'Congratulations.'

'I will marry the brother of my second husband.'

Later Bec left the village and set off for Dar es Salaam with the driver. On the way they were caught in a rainstorm and it became impossible to see through the windscreen. The driver pulled over to the side of the road. The force of water seemed to rock the car. Lightning, cutting through the darkness and the deluge, showed spouts of water twisting from the boughs of trees and the shaking fronds of a field of cassava. Thunder cracked overhead and Bec's phone chirruped and the screen spilled a friendly yellow light. Ritchie was messaging her, asking when she was coming home. Bec called him and when he answered, when she pressed the phone to one ear and put her finger in the other, he was clear and close.

'What's that roaring? Are you standing next to a plane?' said Ritchie.

'It's rain,' said Bec. 'I'm on my way to the airport. Can you hear me? I'll be in London tomorrow afternoon. Hello?'

'I'm here.'

'I thought we'd been cut off. There was a long silence.'

'I was thinking.'

'The vaccine doesn't work. My colleagues think I'm a slave-driver and I think I should stay . . . Hello? I don't think I should be coming back. Ritchie?'

'Perhaps you're right,' said Ritchie.

'That's not what I expected you to say. Are you in the middle of something? There are long pauses.'

'It's the satellite,' he said. 'What you're doing is more important than having fun in London. It'd be selfish of me to encourage your hedonistic side.'

'You used to tell me I should be more selfish.'

'I was wrong.'

'Mum's expecting me.'

The pause was so long that Bec was sure they'd been cut off. The rain slackened. She heard Ritchie's voice again, earnest with a young boy's seriousness, as if there were ways of being he had no patterns of to follow except childhood ones.

'I've been thinking about it lately,' he said. 'There's a lot to be said for a quiet life, a simple, modest life.'

'Then I wouldn't have stories to tell you.'

Did Ritchie draw in his breath? The rain had almost stopped. 'That wouldn't be so bad, if it meant you were getting on with things,' he said.

'I won't tell you what happened today.'

'What happened?' said Ritchie, quick and nervous.

'You said you didn't want to hear my stories.'

Ritchie waited for several heartbeats. 'Tell me,' he said, with a strange wariness.

'My housekeeper's son died of malaria.'

'Oh,' said Ritchie. 'How terrible.' The *how terrible* was right in tune with respect and sympathy, but the *oh* seemed to belong to another conversation. Her brother sounded relieved, or disappointed, that it hadn't been something else.

27

The driver dropped Bec off at the airport at dawn. After takeoff she slept soundly, not waking till the plane descended towards Heathrow. As she marched off the aircraft her vision began to blur. 'Not now,' she whispered. But *gregi* went for her eyes and she had to stop in the corridor with the other passengers streaming round her, dark trunks and appendages whirling through a blizzard of light. She edged back and leaned against the wall.

These were the symptoms: an ache behind the forehead, a fierce itching in her eyes, the detail of the world broken into a snowstorm and blackness beyond. At moments like this, sudden blindness in a transit corridor in the airport, she felt she was a world in herself, alone in the universe, hosting millions of minute life forms striving for mastery over her and each other.

She charted the occurrences and couldn't find a pattern or common cause that triggered *gregi*'s attacks. In the wake of her discovery there'd been a division of the scientific spoils. Bec has pursued the use of the haemoproteus against malaria; the Nickells and others had laid siege to the shanty town, where they'd long ago set up camp, trying to study the human–bird-parasite symbiosis without changing it. The outsiders had done their best not to let the parasite get into them, or if it had, quickly took drugs to get rid of it. They feared for their eyes. A few of the older shanty-dwellers had permanent retinal damage and sat in their doorways, chewing betel and trying to grab the elbows of children running past, so as to have someone to talk to. Bec avoided thinking about this.

As far as Bec knew she was the only person in the northern hemisphere allowing her body to be used as an incubator for *H. gregi*. It took no effort to foster her father's multitudinous avatars, only these occasional feats of endurance; she didn't have to feed them, or stroke them. All she did was count them, and diary the episodes. It had little to do with the vaccine. Her colleagues said she had no good scientific reason to remain infected, as they insisted on calling it. The parasite thrived *in vitro* and was being studied in labs all over the world. They thought she was stubbornly taking a mad risk to prove a point, to get what she wanted. She told herself that it made the deaths of vaccinated children less hard to bear if she endangered her sight; yet the thought of losing it was terrifying. The latest word from PNG was that the shift from temporary to lasting blindness might be sudden. There were days when she considered purging her body of the parasites, yet she never acted. *After all*, she thought, *they have Dad's name. How could I kill the only ones in the family?*

At three in the afternoon, eyesight restored, she left the airport on the Tube, heading home. When she got to Leicester Square and changed trains, she found that a rogue compass quivering in the marrow of her bones pointed her to the southbound platform instead of the northbound, and she went to the Centre for Parasite Control.

She'd hardly put on the light in her office when the hand of Mosi, the Ugandan who was sequencing *gregi*'s genes, crashed down on the door handle and he stepped in, bellowing her name in a crescendo of delight. Bec charged into his grin and hugged him but when she stepped back and looked at him again, trying to keep the welcome fresh, he was wary. He asked her if Maddie knew she was back, and Bec said she didn't know. Mosi asked why she'd kept delaying her flight home.

Alerted by Mosi, the director came to Bec's office, closed the door, kissed her and asked if she could sit down. Her lean old face had impressively clear shadows under the cheekbones and eyebrows and her silver hair was cut close to the head. The brightly coloured glass globes strung on her necklace and hanging from her ears seemed to be ornaments hung on her by a lesser woman to appease her.

'They managed to get you on the plane,' she said.

'I was always going to come back for Christmas,' said Bec.

'To see your friends and family. You're going to Spain to see your mother.'

'Yes.'

'Your brother and his family will be there.'

'Yes, that's right.'

'Friends to see, going out, parties, dancing, catching up. Fun. You've worked hard in Africa, a lot of stress has built up and now you've earned yourself three — is it three? — weeks of rest and relaxation.'

Bec licked her lips and nodded. 'Maybe two,' she said.

'And here you are in your office.' Maddie reached forward and grabbed the top journal on the pile in front of Bec.

'Reading about . . . toxoplasma. Oh! The centennial issue!' She tossed it over her shoulder and nodded at Bec's luggage. 'Have you been home since you landed?'

Bec shook her head.

'When did you last wash your hair, if you don't mind me asking? You look as if you were caught in the rain.'

Bec ran her fingers through her hair, got them caught in tangles and dug in her bag for a brush. 'I went swimming yesterday before my flight,' she said. 'There was a funeral.'

Maddie sat on her hands and rocked backwards and forwards, studying the floor.

'Who died?' she said.

'My housekeeper's little boy.' Bec's face had disappeared behind a thick curtain of hair as she brushed it through.

'What did he die of?'

'Malaria.'

'How old?'

'Three.'

'Vaccinated?'

'Yes.'

'So now you think your work's a failure. You think fifty per cent protection from malaria's a pretty poor return for all the money and time we've spent turning your parasite into something useful.'

Bec threw her hair back, stopped brushing and looked at Maddie.

'Maybe you think you were right all along and we should be infecting children with live haemoproteus. But we couldn't do that, could we? How are your eyes?'

'Fine, thanks.'

'When was your last attack?'

'They aren't attacks,' said Bec. 'It was a bit blurry this afternoon for a few minutes.'

'Maybe it seems to you that all this,' Maddie spread her arms and tickled the air of the centre with her fingers, 'is money badly spent. Maybe you think Europe and America got rid of malaria in their day without any vaccines cooked up by rich foreigners. I used to think that. I used to think there was an infinite number of wrong things to do and one right thing and I had to find it. I used to think my old boss was a disgusting compromiser and a politician.'

'Do you really remember what you used to think?' said Bec.

'I hear somebody called for you today from the Belford Institute. They wanted to know if you got the invitation for the party tonight.'

'It's a party in honour of a man I don't know. His nephew invited me. He's a friend of my brother's.'

'Are you going?'

'Of course not.'

Maddie stuck out her lower lip, fidgeted with her necklace and put her head to one side. 'It's going to be in that new tower near London Bridge,' she said. 'You'll be able to see all over the city. There'll be drinking and dancing. You used to like that. That's why you came back, isn't it? For the past few months you've been slaving, not working. It's as if you've been doing penance for something. What would you have to do penance for? You've never done anything wrong. Stop acting like some crazy Calvinist witch. Go home, charge a taxi to the centre, make yourself glamorous and go out.'

'I don't want to go out.'

'Your housekeeper wouldn't want you to mourn. That's for her. You've worked there long enough to know where you can shove your guilt and pity.'

'It isn't punishment,' said Bec. 'If I wanted to punish myself I'd be one of the people charging around London raving about sex and love and marriage without the faintest idea what they're talking about.'

Bec had a mortgage on a two-bedroom basement in Kentish Town. Ritchie had offered to pay it off and she'd refused. She pushed the door open against the heap of mail in the hall and the unheated air chilled her cheeks with a hint of dampness. Brooding over the things Val had said before they parted, she hadn't emptied the rubbish before she left, and the kitchen stank of rotten banana skins. Nor had she emptied the fridge. All that should have been green there was brown and all that should have been brown was green. A cup of coffee she'd half drunk before leaving had skinned over with pale fur and there were cobwebs on the bathroom ceiling. She opened the laundry basket to pour in her dirty clothes. It was already full; when she lifted the lid the elastic energy in the compressed pile was released and scrunched-up socks and pants sprang out onto the floor.

The phone rang. It was Val. She didn't answer but listened to the voicemail he left.

'Hello Rebecca,' said Val. 'I heard you were back. I was thinking the other day about how you said there was no moral foundation. I thought, "She's right! Why don't I set one up?" Someone's got to keep an eye on things. Merry Christmas!'

Bec's fingers fumbled angrily on the buttons of her jeans, wondering how he'd known she was in London. She threw her clothes violently on the floor, showered and washed her hair and got ready to go out. She whispered to *gregi*, watching with curiosity in the mirror as her reddened lips moved.

'This beauty's no use to you or me,' she whispered. 'You might as well make me blind.'

28

That night Ritchie went out in Soho. He supposed Bruce
Heemingthwaite would be grateful to be invited to join 'a few
of us' (as he put it in the email Paula sent out in his name)
for drinks at one of his clubs, and he was.

'It's so good to see you again,' said Bruce for the third time,
leaning forward and punching Ritchie on the shoulder. Ritchie
grinned and glanced at Midge, sitting next to him. Midge was
tapping and twirling his lighter and staring into space. At the
other end of the table Fred and Art talked quietly.

'I'm the first to admit I fucked up,' said Bruce. A drunken
edge came into his voice and Ritchie's muscles tensed. 'But
the fantastic thing about this sort of time in your life is, you
find out who your real friends are, you know? D'you know
what I mean, Midge?'

Midge raised his eyebrows, picked up his beer and turned
his eyes back to the distant point in space he'd been focused
on. He took a gulp and put the glass down carefully.

'Fred!' called Ritchie. They were close together, on a
banquette and two chairs. There was no music in the club but
they had to raise their voices to be heard above the din of
other people's chatter. 'Fred! You look like you had your tie
removed and they forgot to sew you up.'

Fred fingered the open collar of his striped shirt. He'd come straight from the office. 'They let me keep it,' he said. 'Here.' He took the rolled-up tie out of his jacket pocket and held it out to Ritchie. 'You look as if you need a donor.'

'He needs more like a shirt graft,' said Art.

'Ritchie's got a special offer on his donor card,' said Midge. 'It says "In the event of my death, I wish my fat to be used to help feed the hungry."'

'You've got a donor card,' said Ritchie.

'Fuck 'em,' said Midge. 'I'd rather be made into dog food.'

'Doesn't it say you're donating your cock to the Russian women's netball team?'

'Only for one night!'

'Face transplant,' said Bruce, his voice cutting into the laughter, which faded away.

'What?' said Midge, staring at him with mouth slightly open and nose wrinkled.

'Nothing.'

'Thought you said you wanted a face transplant,' muttered Midge into his beer. 'When are they going to start transplanting personalities? There's a need there.' Nobody spoke for a while. Ritchie ordered another round of drinks.

'Are you getting much work?' Art asked Bruce.

'Yeah! Yeah. Well, no,' said Bruce, looking down at the floor. Making an effort, he lifted his head and smiled at Art. 'It was always going to take a while to come back, wasn't it? The cold shoulders, the divorce.' He glanced at Ritchie, who was running his right hand repeatedly over his mouth and jaw. 'The producers, they'd give me a second chance, but it's your lot, isn't it, they won't wear it.'

'Not my paper,' said Art.

'Yeah, come on Bruce,' said Midge. 'Art works for a poncey paper. They always give the paedophile the right of reply.'

'OK,' said Ritchie, holding up his hands. 'Bruce's paid his dues, OK? Midge, you're out of order.'

Bruce fingered the crucifix on the gold chain hanging out of the v-neck of his sweater. He leaned towards Midge, eyes glittering, and said: 'I remember being in here with you when you were boasting about the little Thai whores you did in Chiang Mai. You said "If they're not white, it's all right."'

Ritchie took Bruce's arm, lifted him out of his seat, took him to the bar upstairs and ordered him a drink.

'Sorry, Ritchie,' said Bruce. 'I fucked up again.'

'It's been tough for you, mate, we know it,' said Ritchie.

Bruce nodded and pressed his lips together. Tears welled up and rolled down his cheeks. He rubbed them away with his sleeve.

'Wait here, I'll be back in a bit and we'll talk,' said Ritchie.

'I'm not looking for pity,' said Bruce.

'I know.'

'I'm good. I'm good at what I used to do.'

'I know.'

'What happened, it's given me depth. You could use me.'

'We'll have a talk about that. Wait here, I'll be back.'

Ritchie went back downstairs to the others. 'What did you have to invite that cunt for?' said Midge.

'It was a long time ago,' said Ritchie. 'Five years, wasn't it?'

'Four,' said Fred.

'It's not about what he's done,' said Midge. 'I've –'

'You've what?' said Art. 'I haven't.'

'I can't even remember how old she was,' said Ritchie.

'Fifteen,' said Fred. 'And you know what happened to her?'

'That's right,' said Art. 'That columnist, what's his name, she ended up with him.'

'Didn't they get married?'

'Now that's wrong. Married at nineteen.'

'I saw her once. Fucking incredible. Legs up to here.'

'What a fucking waste.' Their heads were close together.

'What Bruce did wrong wasn't having sex with a fifteen-year-old . . .' said Fred.

'I thought you were a lawyer?'

'It was that she was on the show.'

'What was it called?'

'Some twattish name.'

'*The Ugly Show.*'

'He had some twattish way of pronouncing it.'

'*The You-Glee Show.*'

'Something like that, yeah.'

'What a twat.'

'It's not the point,' said Midge. 'It's not him fucking a schoolgirl, it's him being lame enough to get found out. That's what he's ashamed of. That's what's fucked him up. I hate entertainers who're too shit-thick to find a way to keep their dirty habits secret.'

'Shall we leave him?' said Ritchie.

'Eh?' said Midge.

'Let's go to Canaan. We'll just leave him here.'

Fred laughed. Art joined in. Midge smiled slyly at Ritchie and stood up. 'Come on then,' he said.

They left and Ritchie stayed to settle up. After he'd paid the bill he went upstairs and stood in the doorway there, half-hidden, watching Bruce alone at the bar with an empty glass in front of him, hunched on a stool, head down. Bruce lifted his head and began to look around and Ritchie quickly moved out of sight and went down into the street to join the others.

It was drizzling. Canaan was only a couple of streets away and the four men spread across the pavement as they walked, joking loudly, brazenly turning their heads to follow the girls in heels they forced to squeeze past them. Ritchie signed them into Canaan and when they sat down it was as if they hadn't left Zeppo's – the same banquette seats, with the leather a different shade of red, the same drinks, everything the same except that there was no Bruce. Now that they were four they spoke in turn. They spoke about their children and their wives, property, their hobbies. They were earnest and gently competitive. It was as if the expulsion of Bruce had induced a need for tranquillity. On the way to Canaan Ritchie had been proud to be leading a group of cocksure swaggerers and he was proud now to be in the heart of a group of good men who with their eagerness and their harmless boasts about their weekend lives reminded him of the friends he'd had at school. Yet purpose ate at his heart.

'He never came to you, did he, Fred?' said Ritchie.

'Who?'

'Bruce.'

'I'm not with you,' said Fred coolly. He took a big gulp of wine.

'Didn't the paper that broke the story try to do some kind of deal with him? We won't publish it if you bring us the dirt on so-and-so, that kind of thing?'

'That would be blackmail, wouldn't it?' said Art.

'*Innocente!*' said Midge, pointing at him.

'It would be blackmail,' said Fred. 'I don't see why he would have come to me.' Ritchie could hear the lawyer in him taking control of his voice, like ice crystallising at the edges of a pond.

'That's what you do, isn't it?' said Midge.

'Privilege,' said Fred, trying to grin, but the ice was thickening. He hid his mouth behind his glass.

'They have ways of putting it that it doesn't sound like blackmail,' said Midge. 'You know what they're getting at but it wouldn't stand up in court.'

'You sound like it's happened to you.'

'I've got a lot of clients. They all like to talk,' said Midge. 'What it comes down to is two things. One, they can't keep it in their pants. Two, the country's full of sneaks and snitches.'

Fred laughed to himself.

'Traitors,' Midge went on. 'People who'll sell you out. Kiss-and-tell girls. Paparazzi. Tip-off merchants. Camera phones. It's like the fucking Stasi. How d'you think a police state works? I'll give you a clue: it's not the police. Watch your friends. Half the country's ready to inform on the other half.'

Ritchie said to Fred: 'Supposing Bruce had gone to you and said look, I've been fucking this fifteen-year-old and they've found out, they'll splash it all over the front page unless I give them some dirt on someone else. What do you say?'

Fred put his glass down slowly on a place mat and turned it round through a hundred and eighty degrees, watching it. They all watched it. He looked up. 'I'd say I charge three hundred pounds an hour,' he said.

Midge and Al sniggered.

'I'm curious,' said Ritchie.

'I'm off the clock,' said Fred.

'You're a lawyer. Lawyers are always on,' said Ritchie.

'Thanks,' said Fred. 'You want some free advice?'

'No, I'd rather give you three hundred pounds.'

'Do you want some free advice?'

'Go on then.'

'The best way not to get caught is not to screw around in the first place.'

'You don't need to talk as if it's me who's got a problem,' said Ritchie.

'It's good advice, Fred, but then I'd have four dozen fucking saints on my books,' said Midge. 'Nobody ever paid for their house in France with ten per cent of Goody Two-Shoes.'

'What is it with lawyers?' said Ritchie to Midge. 'You ask them out for a drink after hours and the next thing they're quoting at you from the Licensing Act and billing you for it.'

Fred made a joke about producers always trying to turn a good time into bad reality TV. Nobody laughed. Fred looked at Art, who looked away. Fred got up.

'Are you leaving?' asked Midge. 'Bye.'

Ritchie watched Midge and hated him, his cleverness, his tailored black suit, hand-made white shirt and gold tie, his ability to be absolutely certain of his place in the world while mocking every place in the world. Yet although he hated Midge, he wanted to keep him as his friend.

'Not going to write this up, are you?' said Ritchie to Art.

'You haven't said anything interesting,' said Art.

Ritchie and Midge looked at each other.

'You invited me,' said Art.

'Yeah,' said Ritchie, looking into his empty glass.

'I'll get another bottle,' said Art.

'Nono nonono,' said Ritchie, holding his hand up. 'I'll do

it.' He called the waiter over and ordered, then said to Art: 'You were pretty hard on poor old Bruce.'

Art frowned. He said: 'It was your idea to leave him there, and it was him' – he nodded at Midge – 'who called him a cunt.'

'"Him",' said Midge. 'That's courteous.'

'You went along, though, didn't you?' said Ritchie to Art. 'What do you think? If you'd been the hack who got the juicy titbit about our Bruce? Would you have used it?'

'I don't do that kind of journalism,' said Art. 'I write about politics for a serious newspaper.'

'Writes about boring for a boring newspaper,' said Midge.

'Come on,' said Ritchie. 'You're all the same. You get some dirt on a popular TV celebrity who falls for a greedy, scheming little girl who can't believe her luck, who knows exactly what she's doing, whose mum, whose parents are probably in on the act . . . you wouldn't hesitate, would you? You'd stitch him up, wouldn't you, you'd destroy his life?'

'She was fifteen!' said Art.

Ritchie folded his arms, leaned back in his seat and turned to Midge. 'They're all the same,' he said.

'All the same,' said Midge.

'But maybe,' said Ritchie to Art, 'you wouldn't crucify him right away?'

'Are you even listening to a word I'm saying?'

'Don't get upset, we're just talking. I'm saying you wouldn't crucify him right away. You might try to use the leverage to get something even more juicy out of him. Here.' He held the bottle over Art's half-empty glass.

'No, it's OK, thanks.' He cleared his throat. 'I should be heading off.' He got up, licking his lips and fumbling with his jacket.

'You're not offended, are you?' said Ritchie, looking up at him with wide eyes.

'No, no.'

'We were only having a bit of fun.'

'I know.'

'Even if you are a treacherous little toerag who'd sell your own sister for a story.'

'Yeah,' said Art, trying to smile. He forced a laugh. 'You're a bunch of fuckers too.'

'That's not a very nice thing to say,' said Midge, seriously.

Art's face lost colour. He seemed to search for a comeback and settled for staring hard into Midge's eyes. Midge met his stare and asked if something was wrong. Art slumped his shoulders, half-lifted his hand in a wave and walked away, Ritchie calling after him to give his love to his wife.

When he'd gone they sat quietly for a while.

'How's Karin?' said Midge.

'You asked me already. I told you, she's fine.'

'You're in a fucking strange mood, Ritchie.'

'Work.'

'Tell you what,' said Midge in a low voice. 'I could murder a line right now. Have you got some?'

'Could make an order,' said Ritchie.

Midge put his hand on Ritchie's wrist before Ritchie could text his dealer. 'I'll go,' he said. 'I know a guy near here. I'll be back in ten minutes.'

Ritchie sat alone on the banquette with the smudged empty glasses disarrayed in front of him. He looked round. A woman in a black dress, bare-shouldered, was sitting at the bar. Ritchie got up, went over to her and said 'Hello.' He wanted to buy her a drink and tell her about the time he gigged with Bono and David Bowie at the Hammersmith Palais. The woman looked at him, turned away, raised her finger and caught the barman's eye.

'Mr Shepherd,' said the barman. 'Is it possible you've forgotten we have a strict rule about unsolicited approaches to other guests?'

Ritchie left the bar, putting out a hand to keep the wall at a polite distance after it bumped into his shoulder. He locked himself in a toilet stall. A sign above the toilet warned that any guest found using drugs on club premises would be expelled permanently. Ritchie took a tinfoil package out of his pocket, placed it on top of the cistern and opened it. He took one of the dark brown pieces from the foil, put it on his tongue, sat down on the closed toilet, shut his eyes and pressed the choco-late against the roof of his mouth.

29

Harry saw the potential for comedy in his cancer. He imagined strangers asking him what he did, and him saying he was head of a cancer research institute, and the stranger asking him what kind of cancer, and him saying 'Not the kind I've got. I'm jealous of people with *that* cancer. If there's a commandment, I'm breaking it. "Thou shalt not covet thy neighbour's cancer."'

But strangers never did pronounce the lines Harry scripted for them. He ended up having to fill in the set-up himself, and before he could get to the jokes, three Os appeared on their faces: two widened eyes and one open mouth. Harry didn't want that. He wanted the cancer and him to be treated as partners in an ancient country story, The Cancer and the Scientist, like the Devil matching wits with a farmer after dark at a crossroads halfway between the farmer's hearth and hell. The three Os deferred to death. He felt like a man introducing a friend who knows a celebrity. It was the cancer they wanted to talk to, hoping for the inside juice. 'Oh, you know Death! What's he *like*?'

Harry's former wife lived in New Zealand. She'd removed herself to the land of her ancestors when she told Harry that he'd made a mistake marrying her, that getting hitched to the first woman he got pregnant had seemed like clearing something complicated off his agenda early when he had other priorities; and Harry hadn't disagreed, or tried to stop her. His post-divorce affairs petered out in his late fifties. An experience with the heartbreaking jollity of an erotic masseuse had put him off paying for a woman's company. At night there was no one for Harry to turn to and demand an embrace and a hearing. His was the only warm body in the house.

He woke up when the first planes from Asia descending into Heathrow shook the darkness. At those times it wasn't so much his own fate that frightened him as a simple disproportion of scale. An image of the Earth as a distinct turquoise speck drifting across a vast yellow sun haunted him and became the gateway to a recurring fit of vertigo in the face of the unknowable. In daylight the fear became a background hum of anxiety about an imminent, important trip he had to make against his will. He caught himself thinking he had to pack and remembered he didn't.

Chemo and radiotherapy were behind him. Surgery couldn't help and he was in a lull before the palliatives got interesting. He didn't have cancer-related tasks to occupy his time. At the institute, he observed a benign conspiracy to peel away his responsibilities. In garrisons preparing for battle, he'd read, officers filled soldiers' time with pointless drills and parades to tire them out and occupy their minds; but what did the officers do? Harry had thought making his own funeral and burial arrangements might amuse him, but that, too, fell short. He'd ordered his own headstone, chosen the material, the font and the text. It turned out you could do it online. It had seemed funny to have:

chiselled deep in black-enamelled letters in a slab of pink Scottish granite. A few weeks later he woke up with his heart beating fast and his face burning, sure that he'd paid twelve hundred pounds to have a scientific in-joke perpetuated in a Surrey cemetery as his memory on earth. He called the mason's yard next day, half-hoping they'd say 'Well, it's not set in stone. Oh no, it is.' But the mason's receptionist told him they wouldn't start work until long after the client was buried. There was always the danger of subsidence if you put the stone up too early, they said. You had to let the grave settle.

It seemed to Harry that laughing at death was a good way to show he wasn't afraid of it, and that carelessness in the face of losing everything was the bearing of the noble man he wanted to be. And yet what was it, he wondered, to enclose death in comedy? Was it nobler to show your bravery by laughing at yourself, or to make the purest comedy by cheating death at the end, and make death the fool?

Often the awareness came to him that in a cold room at the institute, suspended in CryoStor solution, bagged, labelled and kept in a Planer freezer at minus one hundred and fifty degrees, was a large supply of his own cells, drawn from him, genetically modified and cultured ten years earlier. A sample had been infused into his bloodstream then to show that they were safe, and they had not had the slightest effect on him. They were designed for a different kind of cancer. There was no scientific reason why they should have any more effect on solid tumours than an injection of orange juice, yet Harry couldn't stop thinking about them. His cancer was his own;

the cells were, whatever the institute's lawyers might say, his own; why shouldn't he put the two of them together? It would be a family reunion.

Harry remembered how doubtful he'd been that the expert cells would work as they were supposed to. Most things didn't, after all. And yet they *had* worked on those patients. Harry's mind arranged a pseudo-logical argument that he knew was nonsense but found attractive. It went like this:

I thought a treatment designed for one cancer would probably fail, and it succeeded.

Therefore, if I think the treatment will definitely fail in another cancer, it will do better than definitely failing.

The next better thing after definitely failing is possibly succeeding.

So Harry reasoned, and so he yielded to temptation. He admitted that much to himself, never that he was yielding to hope.

30

A river the colour of milky tea flowed through London. Once in a while the sun sparkled on its surface and you saw that it was really made of money, a sediment of macerated currency washed off the cash mountains of Eurasia. The river's looping course at the City and Canary Wharf strained and cleansed the flow as it gushed towards its mouth in Switzerland, leaving a looty silt behind on the banks, and in this fertile tilth sprouted skyscrapers. The tallest grew out of a deposit of Gulf dollars near London Bridge. Its concrete core seemed to have been jacked up seventy storeys overnight, jabbing the skyline wherever you looked.

Harry liked to see London grow tall. As an old man it gave him paternal comfort to watch grand human feats enacted on the scale of skies and horizons, as if when he cheered from the sidelines at the swing of cranes and the pouring of concrete he took part in the future's common fathering. Each topping out seemed a personal victory. The daring of it thrilled his old heart: the boldness of change was all, in wild strokes slashed across the cityscape.

He didn't understand his assistant Carol when she told him she'd booked a floor of the tallest tower for his party. To him the manifestation of the building, its sheathing in glass and the gradual flickering on of its lights were like gestures of the hand of progress. He'd forgotten real people ran it. Carol had noticed the tower one day, thought *Where did that come from?*, decided Harry would like it, made a few calls and fixed a day.

Not long before Christmas, at eight in the evening, a thousand feet above London, the first guests came out of the lifts and wandered towards the glass walls of the banqueting suite to marvel at the ocean of streetlamps and windows fixed in the darkness. A shaggy cloud a block long crept past them over the city, making them tingle with the godlikeness of their position. After a minute they got used to it, and it wasn't interesting any more, and they turned to each other. A ten-piece swing band in white tuxedos played and a close-ranked company of champagne bottles fresh out of the chiller smoked on a long table, attended by Polish boys and girls in white shirts and black waistcoats. In the kitchen more young Poles, in on the bus from crowded digs in the far west, took cling film off platters of canapés contrived as doll's house versions of famous foods: hot dogs two inches long, a stack of cigarettes revealed as crispy duck in micro-pancakes, and infernal lumps of guinea fowl tikka, spiced red and roasted black, in ocarina-sized clay tandoors.

The finance director at Harry's institute had been aggrieved when Carol asked him for money for the party. He was used to chipping in fifty quid for wine and sandwiches. He understood Harry was *a leading scientist*, but he thought it pretty low to make the despised accountant responsible for determining the lavishness of his boss's wake. What would the trustees say? The institute was funded by the government and medical charities to postpone citizens' departure from this world, as far as he knew, not to send the departing on their way with gold-plated hooleys.

The finance director plucked his lower lip, traced thinking circles with the cursor over Harry's pay spreadsheet and realised he'd felt the same grudging sense of obligation earlier in the year when he'd coughed up thousands in maternity pay to a senior researcher who, he knew, had no intention of returning to work after her baby was born. What if Harry, with the biggest salary in the institute, had got pregnant instead of contracting a terminal illness? The finance director tapped in the codes and stared at the screen in horror. How much more it would have cost him! He deleted 'maternity pay' and typed in 'mortality pay'. He looked over his shoulder guiltily and set aside, for Harry's farewell bash, a tenth of what he would have paid him as a new mother. Immediately he felt moved by his generosity and sent Carol an email.

Harry reckoned it was mean and told Carol he'd triple what the institute spent from his own pocket. He thought modest public servants like himself had a duty to stage princely entertainments. 'Am I supposed to live like a monk just because I'm not the director of an oil company?' he asked. An American colleague muttered about the war on cancer. Oh, said Harry, if you knew what a lot of off-ration champagne the prime minister guzzled in wartime while our brave boys were dying! Churchill knew, said Harry, that nothing was wasted like a life without superfluity, without the grand gesture.

Two young women in low-cut dresses, a media assistant at the Wellcome Trust and a friend with only an idea of a job, in heels and dark tights, with a little gold about them, stepped into the party; feared having gone too formal; feared having chosen a *lame* event from many possibles; were relieved by the rasp of trombones, beat of a double bass, bright colours, bare shoulders, smart jackets, pearls on skin, hammering of talk; felt unknown to all; were nervous; had cold champagne offered; smiled at the cute waiter boy; sipped; had tongues tickled; felt triumph in the big city; saw London lit up below; went to the great window; felt dizzy at the distance from the ground; took bigger sips; agreed it was like they were flying over London; saw the flashing lights of an aircraft landing at City airport; said it was weird to be looking down on it; noticed islands of light in the sea of lights; identified the City, Canary Wharf, the O2, Stratford where the Olympics had been; edged away from the window; were offered food; bent to put bite-sized pizzas in their mouths, making their earrings swing and glint; drew the attention of two men.

A lonely geologist in his forties who thought his life had gone wrong tried to make conversation with the jobless one; was told she was *trying to get funding for a pilot multimedia project to enhance public understanding of science*; considered telling her it was a waste of time; found her young, pretty; tried to impress instead with gossip about Harry; reported that Harry hadn't invited his son to the party; was asked which one was Harry; pointed him out, standing by the champagne table in an electric-blue suit, a mauve shirt and a pink tie, speaking to a semi-circle of people, hands in his pockets, rocking back and forward, laughing and talking at the same time; was told by the media assistant how well Harry looked; told her he'd lost a lot of weight, that he'd be gone by spring; accidentally fascinated the women by the casual confidence with which he said this; made his friend feel neglected.

The friend, a handsome young hack from the *New Scientist* who hadn't dressed up, crossed the room on a pretext; joined an American biologist talking to a writer who'd predicted the end of the world in a forgotten bestseller; asked the biologist whether she'd come all the way from America for this; was found to be cocky and trivial; was told she'd come to celebrate a well-lived life; said he'd heard Harry hadn't invited his son; heard from the writer that Harry's nephew Alex was present, at the great man's right hand; stepped back to allow others into the circle; heard someone ask if it was true that Alex would be Harry's successor at the institute; confirmed it; pulled out his iPhone; said he wanted to check that the word 'nepotism' came from the Latin word for nephew; was jeered at and giggled with.

The biologist pulled away from the group and looked around the room, wondering where you could go on the seventieth floor if you needed a smoke. The din was getting to her and she was disappointed by Harry's choice of venue. She'd come here via Shanghai. The duel of the towers, she thought, wasn't one London was going to win. She recognised Alex in the crowd, a tall, restless fellow with a shark's-fin nose and big eloquent hands, nailing some innocent into the ground with sweet reason.

A woman walked into the room with a distracted intentionality, as if the party was a corridor she was obliged to traverse on her way somewhere. She was in her early thirties, with black shoulder-length hair that framed her face in thick-waved strands. She was tanned, with bright black eyes, and a touch of natural red on each cheekbone, visible even under the tan. She had on an indigo dress, plum-coloured tights and black pumps and was too full-figured for modern glamour; a pre-photography ideal of curves above and below a narrow waist, a plenitude that was light in motion but might seem heavy stopped in a picture. A waiter approached her with champagne on a tray.

The biologist asked the journalist if he knew her.

'The good-looking one? Rebecca Shepherd. Malaria researcher.'

The biologist wanted to talk to her, but she saw that Harry's nephew had seen her come in, and was already going to meet her.

31

Bec looked up. A tall man with brown eyes was standing over her, appealing for recognition, but she didn't know him until he said he was Alex Comrie. She looked away towards the room. 'Why does your uncle wear such bright clothes?' she said.

'He thinks his face has become interesting since he became ill. Strong enough for colours.'

'He doesn't look ill. He looks happy.'

'He's full of drugs and life force. He's not at all resigned to it.'

'Nobody's resigned to it,' said Bec.

Yesterday, she remembered, the grave had hardly been big enough for Huru, and Batini had spent a long time pressing him into the hole carefully, with dull satisfaction, like a mother squeezing sandwiches into a child's lunch box.

Alex said: 'He's less resigned. There's a lot of him in the thing I'm working on and he wants me to change the last sentence to say I've found a way to make people live forever.'

'Have you?' said Bec.

'It's a theory. It's hard to make the values stick when it gets complex. If you wanted to make it practical you'd need a computer the size of Wales for each person.' *She's listening,* he thought. *She'll notice the unsteadiness in my voice.* Time had left little trace on her since they'd last met and she seemed as open as she had then. He had a desire to lift her hair aside and press his lips to her neck. *I can't get there,* he thought. In the state of absolute focus on Bec he was able to see that a sadness was distracting her. He wanted to make her smile but found he couldn't stop gabbing on about his problem with Harry. 'It's not the complexity that stops us living for centuries,' he was saying, feeling his tongue flap leatherishly with every *l.* 'To be truly immortal we'd need the power to forget we'd seen it all. To be young you have to be not long born.'

Bec laughed and Alex, who'd seemed a little preacherly to her as he said this, laughed too, not sure what they were laughing about.

'You haven't seen it all,' she said.

'Sometimes I think I have,' said Alex. 'And then I meet someone who reminds me that I haven't.'

Bec regarded him, not wanting to accept that he might mean her, which would oblige her to remember the details of his strange incursion into Cambridge, and to weigh the immense distance of time, her whole adult life, that had passed between then and now. *Too late,* she thought, *I'm doing it.*

'Your uncle surely doesn't think you're going to come up with a way to make him live for ever,' she said. 'He wants you to put his work and your work together so that when he goes he knows he'll have left his mark.'

'He's already left his mark. He's immortal. He has a son. He's got four grandchildren and another one on the way. He's part of an unbroken family line going back to the first eukaryote a billion years ago.'

'We're all cousins in that family,' said Bec. 'Salt of the earth, us eukaryotes.'

'Some of us let our part of the line break,' said Alex. 'Getting together with another eukaryote and replacing yourselves, that's the only way to live for ever. You can't forget, so you make a replacement instead, and the old one dies, and on you fly for another billion years.'

Bec listened carefully. He had a way of stating the obvious with such urgency that it no longer seemed obvious. She could barely remember what he'd been like at Ritchie's party; she kept an impression from then of eagerness, shyness and arrogance. It didn't correlate with the Alex in front of her. He was still eager but the other attributes had faded. He was full of will. It made him powerful. She saw her silence worrying him. He watched her closely as if she might be about to bolt. He had attractive hands, she thought, and there were no rings. Bec hadn't been with a man since Val. It would be nice to be held by him, to touch; why not? She was free.

She asked Alex to show her which one was Harry's son, and Alex told her that father and son didn't get on. Matthew was religious, he said, and there was a rift; he hadn't come.

'What about your replacement?' said Bec. 'Your reproduction?'

'I don't have one,' said Alex. 'We tried. The doctors couldn't find anything wrong with me or my ex. There are still only two of us.'

'That was rude of me, wasn't it. To ask like that.'

'You can ask me anything you like,' said Alex. 'I'll tell you.'

'There was something I was curious about. This woman you call your ex. Is she your ex or isn't she?'

'We've split up, but we're still living together.'

'And sleeping together.'

'For the time being.'

'Those arrangements never work,' said Bec impatiently. She grabbed two glasses of champagne from a tray that was going round and handed one to Alex. 'Either you stay with someone or you leave them. No woman's going to sleep with you until you're single.'

'How ready any woman is to say what no woman will do.'

Bec blushed, swung her head to look over to where people had started dancing and said to Alex: 'Would you like to dance with me?'

'I can't dance.'

'How can a drummer not dance?'

Alex went red. 'You remember,' he said.

'It's not every day somebody plants a drum kit outside a girl's window in the middle of the night.'

'Even for you?'

Bec laughed. 'You gave up easily. I was only eighteen, remember. I thought I might find you shivering on the door-step next day. Come and dance.'

Bec felt her arm being grabbed and tropical cloud colours tumbled into her vision. 'Dr Shepherd!' said Harry. 'I read your last paper! It was wonderful, very clever. But if only they still sprayed with DDT! What do you think of Dietrich and Knapheim's work on DDT?'

'I haven't read it,' said Bec.

'Of course you have!' roared Harry with a piratical grin.

'I've never heard of it.'

'Nonsense, we'll talk about it later. You must come back to the house for the post-party. You see?' he said to Alex, jigging his thumb at Bec. 'That's what I'm talking about. Gets herself infected with some wretched parasite to tackle the problem. That's guts.' He swung his head back to Bec. 'Has he told you about his latest masterpiece? Genius and he won't spell it out! Bloody nightmare! Look at this!' He spread his arms out. 'Look at that!' He gestured to the city below. 'Could they have built this tower fifty years ago? Progress! Action! If it were up to Alex we'd still be living in caves and dying at twenty-five.'

'I went to somebody's funeral yesterday,' said Bec. 'He lived in a house made of mud bricks and he died when he was three.'

Alex saw that this was the sadness, his rival for her attention, and asked what had happened, and Bec told them not to worry; that she didn't want to talk about it.

'Look,' said Alex. He pointed out of the window across London to where a procession of car lights glittered along a foreshortened highway. Thousands of identical white particles of light shuffled west towards the centre of the city and as many identical red particles of light moved east away from it. 'Suppose that's your bloodstream,' he said to Harry. 'As scientists, this is as close as we can get. If we see the cars stop moving, what can we do from up here? How can we make them start moving again?'

'I'm glad you're not my doctor.'

'Here, where we're standing, that's where the doctor is. He can't get down there and he can't grasp the totality. He sees the city getting old. Towers fall. Traffic slows down. Buildings sprout where they aren't supposed to. Medicine's come so far, and even now, even now, the best way we have to stop the city dying is to drop bombs on one part to try to save the rest. And even when we manage to send agents into the city, to help without destruction, we can do as much harm as good, because we don't know every pathway that every citizen takes at every moment, and how they all connect. Suppose we find out that everyone in the city who wears a red hat has gone crazy and is sabotaging the city's water supply. So we find a way to go in and put all the red-hatted citizens to sleep, and the water supply's safe. But then we find out these red-hatted saboteurs, as well as vandalising the pipes, were the ones who'd been delivering bread around the city. So we've saved the city from being poisoned, but now we have to stop it starving.'

'You see how he treats me, in my condition?' said Harry to Bec.

'You've got months yet,' said Alex.

'Alex,' said Harry, putting his hand on his heart. 'Humour a dying man. Put the sentence in. Help me. Help yourself. Give the world hope. Rebecca, persuade him.'

Talk of research gave Bec an urge to leave the party and put in an immediate shift at the lab. She knocked back the rest of her glass. 'Would it be so terrible?' she said to Alex.

'If I agree he'll ask me to do something else,' said Alex.

'What an old bugger you think I am. Trust your uncle.' He counted on his fingers. 'And, has, potential, to, delay, or, suspend, human, ageing. Nine little words. Shake on it.' He held out his hand and Alex shook it.

32

When they were thrown out Harry and Alex led those who didn't want to go home to the foot of the tower. They got into black cabs and drove north across the river to Harry's house.

In the Sixties, when Harry and his brother Lewis, Alex's father, were at university, they inherited money from their grandmother. It was five thousand pounds each, the kind of sum that seems trivial to the rich and vast to the poor and keeps the middle in the middle. The brothers grew up in Derby, where their father designed jet engines at Rolls-Royce. Neither liked the place and left as soon as they could. Lewis's Derby was an endless urban sprawl of smoke-blackened buildings, a hustling, shoving ring of modernity. He moved to Scotland and became a family doctor in Brechin. For Harry, Derby always had too much country in it, all moss in the pavement cracks and shrubs growing out of gutters. To him it was the provinces, practically a village itself, and he couldn't get to London soon enough. He took his inheritance and got a mortgage on a run-down terraced house in Islington, on one of the squares between Upper Street and Liverpool Road, with four storeys and an attic and a long narrow garden.

He and Jenny pointed its black brickwork, replaced its

two-hundred-year-old window frames, sanded and varnished its wooden floorboards, tore off its Thirties wallpaper, replastered the walls and painted them white, fixed the roof, knocked down dividing walls, turned the attic into a library and remade the garden in Japanese style with bamboo, gravel and a skinny pond. Harry hoped the house would become a meeting place for intellectuals, revolutionaries and artists, a drop-in hangout for the eloquent scuzzerati of north London. He imagined future biographies mentioning the house on Citron Square *where the Comries hosted their notorious parties*. He imagined the phrase *the Citron Square set*. He imagined a look – attractive, lean, ready to spring, dressed stylishly in old clothes, confidently witty, learned across the arts and sciences. 'Look at those two,' jealous ankle-biters would say, 'trying to be all Citron Square.'

But nobody dropped in. The Comries couldn't provide the fuel to feed the interest of ambitious intellectuals – free alcohol and drugs, effortlessly seducible young people, access to the already rich and already famous. Harry refused to see this and blamed his wife for desecrating his academy of joyful enlightenment with her gloom and shyness. It frustrated him that he couldn't restore Jenny like a house, choose her clothes and give her energy, and he accused her of carelessness for allowing Matthew to be seduced by the cult of Christ.

Work wasn't enough of a refuge for Harry and he took long weekends away with his brother's family in Scotland. Even so his pride was hurt when Jenny told him soon after Matthew left home that she wanted a divorce. Back in New Zealand she opened a gallery that sold animal sculptures made of seashells glued onto pieces of driftwood. When she was gone Harry found he missed her, or he missed something, anyway.

It was only him left, the house and his enormous dissatisfaction. Over the years he realised the dissatisfaction kept him going and he began to feed it. A few years before his diagnosis they gave him an OBE.

Harry showed Bec round the house while Alex fixed drinks for the others. He took her to the wine cellar and waved at the racks of dark glass circles resting in the cool dim space below the street. 'I spent years on this,' he said. 'I'd go to Bordeaux every autumn, I learned the names of all the chateaux, I subscribed to wine magazines and went to tastings. I had a thousand bottles this time last year. Now even if I drank two bottles every day I wouldn't be able to drink it all before I die. These days I can hardly manage half a bottle before I feel like throwing up. I can have parties and dinners, like this, but there's so much to do before I go, and I get tired easily.' He stroked the ends of the bottles. 'My son doesn't drink.'

'You could give it away,' said Bec.

'Would you like it?' said Harry.

Bec went red. 'I didn't mean to me,' she said.

'You and Alex could share it.'

'We're not going out. He has a partner.'

'He'll leave her. You like him.'

'He spends a great deal of time explaining things.'

Harry pulled a bottle out and read the label. He showed it to Bec, with wide eyes, biting his lower lip, as if it were a magic trick, and said: 'Is that the year you were born?' Bec nodded. 'I think we should drink some of this. You're of the opinion that professional explainers of nature like us should only do our explaining during working hours. Alex can listen, you know. When he was a boy he'd ask me questions and I'd give him an answer and he'd listen and remember.'

'What sort of questions?'

'What are stones made of? Can birds fly upside down? Is it better to be happy than to be good?'

'I wonder how you answered that one.'

'The main thing is not to be happy, but to be lucky. We're close, Alex and I. Closer than I am to Matthew. It's not the blood that matters. Ties of sympathy are what count, don't you think? Alex doesn't understand it's good for children to have many fathers. He thinks you have to yield to evolution where parenthood is concerned. He says he'll never go through IVF again. Personally I reckon Darwin would have given IVF the thumbs-up. If you start saying people have to conceive naturally, where does it lead you? The human race pretty much told evolution where to shove it when we invented the barbecue.'

They went upstairs. A dozen people were arranged around the living room, lit by candles. Candlelight had the power to compel people to sit on floors and lower their voices. There was a smell of hot wax and spilled wine, and a faint trumpet line tootled from a box in the corner. One flame cringed and flickered in the draught from Alex's moving hands. Bec walked over and touched him on the shoulder. He stopped talking and gesticulating and looked up at her eagerly.

'I have to go,' she said. His face fell. He got up and asked her to stay.

'I'm tired,' she said. 'Sleeping on the plane isn't really sleep.'

She waited to say goodbye to Harry. In the short time since he'd come upstairs he'd launched into a story about an argument he'd had with a Russian biologist over the evolution of the organs of the body.

'So I said "What, you think the liver evolved from a

parasite?" and he said "Yes, yes." Harry tugged on an imaginary beard and put on an exaggerated Russian accent. "'And the kidneys?" "Why not?" "And the brain, the eye?" "Please, you are welcome." "The lungs?" "This also evolved in parallel and joined the body." "What about the heart?" Harry punched the air and gave his Russian sudden passion. "'Oh, the heart *brrroke* in!'"

Harry's audience laughed, and Bec kissed him goodbye, and Harry squeezed her hand. Alex followed her to the front door and said he'd come with her and she said that he should stay with Harry; she'd get the last Tube.

'I want to stay with you tonight,' said Alex.

'You can't while you're sharing somebody else's bed.'

'I'll leave her.'

'Don't do it for me.'

'I'll call her now. I'll never go back.' Alex took out his phone. Bec put her hand over Alex's and pushed the phone down.

'No,' she said.

Alex asked if he could see her the next day, and Bec told him she was flying to Spain for Christmas, then going back to Africa. Alex got it out of her that she'd be getting the train to the airport from Paddington at ten and he said he could meet her beforehand. Bec said she didn't think it would be a good idea.

'Write to me,' she said. She had her coat on. She opened the door and stood on the threshold with her hands in her pockets, looking at Alex. He was about to move towards her when one of the women from the party appeared and called to him, saying that his uncle was asking for him. While he was distracted Bec said goodbye and walked off towards Angel.

Alex found Harry coughing and shaking his head in an armchair in the living room. A group of people around him wanted to show willingness to help without knowing what to do; they seemed to be queuing up to touch him. He had a glass of water in one hand and a stained, crumpled white cotton handkerchief in the other. The lights were on and the room stank of cigar smoke. A stubbed-out stogie poked over the edge of an ashtray.

'We were talking,' said Harry. His voice was scratched and weak. 'Now that you're the director of the institute, we think you should let me have some of those cells, just to see what happens.'

'Let's talk about it another time. You should get to bed.'

'Why do you have to be so bloody negative?' said Harry. 'You know what your trouble is? You're too fond of death. You think he's got us licked.' He began to cough.

'Well, he has form,' said Alex.

'I won't have you speaking in that way! When it's *happening*! We're making the breakthroughs! We're getting there and all you can do is tell everyone we'll never arrive.' Harry began to cough. He raised his voice as if trying to make himself heard over another person coughing and the effort made him cough more. 'You come over so smug, so pleased with yourself, so glad to pick holes in other people's work,' he wheezed and hacked phlegm – 'and you're the one with the problem. You're the we'll-never-reach-the-moon man, we'll never know how the universe began, we'll never cure cancer. We'll just potter round the margins.' He bent forward, burying his face in the handkerchief. Alex knelt beside him and told him to stop talking. Harry leaned back, wiped his mouth, was convulsed once more by a long, bubbling hack that sounded as if he was choking on a sword, and shouted at Alex: 'You're a coward! Afraid of death! A bloody coward!'

33

Alex called Harry's doctor, who told him not to worry. Alex stood in the living room, where in the bright light the candles looked like guests who didn't know it was time to go. The best minds in cell biology had got drunk on Harry's wine that night. None had much of a clue about medicine, yet Alex intended to leave and let them look after his uncle. The reward he'd take for giving Harry his immortality concession was a short holiday from caring. He went downstairs, lifted his coat from the hook and stepped out into the open air. For a few moments, while he walked the terraced streets, looking for a taxi, he savoured the guilty joy of walking away from a sick old relative, and thought of what Bec had said. *You can't while you're sharing somebody else's bed.* It was as if she'd told him what he had to do.

At home in Mile End, where he'd lived for so long, he saw objects with the novel idea that he was about to walk away from them. In the kitchen he heard the flicker and hum of the old-fashioned fluorescent light coming on as if it were a tune from the distant past instead of a sound he heard that morning. He stared like a ghost at the dirty cup Maria had left out, familiar and yet, without its physical substance changing in the least, quite altered. It was the black mug he'd brought with him from Scotland when he came to London as a student. Yesterday it had been something that happened to come to hand to hold coffee when he reached into the cupboard. Now it was an object to be transported or lost for ever. 'Have it, it's yours,' Maria would say.

He'd wanted to have Maria once. Where had the wanting gone? Surely, he thought, into all the other things they had. When you loved some*one*, having was being; loving any other thing was just having. He wanted to have Maria once, and now he wanted Bec. He wanted to possess her and didn't want to be distracted by having to have anything else.

In the living room Maria's shawl lay on the sofa where she'd been lying watching TV. The cushions still had the imprint of her body. A partly drunk bottle of wine and a glass were on the table. Wandering from room to room Alex delayed the moment when he would go to bed and lie beside her. He went upstairs slowly, feeling that what he was doing was like murder.

He kept the light off and Maria seemed to be asleep while he undressed. When he got carefully into bed next to her, close enough to feel the warmth of her back and smell her hair, she stirred and without looking round said: 'How was it?'

'It was a grand affair. Lovely speeches. We gave him a good send-off.'

'Did you meet any nice girls?'

'Ritchie Shepherd's sister was there.'

'Is she single?'

'Yes.'

'Did you kiss her?'

'No.' He wouldn't tell her until the morning unless she

made him and he waited, his heart beating hard, for the next question out of the darkness. But no more questions came. Soon he heard Maria's breathing hoarsen, as if she'd decided the dangers of the day had all been found, captured and safely fenced in by her and Alex's community of sleep.

Alex woke early. It was still dark. He got up, dressed, went downstairs and wheeled his bicycle out of the garden. Light rain fell, just slickening the street and putting an oily gleam on the cars. The terms of honour had crystallised in his mind overnight and were presented to him while he waited for Maria to come down, as clear and as arbitrary as a duelling code. He could not have Bec without leaving Maria, and so he would leave Maria. He must tell her that he was leaving her to her face. He must tell her now, because he couldn't wait. But he must not wake her to tell her. She must wake of her own accord. And once he had told her – this seemed the hardest of all to him, but he was sure that it was right – he must let her have the last word.

He sat in the kitchen tapping his feet, watching the big clock on the wall. He got up and stood close to it, watching the minute hand creep through the space between marks. He cleaned his teeth and put the toothbrush back in the metal cup where it stood next to Maria's. He stared at the two toothbrushes angled against each other, one red, one blue, then took his out and put it in his pocket, leaving the red one in the cup by itself.

At quarter to nine he heard Maria come downstairs and the swish of her dressing gown in the hall. As she came into the kitchen she glanced at him and moved to the worktop.

She put on a pair of surgical gloves to protect her hands, took a pomegranate and with a serrated knife cut lines through the skin of the fruit. She opened up the pomegranate and began picking out the seeds and putting them into a dish.

Alex got up. 'There's something I have to say,' he said.

'Say it, then,' said Maria.

'You have your back to me.'

'I can hear you.'

'I don't want to live here any more.'

'Is it about her?'

'Liking her is what's making me go.'

'Liking her? You mean fancying her? Wanting her?'

'We talked about this moment coming.'

'So you're going to her now?'

'She's leaving this morning. She's not expecting to see me. I don't think I'll catch her. She's getting the train to Heathrow at ten.'

He waited for Maria to speak, to have the last word, and as he wondered at himself for daring to cause her such pain, he began to hate her for her silence. It was ten to nine and he itched to leave. He could tell from the care Maria was taking to keep her back to him and the jerkiness in her movements that she was almost crying. The only sound in the kitchen was the ticking of the clock and Maria seeding the pomegranate. The soft rip of pith as her fingers separated the clusters of seeds from each other sounded to Alex as if she were tearing her heart to pieces.

'You'd better go, then,' said Maria.

'I'm sorry.'

'Don't say that. You've been decent so far. Don't spoil it by lying. Don't say anything more. Just go. I'm the loser and there's nothing you can do.'

Alex went over and put his arms round her. She turned and

shrank into him but didn't return his embrace. He felt her tears on his neck and her body shaking.

'Ho ho ho,' came her voice, muffled.

He felt a discomfort beneath his ribs, as if a cat were prodding and sniffing his heart and rolling it between its paws. Crying would be the decent thing, he thought, but the tears wouldn't come. He unclasped his arms from her and left the house.

34

It was nine o'clock. Alex tucked his right trouser leg into a steel clip, unlocked his bike and set off from Mile End against a stiff west wind, under a sky that promised rain and rumbled with jets.

He accelerated between the cherry trees and tight little terraced houses of Lichfield Road, stood up off the saddle, pistoned the pedals, shot round the back of a white van reversing and forced it to brake, barrelled over the Grove Road pedestrian crossing between lines of jammed-up traffic and through the gates into Mile End park, hissed past two schoolgirls in white headscarves close enough to make them yelp, hit the canal towpath, headed under the railway bridge as the fast train to Ipswich crossed, rang his bell, drove a woman pushing a baby buggy out of his way, ducked under Roman Road, past coots fighting in the water, over the hump of the towpath at the Hertford Canal junction, down the far side in high gear with a bang on the bump at the bottom, sliced between a man in a tracksuit and his pit bull terrier, under the concrete bridge of Old Ford Road and the stencilled HOW'S MY GRAFFITI? DIAL 0800-NOBODY-CARES, up the ramp by the lock keeper's cottage and round as the canal turned west, past the chestnut trees of Victoria Park and the line of narrow boats at rest in their own smoke. He ducked under a branch two boat-dwellers carried from the park for fuel, fired his bike through the dim narrow space under Approach Road, came out from under Mare Street bridge's pigeon-infested girders at twenty miles an hour, forced another cyclist to turn sharply into the thin strip of verge and flew under the Lea Valley railway.

Into the long open curve towards Broadway Market he lowered his head and sprinted past the frames of deflated gas holders on the far bank. He dived under the Goldsmiths Row bridge, charged on towards the lock, up the slope, round the wooden shaft of the lock gate with the roar of the weir in his ears and up onto the straight. The loose paving slabs of the towpath rocked under his wheels and he hurtled over three thick white lines and the painted word SLOW. The ringing of the bell filled the murk between the brick arch of the Queensbridge Road bridge and the green water. He passed the painted sign for Ron's Eel and Shell Fish and went under the grey steel bowstring of the East London Line bridge. The towers of the City rose to the south. He put on speed to beat another cyclist to the barriers choking the lock ramp, wove through them, built up momentum and took the steep ramp to street level without changing gear. He pulled out in front of a Range Rover, rushed through the Danbury Street choker, raced across the roundabout, accelerated past the gardens to Goswell Road and jerked into the bus lane. The old clock on its column reported twenty past nine.

The lights were green at Angel and Alex sped across into Pentonville Road, racing and dodging buses, jumping lanes, knocking against the sides of cars with his handlebar ends. He crested the hill, saw the long slope down to King's Cross ahead of him, made a dash for the bus lane, lowered his head, added his pedalling to gravity and built up speed till the slipstream buffeted his face. Just short of the Thameslink station he was boxed in by buses and railings. He jumped off the bike, lifted it over the railings, threw it down with a crash on the far side, clambered over after it, got back on the saddle and sped along the pavement, half riding, half scootering, one foot on the pedals, one hopping off the ground.

Nine-thirty, the clock on King's Cross station said, and the clock on the great red spire of St Pancras far above agreed. Alex kicked on past the British Library. It began to rain. Sirens shrieked around him. He dived steeply into the tunnel at Warren Street Tube, toiled up the far side and with a whoosh smashed through the membrane dividing east from west London. He passed the first white crescents of the ultra-rich. *Nine-thirty-six* said the clock on the Landmark Hotel. He belted past the Western Eye Hospital, jumped the lights, veered off down the Harrow Road, rocketed between a column of taxis and the vaulting concrete of the Westway, took the bridge over the tracks and entered the flow of black cabs streaming into Paddington station. He cut in front of a middle-aged couple heading for the taxi queue and they braked their luggage trolley and a suitcase slid off and span like a curling stone towards Alex's rear wheel and he dodged it and rode between the grey and white columns into the station, past the statue of Brunel, into the roar of a west country express heading out and the smell of diesel under the far-off roof arches. His tyres glided smoothly over the beige tiles, passengers leaped for safety, coffee spilled, cries rang to the girders and Alex rode past McDonald's, WH Smith, Ladbrokes, the West Cornwall Pasty Co. and Costa Coffee, ting-tinging his bell, round the corner, past the ticket barriers, a policeman with a raised hand and a shout that had to be obeyed, but Alex didn't obey until he saw the yellow snout of the next Heathrow train, looked up at the clock on the far wall, stopped and got off his bike with sixteen minutes to spare.

Breathing heavily, flushed through with heat, his heart hammering, his legs tingling, he walked alongside the train, looking in through the windows and over his shoulder in case she was coming up behind him. He went the length of the train without seeing her, thinking how jealous he'd been the night before, watching her dance with other men, and how he'd felt, when she hesitated on the steps of Harry's house before leaving, that she wanted him to give her a reason not to go. He turned round and at the far end of the train saw someone who could have been Bec hurrying to get on board. He ran back and saw her through the glass, sitting at a window seat. She saw him, gave a puzzled smile and got up. Whistles sounded and by the time Alex and Bec reached the train door it was locked and couldn't be opened.

'I left Maria!' shouted Alex through the glass. Bec shook her head and pointed to her ears. She took out her phone, keyed in numbers and held the screen up to the glass. Alex dialled the number and Bec answered.

'I left Maria,' said Alex.

'Not for me, I hope,' said Bec.

'Only for you.'

'You shouldn't have done that. I never promised you anything if you did. I'm not a homebreaker.'

'It was already broken.' He put his palm against the glass.

Bec shook her head. 'I'll write to you,' she said. The train began to move and Alex got back on his bike and cycled alongside it, still holding the phone to his head and trying to speak to her.

'Stop!' said Bec into the phone. The train pulled out of the station and she lost sight of him.

Alex had been silenced. Bec wondered if he'd flown off the end of the platform chasing her train. How lost he'd looked with his hand against the glass. She would have opened the doors to let him in if she could. She waited for him to call again; he didn't.

There were no texts or calls waiting for her when she landed and she sent him a message saying: *I WILL write to you.* A moment later he messaged back *What will you write?*

35

In the days after Val threatened him Ritchie would wake up moaning in the night and reach for Karin, or she would shake him out of his sleep. He found the sound of his own moan in his ears, half actual, half dreamed, worse than the nightmare that caused it. Karin made him tell her what he had dreamed. When he could remember, he gave her a toned-down version of the horrors, missing out Dan's, Ruby's and her dismembered corpses stacked neatly on the corner of a street next to the bins, compressed and bound with string like old newspapers. Or menace came unattached to specifics and he felt a merciless force set against him, as omnipotent as it was without form.

Worst were the nights when he dreamed sweetly or not at all, woke up purged of memories and felt the terror of exposure materialise in him; it would linger, stuck in his gullet like a box with sharp corners.

Gradually the acid of time softened the corners. As the months went by after meeting Val, the intensity of the impression faded, even though that same passage of time must, it seemed, bring the moment when he would be exposed as a cheat and a sex criminal closer; when his family, his home and his work would be taken away.

Ritchie drank. A bottle of strong red wine and three fingers of whisky was standard fare for an evening. He mixed it with ideas of how Val might die. In the first weeks after the meeting with the editor he took shy thought-steps towards murder. He wished Val did not exist; he hated Val; Val didn't deserve life; how much better if he died! But how to kill him in such a way that Ritchie could be absolutely certain he would never be found out? It was impossible. Val was full of blood, and overcrowded England was full of witnesses. What if he could discover when Val went on holiday abroad, to some place where killers could be hired cheaply and anonymously? The Caribbean, perhaps. Without knowing whether Val ever went to the Caribbean, Ritchie tapped the words *Barbados hitman* into Google and pressed the return key. In the instant it took the search engine to return the results he saw he'd incriminated himself. The project of murdering another man, even one as loathsome as Val Oatman, was too complex and time-consuming. It was too much like the unattached dread of his more diffuse nightmares.

One evening at dinner Karin asked him what was wrong and he realised that he'd screwed his eyes tightly shut, bared his teeth and clenched his jaw because it'd occurred to him that he was about to meet a murderer, O'Donabháin, and he couldn't prevent the thought coming up, so close to the surface that it almost formed the precursor of spoken words: *He might do it. He owes me a favour, after he killed Dad.* The grimace in front of Karin and the children was the least he could manage. He would sooner have stood up and howled at the ceiling. He would sooner still have jumped out of himself, like a man jumping away from a poisonous snake. He couldn't bear to be that Ritchie.

From then on he restricted himself to fantasising about Val having a heart attack, or a car accident, or being on a plane that crashed. It was unlikely, but it happened. Why should it not happen to Val? One night before going to bed Ritchie climbed the stairs to his study and instead of turning on the lights lit a candle. He kneeled on the floor in the glow of the flame, clasped his hands together, turned his face upwards and whispered:

> Our Father
> Who art in Heaven
> Hallowed be Thy Name.
> Thy Kingdom come
> Thy Will be done
> In Earth, as it is in Heaven
> Deliver us from Evil
> Deliver us from Val
> For Thine is the Kingdom
> The Power and the Glory
> For ever and ever
> Amen.

He stood up and blew out the candle. 'Thank you,' he added in the darkness.

Against Ritchie's fears Ruby's demand to be on television was a challenge he enjoyed. He forgot that Ruby had used her knowledge of the phone to force him to act against his will. In its intimacy, in the opportunity to show his family the skills of reward, firmness and persuasion he wielded so effectively in Rika Films, the project consoled him. He talked the commissioning editors of the O'Donabháin project into including a title song from him. He explained to Ruby that instead of being on *Teen Makeover*, when she wasn't a teen, and would be with other people, she could sing solo in a special video, a special song about her granddad, which would be on television and the Internet, and maybe even in the cinema!

He'd never loved Karin more, and she'd never been so kind to him. It was as if she knew that he was troubled, and knew not to ask why. She spent her days with the children and split her evenings with them, Ritchie and the stable-block studio. There were times when he wondered what she and the music were up to; when he thought back to the days when it had been the three of them together, the music, Karin and Ritchie. But the thought that Karin and the music might be closer to each other than either was to him was intolerable and Ritchie could not take it seriously. Karin was always around on Saturdays, when the family made trips to the coast or the forest. They would sit side by side at the top of the beach, knees drawn up, watching Dan and Ruby run, halt and whirl by the sea's edge, Karin deep in thought, Ritchie watching her, forgetting his fears for a while.

'What are you thinking about?' Ritchie would ask.

Karin would look at him and smile. 'So many things,' she would say. And Ritchie, who'd only wanted to drink her affection, was glad that she didn't try to tell him what those things were.

Christmas in Spain passed safely. Bec had been in a good mood, drinking a lot of wine to help, she said, resist the temptation to work. She wanted to sit with him and their mother late on the terrace, to talk about the old days. She'd spent a great deal of time sending and receiving text messages and when he asked her who was on the other end, she laughed and said she'd tell him later, but she never did. In the new year she went back to Africa.

Ritchie marked Bec's emails from Tanzania when they came in, meaning to reply to them, but he didn't, and they slipped down the list of the unanswered. The arrival of the emails troubled him more than the contents. The thought that his sister was in a faraway country, pure and isolated among needy Africans, was comforting, as if Bec were safely locked in a convent. Each email reminded him that she was not far away at all. As long as Bec was in Africa she was dear to him. When he thought of a returning Bec, he seemed to hear a cacophony of angry male voices yelling phrases like 'I love my sister!' 'Bec is a good woman!' 'My sister is one of the finest people I know!' When he thought about Bec coming back, he knew he could never betray her, and knew she would always be too virtuous and too obscure to be betrayable. It never seemed to him that there was a difference between these two certainties; and his mind turned again to the hope that Val would die.

One morning after a night of little sleep Ritchie drove to London, blinking and squinting, his head throbbing. As he entered the southern suburbs, he heard Alex's voice on the radio. A headline about British scientists claiming a break-through in the understanding of human lifespan had been read out several times in the first part of Ritchie's journey but it was only when he heard Alex being interviewed that he real-ised who the principal scientist was. As far as Ritchie could understand it was related to some kind of cancer treatment. Ritchie's spirits rose, and his head cleared a little, when he heard Alex's clear, confident voice fill the car.

The interviewer said: 'Now at the moment the treatment you're talking about, and I think it's fair to say it was a break-through when it came along, it only helps people suffering from one fairly rare type of cancer, doesn't it?'

'That's right,' said Alex. 'But what makes this latest discovery exciting is the potential for a similar approach with other cancers. We don't want to raise people's expectations, because it's early, but now that we're starting to understand the chronase complex, expert cell therapy could be a great game-changer in medicine.'

'And not just for cancer? Because your research involves some astonishing ideas about how this approach, if that's the right word, could actually enable human beings to live longer – considerably longer?'

'Haha!' shouted Ritchie, and drummed his hands on the steering wheel.

'That's on the furthest fringe of possibility,' said Alex. 'We need to work one step at a time, and start by giving extra years of good health to people who are in their fifties and suffering now.'

'Alex Comrie –'

'It's important to remember that our success vindicates the pioneering work of –'

'Alex Comrie –'

'– Harry Comrie, who discovered the properties of expert cells twenty-five years ago.'

'Professor Alex Comrie, thank you.'

Alex was in the news. He was on TV. Val's paper had made it the main story on the front page – SCIENTIST FINDS FOUNTAIN OF YOUTH was the headline – and Alex's name was all over the Internet.

Ritchie was glad people like Alex existed, even if his own circumstances didn't allow him to be as good a person as his friend, as good a person as he would like to be. Ritchie felt he, Ritchie, had the misfortune to know the reality of life, which was that people were always trying to fuck you over, and sometimes you had to fuck them back. He found it comforting to know that there were good, hard-working, self-sacrificing geniuses like Alex out there; Alex cloistered in his institute, doing good works and guarding the fire of knowledge, like an abbot in his monastery, like Bec in the convent of Africa.

If only she wouldn't come back, thought Ritchie.

Ritchie saw the limits of Alex's means as the price he paid for the great honour of being virtuous, and his own success as compensation for being punished with the necessity to lie and deceive. He felt a seigneurial sense of tribute in all that Alex had done since he'd drummed for him at college. Yet here was his unworldly Scottish friend, with his eggheaded jottings, being quoted for twenty-four hours around the world. *I hope it won't turn his head*, thought Ritchie. *He has no idea how evil men like Val are, how they only make people famous in order to destroy them later, them and their families.* He remembered Alex's partner Maria; how well Alex had done to land her! Neither had the slightest idea of the danger they were in by creeping out of obscurity.

He called Alex from his office and congratulated him.

'I shouldn't have hyped it like that,' said Alex.

'Nonsense,' said Ritchie. 'You're a media natural.'

'Where did I get that expression "game-changer"? I hyped it up for Harry's sake,' said Alex.

'You worry too much,' said Ritchie, who had no idea who Harry was.

'Did Bec tell you about me going out there?' said Alex.

Ritchie felt a tingling behind his ears.

'What?' he said.

'I'm going to Tanzania to visit your sister. Did she tell you?'

'With Maria?'

'Maria and I separated three months ago.'

'God.'

'Yes, I know.'

'Was it . . .'

'Just . . .'

'I mean . . . God.'

'Just not working out.'

'I had no idea.'

'We're still friends.'

'Why are you going to Africa?'

'Why not?' said Alex. 'You introduced us.'

'What are you up to?' said Ritchie roughly. 'She's bloody busy, you know.'

'Ritchie, are you all right?'

Ritchie couldn't speak.

'I don't know what you mean by "up to",' said Alex. He laughed uneasily. 'She invited me.'

'Fucking hell, Alex, I really don't know if you should be doing this,' said Ritchie, and ended the call. He was trembling. He switched the phone off, dropped it on his desk, picked up the pile of newspapers, jammed them into the bin and kicked the bin across the room, where it smashed the glass door of a cabinet holding some of his awards.

36

Alex succeeded his uncle as director of the Belford Institute, limping in on his first day with a bruised foot from his bicycle flying off the end of the platform at Paddington. In emails to Bec he told her he'd become the senior of a small group of well-paid people who held unending meetings to pass judgement on the hard work and good ideas of badly paid people.

Bec texted him: *It's called 'management'*.

When he applied for Harry's job Alex had his uncle's version of the institute in his head. The cancer researchers of Harry's legends were always fighting, always on the front line – there were no other lines. There were battles, victories, advances, breakthroughs; there were arsenals and armouries, with ammunition and weapons, including silver bullets and the occasional smoking gun. There was glory, sacrifice, heroism. There was faith, belief, heresy, blasphemy, anathema, schism. There were holy grails. In his pitch to the trustees Alex spoke passionately about the Belford Institute as if its scientists were an elite group of warrior saints. But the trustees didn't recognise the institute he talked about. Listening to Alex describe the past institute of Harry's memory they thought Alex was describing the future institute of his brilliant plans. As far as they were concerned the place had degenerated into a random clump of incompatible research teams whose members spent more time spying on and bitching about each other than they did coming up with the kind of discoveries they wanted, the kind that would, as they told each other, *make people look up from their morning coffee*. They assumed Alex knew that after the triumphs of his early discoveries, Harry had become a bureaucrat, and not a good one. But Alex did not know, until he took the job, and found his first task was to chair a meeting of the Landscaping Committee.

Alex found that the trustees were impressed by the way the last paragraph of his paper had travelled around the world. He'd intended to tell them that he did it for Harry's sake and that he was embarrassed by how those few words had skewed the way the paper was read. But he realised, facing the horseshoe of eminent committee-hounds under the portrait of old Lord Belford, that it was too late. He couldn't cast doubt on the last phrase without casting doubt on all his work, and he was too proud for that. He noticed that some of the trustees had copies of the story in Val Oatman's newspaper in front of them during his interview, with its ludicrous headline. The only way he could restore truth would be to attack himself using the same media that was being used to build him up. I WAS WRONG, BY 'FOUNTAIN OF YOUTH' SCIENTIST. MY REGRETS, BY 'IMMORTALITY' BOFFIN.

One day he got a call from Val Oatman, who said he'd heard through the grapevine that Alex wasn't happy with the way his research had been reported. 'You should have called us,' Val said. 'We take these things seriously, you know.'

'I knew it'd be trivialised. But I thought you'd trivialise it in a more thoughtful way.'

'You're important now,' said Val. 'Our readers want to know more about you. Everyone's interested in science when it's about how long they're going to live.'

'And why did you say "Scientist finds" instead of "Scientists find"? You embarrassed me with my collaborators. There were other names on that paper besides mine.'

'We want to promote champions of sciences,' said Val. 'We talked to your media people about it. They're keen. You want to get on with your work, of course, but you've got to remember that you're a hundred times more likely to get your ideas listened to if you're a celebrity.'

'I don't want to be a celebrity,' said Alex.

'We humble scribes have a duty to persuade you. The man in the street can't name scientists any more. That can't be good. Come and see me next week, we'll have lunch.'

'I'm on holiday then.'

'Where are you going?'

'Africa,' said Alex, wondering why he instinctively answered the question when he felt instinctively inclined to tell Val it wasn't his business.

'Nice. Which part?'

Alex didn't want to tell him, yet again he did. 'Tanzania.'

'Visiting a friend?' Alex was silent until Val said 'Hello?'

'I'm not sure it's . . .' began Alex.

'I have a friend in Tanzania,' said Val. 'She's a scientist. Rebecca Shepherd.'

'Did you know I was going to visit her?'

'How would I know that?'

'Did you?' said Alex boldly. He faltered. 'I know the two of you . . .'

'That's in the past,' said Val. 'Don't worry. I wanted to make contact. I wanted you to know that whatever you do, there's an interest.'

'In the science.'

'Absolutely. We'll talk when you get back.'

At the beginning and end of each day at the institute Alex passed a piece of sculpture in the lobby that Harry had persuaded the trustees to let him commission. 'A scientist can spend the public's money on art just as well as some Tuscan spiv in a cardinal's hat,' he said. *Reason IV*, the work was called, scaled down from the artist's original concept, which would have filled an aircraft hangar. As finally executed it was shoulder-high and resembled a metallic scarlet bowling ball dropped onto a worm-cast of hardened dough.

Alex wanted to fly to Bec at the earliest moment, but he'd moved in with Harry, who demanded that if he was going to *swan off to Africa*, he had to give him an infusion of expert cells first. Alex refused. Harry whined, mocked, sulked, made out he didn't care and quivered with indignation. The sense of being denied a therapy he felt he owned invigorated him and it seemed likely to Alex that withholding the medicine might be better medicine for his uncle than the medicine itself. But that would be a life extended by grievance. And if he flew to Tanzania without giving Harry what he wanted, his uncle wouldn't forgive him.

Alex agreed to fetch the cells from the institute's freezer, and to administer them to Harry, on two conditions: Harry's son Matthew must give his consent; and Harry must let Matthew help look after him in the end, as his son wanted.

'Why won't he let me see my bloody grandchildren?' said Harry.

'You know why.'

37

Alex decided that he had to talk to Matthew in person, even at the cost of delaying his trip to Africa. He took the train north. Lettie picked him up from the station.

She was forty-two years old and eight months pregnant, which, she said when Alex congratulated her on it, was a miracle. Tall and heavily built, with short greying hair, she made *miracle* sound like *nuisance* and looked weary. Even as Alex kissed her on the cheek she'd begun to turn and lead him away to the car. Her movements expressed duty, as if she were an agent collecting Alex for a conference.

Alex's consciousness of this was dulled by love; anticipatory love, which, he found, swamps forty-year-olds too. He was confident that Bec would be his and though he was impatient to get to her he didn't resent Matthew's family for detaining him. He felt he was already on his way to the Indian Ocean via the Ribble valley. Love seethed in his belly and people like Lettie were only sights by the wayside on the road taking him to Bec. Whatever happened before Africa, he was sure, couldn't hurt him; he was armoured in love.

All Matthew's children were at school. Sixteen-year-old Rose, with three silver bracelets on her wrist, who watched from the edges and tried to put distance between herself and the others;

Peter, two years younger, who pushed his glasses back up his nose with his forefinger; Leah, a twelve-year-old mood-vane, happy when everyone was together, anxious when two of her siblings were quarrelling and she couldn't be friends with both; and young Chris. Their father was two rungs off the top at Lancashire county council. He had his own parking space at the education department and administered there, in a bright white shirt, from a desk wider than he was tall, rotating half a dozen ties, four suits and two coffee mugs, WORLD'S BEST DAD and Women aren't supposed to make coffee — the Bible says HE BREWS.

The family lived in an old rectory at the edge of the fells, where the pastures begin to be dotted by tussocks of sedge. They were active in the parish; they kept two cars rushing to and fro along the web of thin crooked roads in and out of Preston, Clitheroe and Longridge.

On the drive to the house Alex kept a kind of conversation going by asking about the family while Lettie concentrated aggressively on the road ahead. He asked about Rose.

'She hates it that I'm using her as a childminder now she's sixteen,' said Lettie. 'We had a row about me coming to pick you up tonight.'

'I could have taken a taxi,' said Alex.

'It's fine,' said Lettie, chopping the side of her hand viciously down on the indicator.

'Harry's doing better than the doctors expected,' said Alex.

Lettie shook her shoulders as if to relieve a sudden muscle pain.

'Do you mean he'll recover?' she said.

Through gaps in the hedgerow as they passed Alex saw a

flickering image of prosperous, portly sheep. 'Extra weeks,' he murmured. 'When does lambing begin?'

'I never picked up farming knowledge,' said Lettie. 'I'm not from the country.'

Alex was given Chris's little room for the night. The boy was gracious and serious as he showed Alex around. A poster showing a Napoleonic warship unleashing a terrific broadside of cannon and bodies flying into the air from an explosion on the enemy vessel was fixed to one wall with *Jesus Loves Me* stickers. It was the Battle of Trafalgar, Chris told him. He was going to join the Navy.

Alone, Alex sat on the quilt, printed with pictures of nautical knots. It was a small bed. If he didn't curl up when he slept in it, his feet would stick out of the end. The room smelled of milk. He sent Bec an email and laid his iPhone on the desk. It was dark outside. The window rattled suddenly in a gust of wind. The shaking of the wooden frame seemed urgent and personal, as if someone were trying to get in.

Floorboards creaked. Matthew was in the doorway, dark and smooth, his black eyebrows like fur. He was in his work suit and tie. They smiled at each other and embraced. As Alex hugged his cousin he thought, *We didn't use to do this, now we do.*

'The great scientist,' said Matthew. 'We're honoured.'

'It's good to see you. They keep you late in Lancs.'

Matthew had a habit of pausing for a couple of seconds before picking up his side of a conversation, more, Alex thought, to give his interlocutors time to wonder whether they'd said something wrong than to think about what to say himself.

'I'm not popular at the moment,' said Matthew. 'The young

Muslims say I'm an Islamophobe, the white racists reckon I'm too cowardly to admit I agree with them and the lefties think I'm a fundamentalist. I'm just a public servant. I'm sure the Evil One is glad that we think banning schoolgirls from covering their faces will save us from his power.'

Matthew asked after Maria, and Alex told him they'd broken up, and Matthew looked stricken and repeated his words back to him, moving his eyes across Alex's smiling face. Alex confirmed it and remembered that Matthew wouldn't know why it was a good thing that he'd broken up with Maria or why he seemed happy about it.

'Yes,' Alex said, and cast his eyes down in respect for the broken up with. 'It didn't work out.'

Matthew said he was sorry. He spoke with a beat, as if he were counting off the years his cousin and Maria had been together. Alex wanted to make him understand that it was all right, that it was for the best.

'I'm seeing somebody else,' he explained.

'Oh,' said Matthew. 'I see.'

'It was amicable,' said Alex.

'I'm glad to hear it,' said Matthew.

'We agreed on everything.'

'It was good that you didn't have children, I suppose,' said Matthew.

Peter came up and told them that it was time to eat.

It seemed to Alex that Matthew exercised a mysterious authority over his family, without bullying, without force or bluster. They deferred to him, to his quiet voice, his silences, his steady gaze, his certainty and his routines. He lived by the Bible, but it was not the Bible that gave him authority. There was some inexhaustible, incorruptible pool of confidence in him whose existence steadied everything, and in that steadiness and certainty the six of them, soon to be seven, lived diligently, humbly, admirably. Yet Matthew spoke of the Evil One, as if Satan lived a short drive away across the fells. When, in this peaceful household, did Matthew rally his wife and children to fight the Devil? Over breakfast? And what were the battlegrounds? The friends they kept, the books they read? The children were out in the world. There was nothing cloistered about their schools. If Matthew believed that God and the Devil were at war in this town, how could he bear to risk his family in it?

Throughout supper Lettie helped Alex to food without eye contact, telling him that *he was probably used to more sophisticated food down south.* 'You're famous now,' said Matthew to Alex when they'd finished eating. 'You were on breakfast TV, I heard.' Rose looked up. The other children had gone.

'Was I?' said Alex.

'I'm proud of you,' said Matthew. 'I mean it. We pray for you. Your saviour hasn't turned his back on you, and he guides you in your work.'

'I don't feel guided,' said Alex.

Matthew bowed his head, then broke out warmly: 'You're saving lives. The potter hath power over the clay.'

'Who?'

'The potter. It's from the Bible. Romans nine.'

'Cancer is the clay?'

'No, *you're* the clay.' Matthew poked his cousin in the shoulder, as if Alex were a charming but slow-witted child. 'God's the potter.'

'Oh.'

'What's he famous for?' said Rose. She'd got up to fill the

water jug and was leaning against the kitchen sink, hunched as if resisting the tallness that was being forced on her. She was all elbows and shoulders and impatience.

'Don't say "he" like that,' said Matthew. 'If you've got a question for my cousin Alex, ask him.'

'What are you famous for, Alex?' said Rose, tossing her fringe aside, angling her head back and smiling.

'Counting atoms,' said Alex. 'Trying to work out why they go where they go.'

'Like granddad.'

'I'm following in his footsteps.'

'How is my father?' said Matthew.

'There is something we should discuss,' said Alex.

'You're on a mission. Excellent. Then there's lots to talk about.'

'Certainly is,' murmured Lettie, turning a fork over and over on the table.

'May I leave?' asked Rose.

'Of course, darling,' said Lettie. 'Can you bring the bibles at nine-thirty?'

Rose giggled and asked if Alex was going to do Bible study with them. They looked at him and he said that he would, if they didn't mind an unbeliever sitting in. They protested that they weren't like that.

Once Rose had gone Alex explained to Matthew and Lettie what Harry wanted.

Matthew leaned forward, palms down on the table. 'So these cells won't do him any good, and they won't do him any harm?'

'They're his own cells, with a bit of a genetic tweak, so there aren't any immune system issues,' said Alex, twiddling an imaginary knob with his right thumb and index finger on *tweak*. 'He had the same cell line injected into him fifteen years ago when he was testing them for safety and they had no effect. They've been sitting in a freezer ever since. An infusion of a few million of these cells won't make the slightest difference to his condition. I wouldn't do it otherwise.'

'A few million sounds like a lot,' said Lettie.

'There are sixty trillion cells in a human body,' said Alex, moving his hands apart and holding them out as if demonstrating the size of a gigantic fish he'd caught.

Matthew said: 'If they won't help him, and they won't hurt him, why does he want them?'

'It's his way of praying,' said Alex. 'Trying to turn hope into a system.'

Lettie tutted and exhaled.

'Prayer is when you ask for God's forgiveness and mercy,' said Matthew. 'But my father doesn't believe in that. This is more like when a gambler blows on the dice to get the number he wants.'

'That's a good comparison,' said Alex.

'If you're trying to be nice by saying Harry's as superstitious as we are, I'd rather you didn't,' said Lettie.

'He's wise enough to know the end is close,' said Alex, 'and frightened enough to grasp at the hope that he might get himself a few more minutes.'

'He's proud.' Matthew brooded for a moment. 'I've no objection to letting him have these cells. Do I have to sign something?'

'It's an informal arrangement,' said Alex. 'There's no need for paperwork as long as I know you agree.' He felt the power of being a messenger from the capital. There was a faint roar from the boiler cupboard as the gas jets lit. 'He wants to see you,' said Alex, 'even if you won't let him see the children.'

Matthew widened his eyes. 'Did you persuade him?' he said.

'It doesn't matter. He wants to see you. He wants you to visit the house when you can and be with him. He wants your help.'

'That's quite a change of heart,' said Lettie.

'He hasn't got long,' said Alex.

Matthew's head shook slightly and he looked down, then met Alex's eyes. 'I don't want to keep the children away from Dad when he's dying,' he said. 'But what can I do? He's broken so many promises. He's tried so hard to get them on their own, in the dark places of his house, and turn their hearts against their saviour. The last time we were there I caught him in the laundry room with Leah, asking why God would go to the trouble of creating the dinosaurs if he was going to kill them all and bury their bones before people turned up.'

'Was Leah upset?' said Alex.

'That's not the point,' said Lettie. 'He says he wants to protect the children's minds from religion but all he cares about is getting his own back on Matthew for finding Christ.'

'He knows you won't let the children come to London,' said Alex. 'It's my dad's birthday next month and Harry will be in Scotland with us. We could get together for that. The whole family, on neutral ground.'

Rose came in with a stack of bibles and dealt them out.

'Judges,' said Lettie.

'Judges,' said Matthew, and they looked for the place. 'Lettie, why don't you start?'

Alex had the bible he'd been given open at the book of Judges, chapter one. He didn't know what was expected of him. Lettie began to speak. In Judges, she said, we see a society in turmoil after the death of Joshua. People can't distinguish any more between good and evil, right and wrong. They worship false gods. They have no fixed point of reference except their own selfish wants. They give in to their twisted desires, their fascination with violence and cruelty against others, their craving for luxuries and delicacies they don't need. Why should they do otherwise? There is nothing, they think, to stop them. They don't believe anyone is watching or cares when they do wrong. So God punishes them, and first of all he punishes them through the consequences of their actions. They look at the greed and violence and perversion around them and despair.

While Lettie spoke she was possessed by a passion that altered her voice. It made her louder, more confident. Strong words in her mouth did not inhibit her.

When Matthew took over his voice changed, too. He said that what they saw around them today was a society like the one after Joshua. Young people getting drunk, taking drugs, learning about love from pornography and murdering each other with knives. Their parents unable to stop them because they no longer knew themselves what was right and what was wrong, what was good and what was evil. People looked for answers, but instead of turning to Jesus, and to the Bible, which gives such clear moral guidance, they made sickly cocktails from different bits of religion, a little bit of Christianity, a little bit of Hinduism, a little bit of Islam, Buddhism, shamanism. It wasn't the first time Britain had gone through a time of doubt and rejection of the truth of the Lord, said Matthew, and it would not be the last, but Judges showed us how the cycle of the generations was bound to turn, back towards faith.

He asked Rose what she thought. She spoke with sureness for a young girl. Alex realised that she was giving her parents back their own words, shortened and summarised.

'What about you, Alex?' said Matthew.

Alex, who hadn't read the Bible since he was a child, had skimmed through the first chapters of Judges while the others were talking. He could see no relationship between what Lettie and Matthew described and the words on the page; in the text he read, the Israelites and their deity were a sado-masochistic old couple only kept from divorce by their shared love of killing.

'God and the Jews seem to hate each other,' said Alex.

'It's not to be taken literally,' said Matthew. 'It's about submission to God's law.'

'There's a lot of gangster stuff in it, though, Dad,' said Rose. 'When Ehud stabs the fat king in the stomach and Jael hammers a nail into Sisera's head.'

'That's not what it's about,' said Matthew.

'You wouldn't let me read it when I was younger cause of the language.' She was looking from face to face, lifting her chin defensively against an attack that hadn't happened. 'Why not just tell us how to behave, like other books do?'

Matthew and Lettie folded their arms at the same moment. With a heavy turn of her head Lettie looked at her husband.

'What other books?' he said.

'Never mind,' said Rose, jumping up and saying 'May I be excused?' as she went through the door.

'It's the school,' said Lettie. 'It's too multicultural. She spends too much time with them.' She turned to Alex. 'If you and Maria had children, you'd know how hard it is.'

Matthew put his hand around her wrist and she tugged at his hold, not so much trying to break free as to show defiance; he was holding her wrist quite tightly. 'You have to guide them. You have to show them the difference between right and wrong. You need some equipment. I know you think all this,' she lifted the bible, 'is very silly, but how do you explain life without it?'

'There are no explanations,' said Alex. 'There are no answers, and there's no meaning. There's just life.'

Lettie laughed. 'Is that what you'd say to your children if they came at you with their questions? That there's no meaning, no answers? I'll bet Maria doesn't see it that way.'

'Maria and I aren't together any more,' said Alex. 'We broke up.'

Lettie looked at him in astonishment, tinged with horror, as if he had brought something unwholesome into her house that couldn't be cleansed.

'It didn't work out,' said Alex. 'It was amicable.'

'But you were together for so long,' said Lettie.

Alex shrugged and couldn't stop a smile creeping onto his face, which increased Lettie's horror.

'He found somebody else,' muttered Matthew.

'You had an affair?' said Lettie.

'No!' said Alex, no longer smiling. Lettie had never cared for Maria as far as he could remember. 'No, it was her idea.'

Lettie looked at him incredulously. 'It was Maria's idea that you should fall in love with somebody else? Why would she want that?'

'Lettie,' said Matthew. Alex was blushing furiously and his heart was pounding.

'I'm sorry,' said Lettie. 'It's what happens, I know, but it seems so casual.' She spoke as if she'd forgotten she was speaking her thoughts out loud. He wanted to defend himself but he couldn't tell them how ashamed he'd felt to walk away from Maria when he'd already smiled about it to their faces. Phrases like *It's one of those things* and *It happens all the time* came into his head and he knew that for some reason in his cousin's house they'd fall crippled from his lips.

Lettie got up, one hand on her belly, one hand on the back of the chair, taking care not to let the chair legs scrape against the wooden floor. 'So you and this new girlfriend'll be taking over Harry's house,' she said to Alex. 'Or maybe you'll find a way to sell it.' She turned her back to put a half-eaten loaf away and spoke words Alex didn't catch except the last, which were '. . . two million'.

'Don't speak that way,' said Matthew to Lettie as if he were rebuking a child. 'He can't do that.' He looked at Alex. 'You don't know what we're talking about, do you? Did you ever wonder what was going to happen to my father's house when he dies?'

'You'll inherit it, I suppose.'

'He's made a will leaving it to the institute. He got a lawyer to draft a covenant so that the only thing the institute can do with it is let the director live there for free. You, in other words. As things stand you'll have possession of my father's house when he's gone.' Matthew turned to Lettie. 'He does look surprised.' He said to Alex: 'I would rather you didn't let Dad know that you know. He told me he wanted to make a stand.'

'You saw him?'

'I hadn't seen him since he got the diagnosis four months ago, so I went to London. He wouldn't let me into the house. We stood and talked on the doorstep. He said, "The old intellectuals in London are dying and the young ones can't afford to live here."'

'I'll move out,' said Alex.

'There's no need.'

'I'll move out as soon as I get back. And you'll be seeing him again and looking after him. He'll change his mind.'

'It's unfair,' said Lettie. 'You don't have a family.'

'Lettie,' said Matthew.

Shaking her head, Lettie said she was going to bed. Matthew rose, apologised to Alex, said goodnight and followed his wife out.

Alex was only alone in the kitchen for a moment before Rose came back and began to fill the dishwasher. He offered to help.

'It's all right,' said Rose, smiling as if it was ridiculous that he could do anything with the chores except get in the way. Alex stayed where he was and watched her work. *Where did she get the grace?* he wondered. *Did she pick it up from Lettie?*

'What's the point of living, then?' said Rose, slotting plates into the rack. She turned round and folded her arms. 'You said there are no explanations, no answers and no meaning.'

'You were listening outside the door.'

'So, what's the point?'

'Living doesn't have a *point*,' said Alex. 'And yet we're living.'

'That's not very clever.'

Alex stood up and began flapping his arms up and down.

Rose shook her head and laughed at him and Alex said: 'The first thing you feel when you're born is time. Time, you see?' He looked around and blinked as if he could feel time on his face like the wind, as if he could smell it. 'Everyone around you is moving through time and changing. That's the journey you're born into. You're born on the wing. Flying through time, on a great migration.' As he talked he trotted around the kitchen table, flapping his arms heavily as if he were a weary bird. 'And then, still travelling, you give birth yourself.' Still flying around the table he used one wing to make an extravagant natal gesture.

'I hope there's somebody there to catch the egg,' said Rose.

'Come on! Follow me! Come on!' Rose sighed and shook her head and with her hands in her pockets began to trudge round the table after her uncle. 'Take your wings out of your pockets!' said Alex. 'Fly! And when your child looks back at you and asks: "Where did we start this journey?" you remember that you asked that question, too, and never got an answer. You never found out where you were going. But when you die, you'd rather still be flying. And the others around you, your children and your friends, the great flock, they're still flying on.'

'If you have children.'

'Your bluntness is a great cauteriser.'

'I don't know what that means.' Rose was annoyed. 'Being clever's not everything, you know. People are never clever enough to work out right and wrong for themselves. They need to be told by a higher power.'

'Is that what your parents think?'

'Yeah, but they're not strict enough,' said Rose. 'I've got this friend, he's a Muslim, and he was saying how every thousand years there's got to be a new religion, because the old one gets soft and bends the rules. So there was the Jews, and they got soft and there was the Christians, and they got soft and now there's Muslims.' Her eyes were shining. 'Don't tell Mum and Dad I said that.'

Later, in Chris's room, Alex called Bec, although he knew it was long past midnight in Tanzania. He knew she wouldn't answer, but was disappointed when she didn't. He wanted to tell her what had happened, how when he thought of her he couldn't stop smiling, and how he'd forgotten that it'd look as if he didn't care about Maria, when it wasn't like that at all; and about Harry's spiteful legacy. He wanted an audience that would turn his shame into goodness. The phone rang out and every few rings there was a click as if Bec was picking up but it was only some kind of interference in the cosmos. The joy of anticipatory love Alex had felt was destroyed and he doubted everything. What a prick he'd been to smirk about Maria; what a fool he'd been to say that he'd *found someone* when Bec had made no promises and they hadn't so much as held hands. He began to think over the lines in the messages she'd sent him, lines he'd read so many times and found so tender, and find alternative, cooler interpretations of each phrase she'd written. The thought that he could fly to Dar es Salaam and fly back two weeks later with Bec as nothing but a friend ran freezing through his body.

He bumped his head against the lampshade as he was undressing. He switched off the light, laid his head on the springy pillow and listened to the window rattle and the prickle of raindrops against the glass. Why, he thought, did Matthew admire his medical work, when he was delaying the entry of souls into heaven by keeping people alive? Why did the believers love the healers who brought them back from the brink of everlasting light? Harry was dying without the hope of paradise, but Alex knew that when Matthew came to face old age and the illnesses that would kill him he would cling to life no less tenaciously than his father.

38

There was something that sickened Ritchie about Bec's principles. Was she really so good? If she was so kind, why had she gone through so many men in her life? She'd barely broken up with Val before she'd moved on to Alex. Long ago she'd confessed her part in the terror that their father had delivered to his bedroom on the night before he left on his last tour. The evil yellow eye of that cruel bird, the sweep of its wings and the hellish shadows they cast on the wall, the dagger of its beak! The scream seemed to come from within the bird's skull, even if the sound came from his own throat.

It occurred to Ritchie for the first time that if he chose to dig up dirt on his sister, he would find something. She already came to him with her problems. *Of course I would never do that*, he thought.

He began to resent the way his sister, comfortable in her malaria-healing saintliness, would never know how loyal he had been to her, and the terrible punishment that he faced from her ex-lover as the reward for this loyalty. It was unjust that he, Ritchie, should suffer like this, when it was Bec who had made Val angry by saying she would marry him and then changing her mind. She would never appreciate the sacrifice her brother was making in order to protect her from the consequences of her own selfishness. This was the woman who presented herself as a superior guardian of their father's memory, when she wanted to let the world forget him, and he wanted the world to remember!

Let it be that way, then, thought Ritchie. If he had to be the one to understand it was nobler to make peace with O'Donabháin, so be it. If he had to make the secret sacrifice of not betraying his sister, well and good. Let God be his witness: he did the right thing. And if he was to be a martyr, why not make it harder for himself? Why not help Val dismantle another obstacle to Bec's exposure in a national newspaper, her lack of fame? When Ritchie realised Alex and Bec might be falling in love, just when Alex's research was giving him a tinge of celebrity, his instinct had been to keep his sister and his friend apart, to keep Bec safe in her obscurity. But he, Ritchie, was going to be a martyr for his sister, so there was no need for that. He'd help her and Alex to be together. He'd encourage them. He'd sing at their wedding if they liked. If Bec was neither too good nor too obscure to be the subject of national scandal, all that stood between her and disgrace would be her martyr-brother, who would hide his goodness, who went unappreciated, the secret philanthropist, the doer of good deeds for the perpetually ungrateful. He wouldn't betray her, not because he couldn't, but because he chose not to.

Ritchie wasn't resigned to exposure, arrest, disgrace and divorce, but he was afraid to seek help from the lawyers and showbusiness intermediaries who might make his problems go away. He looked for an alternative sacrifice, an enemy with a secret whom he could stitch up. He knew Lazz did coke backstage during *Teen Makeover* rehearsals, when *vulnerable young people* were only a few yards away, but Lazz wasn't an enemy. For all his coldness, Lazz was a star, Ritchie's star, and Ritchie couldn't bear to break the star's exquisite points.

The last hope he was left with was the film about his father's killer. Ritchie sensed that there was a cryptic accountancy of darkness, that the public was prepared to tolerate a certain amount of balancing and rounding up between different columns where sin and suffering were concerned. A distinguished film director, for example, might be able to take figures from the 'suffering' column – parents taken to Auschwitz, wife murdered – and transfer them over to the 'sin' column – committed statutory rape of a thirteen-year-old girl. This was acceptable because, in some mysterious way, the figures all seemed to represent the same general quality of darkness, a more palatable and universal medium than wickedness, stoicism, evil or self-restraint. In sum, there was no darkness received and darkness expended: there was only darkness. Ritchie believed his interview with his father's killer would cast a kind of balancing darkness over him that would make his indiscretions with Nicole more fitting and forgivable in the eyes of society, and that this held whether society was touched by the film, or appalled.

None of this would keep his family together if the story broke, and this weighed heavily on Ritchie's heart, and kept him reaching for the bottle.

39

When Alex returned from Lancashire he went to the institute, used his passcode to access the freezers in the basement and took out a bag of his uncle's genetically modified cells. He took a cab back to Citron Square and went up to Harry's room, taking the stairs three steps at a time. Judith, the agency nurse who now attended his uncle, followed behind with an IV stand. She pushed Gerasim out and left him whimpering on the other side of the door.

Harry lay on his bed with a ramp of pillows raising his head and shoulders halfway upright. He wore a black waistcoat and a white shirt with the sleeves rolled up. He was freshly shaved. The scent he'd rubbed into his chin was an aromatic squawk in the gamy bachelor reek of the overheated room, a deep smell of old books and decades-worn wool and painstaking ablutions. On the wall above Harry's head was a faded reproduction of *The Boyhood of Raleigh* that had hung in his parents' house in Derby when he was a child.

Alex's boots clomped on the white-painted floorboards and made them creak. He dropped an orange Sainsbury's bag on Harry's lap. The thin plastic made a crinkling sound as its wrinkles relaxed. Harry looked inside the bag and took out a litre plasma sachet filled with clear liquid. He turned it over in his hands. It was cold to the touch and had his name written on in his own handwriting from fifteen years ago.

'Sainsbury's,' he said. 'Son of a gun. My genetically modified self should be a Waitrose product.'

Alex hooked the bag on the IV stand. On the table by Harry's bed a wind-up travel clock in a clamshell case of cloth-covered tin ticked fussily, the alarm hand set to seven-thirty. Next to the clock was a horn comb with one broken tooth and a photograph in a silver frame of Harry and his brother, Alex's father, as boys on Filey beach, with bleached hair and little nipples and teeth white against their summer-darkened skin, eyes squinting at the sun. As Harry's condition worsened the cluster of objects had seemed to creep closer to him.

Alex and Judith washed their hands, put on rubber gloves and set up the infusion kit. Judith spiked the line into the salt solution, closed the clamps, connected the bag of cells, arranged the bags and lines on the stand and fed salt solution into the drip chamber. Alex sat on the bed, ripped open a sterile catheter bag and lifted Harry's hand. He swabbed a spot and Judith stuck the catheter in. She fed the line into the catheter tube and flushed it with the solution. Alex got up, opened the clamp in the line from the cell bag and adjusted the flow. The bag began to empty into Harry.

How strange it would be, Harry thought, if something happened; if his muscles filled out, his skin turned pink and taut, his voice strengthened, his cancer shrank, his innards cleared and glistened and he could eat, talk, run, sing and laugh, eat meat and smoke tobacco.

'You think I'm a fool,' he said. 'You know it won't do me any good.'

'Who knows what good it did you last time?' said Alex. 'Who knows what diseases you didn't get?'

Alex was woken in the night by someone coming into his room. He switched the light on as Harry sat down on the edge of his bed. He was in pyjamas and a dressing gown and had a glass of wine in his hand. Alex asked what time it was, and when he asked it, realised the question he'd wanted to ask was 'How old am I?'

'I couldn't sleep,' said Harry.

'How do you feel?'

'Excellent.'

'Different?'

'The river cannot enclose the same foot twice. Do you mind if I sleep here?'

'Yes.'

Harry knocked back a gulp of wine. 'You're selfish. And you're going to bloody Africa tomorrow.'

'You don't need me here. You've got Judith now, and Matthew will be coming and going, and so will I. When I get back I'm going to move out for a while. I'll rent a place close by.'

The corner of Harry's mouth turned down and he looked into his glass. 'Matthew snitched on me, I suppose. He told you about the house. Don't those Christians have some kind of commandment about not ratting on their elders? I'm not going to change my mind. If he tries to make me I'll leave the house to you outright.'

'I wouldn't take it.'

'Children aren't what you think,' said Harry. 'He's more disappointed in me and his mother than I am in him. He's my son and I have the will to choose the child I like the best and it happened to be you. It could have been Dougie. It could have been a kid off the street.' He looked up, gave Alex the chance to speak, and when Alex said nothing, only blinked at him and went on. 'You have children — who knows? You treat them like princes and princesses, you tuck them up at night in soft beds, you spend your last penny on them, you teach them everything you know, you love them and tell them how wonderful they are, and they turn into liars and whores and thieves. They betray you. Or you smack them about the head, put them to work when they're six, starve them, abuse them, tell them they'll never amount to anything, and they make it their university. They flower. They rule the world.'

40

Bec sent a car to collect Alex from the airport in Dar es Salaam. He hadn't slept on the overnight flight from London. On the way to the villa where Bec's group was based his eyes ached and his head spun. In the streets he had a muffled sense of diesel fumes, criss-crossing streams of motorbikes, searing light and black shade. The sense of journey's end gave him a hollow, adrenaline wakefulness.

She was busy. She met him with a distracted smile and a kiss on each cheek and they talked with awkward formality in her cluttered office. The heavy old desk – some colonial antique, he supposed – impressed him with its varnished darkness and in his disappointment he instinctively wrote off his new power and fame and threw together a hallucinatory architecture of Bec's psychic estate, vast, aristocratic and fortified, into which he'd slipped by chance, and might easily be found out: her neo-imperial set-up in Africa, great project, researchers, local staff, famous and powerful brother in England, former lovers, and she, the mistress at the heart, aloof. Batini came to show him his room. Bec said she'd be finished at four and he sloped off with his luggage, to sleep.

Bec had hoped to finish the vaccine trial by the time Alex came; she'd looked forward to seeing him. But in the end there were still villages to go round with questionnaires and booster shots. When he appeared in her office, pale and tired from his journey, filling space with his long limbs at rest, she felt a shiver of nerves, if it was nerves. The sleepless flight had taken away his fidgety restlessness and she saw a stooped, brooding man harrowed by excessive emotional algebra. He looked at her, she thought, with curiosity naked of decorum, as if she were nature itself.

Bec found it hard to concentrate on the way to the villages, when she'd meant to chew on some data on the laptop in the back of the car. She'd taken trouble to shove necessary tasks into earlier and later days and arranged for the other researchers to be out in the districts so she and Alex could have one evening to themselves. For the rest of the time, she'd collected brochures for him about safaris and Kilimanjaro. Why, she wondered, hadn't she told him this? And why stand behind the ugly old desk in her office, as if she were interviewing him?

He must have imagined she was afraid of him, or putting on a performance of authority. She knew he hadn't come for a jolly walk and dinner and to post pictures of zebras on the Facebook page he never touched. She searched for the memory that the worn-out, not-giving-up Alex echoed with. Her father at the end of a day spent clearing fallen branches from the coomb, or had that been Ritchie? Joel sitting on the tailgate of the car, head between his knees, after failing to place at the cross country in Crystal Springs? Or her favourite engraving of Don Quixote from the old edition in her grandfather's house? *That's him*, she thought, *the doleful, hopeful knight.*

When she got back, before going to find Alex, she asked Batini's opinion about her choice of earrings, and Batini discussed it with her very seriously.

Alex woke refreshed in a strange bed. It was late afternoon, he guessed. Over his head was a metal ring with a furled mosquito net. From where he lay he could see a rhomboid-shaped section of clear sky, a faintly inky yellow, that mysteriously had depth without having features. He'd forgotten his resentment that morning. He remembered Bec seeming distant, looked at his phone, saw that it was after five and hurried to wash and to dress in his new linen clothes.

He found her on a cane armchair on the verandah, waiting for him, it seemed. The evening chorus of birds and insects was beginning and the horns of mopeds rasped from the street. Beyond the trees at the bottom of the garden the concrete shell of a half-built apartment block turned a soft spider's-web colour as the sun went down. She turned towards him and rose and her eyes and earrings glinted in the last of the daylight. She'd put her hair up. She began to speak and Alex heard but didn't take the trouble to lay hold on the words of *how did you sleep I'm sorry I didn't wake you but you looked so peaceful it's probably too late for the market but there's a nice place down by the seafront where we can have a drink before dinner.*

'That sounds good,' he said. He'd repeated to himself as he got ready that he must compliment her on the way she looked, however she looked. But now that she was in front of him whatever he could have told her about her appearance seemed cheap and beside the point. A few weeks ago he'd been told he was a leviathan of science, talked confidently on live national radio and global news channels, and gave presentations on cellular timekeeping to conference audiences of hundreds of people. Yet now the memory of his failure of eloquence and resolution in the rain in Cambridge was stronger.

'Let's sit here for a while,' he said. He pulled another chair close to Bec's and they sat down with his knees almost touching the hem of her cotton skirt, printed with a cherry blossom pattern. They asked each other catch-up questions until a taut bubble of unsaid things pushed between them.

'I wonder what it is about a person that gives you a sense of what they are before you know them,' Alex said. 'It must be the way they look, and the way they move, I suppose. It's not much to go on and I don't remember being trained to do it.'

'There are the things they say,' said Bec.

'Yes, and the things they do, but before that, there's another language. You read it and you don't know you're reading it. It's written in a fine script. The eyes are a millimetre wider, or narrower, the eyes a fraction brighter.' Alex lifted his index finger and thumb together in front of his eye and squinted through it as if it were the eye of a needle. 'The smile, the head, the way she holds herself.'

'Oh, it's a woman!'

'These movements, these dimensions – they're too minute and complex to measure.'

'Would you want to?'

'Beauty helps.'

'There we go.'

'But it's not the thing itself. The thing itself is what's encoded there and how you read it.'

'Give me an example.'

'A woman I'm thinking of. She is attractive, as it happens, and clever, but that's not the thing. When I met her, and before I talked to her, I read in some way that her mind was wide open. You hear people say *open-minded, I'm keeping an open mind* and what they mean is they're opening a little hatch in their closed minds and taking a look outside.' He made a hinge with the heels of his hands together, swung his hands open and mimed a lookout. 'This woman is different. She really has one. And the idea of a mind that actually is open is scary.'

Bec smiled. 'You're saying this woman has no restraints.'

'I'm sure she does. But I don't think she trusts them unless she made and tested them herself.'

'You make this woman sound like some kind of pioneer in the wilderness of her own brain.' She laughed.

'You must know her,' he said.

Bec was going to say that Alex saw what he wanted to see, but hesitated. It wasn't so much that she liked what he said about her as that she liked to see him want to take her into an idea he'd made. Alex took his moment to lean forward to kiss her, and she responded, and for some time, before they were interrupted by one of the drivers coming to ask if they wanted the car, the crickets were drowned out by the creaking of hundreds of strands of woven cane.

They went out and got a little drunk and Bec told him how hard it would be to spend time with him after that night. 'I'm nearly finished but there are ragged ends,' she said. 'I thought you could go on a safari. I don't know if you're interested in lions.'

'Smug beasts,' said Alex. 'Complacent.'

'They have zebras.'

'Too retro, too Eighties.'

'Leopards.'

'Leopards are cliquey. Couldn't I travel around with you? I could be your unpaid apprentice. I'm more on the theoretical than the practical side. Perhaps they'd be interested in quantum theory and protein folding out there in the countryside.'

'We might find a space, I suppose,' said Bec. 'Dr Katanga needs a dogsbody.'

Later they drove up the coast and walked along a quiet beach. The few jagged white lights inland seemed to have nothing to do with human life. Their feet sank half an inch into wet sand and the darkness out at sea was warm, unflawed. Bec cut her bare foot on a white shell and bled and put her hand on Alex to help her limp along, hopping forward and letting him take her weight on his shoulder. She lay down laughing on the sand and he licked the blood off her foot and spat out the grains. They walked into the darkness and the water lapped around their ankles and Bec drew in breath and said that it stung. A single red light on the mast of a fishing boat ducked and rose in the swell offshore and they heard the distant clack of its old engine. They watched the light rise and fall, a pattern in the void.

'I'm glad you came,' said Bec.

After they first made love Bec noticed a strange trick of time, where the memory of the night split into two: her memory of what happened, and her memory of what it meant. She remembered details. She remembered his eyes, the rush in her chest, how his lips were softer than they looked, his back muscles stretching under her hand, his fingertips, the moment he pushed into her, her gasp, her laughing when she came, some of the things he said. None of these was the memory of what it meant: the beginning of a time when being with Alex for ever became something that would happen unless she stopped it.

One night, in the yard outside the villa, the generator started up. Alex turned his head and saw Bec asleep next to him. Her lips moved and she began to whisper, too faintly for him to make out the words, exposing the dark seam of things he didn't know and experiences he couldn't share because they'd already happened. Her whispers must bubble up from the same source as the blood dried in the pinpricks in her fingertips, the scars on her wrist and the microscopic creatures living in her veins, towards which he felt a queer rivalry. Suppose happiness were luck, as Harry said; his luck was so solidly embedded in the woman next to him that should he lose her now he couldn't imagine being lucky again.

He wanted to stay with her, and he wanted a child with her. In some part of him he was aware how much unhappiness lay ahead if, as was quite likely, he could have one but not the other, and yet he managed to keep that part of himself sealed off from the part of his mind that made plans.

When he'd left London he was so drenched in accolades that for a while he saw his chronase complex theory bowling forward into eternity, passing from generation to generation as resolutely as any gene set, like a virtual child. But Africa struck him with its youth and its intent. He saw the daily tide of children in uniform walking to and from school and wanted to stake a claim. Through Bec he should have lived malaria day and night yet he was oddly blind to the disease and hunger, the cruelty of the daily strive and hustle, the dullness of being poor. To Alex, Tanzania was flowering. To come from the fat, spoiled, ageing north to Africa and find Bec was like coming from the world of scientists into Ritchie's party and finding her among the musicians. She was his guide between the worlds.

Bec opened her eyes, smiled at him and stretched like a cat, pedalling the sheet off her body. She saw he was thinking about something, with a trace of the furrowed brow, as if he were about to make a judgement.

She was struck by how safe she felt and had the urge to give her ease a prod, to test it. 'Let me guess,' she said. 'You're thinking, "I liked sex with her so much that I want to do it again with someone else just to make sure she's the best."'

He laughed, but the thoughtfulness came back.

'What if you and I didn't sleep with anyone else?' said Alex. 'For the rest of our lives?'

Bec considered the strange extremity of the proposition. She remembered how strange it was that it should seem strange. Most of her friends had made that promise to their partners. She didn't like to be reminded that she was unusual. Ever since Joel, ever since Papua New Guinea, she'd worked longer hours than anyone around her, and when she felt like it, taken the sex that had come her way; since Val, the sex had fallen off. With the vaccine trial soon to wind up, she'd go back to London; would she end up spending nights in the lab again? She'd felt an arcane spasm of having been betrayed when her feminist friends, those most ardently for independence, polyandry, self-definition, had suddenly dived headfirst into permanent, monogamous domesticity. The betrayal wasn't the dive; it was that they never admitted to making the choice, as if setting up house together were some extraordinary accident that they were making the best of.

She ran her hand down Alex's spine, pressing her forefinger lightly into each vertebra as if she were counting them. 'Would I have to read your work?' she said. Even to discuss hypotheticals seemed a step towards consent.

'You mean you haven't?' He was disappointed.

'You don't know the names of all the parasites.'

'Try me,' said Alex.

'What's the most famous parasite?'

Alex lifted his head from Bec's breast. 'The Queen.'

'The cuckoo,' said Bec. 'It lays its egg in another bird's nest and gets the parenting for free. Hey, don't stop that, it's nice.'

The mosquito net stirred as Alex sat up and looked at her keenly. One side of his body was illuminated by the security floodlights in the garden leaking through the gaps between the slats of the blind. 'Perhaps those other birds wouldn't have chicks any other way,' he said.

One of the villages where Alex came to help was a prosperous, bleak place of cube-shaped mud-brick houses with the white render stained and crumbling away. The late afternoon sun gilded the villagers' cheeks and flashed off rooftops' unrusted spots when they walked towards the schoolhouse. The air smelled of fresh-lit charcoal. Bec looked back over her shoulder and saw Haji Katanga carrying a box of questionnaires and a few yards behind him Alex in a white shirt, pale grey jeans and dusty boots stepping carefully along with a tray of vaccine vials just out of the cooler. He led a ragged V of children, dogs and chickens down the road between the houses. He was watching the vials to be sure he didn't tip them over and Bec saw how he was distracted by the way the curls of frost vapour coming off them caught the reddening sun. His head bent lower and lower and he walked more and more slowly until he stopped and the children and dogs gathered round to see what had fascinated him. She saw him gradually become aware of their interest; try to explain, with enthusiasm; remember what he was supposed to be doing; look up at her encouragingly; lead the ragged procession rosily on.

'Dr Katanga, your man is slacking,' she said to Haji.

Haji looked over his shoulder, then shook his head at Bec. 'You can't get good labour these days,' he said.

Later she looked up from the line of children and mothers to see Alex in the distance, standing around a tall local drum with a group of older boys. They were showing him how to play it and he shook his head, stopped them, held up two sticks he'd found and performed a drummer boy roll, and they shook their heads and stopped him and beat the drum with their hands, and he shook his head and stopped them, and so it went on.

In the last weeks of the vaccine trial Bec thought about the future and found that Alex was in it, and found she liked him being there. It was a luxury to lie naked, skin to skin, in the smell of sex, with a man who not only knew what she meant when she complained about the basolateral domain of the hepatocyte plasma membrane, but could reassure her that her work was worthwhile.

'It's like an epic poem,' he said one night, bouncing slightly with enthusiasm as, more at ease with her, he'd begun to do. 'The races of humans and haemoproteus on one side, the mosquitoes and malaria parasites on the other.'

'Who's in charge?' said Bec.

'You. In a plumed helmet, mounted on a great black horse, raising your mighty syringe, turning to the ranks stretching out on either side of you and calling on the bugler to sound the charge. Damn it, a spy in the camp! Did you hear that?' He twisted round, clapped his hands in the air, examined his palms for insect guts and clapped his hands again, chasing the pulsing whine that had infiltrated their net.

'Did you take your Malarone?' said Bec.

'Don't I get immunity by sleeping with you?'

'No. You're not the first person who's said that,' said Bec, picking at the sheet. Without thinking, she let her mouth twitch and her look turn inward toward to the memory of a one-week affair with a Kenyan immunologist years before. Alex noticed and fell back on the bed sullenly and she pressed herself against him and put her hand on his heart. 'But you can be the last.'

'That sounds like a promise,' said Alex, looking for a catch.

'If you'll still have me,' said Bec. 'I'm not easy.'

'Easy's soft,' said Alex. *She made a promise to Val too*, he thought; *is that the catch?*

Bec read his doubt. 'This isn't like somebody springing a ring on me and me taking it,' she said. She felt summoned to bring an affirmation into words, some simple, solemn and binding expression, but the society to which she belonged, it seemed to her, had taken away the scripts and parts from the old play of women and men without providing new drafts. So she was free to improvise her vow, and freedom, it was understood, was good, and the first thing a free modern woman did when she had to come up with a sincere and life-changing promise was to reach for some rotten cliché. And it seemed unnecessary; she had the feeling that it'd all been settled long ago, and they were already together.

'I have to say something,' she said, and her voice cracked a little. 'I want to stay with you. Wait, that's lame.' She put her index finger to her lips in thought. 'I'm *going* to stay with you. How's that?'

Alex swallowed, held her shoulders and stared into her eyes as if wanting to endlessly devour and recreate her. He too felt that he was groping for the response in an ad lib sacrament. 'I do love you,' he said.

'But?'

'Somewhere along the way *I love you* got small. It's not enough. I want better. I want to plight my troth.' He looked as if he was ready to be laughed at for this, but although Bec wasn't sure what he meant, the words made her press herself against him, push her tongue into his mouth and open her thighs around his hips.

Next day she took down from the shelf an old Chambers dictionary, left behind by the Tanzanian professor who owned the house when he emigrated to Canada, and looked up *plight*. It meant pledge, or promise; from an Old English word *pliht*, meaning to risk. She looked up *troth*.

Troth, it said. *A variant of truth.*

Not long before Alex was due to go back to London, Bec managed to clear time for a day excursion to Zanzibar. They made it early in the morning to the jetty and waited for the ferry. There were few other passengers. A family sat on a pyramid of suitcases, children standing lookout on the apex, elders hunched at the base; a young man with his short-sleeved shirt hanging open over his bare chest squatted on the corner of the jetty, looking out to sea; a pair of American missionaries in caps and knee-length shorts with camera straps slung across their chests were talking about their home town. Bec sat on a bollard and Alex sat beside her on the jetty deck, his head at the level of her ankle, letting his feet kick over the edge. There was no wind. The water was like turquoise milk. The line of the horizon was invisible in the haze. Alex looked up at Bec, who seemed to be searching for something, shading her eyes with her hand. Alex had burned on the second day and his face and neck were smeared with high-factor sunblock.

'What's going on with you and the sun?' he said. 'He spends the whole day on your skin and leaves it magnificent and whenever I try to spend time with him he just beats me up.'

Bec jumped off the bollard and sat down next to Alex. 'You really are jealous, aren't you?'

'You keep exalted company.'

'Who?'

'Well, the sun, for one. And Ritchie.' He laughed to show he didn't mean it and showed that he did.

'He's my brother! And your friend!'

'He didn't want me to come here.'

'He's being protective. And proprietorial. He likes to play the father figure with me.'

'You went to a fancy school.'

'A bad private school for the daughters of officers to learn to be good wives. They were upset that I wanted to be a scientist.'

'You went out with a newspaper editor.'

'You're the one who found out how to make people live for ever,' said Bec, putting her arm round his shoulder. 'You're the exalted one.'

'I said it was theoretically possible, for Harry's sake, and now I'm stuck with the hype.'

Bec put on sunglasses. 'Is that better?' she asked.

Alex drummed his hands on the edge of the pier. 'Look, pelicans,' he said, and sang

Mr Sheen shines

Umpteen things clean

'What is it?' said Bec.

'Nothing.'

'You sang one of your jingles.'

'I want to know why you went out with Val,' said Alex, turning away from the pelicans and looking Bec in the eye.

'He was attractive, and powerful,' said Bec. 'It started out of curiosity and sex. I thought I was being kind to a man who'd lost his wife but I think I was letting myself be flattered. And given treats. He had a lot to offer in the way of treats and dressing up. I thought he was kind, but he wasn't. He was only kind to *me*. I should have known that the tone of his newspaper came from him but I didn't get it until I gave the ring back.'

'You were going to marry him?'

'I was stupid.'

Alex looked behind him sharply as if he'd been stung by an insect. He was responding to an instinct to throw something violently into the water, but there was nothing within reach.

'Why was he kind to you?'

'He wanted a new and fitting wife.'

Should I ask if I am fitting? Alex wondered. 'He could still have been in love with you,' he said, and Bec didn't reply.

A faint stream of foam appeared in the haze towards Zanzibar. 'He called me before I left,' said Alex. 'He said he wanted to promote me, said there weren't enough famous scientists. I felt he knew I was coming to see you, I can't imagine how.' It occurred to him as he spoke that Val's paper had run the most prominent and hysterical story about his findings; the rest of their media had taken their cue from it.

'Did he talk about me?' asked Bec.

'He described you as a friend.'

'That's all right, I suppose. I treated him badly and just like that,' she snapped her fingers, 'his hinges broke. He started speaking all in capital letters. It's true I don't know how to

282

behave. Who does? It doesn't mean I don't know the difference between right and wrong. My dad didn't go to church or push God on us and he knew the right thing to do well enough to get . . .' She was going to say 'get killed' but wasn't ready, even in front of Alex.

The ferry arrived, a hydrofoil with no outside deck. From inside they could see nothing through the windows except a bright, foggy azure. The crew put an old Sylvester Stallone movie up on a small screen at the front of the passenger seats and piped the soundtrack through the PA at deafening volume.

There was a line of passengers waiting on the jetty to go back to Dar when Bec and Alex disembarked in Zanzibar, and a group of delicate, abused-looking cats with patches of fur missing and an odd number of eyes. As he approached the queue Alex was gazing at the mould-blackened façades of Stone Town, imagining himself a slave brought for sale in the days of the Sultan, when he felt Bec grip his elbow.

'That guy in the green polo shirt,' she hissed. 'Don't look! I don't want to talk to him. Don't let him see me.'

Alex took a peek, doing his best to hide the slinking Bec with his body. The identified threat was a paunchy, shaven-headed European with dark glasses and a beard carrying a small leather shoulder bag and squinting at an iPad. He glanced up.

'He's looking our way,' said Alex out of the side of his mouth. 'If you weren't walking in that daft way he wouldn't have noticed you.'

'Make him look away,' said Bec, who had bent her body forward parallel to the ground.

Without breaking stride Alex stooped down, picked up one of the cats by the nape of the neck and tossed it in a shallow

283

parabola in front of the bearded man. The animal flew through the air, shrieking with indignation, landed on its feet with a gentle thump, sank onto its hind legs and coolly resumed licking its crotch. Alex and Bec increased their walking speed as they powered towards the wharf, then heard a faint shout of 'Rebecca? Dr Shepherd?' behind them and broke into a run. They trotted into Stone Town, pursued by small boys selling drinks and roses and tours of the city. Bec stopped in an alleyway by an ancient wooden door studded with brass knobs and leaned against the wall.

'He recognised me,' she said, over the din of urchins grabbing their forearms and waving Chinese vendibles in their faces.

'I'm sure it won't be the lead item on the Zanzibar nightly news.'

'I didn't realise how quiet it was until you threw the cat.'

Up the street they found a hotel in a converted merchant's house and sat with beers in the shade in a colonnaded courtyard. A tiny fountain spat and gurgled in the centre of the yard and every few minutes a dappled shadow crossed the sunlit part as a flock of doves flew overhead.

'His name's not important,' said Bec when Alex asked who they'd run from. 'He's from the Karolinska. I couldn't bear to have a conversation with him. He was one of the researchers who stopped me doing what I wanted to do with *gregi*.'

'Actually stopped.'

'You know what I mean. He campaigned against it in journals, on the conference circuit. He was one of the ringleaders.'

'You told me it was the World Health Organization and the Tanzanian government who stopped you trialling the live parasite.'

'Under the influence of those carpers.'

I see why Harry liked you, Alex thought. He said: 'What about the eyesight issue?'

Bec fumbled impatiently in her rucksack and banged a plastic pill bottle on the round mosaic-tiled table top, which rocked from side to side, its cast-iron frame ringing dully on the flagstones. 'I've had *gregi* in me for six years, the population is stable, and my eyes are fine. I get the occasional episode, that's all. If I ever need to get rid of them, I take two of these a day for a week, and they're gone.'

'Why don't you take them?'

Bec stared at him, stiff and with her eyes narrowed, as if she thought he must be pretending not to understand.

'It's named after my father,' she said.

The response *Just because of that?* travelled from Alex's mind to his mouth, but instead he said: 'Of course.'

41

Ritchie had been surly at dinner on the eve of their father's last tour, Bec remembered, shovelling food into his mouth with the fork held at right angles to his fist and his fringe falling over his eyes. Later, when the summer darkness fell and Bec was in her room, tying the laces of her walking boots, she'd heard Ritchie yell 'Fascist!' and his door slam shut.

She put her nightdress on over her clothes and opened the window. The air smelled of chestnut blossom and the sound of the stream came up from where it rushed through the coomb at the foot of the garden. She got into bed with a book, but she couldn't read. There was an owl call from outside and a plastic box flew in through the window and bounced on the floor. Bec got out of bed, grabbed it and ran back under the covers. She opened the box. It had a mirror in the lid, like a make-up compact, and three troughs of cream – one black, one green and one brown. She heard her mother coming, snapped the box shut, hid it and pulled the quilt up tight around her neck. Her mother put her head round the door and asked if she'd seen her father, and when Bec said she hadn't, her mother told her it was time for her to go to sleep. She kissed Bec, switched off the light, went out and closed the door behind her.

Bec stared at the darkness through the window. As her eyes picked up the faint gradients of blacks and browns the square of nothingness began to take on substance and form. What had seemed like an opening into pure night now puckered and solidified into a shape, as if the air was curdling. A pair of disembodied eyes opened, their whites so pale as to seem to shine, like the moon. They swivelled and came to rest on Bec. A few inches below the eyes, two rows of teeth appeared, parted and let out a voice.

'You haven't cammed up,' said her father.

'I didn't have time,' said Bec. She got out of bed and carried the box to the window.

'You have to blend into the darkness like a panther,' said her father, taking the box from Bec's hands and opening it. Reaching through the window, he began to dab and smear camouflage cream onto his daughter's face.

'What about my eyeballs?' said Bec.

'And nor does the panther have black teeth. We must give our prey a chance.'

Once he'd darkened Bec's face and hands to his satisfaction, her father lifted her out of the room and set her down on the flowerbed under the window. From the far end of the house Bec could see the grey light cast by the television shrink and brighten.

'Ready?' said her father. 'Remember the rules?'

'Don't make any noise. Don't leave anyone behind.'

'And?'

'That's it.'

'Good girl. If we find the poacher, you wait while I work my way behind him.' Bec's father took a small pipe hanging from a cord round his neck and blew into it. It was a reedy, lonely call. 'As soon as you hear that sound, clap your hands and shout, scare our friend, and I'll nab him. Let's get cracking.'

Bec followed her father through the garden, through the back gate and along the path that ran downhill along the edge of the coomb. When they smelled the stand of pines that marked the fork in the way, they turned right into the thick wood that grew on either side of the stream, in the deep, narrow cleft in the hill. The path ran closer and closer to the stream, over ground ribbed with old roots and tasselled with the remnants of the spring's bluebells. Bec stepped on a twig and she and her father stopped. Her father looked round and Bec knew she had made a mistake but her father pointed to the sky. Bec looked up to see the Milky Way like something frantic that had been frozen there.

The path now ran just above the water. Bec's father signalled to her to get down on all fours and they crawled forward to a thick root that rose up across the pathway. They hid behind it and raised their eyes over the top. Ahead of them they could see where the stream opened out to a set of pools, with clumps of rushes and partly submerged alder trees. Bec followed her father's pointing finger and saw their quarry twenty yards away, standing still in the shallows on one leg, head hunched into his shoulders, the crown of feathers serrated against the water and the long beak sticking out like the peak of a cap. Bec's father looked at her, pointed to her, pointed to his ear, pointed to the bird-caller, pointed to her again, mimed a handclap and a shout, and made a thumbs-up sign. Bec made a thumbs-up sign in return. Her father stared at her, blinking a little. It was only for a moment. He pressed his lips together, cupped her cheek with his hand, got up and vanished silently into the trees.

Bec settled down to watch the heron. How could it stand

for so long without moving, with one foot in the cold water? Was it asleep? Was it waiting for a fish? She yawned. She mustn't fall asleep. She had heard that soldiers who fell asleep on guard duty were executed. She would never fall asleep if she thought she'd be executed for it. She was cold and wished she could jump up and down. She would be as patient as the heron, as invisible as the panther and as brave as her father. He'd spent nights without shelter in the snow and the jungle with men he called 'the blokes'. Bec wanted to be a bloke, although she wasn't sure what a bloke was.

She heard her father's bird call. She stood up, clapped her hands together and shouted 'Heron! Fly away, heron!' The heron unfurled its great wings, hopped lazily into the air and skimmed across the water to the far side, disappearing among the trees. Bec listened. She could hear nothing except the sound of the water. Could her father have made a mistake? Could something have happened to him? What if he'd slipped on the rocks at the edge of the stream and broken his leg? How would she find him?

'Dad!' she shouted. 'Dad!' After her second shout, she heard his bird call. A few minutes later something touched her shoulder and she wasn't surprised, she knew it was him.

'It got away,' she said.

Her father lifted a net hanging from his right hand. Something twitched angrily inside. 'It did not,' he said.

Bec asked how he'd caught it.

'One day I'll show you,' said her father.

They walked back towards the house. Bec's father held her hand. She asked him if she was one of the blokes.

'You're my best bloke,' said her father.

'What about Ritchie?'

'He's my best son.'

'You've only got one!'

'How lucky it is that he is the best.'

'Did you ever take him out at night to catch a heron?'

'Ritchie doesn't like being in the woods at night,' said Bec's father. 'He doesn't like camming up.'

'Did you ask him?'

'Your brother's going to get what he wants. He's going to be rich one day.'

'Can I say a bad word?'

'If there's a good reason.'

'He told me rich people are bastards.'

'There you are,' said her father. 'He's interested in them already.'

They came to the house. Instead of hoisting Bec back through the window of her room her father led her round to the front, where they could see that Ritchie had his light on upstairs. They heard him strumming his guitar.

'Shall we put the heron in Ritchie's room?' asked her father.

Bec thought about this. If they did, her mother might find out what had been going on. She would see her husband and daughter with black and green warpaint smeared on their faces, and be angry with him for leaving her by herself on his last night, and for conspiring with Bec, and angry with her for hunting herons when she was supposed to be sleeping, and for lying. Whereas if her father put the heron away somewhere safe, or just let it go, they could slip back into the house, wash themselves in secret, and never be discovered. And yet she was tremendously curious to find out what Ritchie would do if he found a tall grey bird with a long sharp bill unexpectedly flapping around in his room.

'Yes,' she said, and her father nodded, clamped the net with the struggling bird between his teeth, and began to climb the wall of the house, fitting the toes of his boots and his fingertips between the cracks in the stones. A few minutes later she heard Ritchie scream.

While the household was distracted she cleaned her face and went to bed and by the time her father came to kiss her goodnight, she was asleep. She didn't see him alive again. Ritchie told her that very early in the morning, when their father left, he'd taken the heron with him to release in another part of the country.

A month later, at her father's funeral, Bec met the blokes. Some of them were handsome, watchful and quiet, like her father, like the heron. They preferred the edges of crowds. Others she didn't like, crop-haired men bursting with secretiveness, swollen-chested in smart uniforms they obviously hardly ever wore. She understood that these were not the people who were supposed to have killed her father. Angry Irish men were supposed to have. The blokes and the Irish men were on opposite sides. They were enemies. They fought each other over there in that place, in Northern Ireland. That was the fighting place they shared, and the blokes had come out of that place here to Dorset to claim her father for themselves. They thought his death belonged to them, so it belonged to that fighting place across the sea, and Bec didn't like that. The blokes surrounded her family. Her mother looked beautiful in black, and the blokes were afraid of beauty; it was too strong for them, it made them shy. But Ritchie, who'd cut his hair and become kinder and more gentle since their father's death, was fascinated by the closeness of the Marines. He seemed to find it easy to talk to them, and they to him, and

Bec saw that her brother could easily become a bloke. When the earth first hit the top of the coffin, she felt its hollowness, that it was a wooden box with her father in it, in a way she hadn't when the Marines had carried it on their shoulders. For a moment the hope rose up in her that sometimes death might not be the last thing that happened, not to everyone. That some people might live for a bit, then die, then live some more. Why not? But she already knew that this couldn't be.

By the time she was at university she knew much more about the sort of things her father and the blokes did. In the library her mind would bite most cleanly into her studies when she could bring her dreams to bear on what she read, and her memories would bind to the nubs of learning on the page. When she first studied the life cycle of the parasite that causes malaria, she thought how brave the parasites were, dropped from a mosquito into the vast, hostile, unknown territory of the human body, hiding out in the liver for days, disguising themselves to pass for human and bluffing their way past the phages standing guard on their way to the heart. How dangerous and difficult the parasites' journey to the heart was, through the heart and into the lungs, paddling upstream, against the flow of blood. If they made it to their target, they would begin their work, and this great, powerful, infinitely complex regime they had infiltrated, this human body, would sicken and perhaps be destroyed. The parasites killed the world around them; but their aim was not to kill. Their aim was only to live, and to multiply.

42

A demonic shape tore into the lamplight when Ritchie's fingertips were stinging from a Joey Santiago riff and he half-fell,
half-jumped from his chair. He screamed, clenching his bowels,
shielding himself with his guitar, but the beast was everywhere
at once, on the ceiling, on the floor, on every wall, with
carnivore eyes and a beak like a dagger. Ritchie couldn't tell
where wing ended and shadow began. Just as he began to
understand that a giant bird had entered his sanctuary he
screamed again and pushed his back against the door, pressing
the guitar sound box to his loins. Behind the bird, by the open
window, was its devil master, in the shape of a man, with skin
mottled black and pink, staring at him.

Ritchie stopped screaming, squeezed two tears out of his
eyes and sank to his haunches. Fear became anger and he raised
his guitar by the neck and with a marvellous splintering sound
smashed it on the floor: his first.

'Rock and roll,' said Ritchie's father. 'You make too much
noise. Now your mother's going to come. I wanted to talk
to you.' He looked over to where the terrified heron was
hiding in the corner, went to it and broke its neck. He tucked
the dead bird under his arm and stepped onto the window
ledge.

'Tell Bec I let the heron go,' he said. 'Look after the women. We'll talk when I get back.' And he dropped out of sight.

On the plane to Dublin twenty-five years later the death of the heron came to Ritchie, as he had enriched it over the years, half-knowingly. There were two things he knew that Bec didn't know whose secrecy pleased him. One was that his school had cost twice as much as Bec's. The other was that his father had killed the heron. Nothing he'd seen his father do and nothing he'd heard him say had impressed him like the calmness and lightness with which his father had wrung the bird's neck at exactly the moment when its continued survival became an embarrassment. It seemed to Ritchie that you could read thousands of books and never get such a lesson in that kind of beautiful rightness, the manliness and dignity of a moment when generosity turns perfectly to ruthlessness. At that moment, the act justifies itself; but a moment too early and it is cruelty, a moment too late and it is weakness.

In the arrivals hall of Dublin airport Ritchie dialled the number he'd been given and met a red-faced man who looked old for the gel in his short, spiked hair. Mike worked with Colum O'Donabháin at the community centre. He led Ritchie to a car with the first blush of rust on its wheel arches.

'Not got your camera?' Mike said as they got in. The car smelled of dogs.

'I explained in my letters,' said Ritchie. 'I thought the first time it would be better to keep it one on one.'

'When you see the documentaries, that's the big moment, isn't it? When they meet for the first time.' Mike offered Ritchie a cigarette and lit up. 'This is a hard day for you, Mr Shepherd.' He opened the window and blew smoke out into the damp air. 'Listen to me talking. What the fuck do I know about making films, now? I love the documentaries, though.'

Ritchie had left it till a fortnight before he was due to meet O'Donabháin to consider the professional help he'd need to make his first film. By the time he realised that six years' experience making studio-based entertainment TV for a national network was thin preparation for going out into the world and capturing a story, it was too late. He'd had time to lunch a couple of directors, thinking he might take one of them along, but hadn't trusted them. They'd been too eager. They asked what there was in the way of Shepherd family videos. They'd wanted to make the film their own.

'Are we going?' he said. O'Donabháin's friend had put the keys in the ignition but not switched on the engine. He sat back smoking. The windows were steaming up. *Was he a terrorist too?* thought Ritchie. *Is he still?*

'I've known Colum O'Donabháin twenty years,' said Mike. 'I don't know you. You've got to look after yourself, and I've got to watch out for him. So I have to ask. It's not revenge you're after, is it?'

'No,' said Ritchie. 'I explained it in my letters.'

'Not wanting to humiliate him, or put him on trial again?'

'No.'

Mike started the car and drove off. 'North Dublin. It's handy for the airport,' he said and laughed. 'The probation fellows, they think he's a success story.'

'Really?'

'Working in the community centre, looking after his mum, writing the old poems. They think he's a success, the bloody fools.'

'He's not rehabilitated?'

'Oh, he's habilitated all right. He's habilitated all to hell. Did you read any of the poems?'

'Not yet,' said Ritchie. He'd taken a look, but they hadn't made sense to him. There'd been nothing in there about killing people, as far as he could tell; plenty about mothers and the seashore.

'Here,' said Mike. He opened the glove compartment, took out a thin book and gave it to Ritchie, who recognised the manila cover, the woodprint of a gull and the title, *Surrender*. The book had a bus ticket sticking out of it. Ritchie opened it at the marked place and saw a poem called 'The Clapper'.

'Colum said to make sure you read that one before you met him,' said Mike.

The Clapper

Heavy in my pocket, cold warmed by my hand
It was with me at the fair
I had it by me tea and dinnertime
It had no place to be at night,
While I was sleeping, there it lay somewhere
Sleeping well, thanks.
You couldn't say it was a handsome thing.
Sure though, it did belong to me.
I thought no more of hiding it
Than throwing it away.
Twenty Rothmans, that was what
The woman at the counter shouting
'Mary, mother of God!

Dear sweet Jesus
Satan!
The boy is carrying a clapper!'
I ran out of McGinty's News and Tobacco
The sky was bronze.
Bell-bronze, from Parnell Road to Ballybough.
The sky began to ring.
Since then I've known its whereabouts
No sleep, no sleep, the clapper jings the sky.

Ritchie closed the book and put it on the dashboard. They'd come off the motorway and were driving through a council estate.

'What did you make of it?' said Mike.

'I didn't understand it,' said Ritchie.

'That's two of us, then,' said Mike. 'He's proud of that book, mind you, so don't tell him.'

They parked outside a whitewashed two-storey council semi. Mike got out. Ritchie couldn't move. His heart had begun to beat rapidly when the car stopped and he was struck with horror and surprise that he had deliberately put himself in this position. Only now that he was about to meet the man who killed his father did he realise his imagination had always seen it as if it was in a finished film, where O'Donabháin was alone and Ritchie had the camera, the film editor and the audience on his side. In those imagined meetings anything Ritchie didn't like had been edited out.

Until this moment his father's death had seemed like something he, Ritchie, had inherited. Now he saw that it still belonged to his father, that his father shared ownership with O'Donabháin, and that Ritchie couldn't simply turn up and take possession of it from his father's executioner. He, Ritchie, was only the son and heir; O'Donabháin had been there.

Mike leaned down and looked into the car. 'This is the house,' he said. 'You're expected.'

Ritchie got out of the car, wondering if Mike could tell he was trembling. A group of teenagers opposite watched him and spoke and laughed among themselves.

Ritchie followed Mike up the flagstones to the patterned glass door and rang the bell. They heard slippered feet creak up, a blurry shape materialised behind the swirls in the glass, and the door opened. O'Donabháin's old mother, in a v-necked sweater over her dress, glanced at Mike and Ritchie and stood back against the side of the stairs, gesturing down the hall. *She should be begging my forgiveness for giving birth to a monster*, Ritchie thought, but he only saw loathing on her face.

Colum O'Donabháin was standing in the low-ceilinged living room by the flames of a fake coal fire, in front of a blue velour armchair, his hands by his sides. There was a clean glass ashtray on the coffee table and a pile of half a dozen slim paperbacks combed through with coloured Post-it markers. The contrast between the dimness of the room and the brightness of grey daylight through the picture windows behind O'Donabháin made it difficult to see his face.

Mike introduced them, growing more nervous as he looked from one man to another; they stood still and stared. He finished and waited.

'Will you take a seat, Mr Shepherd,' said O'Donabháin, waving to a sofa with a tasselled cover facing the fire. Ritchie sat down at the end of the sofa furthest from O'Donabháin. He still had his raincoat on. O'Donabháin lifted a copy of a newspaper Ritchie didn't recognise, dense with print, from the armchair, dropped it on the floor and sat down.

'Is it all right to leave you two together now?' said Mike. Ritchie and O'Donabháin looked at him and O'Donabháin nodded. Mike went out, closing the door to the room, the draught excluder scratching over the synthetic fibres of the turquoise pile carpet. The latch clicked shut.

Ritchie and O'Donabháin sat without speaking for what seemed a long time. Ritchie glanced at O'Donabháin. O'Donabháin was looking into the fire. Ritchie's eyes had adjusted to the light. O'Donabháin was wearing an old taupe polo shirt, too tight for him, with a red collar.

O'Donabháin lifted his head and looked straight at Ritchie. 'How can I help you, Mr Shepherd?' he said. His voice was firm. *He thinks he is a priest, a judge*, thought Ritchie. There wasn't the humility Ritchie had expected O'Donabháin to feel, to pretend to feel. No sadness; no conscience. Ritchie stared at O'Donabháin's fat hands and thick forearms, bare and fuzzed with curling white hairs, still strong, and remembered his father's grin when he tantalised Ritchie with the beginning of a story, and Ritchie would shout 'Tell me, tell me!', and remembered the coroner's report, and knew that these were the hands that helped strip his father naked, these were the muscles that pulled the rope tying him to the chair so tight that his father bled from it. That was the hand that made a fist and punched his father two dozen times in the head, broke his jaw, knocked out five of his teeth and fractured his skull when he was bound, naked and helpless. 'Tell us! Tell us!' *It is the same hand. This is the same man*, thought Ritchie. Prison, poetry, age, it didn't mean anything. *It is the same man.* Those were the arms that tortured his father and those were the fingers that pressed a pistol to his temple and pulled the trigger and shot him dead.

Ritchie felt hate for O'Donabháin fill him, inflate him. His hate for O'Donabháin, his desire to see him literally crushed, his bones snapped and his flesh mashed and the remnants fed to pigs, became so strong so suddenly that he could hardly breathe. He stood up and turned his back to the man he had come to Ireland to visit, clenching his fists.

'Are you all right there, Mr Shepherd?' said O'Donabháin.

'I didn't think I was going to hate you so much,' said Ritchie slowly, not turning round.

'I did wonder if you were coming here with a notion to kill me,' said O'Donabháin. 'And I thought, "Why not? Let the boy have a go if he wants."'

Ritchie turned round, taking deep breaths. Seeing O'Donabháin looking up at him made him feel better. Perhaps O'Donabháin's eyes had widened a little.

'Of course then you wouldn't have had me to put in your film,' said O'Donabháin.

'Would you have resisted?' said Ritchie.

'If you'd tried to kill me? Oh certainly I would have resisted. I wouldn't want you to be in the pokey on account of bumping me off.'

Ritchie sat down, considered, began to speak, hesitated, and went on.

'I expected you to be different,' he said.

'How so?'

'You don't seem punished.'

'Beaten, you mean?'

'I mean what I said. Punished.'

'I've never known what that meant, to be honest. If you

mean humiliated, I was punished long before I was put away. The priests and the RUC and Long Kesh took care of that. If you mean "did society take its revenge?" I can't live in the north any more. I was in prison from the age of twenty-seven to the age of fifty-two. But then there's people whose idea of heaven's a little room with a bed and a TV and a pot to piss in.'

'That's not what I meant,' said Ritchie.

O'Donabháin looked into the fire and waited. 'You mean remorse,' he said.

Ritchie didn't say anything.

O'Donabháin looked Ritchie in the eye. 'I was fighting for a cause. Still believe in the cause. Not so much in the fighting. Your father and I, we were soldiers then.'

'He was a soldier. You were a torturer.'

'Your boys had them too. I was just an amateur.' He bent his head a little and Ritchie glimpsed something in O'Donabháin that was neither the defiance he'd seen when he met him nor the guilty torment he'd expected. The flood of hatred that had choked him ebbed.

'I was angry with your dad,' said O'Donabháin, his voice stronger, as if he were angry still. 'Having to play the fucking hero, just to protect a piece of scum who'd grassed up our cell in Derry and didn't worry about setting up a couple of RUC for us to take out two weeks later. He was playing both sides against the middle, and we knew that, and so did Captain Shepherd. The ratbag whose name he didn't give us wasn't worth it. It was like I was trying to help your father, and he wouldn't let me. You know sometimes you're pulling on some-thing and it won't come loose, and you go mental, and you lay about you and damage everything? It was an operation.

I was trying to get the truth out of someone, like pulling a tooth, and it wouldn't come. I forgot there was a man there for a moment.'

Ritchie was leaning forward, his hands squeezing the edge of the sofa cushion.

'We weren't ready, the three of us. We weren't ready on any level. None of us had ever interrogated anyone before. None of us had met anyone like your father before. Where would a bunch of Taigs ever sit at the same table as an English toff who'd been to private school and Cambridge?'

'Oxford,' said Ritchie. His mouth was dry.

O'Donabháin took a deep breath. 'What I'm saying is, if we hadn't abducted him, we wouldn't have met him socially.'

'Do you have nightmares about it?' said Ritchie.

'No. That wasn't the answer you were looking for, was it?' O'Donabháin folded his arms and looked up at the ceiling, then leaned towards Ritchie, speaking quietly again.

'Before we took him, when I knew what we were going to do, a guy lent me this film on cassette. It was a French film about the Resistance – *Army in the Shadows*, do you know it? There's a scene in it where these Resistance fellows, one of them's grassed the others up, so they take him to this house, and they have to get rid of him. But none of them has ever done anything like it before. They end up discussing it in front of the man they're about to top off, and he's got to sit there and listen.' O'Donabháin gripped the ends of the armrests of the chair and shook his head. Was he teary? Ritchie couldn't tell.

'It was twenty-five years ago,' O'Donabháin said. 'The man I was then, he's a stranger to me.'

His eyes were dry, Ritchie saw, but the thought that they

might not have been showed Ritchie the possibility again of something in Colum O'Donabháin that he could reach out to and hold. *If the man had wept*, Ritchie thought, *I would have gone over to him and put a hand on his shoulder.*

'Did you read the poem?' said Colum.

'Yes,' said Ritchie.

'What did you think?'

'Interesting.'

Colum shook his head. 'You can carry out an action,' he said, 'a bad action, and know you've done it, but nobody else knows, it's private. And the thing about being exposed isn't just that everyone knows what you've done. It's that you don't really know what you've done until you know that everyone else knows. When I went into that newsagent, I knew that two days before, I'd beaten a man up and done him in. But it was only when I saw the headlines in the papers that I knew what I'd really done.'

'I know what you mean,' said Ritchie.

'Do you?' said Colum, looking at Ritchie in surprise.

Ritchie blushed and licked his lips. 'I'd like to make this film,' he said slowly. 'I can't offer you any money, of course.' He understood what he'd seen in Colum. 'I can offer you forgiveness.'

'Do you think I want that?' said Colum.

'Yes,' said Ritchie. The more the word 'forgiveness' settled in his mind, the more it eased him.

'D'you think you have it in your power to forgive me?'

'If not me, who?'

'Your father can't,' said Colum. 'That leaves God.' He cocked his head and looked down at the carpet. 'What a brave foolish man your father was. He never asked us not to kill him, and

303

you know,' he looked up at Ritchie, and again Ritchie had the uncomfortable feeling that Colum and his father had been intimates '– if he'd just given us the name we wanted, we might have let him go. He never saw our faces.'

'Would you be prepared to talk to me like this on camera?' said Ritchie.

'We were talking about forgiveness,' said Colum.

'That's what I can offer you.'

'Ah but it shouldn't be a bargain, should it? Would you not forgive me unless I was in your film?'

Forgiving Colum in any circumstances seemed like cool water Ritchie could drink in a dry place. 'I do,' he said, and saying it gave a sense of contentment that amazed him. He stood up, walked over to Colum and held out his hand. 'I forgive you,' he said. 'I forgive you, Colum.'

Colum didn't get up, but put his hand in Ritchie's. Ritchie squeezed it and shook. *I am doing this*, he thought. *This is real. I am forgiving my father's killer. I am doing a good thing. I am holding the hand that killed my father.*

Colum let go and Ritchie sat on the arm of the sofa closest to him. 'The film would be about an hour and a half long,' he said. 'You and me talking; you being interviewed; me being interviewed; archive footage. We'd have to restage this first meeting.'

'What about your mother?' said Colum.

'What about her?'

'What about your sister?'

'What about her?'

'We didn't take anything except his weapon,' said Colum. 'Your father's. We didn't take his wallet or what was in it. We had a look inside. There was a picture of the four of you, the family. I was surprised to find it there, with him being under-cover. It wouldn't be right to do this without your father's wife and daughter.'

'Maybe they aren't ready yet.'

'I don't mind waiting.'

'Maybe they'll never forgive you.'

'Then there won't be a film.'

Ritchie lifted his thumbnail and bit it.

'What was the last thing he said?' he asked.

'He said, when he knew it was coming, he said: "Tell them I wasn't frightened in the end."'

'And then you shot him?' Tears suddenly oozed out of Ritchie's eyes.

'Yes.'

'What did you say before you shot him?'

'I didn't say anything. I just pressed the gun into the side of his head and shot him.'

43

Late in the afternoon, in the porch outside the kitchen of Bec's villa, Batini chopped onions and aubergines for the evening meal. She'd mopped the floors, changed the bedding and handed over the dirty sheets to the laundry truck, and then she'd sharpened the knives. From the front yard round the corner she heard a dog whimper as it yawned and the clang of the door set in the main gate of the compound. She recognised her sister's footsteps shuffling across the yard and Zuri came round the corner and greeted her.

'Go on cooking,' said Zuri in Swahili, waving at Batini when the greetings were over. 'I'll make us some tea. I couldn't call, I've no credit. What are you making?'

'Curry.'

'Where'd you learn that?'

'The old housekeeper.'

'Do they like that, then?'

'One of them is Pakistani from England.' She shrugged. 'The English English like it too.'

Zuri wrinkled her nose and sat down with a sudden exhalation of exhaustion on a stool at the corner of the table. She wobbled the table from side to side contemptuously and pinned it in place with her powerful elbow.

'You should get your husband to fix that,' she said. 'Where is he?'

'Looking for work. The Chinese opened a factory.'

'Do you have any of those biscuits? Why can't he get a job here? Drive one of their cars?'

'He doesn't know how. They need a driver, too. They've got anyone driving cars, even her.' She put the kettle on and threw the chopped vegetables in a wide shallow pan.

Zuri took a paper twist of pumpkin seeds out of the plastic bag she was carrying and began to eat them, spitting out the husks. 'I thought she was blind,' she said.

'Not all the time,' said Batini uncertainly.

'Doesn't she have a man these days?'

'Alex,' said Batini. She laughed. 'He's just visiting.' She turned away from stir-frying. 'He keeps trying to help me with the washing up.' She covered her mouth with her apron and doubled up laughing. Zuri increased her seed-processing rate.

'He has a huge nose like a beak,' said Batini.

'Don't let the food burn.'

Batini went back to frying. 'I hear them. They're in the room above me.'

'Heh.' Zuri was knowing. 'And she's thirty-three, and no husband, and no children? And I suppose he's got no wife and no children either? How old is he?'

'Older. Forty at least.'

Zuri shook her head. 'What's wrong with them? Is it something about the climate there?'

Batini switched off the gas, folded her arms and stood over Zuri. 'I like Bec,' she said. 'She doesn't need to have children. Why should she? She has a house of her own and a big salary.

I'd like to live like that. Why not?' She put her hand on her belly and gestured with the other. 'I say to my husband "Where's the condom?" and he says "You want me to wear one of them, you get the condom," and I say "You're the man, you wear it so you get it, you get your own underpants and your own t-shirts and you wear them, why should I choose your condoms?" Of course he never has any.'

Zuri inclined her head to one side and lifted her eyes to the sky until Batini stopped talking and relit the burners.

'Well, you're pregnant now,' Zuri said with satisfaction, and after a moment, while Batini scraped angrily at the bottom of the pan, said: 'You're very nice about her when her vaccine doesn't seem to work.'

'She never said it would protect completely,' said Batini. There was a sharp hiss from the pan as tears splashed into the hot oil. She wiped her nose with the back of her hand and sniffed. 'I don't want to think about Huru now.'

A crash of metal against metal and breaking glass came from the street outside. There were shouts and screams and the continuous blare of a horn. Batini and Zuri ran to the gate and saw that one of the vaccine project's big white Toyotas had smashed head-on into the wall of a neighbouring villa. Bec was still gripping the wheel. She was saying 'Sorry, sorry,' over and over. Two doctors were trying to open the back doors to get out and in the seat next to Bec, Alex was slumped forward, forehead on the dashboard.

44

The failure of Bec's vision was sudden, extreme and short-lived. Her eyesight was good when she was slowing down to drive into the compound; completely gone just before the car hit the wall; and almost back to normal a few seconds later, when she turned to the passenger seat to see Alex not moving, blood creeping busily across the thundercloud-coloured plastic. *There isn't much blood*, thought Bec. Then she thought: *I've killed him.* She put her hand on his shoulder.

'Is he dead?' she said. Haji had already got out of the back and was peering at the side of Alex's head when Bec shouted that they had to help him. She had both hands on his shoulder, feeling that she must carry out some action, push, pull, support. She had the wild thought that the warmth of her touch might bring him back to life and at the same time a strange remote voice inside her was saying *So, Bec, you're responsible for the death of Alex; nothing but remorse from here on in.*

She felt him sigh and shift and he said, distinctly, 'Ow.'

'Oh thank God,' said Bec.

'Careful, young man,' said Haji, who to Bec's astonishment didn't seem surprised that her lover had come back from the dead. Alex lifted his head off the sticky dashboard. Bec's first impression was that his face was destroyed, and the horror of this made her calm and she pulled wet wipes from a dispenser and began to clean his face and saw that it wasn't as bad as it looked. Haji held her wrist and said she should wait and asked Alex how he was feeling.

'How are you feeling?' said Bec, as if she'd said it first. A crowd had formed around the car; it was the most thrilling entertainment the younger children had seen.

'That *gregi*,' said Alex groggily, leaning back. 'It finds its way to stick it to you.'

'I'm sorry. I'm sorry,' said Bec.

Haji fixed him up in the kitchen with three stitches. Batini, Zuri and Bec watched Haji run the needle and thread through the skin of Alex's forehead and cover the wound with gauze, lint and tape. When it was finished and the doctor stepped back and Alex grinned at Bec, one eyebrow crinkling the edge of the tape, she stopped biting her lip.

'Sorry,' she croaked, feeling small in the shadow of the enormity of her selfishness.

'I should've worn the seatbelt,' said Alex.

'I could have killed you,' said Bec.

Her attachment to her internal colony of haemoproteus had never seemed so sentimental. It seemed childish, the indulgence of a woman who'd gorged on freedom. It occurred to her for how harsh her father would have been towards anyone who put the group in danger in order to commemorate one who'd fallen.

That night she shook the bottle of anti-parasitics in Alex's face and told him she was going to start taking them. But she didn't start that night, and she didn't start the next day, when Alex flew home. She intended to, but didn't, all through the winding up of the trial, and when she moved back to London at the beginning of February, and Alex began to live with her in her flat, the seal on the bottle was still not broken.

Only two weeks passed between Alex leaving Tanzania and Bec moving back to London, but it seemed a desert to Alex, who missed her badly and had been deprived of his usual refuge of sub-microscopic flânerie by his new job and the conclusion of his chronase complex work. He shuttled between the dreary Byzantium of the Belford Institute, where, he discovered, the leader of one faction had reorganised his research group into an attack team tasked solely with discrediting the work of his American rivals, and Citron Square, where Harry was fading peevishly away, complaining of neglect and demanding to be left in peace.

It left time for Alex to brood and to build the epic thoughts that put him and Bec and the child they would have in the same narrative as the billion-year past and future of life and earth. Pedalling at high speed and singing across London, making his Belford colleagues suck air through their teeth with his teaspoon drum breaks on the rims of coffee mugs, he would be weaving visions together, the vision of a small, specific mittened hand, his daughter's, held in his at the zoo, while he explained each animal's strong and weak points to her, and the vision of a limitless cloud of human beings floating towards an eternally setting sun, like dandelion seeds carried on the wind, as if the two visions were the same picture.

Since moving from Imperial College to the Belford Alex had been struck by the fecundity of scientists who seemed less in tune with the rhythm of life than him, awkward, inarticulate, lumpy, unfit, plodding; men and women whom he felt should be less likely to be favoured by nature the bouncer than he was, yet who had children, two, three, five, who belonged. Perhaps, he thought, it wasn't given to him to belong, and when he died, his chronase clock would stop forever. But he had been given another chance with Bec to prove that this was not the case.

Alex saw that there were obstacles. He saw that Bec, who took contraceptive pills, might not want to have children; that they might not conceive; that she might feel it was too soon. He was wary. He remembered difficult conversations with Maria. He didn't know how to bring it up.

In February, a few weeks after Bec returned to London and Alex moved in with her, they took Harry to Scotland for the seventieth birthday of his brother Lewis, Alex's father. On the eve of their flight north Alex came home from the institute to find Bec on the floor of the living room next to a large box marked with the Apple logo. She sat cross-legged on the laminate surface in black leggings and a Norwegian jumper, trying to fix together two sheets of candy-striped wrapping paper. Through the French windows behind her the last blue light before darkness showed the rusted barbecue and rotted hammock in the backyard.

Two days earlier they'd bought Lewis an antique globe as a birthday present. Alex got down on his knees beside Bec and twisted his head to read the specs of the laptop the box apparently contained. 'That's quite a stocking filler for my old dad,' he said.

Bec lifted the box, slid the doubled paper under it, wrapped it round and began fixing it with tape. 'It's for Batini,' she said. 'She sent a message asking me to get her a laptop. She's going to do a course. They have fast Internet in Dar now.'

Alex held the folds of gift wrap in place at the ends of the box while Bec taped them down. She began unrolling a length of brown paper.

'Haji's in town,' she said. 'He's coming round later to pick it up. He'll take it back with him. Hand me the scissors.'

Alex tucked the handles of the scissors gently in Bec's palm. 'That's a lot of Mac for a small lap,' he said.

Bec stopped what she was doing and looked him in the eyes. 'Yeah, there's guilt,' she said. 'Her son died when she wasn't there to help. The boy's grandmother carried him ten miles over the hills in the middle of the night to get to the clinic but he was already gone when they got there. We vaccinated him and I told Batini it was a good thing, when it only made him half-immune. We keep telling people they have to go on covering their children at night and treating their nets, but if some group of big-shot international medics comes in with a vaccine and gives it to their kids they think, "Oh, they're protected now, I can save a few shillings on the permethrin." Wouldn't you?'

She faced Alex and bit her thumbnail. 'Since then she's married the brother of her dead husband and she's already pregnant by him. I spend six years and tens of thousands of pounds of other people's money getting a doctorate in parasitology, I trek around Papua New Guinea and find an unknown species, I persuade dozens of people to spend millions of pounds and years of their lives making a malaria vaccine and in the end I can't save Batini's boy. And in a few months' time, without an ounce of science, she has a baby. It's the oldest medicine there is. Lose a child, make a new one. Try to beat the malaria parasite at its own game. It reproduces, you reproduce back.'

'Let's, then,' said Alex.

'Oh,' said Bec, who hadn't intended to make that case, or any case. It hadn't occurred to her that in her musings about the irony of Batini's situation she might be Batini as well as Batini might be Batini. In being the knowing Englishwoman in Africa, conscientiously aware of the unclosable gulf between her and the Africans, she'd accidentally identified a way to close it.

'It's not replacement,' she said. 'People can't be replaced.'

Alex remembered how when he opened the fridge every morning he saw Bec's bottle of anti-parasitic drugs sitting in one of the door shelves, between the mustard and the mayonnaise, the seal still not broken.

'People find different ways of keeping the ones they loved among the living,' he said cautiously. 'Children. Memories. The names of things.'

'Are you doing that on purpose?' said Bec.

'What?'

'Touching that.' She pointed, and Alex realised he was scratching the small scar left from where he'd struck his head in the accident. He blushed and denied it.

'You and Maria gave it a good old go, didn't you,' said Bec.

'IVF, you know, it's not like going to the dentist.'

'Why do you want to have children so much?'

'We're not required to have reasons.'

'That's true,' said Bec. 'I told you I'll get rid of my haemoproteus, and I will. I'll start tomorrow. Just understand that it's not blocking anything. Not in a medical way. Not in any way.'

'Good.'

'Don't be jealous of it.'

'That would be stupid. Just because it was named after your father.'

'You're not required to have reasons for having children, you're right, but is there a reason?'

'I want us to belong,' said Alex.

'To what? Society?'

'To time.'

45

Alex's mother Maureen laid bricks in the garden on the morning her sons were due to arrive. She wanted a brick and turf bench, ready to plant with camomile for spring. She hurried with the trowel and the spirit level, on her knees in the balding grass, checking the sky. She'd mixed too much mortar. She hated to think of unused mortar hardening and having to be thrown away. The council didn't recycle it, like so many things. The week before, she'd biked all over Brechin trying to find a place to recycle a single watch battery and got the unheeding politeness dealt out to the harmless old. In the end she posted the battery to the Chinese company that made it, with suggestions for a better way of doing things. The postage cost five pounds.

She was full of ideas for better ways of doing things. The organisations she belonged to, the local Green Party, the Mearns Alliance for Justice in Sri Lanka, Paint Against Poverty and Women for Fairness in Farming tried to nominate her as their leader and send her to conferences. She declined. She wanted the world to be a weaponless sea-garden without borders, criss-crossed by railways, cycle paths and sailing ships, powered by modest numbers of wind turbines and solar panels, with a global network of small communes that would farm organically, hold festivals and exchange handicrafts. But when she imagined how this world might be imposed on the real one, on the actual human beings she knew, with all the weaknesses and prejudices that were the substance of their lives, she saw that bringing her utopia about would involve the very war, cruelty and misery it was supposed to end. All her life she'd been visited by guilt, about being fed while others went hungry, having gone to university while others couldn't go to school and indulging in travel to satisfy her curiosity. As a virtually atheist churchgoer with Gaian leanings she repented weekly of more human wickedness, itemised in *The Guardian*, *The Observer* and *The New Internationalist*, than a chapel full of Catholic sinners.

Lately it'd come to seem that there was something self-defeating in her guilt. She was long retired from her part-time job as a history teacher, and had hours to fill. Why not make the bench herself? But then wouldn't she deprive skilled local labourers of work? But if she hired people to do it, wasn't she feeding the consumerist-capitalist machine that was destroying life on earth? It was clear to Maureen that the best way to save the world's oceans, forests and wildlife was for human beings to die out altogether, but then who would be left to make gardens? There would be more whales, but who would praise them?

For Maureen the arrival of so many family members at once was a holiday. Her mind would be called away to her sons' obscure problems from the immediate issues that normally hemmed her in: the plight of the Palestinians, the suffering of women in Afghanistan, human rights in Eritrea. She'd been unable to sleep the night before, thinking about what would happen to the girl in the factory in China – she was sure it would be a girl, for some reason — when she opened the envelope with the battery and Maureen's note of complaint in English. Unable to understand it, the girl would seek help; would be forced by her supervisor to pay for a translation out of her own wages; would have to take a second job to pay off the resulting debts; would fall behind with the rent, break up with her husband, lose her children and either become a prostitute or throw herself into the glutinous, polluted river that surely flowed through the town. All this would be Maureen's fault.

Against this sort of everyday crisis of conscience her children's concerns struck her as distractingly exotic, like Alex's curious obsession with having a child, over which, it seemed, he'd broken up with the perfectly nice Maria. Bringing up Alex and Dougie had been fine, a way to be selflessly selfish; Maureen had liked having them around. But if she hadn't had any it would have been fine too. She knew childless men and women who floated through life on a boisterous raft of friends, nephews and nieces, and bechildrened couples who ached with purposelessness after their children left home. Alex wasn't lonely. He had friends, had sex, fell in love. Why, she wondered, did he want a baby so much? Maureen felt they should hand out medals to the childless. In the Soviet Union, she'd read, mothers who had ten or more children were given medals. Hero Mothers, they were called. What kind of a hero would Alex be? There was no word in English for a father or mother without children. They were like orphans in reverse.

Maureen didn't like to admit that her other son had problems. If Dougie did he had so many that they were his medium, his nourishment. It was Harry who was upset about what had happened to Dougie, when to her mind nothing could really be said to have *happened*.

Maureen laid the last brick in place, tapped it level with the handle of the trowel and scraped off the residue. She stood up, stepped back and realised she'd made a mistake in her design. She'd found the drawings in a book about medieval gardens and as she worked out where to put it, and began building it, she imagined two people sitting talking on the finished bench on a summer's day, like the courtly lovers depicted in the engraving in the book. One of the people was herself, her hands on the brick warmed by the sun, in the smell of flowers and the sound of bees. The other person, she realised now, was Harry, and after this week, he wouldn't be coming to their house any more. He would never sit with her on the bench she was making out of brick and earth and camomile.

She walked quickly to the house, managed to pull her gumboots off after several shaky tries and passed through the barking without paying any attention to the dog Erasmus, without paying attention to anything. She went upstairs and mounted the retractable steel ladder that led to the attic.

Lewis, sitting in front of a box camera, turned from the lens to see his wife emerge from the centre of the floor. He gripped the remote shutter mechanism and watched warily to see what she would do.

'They'll be here soon,' said Maureen. 'You should get ready.'

'In what does readiness consist?' asked Lewis.

'Your hands not smelling of chemicals.'

He saw how unpeaceful her face was, dropped the shutter cord and rolled in his chair to a workbench crowded with plastic flasks. He lifted one up and shook it. 'Recycled fixer,' he said encouragingly. 'Works as well as the old kind.' She stared at him, blinking, and withdrew.

Lewis rolled back to the white crosses painted on the floor marking his self-portrait position and bent to pick up the dropped shutter cord. He couldn't reach; he'd have to get out of the chair and go down on his knees to pick it up, and then how would he be able to stand?

The misery of the supermarket lay ahead. He liked peace and smallness and found it bearable to be what he'd been since his doctoring days ended, another of so terribly many white-haired old men in synthetic fleeces roaming the high street, performing archaic duties like posting letters and buying newspapers. He'd become a GP because he liked the idea of meeting patients alone, one at a time. Now he had to face the horror of his family as society. Harry would come with his noise and brightness, for the last time. His evangelical nephew Matthew would come with his wife and their army of children. His dreaming son Alex would come, bringing a new woman who sounded like some fiercely bright star. Harry's work on cancer seemed remote and glamorous to Lewis, even though he'd seen his share of oncological horrors, even though he'd once put a patient on one of Harry's trials, and the patient had lived long enough to get dementia. *No, not that*, he thought. A lifetime of general practice had shown Lewis that the true scourges of Scottish rural life were loneliness, back pain, sexual ennui, gluttony, drunkenness, sloth and infantilism.

And Dougie would come; but Dougie was all right, whatever Harry said.

For a long time everyone thought it was part of the game, for a bright, happy, lovable middle-class boy to go to university and do the opposite of what he was supposed to do. Everyone knew 'supposed to' wasn't really 'supposed to'. You pretended to believe you were supposed to study hard, be thrifty and plan for the future; you pretended to break those fictitious rules by missing classes, handing in essays late, going out on the lash, getting into debt and giving the impression that you only lived for the moment. A show of rebelliousness was expected before you quietly acknowledged that you were, after all, supposed to do the things you'd pretended to believe you were supposed to do. Two terms passed before anyone realised that Dougie's rebelliousness was genuine. He really was doing no work, even though he was consuming crime thrillers at the rate of five a week, when he was supposed to be studying philosophy. He really had spent all his money, and borrowed heavily. He was an actual outsider; not an outsider who has a tight, loyal group of outsider friends but an outsider who has no friends at all. No friends, that is, at Edinburgh university. Only after he dropped out, got a girl pregnant – she had an abortion – moved to Glasgow, got a job as a postman, had a child, had another child by another woman, married her and separated did he acquire friends who would stand by him and swear he was a good lad.

For Harry, this meant that something had happened. Something had gone wrong. He was an Enlightenment man, a believer in equality and meritocracy. He wanted to see the clever poor get a leg-up into university and the brightest of the middle classes barge aside the dullard children of the rich. It had never occurred to him that equality and meritocracy might mean his own nephew becoming a postman.

'I believe in social mobility,' he said. 'But only up, not down.'

Maureen said Dougie was still the same man. The world

needed letters to be delivered, and there was no shame in being a postman. It was a useful job. If the world really was going to be a more equal place finishing university wouldn't be a heritable thing. Dougie, Maureen said, might not have made it as a husband, but he was a success as a father. He loved his daughters.

But Dougie undermined her. He was so sure that everyone in the family thought he was a failure that it made him confident. His certainty that nobody cared what he said or did meant he felt free to say and do what he liked, not thinking anyone could be hurt by it.

46

It was drizzling when Alex, Bec and Harry arrived at Lewis and Maureen's place, in a rented car from Aberdeen airport. The fine drops settled on them like an aerosol and Bec's shoes sank into the luxuriously large gravel chips of the drive, shining like beach pebbles. The old house sat at the top of a lawn sloping down to the road, surrounded by rhododendrons and Scots pines. It was made of blocks of grey stone and the window glass was black and lifeless. Alex opened the front door and they went into the tiled porch, where there were lines of boots and coats, a sack of potatoes, a portable generator, a reproduction of Leonardo's Vitruvian Man, chilliness and silence. The inner door opened and warmth, sounds and smells came to meet them: Alex's parents, the bark of a red setter, its paws on the guests' bellies, swishing its tail, clacking its claws on the tiles and panting round their ankles.

There was a smell of chicken stock and resiny smoke and from a doorway off the hall Bec heard the snap of pine logs burning. She kneeled down and plunged her hands into the lush hair around the dog's neck.

'Harry's asleep in the car,' said Alex. 'He started pointing out the places we used to go for walks and it tired him out, I think.'

'Oh!' said Maureen, trotting away to see to him.

Harry was put to bed and Alex set off for Montrose to pick up Dougie, who was coming from Glasgow, and Rose, who was coming ahead of the rest of her family. Lewis and Maureen went for groceries. Bec found herself alone in the room she would be sharing with Alex.

A black and white photograph of nineteenth-century ancestors hung on one wall. A yielding lilac carpet absorbed her footsteps and muffled the creaks of the floorboards underneath. There was a smell of burnt dust and potpourri. Stuck to the back of the door was a hand-drawn evacuation plan with instructions to BANG GONG IN EMERGENCY. Bec looked round and saw a dinner gong on the chest of drawers. She tapped it with her fingernail and the sound shimmered out across the room and lingered. On one side of the bed, next to the lamp, was a candle in a holder and a box of matches. On the other side, resting by an alarm clock, was an old-fashioned policeman's truncheon with a leather wrist strap. Bec picked it up. Her fingers fitted into the grooves on the grip and she felt its weight. She looked over her shoulder. The door was half open. Harry was sleeping on the other side of the house. She'd heard the cars leaving with Alex, Maureen and Lewis in them. The last time she'd seen the dog Erasmus he was settling down on a blanket by the fire.

Bec went over to the gong, drew back her hand and whacked it with the truncheon, so hard that it fell off the chest of drawers. From out in the hallway, she heard a series of thumps and somebody swearing. She went into the hall and reached the top of the stairs to see a man in a shiny suit getting up from where he'd fallen on the landing. He looked up at her. He had piles of long, slightly greasy blond hair coming down over his collar. The colour in his eyes was a startlingly opaque turquoise.

'Amazons with clubs,' he said. 'This is too much for the folks to have organised.'

Bec realised that she had the truncheon held above her shoulder. She lowered it. 'Are you OK?' she said. 'I felt like banging the gong.'

'You banged it, love. You banged that gong. I'm Dougie, by the way. The folks probably haven't mentioned us. I'm their son, the unsuccessful one. Who are you?'

The way he looked directly into her eyes made her uncomfortable and she looked away. Dougie's suit was made of synthetic, slightly reflective silver-grey material. The edges of the lapels were frayed. His yellow shirt had the top two buttons undone and the points of the collar disappeared into his blond locks.

'Alex went to pick you up,' she said. 'I should tell him you're here.' She went to the bedroom to fetch her phone and Dougie followed her in and sat on the bed while she made the call.

'I wasn't expecting to get picked up,' said Dougie. There was something about the way he widened his eyes as he said it that reminded Bec of certain boys in her primary school when they were explaining to the teacher that they hadn't done anything wrong.

'He's on his way,' she said.

'I'm gasping for a fag,' said Dougie. 'So're you a doctor, like?'

'I'm a medical researcher.'

'One of the brainy ones.'

'Didn't Alex tell you we were going out? We've been living together for two months.'

'I thought he was seeing some lassie in Africa. Oh, that's you? Oh!' Dougie laughed. It was an involving sound and Bec laughed with him. 'Could've put my foot in it there, eh? I tell you what, the two of you, you're like some crimefighting couple out the comics, out of Hollywood. Only with germs instead of criminals. Good on you. I could never . . .' Dougie shook his head and slapped his forehead. He took a pack of Silk Cut out of his pocket and offered one to Bec, who refused.

'Don't they mind you smoking in the house?' said Bec.

'Aye, you're right.' He looked down at the cigarette turning between his fingers, sullen for a moment, then brightened. 'D'you fancy a pint in town? There's a no bad wee place.'

'I'd better not,' said Bec.

Dougie stood up and went on talking with the unlit cigarette in his mouth, gesturing with a plastic lighter. 'I'll bet they never offered you a drink, eh? They're decent people, the folks, but they've got an English sense of hospitality.'

He led Bec to the sitting room and spent time with her choosing a bottle from the drinks cupboard. Each time she told him that it didn't matter, or said yes, that a bottle would be perfect, he'd suggest a different combination. They went outside in the end with a carton of orange juice, two tumblers, a bottle of vodka, a spoon and a bowl of ice and laid them on a garden bench.

The brothers were tall, the same height; Dougie had more brawn, more shoulder. The nose looked as if it had been broken. When he spoke, he flicked his hair back and shifted his weight from foot to foot. When it was Bec's turn he became still. It was hard to believe Dougie and Alex were related, and hard to understand how two brothers who'd been born a few years apart and gone to the same local schools ended up with such different accents. Alex's had a slight lilt, and he rolled his r's, but otherwise there wasn't much to distinguish it from her own southern English accent. With Dougie, Bec had to concentrate to understand him.

'My brother was into being part of the ruling class,' said Dougie. 'I was never into that. I'm more like a man of the people. No offence, but you make your choices. My family's part of the whole colonial set-up here.'

'Is there a colonial set-up here?'

'Oh aye. I'm no saying anything against them, they're good people. And you're a good person, I can see that. I'm no like a revolutionary or a nationalist or anything, I'm no bright enough for that. I'm just saying Alex the genius and the prophet Matthew and the folks: I'm no the equal of them, and they're no the equal of me. There's places I go that they can't, and vice versa.'

'What sorts of places can you go to that they can't?' asked Bec.

'Bad places,' said Dougie. 'Are you sure you're no wanting a fag?'

'I shouldn't,' said Bec. She'd quit when she was twenty.

'You want one,' said Dougie. He slipped a cigarette between her lips and lit it and Bec took a couple of draws.

A car turned into the drive and she dropped the cigarette and put her foot over it. For no reason she could understand she felt as if she'd done something wrong that she didn't want Alex to know about.

'He's been a postman in Glasgow for fifteen years, but he started speaking like that as soon as he moved there,' said Alex later. 'It's artificial. He put it on and it stuck.'

Alex hadn't told Bec that he'd cleared his brother's debts

and saved him from having his flat repossessed. She didn't seem interested in how much money Alex had. When he moved in with her he offered to pay rent; she grinned and said 'All right.'

He hadn't meant to make his brother a gift of the money, and when, after two refusals, Dougie accepted it, he promised to pay it back. Now Alex saw how unlikely it was that Dougie would ever be able to do that on a postman's salary, with two young children by two different, estranged mothers, both of whom were supposed to be getting maintenance from him. Alex knew he could tell Dougie not to worry, turn it into a gift. Sometimes he thought he would. But then what would stop Dougie going back to the bookies, the loan sharks and the dodgy schemes? So the debt lingered, its existence known to no one except the creditor and the debtor.

Throughout the evening meal Dougie caught Bec's eye, trying to make her laugh. When Bec and Alex went to bed Dougie winked at them and started singing Get It On, empha-sising *bang a gong* by miming ski poles and rocking his head as if it were loose.

Later, Bec came out of the bathroom in a t-shirt and stood over the naked Alex. He raised his hand and touched her. Bec lifted the truncheon and felt its weight and length. She'd never had anything inside her except men and her own fingers; never bought a toy, afraid it might diminish the real thing, for which her friends teased her. The truncheon was smooth, heavy, made of some black hardwood.

'Am I competing with that?' said Alex.

'Oh now,' said Bec, putting it down and taking Alex in her hand. 'It's a cold, dead, nasty thing, and you're alive.'

Later they lay naked and contrariwise on top of the covers,

almost falling off the bed, Alex with his tongue between Bec's legs and Bec with his cock between her lips, and the door opened. They heard a girl's voice say 'Sorry!' and the door closed. Between the opening and the closing of the door it seemed to Bec that there was a long pause, as if whatever shock Rose had experienced at seeing her uncle and acting-aunt in a mutually devouring six and nine in her grandparents' guest room was overmastered by curiosity.

47

Next morning, as a birthday treat, Lewis was left alone in the attic while the others went mushroom hunting. It was February, but mild, and Maureen said she knew a place where blewits had appeared the week before. They walked into the woods with Erasmus galloping ahead, Maureen walking arm-in-arm with her brother-in-law. A lukewarm white sun made the moisture glint in the mud on the track and layers of decayed brown leaves squelched under their feet like seaweed. Dougie clipped a leash on the dog and the two of them dragged each other forward; Dougie hoisting Erasmus off scented fascinations in the undergrowth, Erasmus jerking him violently ahead in revenge.

Alex trudged alongside man and dog, cast into gloom, for some reason, by the sight that morning of Bec's still-sealed bottle of anti-parasitics in her open toilet bag.

'Like old times, eh,' said Dougie. 'You and me out with Uncle Harry. Hot on the trail of the secrets of the universe.'

'Harry won't be coming here after this. We're Harry now, you and me and Matthew. Where's the new young Alex and Dougie?'

'Christ, a new young Dougie, that'd bum my betters out.'

'You couldn't bring your kids here, I haven't got any, and

Matthew's teaching his that God made the Earth in seven days. It's like the Enlightenment's coming to an end, right here in Brechin.'

'It's incredible,' said Dougie.

'Yes,' said Alex, with passion.

'It's incredible how you sound like Harry.'

Rose matched Bec's pace and the two of them fell out of earshot of the others. Rose's hair was tucked into a snood and she was wearing a long dress under her waterproof jacket. Her costume made her look, thought Bec, like a young Hasidic Jewish woman. Up ahead, she saw the brothers talking, Dougie struggling to control Erasmus. She saw Alex's hands come up and describe a circle in the air and his mouth opening and closing.

And the human cell is like a world in itself . . . she subtitled.

'I saw you and Uncle Alex last night,' said Rose without looking at Bec, her balled fists pushing her pockets out.

'Did you?' said Bec. 'I thought I heard someone come in.'

'I opened the wrong door by mistake. Aren't you afraid you'll go to hell?' Rose turned. Her eyes were narrow with anxiety.

'Why should I go to hell?' said Bec.

'For fornicating with Uncle Alex.' Rose stopped and faced Bec. There was something knowingly provocative about her. 'I see why you and Uncle Alex got together,' she said. 'You've got this idea there's no good and evil, it's all *oh it depends how you look at it*, bleh bleh bleh. I don't understand how you could have been out in the world and got by so long without getting into trouble. The Evil One must have something terrible planned for you.'

'There's no Evil One,' said Bec.

'Huh! I've seen him.'

'Really?'

'In dreams, I mean,' said Rose hastily, as if apologising for implying that she knew a celebrity personally. 'He's big as a house, with eyes like traffic lights stuck on red and claws like knives and a necklace made from skulls of little kids.' Her eyes were fixed on the middle distance and the words flowed easily. 'There's no other way to stop people sinning and being cruel and messing stuff up. They're too greedy and nasty to do what God tells them if they aren't afraid of hell. You should be afraid. If you go to hell when you die they cut your fingers and toes off one by one, and they take your skin off with a rusty knife, and they lower you into a lake of boiling salt —'

'Rose, stop,' said Bec, putting her hands on her shoulders and shaking her gently. Rose stopped talking and marched on up the track with her head and shoulders bowed. Bec walked beside her, trying to remember if she listened to her mother when she was sixteen. And if not, what did *bringing up children* mean?

'Anyway, you had a good long look,' she said. 'It must have been an interesting sight.'

'He's a lot older than you,' said Rose absently.

'Do you think seven years is a lot?'

'Yeah!' said Rose, spreading the vowels over three notes, up-down-up. She was jolly for a second and gloomy again. 'Why do they always want to put it in your mouth?'

'It's a good question,' said Bec. 'And why do we let them?'

'We want them to be happy,' said Rose in a small voice, and asked Bec hurriedly when her first time was.

'I was fourteen and he was seventeen,' said Bec. 'I let him

332

take my clothes off one night in a paddock in Spain. He kept saying he was going to show me something and there I was, starkers, still waiting for it. He wasn't too bright. I think the thing he wanted to show me was my own nakedness, because he wanted to see it so much. It didn't occur to him that I might want to see *him* naked. It was a bit of a fumble. It happened. It was a *first time*.' She waited, then said: 'What about you?'

Rose gave no hint that she'd considered answering the question. 'It's a shame you and Uncle Alex are going to burn in hell fire for eternity,' she said. 'Maybe if you repented and accepted Jesus as your saviour you'd get off.'

'Where did you learn this way of speaking?'

'Bible camp,' said Rose. She stopped, leaned in close to Bec and whispered: 'I've got a boyfriend, but you mustn't tell anyone.' She gripped Bec's forearm, her eyes widened and she said through her teeth: 'You've got to promise.'

Ahead of them Dougie leaned out of the trees, waved, pointed and disappeared. A moment later Erasmus charged out and led them through patches of nettles to a grove of ash and oak. Maureen was darting round the base of trees, plucking out fungi and putting them in a basket.

Dougie squatted contemplatively in front of a fat purple mushroom with his eyes half-shut, a cigarette high in the corner of his mouth as if his lip had snagged on a fixture.

'What d'you say this is called?' he said.

'Blewit,' said Maureen.

'Blewit. That's the mushroom of my life,' said Dougie, plucking it.

Maureen told him not to smoke around the mushrooms. Dougie tossed his find into her basket and with sudden boylike effort scrambled up a shallow bank, spraying dirt from the soles of his city shoes, to where Alex was easing Harry into a sitting position on a rug he'd laid on a fallen tree. 'Hey Uncle Harry,' he shouted, 'tell us again how Charlie Darwin got all those animals into the ark?'

'If you'd paid attention like Alex when we were in these woods thirty years ago you might be where he is now instead of delivering catalogues for a living.'

'Never had the geek gene, Uncle Harry,' said Dougie. 'I do Christmas cards as well.'

The men's voices sounded thin and clear among the trees. Alex called to Bec that he was coming down to show her how mushrooms should be hunted.

'We'll just leave you the poisonous ones,' Bec called back. Her cheeks and the tip of her nose were pink in the cold and vapour puffed from between her lips as she spoke. Alex became aware of the smell of moss and mulch and wet bark in the raw, damp air, the questing busyness of Rose among the tree roots, thought of the warmth of Bec close in his arms that morning, and was ashamed of his pessimism.

'If you find any magic ones, they're mine,' said Dougie. Alex watched Bec turn her eyes to him.

Harry said to Dougie: 'You couldn't prise even one of your daughters away from her mother for your father's birthday?'

Dougie threw his cigarette down and stuck his hands in the pockets of the old parka he'd borrowed from Lewis. 'The old man doesn't care, he just wants left alone.'

'Did you actually try?' said Alex.

'Sorry, Einstein,' said Dougie. 'Couldn't order up a kid for you. Maybe try organising one of your own next time.'

The women had been discussing the provenance of an

ear-like fungus Rose had found growing on an oak tree and didn't hear the conversation around the log. Bec heard a swish of foliage and Alex came up to her, looking pale and furious, and said there was something he'd forgotten to do. He had to go back to the house. She asked if she should go with him and he said that there was no need, he'd see her later; and he was off.

Dougie was looking uneasily down at them from the log, fresh cigarette twitching in his fingers.

'Did you say something to your brother?' said Maureen.

'No,' said Dougie. Harry turned to him and raised his eyebrows and Dougie said: 'We were talking about kids. He might have got the wrong end of the stick. Why does anyone listen to what I say? I'll go after him.' He went off after his brother, and once he was out of the wood, two miles from the house, realised that the rest of the day would go better if he took time out to sit in Caffè Nero in Brechin with a whisky miniature slipped into a black coffee. He cut across the fields towards town.

In the wood, Bec, Rose and Maureen worked among the lichen and leaf mould, feeling with their fingers for the cool plush of mushroom caps. The mushrooms parted from the earth with a snap like a single hair pulled out.

Bec knew how many girlfriends Alex had brought to meet his parents before Maria; and perhaps Maureen had been fond of Maria. What were parents supposed to do, after all, when their son brought home half a dozen women over twenty years, introducing each one as the woman he loved? It was easy to decide that they weren't supposed to do anything, that they were to be *really cool about it*. But it was the mother who ended up stripping the bed and washing the sheets when the latest woman had gone. If Maria wasn't *The One*, they might reasonably think, why should Bec be?

'I'm in love with your son,' she said to Maureen.

'Good,' said Maureen, turning to her seriously and nodding once, as if Bec were a child who'd just come and told her she'd tidied her room without being asked. Bec felt the particular sense of foolishness you feel when you hear a profound, difficult, rare truth, one you've come to by yourself, echo in the mouths of others as a commonplace thing.

Maureen looked up over Bec's shoulder, with a smile unmistakeably kept fresh from when she and the beneficiary had been younger. 'Are you all right, Harry?' she called. Bec had forgotten he was there, uncharacteristically quiet on his log. The focused warmth in Maureen's voice, when she had been so reserved, nudged Bec into outsiderdom.

'Do you remember that old ash? The freak of nature?' said Harry. 'Is it still there?'

'Let's go and see,' said Maureen, putting down her basket and going up to him. When Bec next glanced up the two them had gone.

As Bec filled the last box and stashed it in a rucksack Erasmus started barking. Rose laughed and said he'd found a squirrel. Bec saw the dog under a pine tree deeper in the wood, up on his hind legs with his forepaws against the trunk, head wagging as he watched something moving in the branches. She told Rose she was going to find Harry and Maureen and climbed up the bank.

Beyond the fallen tree were clumps of holly bushes. In the distance Bec could hear running water and without thinking she began to move silently, as her father had taught her. At the edge of the second line of holly the ground fell away in a gentle slope scattered with young birches, the mossy ground thinly sprinkled with their leaves. At the foot of the slope were two ash trees joined by a thick branch that had somehow fused, and close by were Harry and Maureen, not moving, their arms round each other. Harry sat hunched on a stump and Maureen stood with her shoulders bowed, her lips pressed hard against the sparse stubble on Harry's head.

Bec went back to where she'd left the rucksack.

'They're coming,' she said to Rose. 'Let's go on ahead.'

Back at the house, she found Alex in the bedroom, sitting on the floor at the foot of the bed, staring at her bottle of anti-parasitic pills.

'I went crazy,' said Alex. 'I was angry.'

'I saw that.'

He told her what had passed between him and Dougie. 'I came back here sure I was going to do something radical about these pills,' he said. 'I thought I could break them open and put some in your food.'

'What an interesting idea.'

'I thought I could grind them up in my mum's food processor. I got as far as the kitchen, and wondering what blade to use, and then I started thinking that perhaps it wasn't the best course of action.'

Bec took the bottle. The seal was intact. She twisted the cap off, pulled off the foil, shook a couple of pink and black capsules onto her palm, rolled them like dice, put them in her mouth and swallowed them. She shrugged. 'There,' she said. 'You see?'

At noon, Dougie slipped into the house, smelling of cigarettes and breath-freshening mints, and soon afterwards, a seven-seater people carrier rolled up to disgorge the Lancashire

Comries. The children rushed through the porch and when Lettie came in a few minutes later she saw Harry in a chair in the hallway, jacket hanging off his ribs, mouth stretched back in a lipless smile, his arms round Leah and Chris, murmuring to them. Lettie called to her children and they stepped away from Harry guiltily and she commanded them to go and play in the garden.

'My dear, we were talking about the seaside,' said Harry. 'What harm can I do now? Down in my plot the worms have got their bibs on.'

'I haven't seen you for ages,' Lettie said to Harry. She turned her child so that his head was over her shoulder, away from his grandfather.

'This must be little Gideon,' said Harry. 'Let's have a look at the chap.'

'Oh, he likes it up here. How are you feeling?'

Harry laughed wheezily. 'Bit worse than chicken pox.'

'I'm sorry to see you suffer like this.'

'That's nice of you.'

Lettie spoke slowly and carefully through the wobble in her voice. 'I pray for *you* every night. I want you to get well. You take advantage of Matthew's love. You can't just take the grand-children and throw the parents away.'

'My wish for the children to entertain the notion of God as wonderful myth isn't the reason you hate me.'

'I don't hate you at all.'

'You hate me because I'm not leaving you the house. You'd find a way to let me spend time with the kids if I changed the will.'

'Which you're not going to do.'

'My dear, it is my property.'

Matthew came in and bent to embrace his father.

'I was asking Lettie if I could hold my new grandson,' said Harry.

Matthew looked at his wife. 'I don't see why not,' he said.

Lettie put Gideon into the old man's trembling arms. She didn't let go, but allowed herself be pulled closer to her father-in-law, so that once Harry had the baby cradled against his chest and was looking down into his face, she still cupped Gideon's tiny head and touched his feet. The child was eyes and a glimpse of movement through a coral of adult fingers. Caressed, manhandled and confused, Gideon began to scream, and Lettie took him and shuffled away, bouncing him and murmuring.

'It was hard to get her to come,' said Matthew.

'We were getting on quite well,' said Harry.

Come two o'clock everyone was gathered in except for Lewis. Bec volunteered to round him up and she was directed to the attic.

As she put her feet on the upper rungs of the ladder and raised her body through the hatch she smelled chemicals and heard the purr of an extractor fan. Lewis, in a shirt and tie, stood behind a workbench arrayed with flasks and trays. He'd rolled up his sleeves and was examining a photograph through a magnifying glass. There was a pile of prints in front of him and more scattered over a green baize easel propped up at a shallow angle. The skylights had been blacked out and the workbench was lit by a single cone of harsh light from the ceiling. In the shadows at the edges of the room Bec could see a box camera on a tripod and shelves of identical red-bound volumes.

'Time,' said Lewis. He lowered the magnifying glass, put

the print down and looked at Bec. 'Time to eat, that's what you came to tell me.'

Bec stepped off the ladder and came up to the workbench with her hands in her pockets. 'Your lab smells different from mine,' she said.

The print Lewis had been studying, she saw, was a colour photograph of his own face, with every line, hair, wrinkle and pore detailed in high contrast.

'From this morning,' he said. He riffled through the pile of prints and pulled one out. 'From a week ago. Look.' He pointed to a line in his cheek. 'D'you see how it's got deeper, just in a week?'

Bec studied the two photographs carefully, but couldn't see a difference.

'Look at it through this,' said Lewis, handing her the magnifying glass.

'Oh yes,' said Bec, who still couldn't tell the lines apart. 'I see now. That's remarkable.' She looked over her shoulder and saw that the red volumes had dates stamped on their spines in gold.

'May I?' she asked. She took out one of the books, marked April–June 1997, and flipped through pages of photographs of Lewis's face taken at the same distance from the lens, in the same light. The skin flickered and stretched as the weeks went by but she couldn't see him age.

'How far back does it go?' she said.

'About fifty years,' said Lewis. 'One photograph a day. I'm going to write a paper but I want to work on it for a bit longer.' He lifted his jacket off the back of a chair and put it on.

'You look smart,' said Bec.

Lewis took the album from her hands and leafed through it. 'It doesn't go only one way,' he said. 'Here.' He showed her two consecutive pages. 'You can see that from Tuesday to Wednesday I actually got younger.'

'Mmm,' said Bec. She couldn't see it.

'The overall direction's the same,' said Lewis. He banged the book shut, looked embarrassed, then seemed to rally and bent his head closer to Bec. 'I wanted to see it. I could've taken pictures of trees growing, but it's not the same.'

'Or your children,' said Bec.

'That wouldn't have been fair,' said Lewis gravely. 'It's hard enough to deal with the difference between the self you know and the self others see. I don't want to show Alex or Dougie their third self, the self time sees. Time, and no one else.'

He looked at Bec from under his eyebrows. He resembled Harry for a moment. 'Alex is more like his mother, you know.'

'Is he? He has his worlds.'

'Harry put as much into bringing him up as I did.'

'You spent more time with Dougie?'

'I spent more time in the surgery,' said Lewis. 'I spent more time in the attic.'

48

The thought of eating made Harry nauseous. A sip of wine burned its way through him. He could tell that Lewis was longing for the social ordeal to end and to be able to climb the ladder back to his studio. Once Lewis had opened his presents and cards, thanking them and parrying their smiles with his glass, Harry made a toast to his brother, but his heart wasn't in it. He lost his way and ended in a mumble. The silences lengthened. The children bent over their food, and when Harry, Bec or Alex tried to speak to them, they looked at their parents. Lettie would shake her head; Matthew would whisper in his wife's ear and nod, and the children would respond with embarrassed words.

Rose's nose wrinkled the moment the *pièce de résistance*, a roast sucking pig, began its portage from oven to table. Her great-uncle attacked the animal with the carving knife, breaking the crisped skin with a sound like cracking ice, and she pushed her chair back and turned her body to the side. When Lewis tried to put meat on her plate she shook her head and held up her hands and said that she wasn't allowed to eat pork.

'Yes you are,' said Peter, with his mouth full.

'We seem to have a doctrinal difference here,' said Harry.

'Rose, you don't have to eat it if you don't want to,' said Matthew in a hard voice.

'It's not about wanting,' said Rose. 'It's about how you're all going to hell and I'm not.'

Leah disgorged a lump of half-chewed pork. 'I don't want to go to hell,' she said, and began to weep silently.

'Oh my goodness,' said Maureen. 'Does it matter?'

'It's in the Bible,' said Rose confidently.

'You don't know Scripture better than your father,' said Lettie.

'I can read as well as he can,' said Rose.

'Touché!' said Harry.

'We'll talk about this later,' said Matthew to his daughter. 'Jesus says we can eat whatever we like.'

'That's not what it says in the Old Testament. You can't pick and choose.'

'Am I going to hell, Mum?' said Leah. 'I ate pork.'

'Of course not, darling,' said Lettie. 'Christ gave us a new dispensation.'

'I'm not going to hell,' said Peter, stuffing his mouth with pork and gnashing in his sister's face.

She recoiled. 'You are,' she said. 'You're going to burn in eternity in hell fire, and every day demons are going to cut you up and eat you slowly, and the next day you'll be whole and it'll start again, for ever and ever.'

Leah wailed and ran round the table into her mother's arms.

'You've got a good old schism going here,' said Harry.

'Keep to your own realm, Dad,' said Matthew.

Lettie said: 'Why do you want your son's family to be unhappy?'

'I'm merely observing,' said Harry. 'It's fascinating.'

'He who gives no love gets no love, and ends up alone,' said Lettie.

One by one they became aware that behind Leah's soft weeping another sound, similar but stronger, sniffing and sobbing, was building. Something extraordinary was happening to Bec's face; her eyes were squeezed together and swollen and her mouth was turned downwards like a mask in a Greek tragedy. It had happened so quickly; her whole face seemed to shine with tears. As the table fell silent, the noise from Bec grew louder. Her shoulders shook and she began sucking in great lungfuls of air and pushing them out with roars of anguish that drained the blood from the children's faces and froze the others to their places.

Alex helped Bec to her feet and took her to their room. She wept for an hour, sitting on the bed and squeezing her knees to her chest, then lying down, curled in a foetal position, as the sound of anguish ebbed. Alex held her but in the beginning she was hard, rigid; it was as if she didn't feel him. As her weeping became quieter she softened and finally pressed herself against him.

'It's dying,' she said.

'It's alive in labs all over the world. You did that.'

'It's dying in me.'

Alex tried to pull his arm, which had gone to sleep, out from under her, and she said, 'Was I crushing you?'

Shaking his arm to restore the circulation Alex assured her that he'd still be able to use it and Bec made a small sound, perhaps the last sob, perhaps a laugh.

'Holding on to the woman to stop her being washed away,' she said.

'It seemed like a freak wave.'

'Came from nowhere!' said Bec, eerily conversational, and Alex had the sense that they really had been on the deck of a ship, and that he'd clutched his lover to stop the water snatching her and taking her under, and that now they were all right.

Bec sat up on the bed with her legs crossed, looking down at her fingers, picking with extreme concentration at the skin below the cuticles, as if there were stray threads of skin that refused to be pulled off. 'Now you know how I was when my Dad died.'

Alex watched her picking. Her face was covered by hanging hair. 'Was it really about that?' he said.

Bec looked up and it seemed to Alex that she was appraising him from far away.

'I thought I was going to be brave,' said Bec.

'You have been,' said Alex. 'You took the risk to show you could live with those parasites, and it didn't work out. It's no shame.'

'That's not bravery,' said Bec. 'Bravery's where you get intimate with the mechanistic side of life without giving up on the idea that it doesn't have to be eat or starve, kill or die, fuck or fail.'

'Are we talking about parasites or people?'

'Both.'

'Ah,' said Alex humbly, conscious that it reflected badly on him to be surprised that Bec should harbour such thoughts.

'Does it never frighten you?' she asked.

'A machine that can conceive of mercy isn't a machine.'

'It frightens me. So, that was the bravery. Sharing space with merciless little lives and accepting them. Now it's finished.'

'You're still full of bacteria.'

345

Bec smiled and sniffed and caressed his cheek. 'You say the most thoughtful things.'

Alex said: 'There's only one kind of life you could share space with who'd learn from you what mercy is.'

Much later, while Alex was in the shower, she took her sheet of contraceptives, popped the pills out of the foil and arranged them in a line along the bottom of the window frame, spacing them evenly.

Alex came out of the bathroom with a towel round his waist, cold air chilling the water drops on his chest. Bec was standing by the open window with her arms folded. She watched him while he picked up the empty square of foil, examined it and dropped it on the floor. He kneeled down, hooked his forefinger into his thumb, and flicked one of the pills into the darkness. Bec kneeled next to him and they worked their way along towards each other, flicking the pills away until there were none left.

A cry came from below.

'Ayah, that stung,' said Dougie. 'What's that you're flicking?' A cigarette brightened and they heard him blowing out smoke.

'Contraceptive pills,' said Bec.

'That's not how you're supposed to use them.'

49

Harry was in the hospice for a few weeks and came home to the care of Judith. Alex was often there and Matthew came when he could. He took days off to drive down from Lancashire.

Harry lost the desire to eat. He subsisted on peeled orange segments, lukewarm soup and weak tea. Judith would wash him and help him go to the bathroom; sometimes Alex and Matthew would do it. His pee turned black and his shit white. His yellowing skin itched maddeningly. The whites of his eyes looked like pale egg yolks. He was on morphine; it was never enough.

They read to him, and while they read, Gerasim curled up and slept on a blanket by the door. Harry preferred Conan Doyle and Stevenson. He listened to Louis Prima and Nat Gonella. If Matthew didn't press him too hard, he'd talk about his childhood in Derby, and about Matthew's mother. 'She said she was depressed,' he said, 'but she was just shy.' Dougie came, and Bec, and Rose wearing an English headscarf. She told him that she'd read his book about evolution, and that he was wrong, which would have made him laugh if he could. She left him with a kiss on the forehead and a fist-sized earthenware pot holding a plant that was, she said, about to sprout a red chilli pepper.

Harry had his bed moved closer to the window. Each morning he would peer into the tiny cluster of glossy green leaves in the pot. He poked with his shrivelled fingertips at the point where the leaves met the stalk. One day Judith came in to find Harry sitting up in bed, his eyes filmed by tears, unable to speak. He pointed to the plant. An orange nib of chilli had broken out of its bud.

There were times when he was sure he was about to die, and people gathered, and he didn't. He heard them murmur 'false alarm' in the hall outside. He found the strength to open the drawer holding the key to his bedroom door and put it in the breast pocket of his pyjamas. He got Judith to fetch a particular bottle of wine from the cellar, pack it in a box with a note he dictated to her, wrap it and mark it *For Bec*. The chilli on the windowsill reddened and swelled.

One Friday evening, with Matthew due to arrive, Judith went to make tea, leaving Harry alone. He raised the covers and swung his feet onto the floor. His limbs were useless now; if he stood up he felt his bones would collapse in a neat heap. Also, it hurt. And yet he would try. He braced himself with his hands on the edge of the bed and with an effort pushed himself into the standing position. He stood there, trying to lock his knees straight. Perhaps some forward momentum would help. He tried to drag one foot forward without lifting it and fell on the floor. *Ow.* He moved towards the door, propelling himself with the sides of his legs pushing and his hands dragging. His head and his body felt peculiar, as if they were expanding and contracting. He wasn't sure he would make it back to bed.

He reached the door, his pyjama trousers halfway down his thighs, horrible pains streaking through him, and got the key out of his pocket on the fourth try. He put it between his lips and clawed at the door panels to get himself in a kneeling position. He took the key out of his mouth and put it in the lock. His first attempts to turn it failed. When he got both hands onto it, he managed to turn it and heard it lock. He sank down onto his bony behind with his back against the door.

Judith returned and tried to get in. A tedious conversation followed, where he could hear her calling his name, but she couldn't hear him telling her that every time she rattled the door, it was as if nails were being driven into his back. He heard her on the phone; she moved away. He drifted off into a dream where his body was the banner of an army, tied at the wrist and ankle to a tall pole, that fluttered in a strong wind as the host marched up a winding road towards a far-off city.

He was woken by knocking and the voices of Matthew and Alex on the other side of the door, calling his name and discussing whether they should break it down. 'Don't,' he said, but only the faintest croak came from his throat. It seemed to him that he was about to stop being. It was certainly getting hard to keep his head in place. It was at this moment that he'd imagined himself feeling remorse for the way he'd treated his son, who'd shown him nothing but kindness, patience and tolerance since Lewis's birthday, and wishing he'd shown more love in return; regretting that he hadn't left the house to him and his children.

Any other's knowledge of his bravery in facing death alone meant that he was not alone, and made him less brave. This was the only true courage, Harry thought, to face death alone and not to cry out, not to whimper or flinch, to affirm his humanity by accepting that from one moment to the next he would go from something to nothing.

But he heard Gerasim scratching at the door. It was as if existence was burrowing its way towards him, as if life was clawing its way through the wood, bursting through the sagging flesh around his ribs to reclaim its place inside him, as if his dog were leading a busy, trumpeting, cartwheeling column of all he remembered and all he had loved. And it came back to him that a life witnessed only by yourself is not a life at all, and that even if the only touch of love you ever receive is the mother's first hand on you when you are born, it is still worth all the trouble of the universe. Harry tried to move, but it was too late. He couldn't open the door. He died, not frightened but preoccupied, busy in the act of trying to change his mind.

PART THREE

50

It was easy for Ritchie to pretend that time was not moving him closer to disgrace when all he had to ignore was the quiet count of the calendar. When the snowdrops turned up, and the crocuses began to congregate around the tree roots in their tawdry purples and yellows, he managed not to see them. When the daffodils arrived, it was more difficult. By the time he woke up early one morning to find it was already light outside, that a fuzz of buds and blossom was softening the outline of the branches and that the birds were not so much singing as cheering in his white, unshaven face, he had to accept that spring had arrived. It seemed to him at that moment, standing in his pyjamas in the kitchen doorway, that this dawn was the beginning of one long, terrible day that would last three months, and that with the evening would come eternal shame.

The change of season coincided with his awareness of a change affecting his sister. She was growing into a more flamboyant and ubiquitous condition, dangerously close to fame. At the end of March he heard from his mother that Bec and Alex were moving house. Stephanie was surprised that he didn't know. When she told him about the big house in Islington, how Alex's uncle had left the house to the institute when he died, to be lived in by the incumbent director and his family, which was Alex and Bec, Ritchie envied their luck. It seemed unjust that he should have had to work like the Devil to secure his rich man's estate in Hampshire, only to have his sister end up in metropolitan splendour without really trying. Ritchie didn't get in touch with Alex and Bec. He didn't see why he should. It was up to them to tell him their news. He shouldn't have to solicit it. If they didn't want to speak to him, even to send him an email, he would leave them alone, in their pretentious new digs, never letting them guess how good he was being to refuse to betray Bec.

And yet, to Ritchie's indignation, they couldn't leave him alone. His sister was all over the media one day on account of her malaria vaccine. The jab had been a success, apparently. To Ritchie, it seemed undignified for a scientist to be posing and pontificating all over TV, radio, the Internet, the papers. First it was Alex with his cancer, now Bec with her malaria. Humility became the wise, Ritchie felt. They'd worked hard in their dingy labs, sweating over tedious calculations and test tubes and formulas or whatever, and they'd done well. To be flaunting themselves in public as they were was inappropriate. Did Bec realise, Ritchie wondered sadly, how ephemeral fame was? Did she realise that her picture only appeared on the front of so many papers because she was pretty? It put him out that on the day the news broke the BBC website gave the malaria story more prominence than the drama of *Teen Makeover*, where they were down to the last three contestants. It seemed odd to him that none of the stories about Bec mentioned that she was Ritchie Shepherd's sister.

Ritchie sent Bec a bunch of flowers with a card that read *You're more famous than me!!!* She called to thank him. He was glad to hear from her. It seemed that he was as fond of her as he'd ever been. He became sentimental and nostalgic, and they talked about the first holiday they'd taken with their mother after their father died, and how strange it had been on the beach without him, how brave the two of them had been to charge into the waves and swim in the cold North Sea. Ritchie remembered what a relief it had been to his fifteen-year-old self to hide from the adulthood that was pressing in on him and partake of his little sister's childhood, to play with her in the water as if he were a young boy her age. He felt so warm now towards Bec, such a sense of refuge, that he dared to ask her whether she'd think again about her opposition to his film.

'What was it like when you met him?' asked Bec. 'O'Donabháin.'

'In the beginning I hated him,' said Ritchie. 'But when I forgave him I felt better. More whole.'

'Whole?'

'Yes.'

'The closure you talked about.'

'Yes.'

'Do you think that's what I should do? Forgive the man who murdered Dad?'

'Forgiveness doesn't justify him. I think it hurt him to be forgiven by me.'

'You're saying that I should forgive him to punish him. That doesn't sound forgiving.'

Ritchie held the phone away from his mouth, swore under his breath and said to Bec: 'If you can find it in yourself to forgive him in any way, it would be a good thing to do.'

Later, Ritchie's assistant brought him a copy of Val's newspaper and drew his attention to a two-page spread under the headline SCIENCE'S GOLDEN COUPLE. There was a large photograph of his sister and Alex, made over, styled and primped, grinning smugly on what appeared to be a velvet chaise-longue. They looked almost regal, Ritchie thought. He couldn't bear to read the text. The smaller photos, scattered across the pages, told him all he wanted to know about the kind of bollocks Val's reporter had written. There was Saint Rebecca, in white, of course, bending over a big-eyed African child. There was Saint Alex, in a lab coat of the inevitable angelic colour, standing over a patient who was gazing up at him as if Alex was going to save his life, which perhaps he was, but still. Saints, Ritchie felt, should be obscure and humble until their day of martyrdom. And Bec and Alex weren't saints. Ritchie would only have to do a little digging, he was sure, and he would find their other side. The way Val was setting his sister up for a fall was diabolical, and yet there was something about it that made him want to laugh, her innocence, her ignorance that her brother was to thank for this celebrity. Once Val's paper had established the legend of Bec and Alex, others followed.

Ritchie thought about suicide as a way out. But he had always flinched at the proximity of possible harm, the edges of train platforms, the mere presence of razor blades in the same room. He was afraid of pain; he feared mess, he feared fear, how he'd feel if he'd sliced open his wrists and watched the blood well out of them into the bath or how the belt would feel when it tightened round his throat. He thought about confessing everything to Karin and asking her to forgive him, for the sake of the children and for the memory of their happiness together, the good things they had done. But these weren't plans. Ritchie didn't imagine killing himself or confessing what he'd done because he thought he would do these things. It was a personal art, a way to dilute his intentions in a nobler current, to make himself feel better about whatever it was that he was actually going to do. But he didn't know what he was going to do, and the deadline Val had given him was only a couple of months away.

At the beginning of May, Ritchie heard that Val had gone mad. At first it was gossip in pubs and clubs. Then there were snatches on the Internet and paragraphs in *Private Eye*. Val had, it was alleged, sent an email to every member of the paper's staff, to the entire board of directors and to the proprietor, saying, 'When was the last time you cunts prayed to almighty God?' Another story was that he'd gobbed on the news editor in a meeting and ranted about how his myrmidons were hypocrites who whored and lied and cheated on their expenses. The trigger for his rage was an edition of the paper that featured a denunciation of the government's lax attitude towards fiends who preyed sexually on children, opposite an unrelated article speculating over how much money a fifteen-year-old tennis player would make as a professional model. The story was accompanied by a picture that could only have been taken by the photographer lying on the ground and shooting up between the girl's legs. There were stories saying that Val had left the paper 'by mutual agreement'. Then the stories dried up. Ritchie asked around, masking his raging hunger to know, and found out that Val's behaviour had crossed the line into clinical insanity. He'd been sectioned. He'd been put away.

Val's physical attack on him, which Ritchie had managed to

put out of his mind, was now safe to mull over. It made sense as the act of a madman, as did Val's peculiar referral to himself in the third person. 'Mr Oatman does get carried away sometimes,' Val had said. The sense of reprieve made Ritchie weak and weepy. He'd woken up into this nightmare for so many mornings, and now it turned out that it had been a sick man's dream. Ritchie knew that whoever had betrayed him – perhaps Nicole herself, perhaps Louise – might betray him again. He supposed that Val had confided in others. Yet because he wanted it so much he began to hope that he would not be exposed. He bumped into the new editor, who seemed decent, at a party. You could never tell with journalists, of course, but he was friendly, normal. It was as if Val had never existed. Ritchie began to drink less and had dinner with Bec and Alex at a nice restaurant in Clerkenwell. He kept his cool. He made them laugh. He didn't mention the O'Donabháin film, and began to think that, over time, he could wear Bec down about it merely by being pleasant.

The season finale of *Teen Makeover* was a wonderful night; the winner was a sweet fourteen-year-old boy they'd put in a beautifully tailored suit, a short-arsed chap with red lips, huge cow-eyes and a voice like caramel. The studio audience, it seemed to Ritchie, was superbly picked for brightness, enthusiasm and prettiness, and the new guidelines he'd set for what they should wear gave the cheering, jumping mass of teeth and hair and slim bodies a vibe of hysterical wholesomeness the BBC was sure to like. Five million people watched. A million voted. At the party afterwards Ritchie hardly left Karin's side. He stood at the innermost of concentric rings of power and celebrity, where people came up to them as if they were king and queen, and Ruby and Dan played with

Lazz and Riggsy around them like princes and princesses of the blood.

A few days later Ritchie had Midge over. They kicked a football around with Dan and went upstairs. Ritchie wanted to play Midge some rare Willie McTell but Midge couldn't sit still. He kept reaching inside his t-shirt sleeve and scratching his shoulder. He wrinkled his nose and flexed his forehead as if he was wearing glasses that didn't fit.

'Ever heard of the Moral Foundation?' he asked Ritchie.

'Eighties electro-pop,' said Ritchie. He was sitting on the floor by the record player, surrounded by sleeves and vinyl discs. 'Here's one he recorded as Red Hot Willie Glaze.'

'The Moral Foundation,' said Midge. 'It's a website. It's the fucking celebrity secret police online. Are you sure you haven't heard of it? They run a scandal every Sunday at six a.m. They've been going for weeks now. Every Sunday morning somewhere in the country some poor cunt's up before dawn, pressing refresh on his browser, waiting to see his life destroyed.'

Ritchie stuck out his lower lip and tilted the record, watching the light break up in the grooves etched by Blind Willie's voice. He didn't want to listen to Midge. He wanted to listen to the scratchy howl of a long-dead alcoholic guitarist who'd sung his sorrows and his sins into a microphone and then died. He wanted hard-luck stories with endings, sealed by death. But Midge wouldn't stop talking.

'It's your sister's ex who's behind it. Val Oatman. He's the grey eminence.'

'I thought he was in the loony bin,' said Ritchie.

'You don't go there now,' said Midge. 'It comes in a bottle. You don't go into the loony bin. It goes into you, three times a day before meals. I don't know if he ever really lost his marbles. Have you honestly not heard about this? Everyone's talking about it. That's how that ManU player got nailed last week.'

The Foundation's modus operandi, Midge told him, was to contact its target and tell them that a particular day had been set aside for a revelation 'concerning you or someone close to you'.

'That's what they say,' he said. '"Concerning you or someone close to you." But they don't tell you what the revelation is, or who it is, whether it's you, or your partner, or your kid, God forbid. And they say, "Do you wish to supply information?" They've got a whole fucking system. One of my client's had the treatment.'

'Lazz?'

'I'm not going to tell you. The less you know the better. But yeah, one of my clients got the call. He, or she, has a skeleton in his closet. Who doesn't? They were fucking clever. They wouldn't say exactly what they knew, but they gave enough hints that he, or she, thought they couldn't risk it. D'you mind if I smoke in here?'

'Yes,' said Ritchie. 'Have another beer. What did he do?'

'Or she.'

'Or she.'

'What did he do? He shopped someone else, what d'you think?'

'It sounds like blackmail.'

'It's a grey area, apparently. It's all to do with how specific they are.'

'He didn't shop another one of your clients?'

'Do I seem like a fucking doormat to you? No, of course not.'

Two weeks later Ritchie was alone in his office early in the morning when his mobile rang with a call from a blocked number.

'Mr Shepherd?' The woman had a slight Essex accent. She spoke with great confidence. 'This is Maggie calling from the Moral Foundation. Is it convenient to talk now?'

'No,' said Ritchie.

'We'll continue to call you, Mr Shepherd, until you have time.' The woman paused, then went on. 'Are you aware of the Foundation's work, Mr Shepherd?'

'No.'

'We're a not-for-profit organisation, set up to make the public aware of immoral behaviour by prominent people.' She spoke quickly and without any dramatic inflection, like a cabin assistant making a safety announcement.

'You're a sanctimonious, holier-than-thou, dustbin-rummaging scandal sheet.'

'So you are aware of our work.'

'What do you want?'

'Do you have a pen and paper handy, Mr Shepherd? I'd like you to write some things down for me. The first thing is a date. It's the twenty-eighth of February next year. Do you have a note of that, Mr Shepherd?'

'Why the hell should I? Who do you think you are?'

'It's important that you know the date, Mr Shepherd. On that day, at six a.m., we shall be publishing, on our website, information about immoral behaviour, concerning you or someone close to you. It will concern one or the other, but not both. Do you understand?'

'What if I haven't done anything wrong?'

'I'm not authorised to discuss what you might or might not

have done, Mr Shepherd. I'm just informing you that on the twenty-eighth of February—'

'Isn't there a law that says a man's supposed to be told what he's accused of?'

'If you've done something wrong, Mr Shepherd, you must know what it is. If you are a good and righteous man you have nothing to worry about.'

'Can I speak to Val?'

'Mr Oatman doesn't take calls, Mr Shepherd.'

'Tell me what you're going to write about me.'

'I'm not authorised to discuss what you might or might not have done, Mr Shepherd. I can only suggest you look at our website to see examples of notable people we've caught sinning in the past. In your case I can only give you a hypothetical example of the kind of thing we might know about you. It might be, for example, that we know you had sex with a child who appeared on your show. But I must stress that's a hypothetical example.'

'If Val's so holy, why's he set himself up to make judgements on us, as if he were God? Isn't that some kind of sin?'

'You'd have to ask Mr Oatman about that, Mr Shepherd.'

'Can I speak to him?'

'Mr Oatman doesn't take calls. I have to give you a code, Mr Shepherd.'

'What code?'

'Can you write it down for me, Mr Shepherd? It's very important. It's A35ZX47. That's your code.'

'Why should I write down your fucking code?'

'Please don't use profanity, Mr Shepherd, it won't help you. You're under no obligation to write the code down. But you need it to verify your identity if you choose to guarantee your exclusion from Foundation scrutiny by giving us information on the moral failings of another person close to you.'

'Such as who?'

'I can only give you a hypothetical example,' said Maggie. 'A hypothetical example would be if you had a prominent sibling. A brother or a sister.'

'I know what sibling means, you condescending bitch,' said Ritchie.

'Please don't use profanity, Mr Shepherd. It's out of keeping with your status.'

'You know I don't have a brother.'

'Would you like me to repeat the code, Mr Shepherd?'

'You're the sinner! You! Trying to get me to betray my sister to save myself. You can tell Val I won't do it. Write what you like about me. I'll see you in court.'

'Would you like me to repeat the code, Mr Shepherd?'

'Tell me if you like, it won't make any difference,' said Ritchie, and wrote it down.

51

Bec wasn't aware of being happy that spring. She only thought about it when one of her friends told her she seemed happy, or when she noticed a man watching her curiously in the street and realised she'd been walking with a smile on her face.

Her paper reporting on the trial of the malaria vaccine was published and although it still seemed to her that it was a failure, everyone else appeared to think half-immunity for infants was a worthwhile thing. Multiple vaccines, that was the buzz; they'd overlap. Melinda Gates called to congratulate her. Vaccine company reps and panjandrums from the WHO sprinkled themselves into her diary.

The centre arranged dozens of interviews, and for a few days old friends who'd lost touch sent messages to say that they'd seen her on a website or in a magazine or heard her on the radio. It seemed to Bec that Alex never had to go into a supermarket and see a stack of newspapers with his face on the front of every one, as she had. Bec didn't understand why they couldn't use a photograph of a sad African child in the way they usually did. In each interview, Bec told the journalists that they should talk to the Tanzanians. They wrote down the phone numbers and email addresses of Issa, Mosi and

Mbita, but if they did contact them, nothing they said ever appeared.

Alex told Bec the covenant in Harry's will was so ingeniously worded that, if they didn't live in the house, it would stand empty. There seemed nothing to do except move in.

Matthew took everything away, apart from the wine, which Harry had bequeathed to the new tenants. One bottle came in a box addressed to Bec personally. *Chateau Lynch Bages, Grand Cru Classé, Pauillac*; it was dated 1972. A note that came with it read:

My dear Bec, I wanted you to try this, harvested in the year my favourite son was born. I wish I could be there to drink it with you. I'll take ties of wine over ties of blood any day of the week. Your oblivious uncle-in-love,

Harry

She read the note several times, folded it and put it away somewhere safe without showing it to Alex. She asked him what year Matthew had been born.

'1971. Why?'

'So he's a year older than you? I just wondered.'

Alex and Bec's possessions diffused rapidly through the house. Their books took up barely a quarter of the bookshelves and they didn't have curtains. They liked the bareness of the rooms, the few items they had spread out in a house of white walls and floorboards whose varnish was wearing thin.

They got used to the patterns of daylight, darkness and lamplight furnishing the rooms in a way their scatterings of things didn't. They put the bed they'd brought from Bec's house into the big first-floor room Harry had used as a sitting room and spent a great part of their weekends in it. They felt as if they were squatting in the house of a rich family who might at any moment return. Lying in bed on Saturday mornings they imagined who would burst in on them. A tanned white-haired man smelling of musk, said Bec. In a black suit, black tie and sunglasses, said Alex. Wearing driving gloves and carrying a shooting stick. He would open the stick, sit down on it, peel off his gloves carefully.

'Watching us all the time,' said Bec.

'Of course. Then he'd take out a gold cigarette case, remove a cigarette, light it with a gold lighter, inhale, and rest his hands on his knee.'

'Would his legs be crossed?'

'I think so. Big gold ring on his smoking hand. And then he'd say, with an Italian accent . . .'

'Fuck, per favore!'

'No, no,' said Alex. 'He'd say, "Please, would you mind waiting for my wife, she loves to watch intruders fucking. She's just parking the car."'

But they weren't intruders, and they weren't poor. Between the two of them they were bringing in more than a hundred and fifty thousand a year. The actual family they were waiting for, Bec knew, was a lanky man in his early forties and a red-cheeked woman about seven years younger, a little overweight, with a baby in her arms.

What Bec did feel the house lacked, as long as they hadn't started filling it up with their own children, was people. They were talking about giving a room to a deserving post-grad when Alex got a text from Dougie asking if he could stay with them while he looked for a job in London. The way Alex put it to Bec made her think that he expected her to say no, but she was glad. 'We'll put him in Matthew's old room,' she said. 'We can get another bed.'

May and June were warm, the air still and the sky clear in the long dawns when the plane and chestnut trees in the streets, squares and parks unclenched their leaves. To the ears of people sleeping in the grass on hot afternoons, the aircraft and the traffic came like ocean surf beating on a reef, far from shore. Cafés and pubs spilled their tables and drinkers outside and the fractal branching of brick terraces smelled of hot tar, firelighters and grilling meat. Boys rocked bare-chested to the park with cans and footballs and slyly watched girls unclip their bras to tan their backs. The sighs of cricket and tennis crowds eddied from open car windows and Asian boys' sound systems in tiny tricked-out cars shook the city like thumbs plucking at slackly strung strings. As it was the change of season memories of a hundred years of summer songs, on every continent, came to the surface in the heads of the old people of London. Flags hung limp and the city's towers and spires and battlements, its wheel and clock, grew legendary in grainy haze. Strange, beautiful faces appeared that were only ever seen outside when the sun shone.

One Sunday afternoon Alex and Bec borrowed a bike for Dougie and the three of them cycled along the canal to London Fields to meet a couple of Bec's schoolfriends. They took wine and food and sat around their picnic with the bikes laid on the grass beside them forming an outer circle of wheels. Across the expanse of grass were scores of other circles of picnickers and bicycle wheels. Some had brought barbecues in tinfoil boxes and the half-dozen columns of smoke gave the park the appearance of the courtyard of a caravanserai. They talked until the shadows lengthened. Everyone around them was conversing as if the reporting to each other of their lives, their moods, their memories and their dreams was the qualifying condition of their existence. Where did all these conversations go when they died, Bec wondered? Were people learning and growing when they sat and chatted for hours on these summer days? Were they drawing conclusions? Some of the groups in the park – perhaps her own – were only talking in the way humming a tune is making music, while the real exchanges were between eyes, light and bodies. Her friends stretched and tossed their hair in their summer dresses, and Alex answered them with his own smiles and frowns and leanings forward and hand gestures, without ever interrupting the flow of possession that passed between her and him. But Dougie didn't flirt with Bec's single girlfriends as she'd expected, or try to impress them with his extreme self-deprecation. He had an unexpected talent for shyness around strangers and Bec wondered how it was that he'd been so confident with her.

They mounted their bikes and rode to Broadway Market, where they sat on the edge of the pavement and drank pints, then went to a club in Shoreditch. It was early for the club, the queue hadn't built up outside, and they sat at the edge of the empty dancefloor. After half an hour the music started, the lights began to twist and track spots of colour across the floor and the room filled up. Alex and Dougie stood a little to one side. Bec saw that Dougie was asking Alex for something and Alex was refusing. Dougie seemed to find the rejection funny. He said something more; it looked like a joke, or perhaps Dougie asked again, because Alex shook his head and looked down into his drink as if he were ashamed. A song began that Bec liked and she tried to pull Alex onto the dancefloor. He laughed and refused.

'If you could only rock me in your arms,' he said. He stayed talking to one of Bec's friends while Dougie, Bec and the other friend merged into the dancers. Dougie couldn't merge, he stood out, and made a virtue of his standing out. He wore a short-sleeved shirt he'd picked up at Oxfam, white with a pattern of bluebirds, three buttons open, and danced with his arms held away from his body, moving his hips as if he were about to begin bending into the limbo position, throwing his long blond hair from side to side with sharp twists of his head. His thumbs and fingers made snapping motions without actually snapping. There was something of the ruined hero about him, as if in his head he was dancing with a long-lost love. Bec leaned in close to Dougie's ear to make herself heard over the music and asked if he'd like a drink. He smelled of sweat and soap.

'It's my shout,' said Dougie. 'But I'm skint.'

'Were you trying to get a loan from Alex just now?' asked Bec.

'Aye,' said Dougie. 'It's OK. I'm a wee bit behind on paying him back for an old loan, as a matter of fact.'

Bec put twenty pounds into Dougie's hand and he told her he'd pay her back as soon as he found a job.

The three of them cycled home drunk at one a.m., when the streets teemed with clubbers. Bec was ahead. She cycled past a group of skinny men in tight trousers and pork pie hats. They turned their heads, stopped and watched after her. The hem of her dress was billowing up over her bare legs and one of the men yelled something in her wake, bending backwards and gesturing at his crotch. Coming up behind him Alex reached out and grabbed the hat off his head and accelerated away. Bec heard the commotion and looked round to see Alex pedalling frantically towards her wearing a pork pie hat and shouting 'Go! Go!' A man was sprinting after him until Dougie, bringing up the rear, stuck out his foot and upended the pursuer into a heap of arms and legs. They cycled off up City Road to Angel and rode round and round Citron Square before going into the house. Alex and Bec rode side by side, holding hands, Bec with the stolen hat on her head, while Dougie cycled behind them with his hands off the handlebars, clapping and chanting: 'Science's golden cou-ple, science's golden cou-ple, da rah rah rah, da rah rah rah.'

They went inside and sat slumped around the kitchen table. Dougie poured them all a shot of spirits, which none of them drank.

'Chess set's laid out,' said Dougie. 'The dust gathers.'

'The one in your room? It used to be Matthew's. It was the only thing he left behind.'

'Pool's more my game,' said Dougie.

'You used to play chess,' said Alex. 'You used to beat me.'

'I don't remember,' said Dougie.

'You used to beat me every time.'

'It was Matty boy.'

'It was you. I always wondered what was going on between the queen and the pawns,' said Alex. 'Are they her soldiers, her servants or her children?'

'Her kids,' said Dougie. He ran his fingers through his hair. 'A big line of kids. It's a big family.'

'And loyal,' said Alex. 'Ready to lay down their lives for their parents.'

'If the pawns are children,' said Bec, 'the king isn't the father. He's so feeble. He must be ill, or very old. He makes these little tottering steps, one at a time. I think the queen is much younger, and very good-looking, and she's always going off and leaving the king. She tells the king it's for his own protection, and maybe that's what she tells herself, but I think it's so she can spend more time with her lovers.'

'Her lovers?' said Alex. 'You mean the knights?'

'They wish!' said Bec. 'They're too much in love with themselves and all their fancy sidestepping for her to be interested in them. And not the bishops, either. The bishops are only interested in sex.'

'Because they look like little penises?' said Alex.

'I think the queen loves the rooks,' said Bec. 'She likes them because they're strong, straightforward and patient. They're reliable, but they're still mysterious, because they're not easy to get to, and they're conflicted, because they're loyal to the king.'

'There are two of them,' said Alex. 'How does she choose?'

'Maybe she doesn't have to,' said Bec. After a moment's silence, all three of them laughed.

Bec took off the hat and gave it to Alex. He turned it over in his hands and smiled. 'Eminent scientist steals hat,' he said. 'I'm interviewing post-docs all day tomorrow.' He went to bed. Bec told him she'd come soon. They heard him singing softly as he walked upstairs.

A Mars a day

Helps you work, rest and play

'How come you're so chilled for a brainy chick?' said Dougie. 'See if it was me, just the thought of having to make choices for other people, and give them a hard time if they didn't jump to it? I couldn't handle it. And when there's life and death at the end of it all. I can hardly run myself, like, and you bring other people into the mix: no way.'

'It's the same for your brother.'

'Aye,' said Dougie. 'But he's no one for shaking his booty on the dancefloor. Everything with Alex comes from talking.'

'He got the hat for me tonight.' Bec wondered how to tell Dougie that his eyes, seeking her own, made her uncomfortable, without using the word 'uncomfortable'.

'Hey, I'm no saying he's no a superior human being to me. Of course he's a better man.'

'You don't know all there is to know about him.'

Dougie got up, came round the table, put his hand on Bec's shoulder and when she looked up to see what he was doing he tried to kiss her on the mouth. Bec turned her face away, stood up and took a step back.

'No,' she said.

'Sorry,' said Dougie. He looked beaten and scared. He sat down and hung his head so that his hair covered his face.

'Don't hide your face,' said Bec. 'Why did you just do that? You're not so drunk. You know I'm in love with your brother.'

'I'm sorry,' said Dougie. He looked up. 'I'm such a fucking arsehole. Everybody knows it. The folks must've told you. Alex must've told you. It's always the same. When anybody decent tries to give me a hand up I end up trying to take what I'm not entitled to. I'm just a fucking loser, Bec. I shouldn't have come. I'll pack my stuff.'

'Don't feel sorry for yourself,' said Bec. 'You're not going to get out of this by telling me that you know you're a loser, or by running away. You know I'm in love with your brother, don't you?'

'Aye.'

'And you know he's in love with me.'

'Aye.'

'Do you know we're trying to have a baby?'

'No, I didn't, but that's fantastic, Bec, fantastic, I'm really happy for you.'

'So why did you try to kiss me?'

'Cause I'm an arsehole.'

'That's not an answer.'

Dougie lifted his head and a trace of pride narrowed his eyes. 'Why? Because if I kissed you and I died in the night my life would've been worth something.'

'You're a real prick.'

'I know.'

'It's such an insult to me to think I'd –'

'Aye but Bec, that's the thing. I don't think. That's always been my problem. Forget about me, I'll pack my things.'

'So you're going to run away?'

'I can't stay here if my brother knows I tried to get off with his – with you.'

'Do you want to leave?'

Dougie shook his head.

'I like having you in the house. But you've got to behave. You don't think I gave you any encouragement, do you?'

'No.'

'You're funny, you're not bad-looking, and you're not as stupid or obnoxious as you pretend you are. This town is full of single women.'

'I know the score. You're a good, generous lassie. You'll give me any woman in the world except yourself.'

'If you talk like that, you'll have to leave.'

'Aye,' said Dougie, and lowered his head into his folded arms.

'Head up,' said Bec. Dougie obeyed. 'If you promise never, ever to think about trying to touch me in that way again, you can stay, and I won't tell Alex. Can you promise me that?'

'I don't like you keeping a secret from Alex on my account,' said Dougie.

'I don't like it either. Maybe having it on your conscience will make you better behaved. What do you say? Do you promise?'

'Aye,' said Dougie.

Bec went upstairs, got undressed and climbed into bed next to Alex. When she pressed herself against him he stirred and said 'Hello.' Bec ran her fingers over his chest, down over his stomach and on lower, as if straying arbitrarily. His cock was already hard when she touched it; it gave a tiny kick.

'Let's not get drunk again for a while,' she said.

52

Alex couldn't find a good reason for his unease about Dougie living in the house. Anything that had a conclusion couldn't be obvious. Things that stood to reason didn't. If it was considered *natural* to feel uneasy about his brother, whose behaviour was so careless and who owed him a huge debt he'd never be able to repay, living under the same roof, Alex suspected it wasn't natural at all; that once it had been *natural* to hang thieves, beat wives, kill atheists, smother children born crippled and abominate homosexuals. He'd come to think of Dougie as someone whose particular genius was to be forgiven, over and over again. Giving part of the house over to a man he didn't want to be there made Alex feel he'd atoned for getting the property in the first place, and he remembered how much time Harry had spent in Brechin when he was growing up.

In the dealings Matthew had had with Alex as he emptied the house of his father's possessions he'd been cool and serene. Alex told him that he was sorry, that Harry had been wrong.

'Dad did what he wanted. He followed his desires,' said Matthew.

Alex told himself that he and Bec were only looking after the place for a season or two. The fact that there was a third resident made it seem more provisional. Alex didn't want to fill the house with new possessions. The city outside the walls of the house seemed cluttered and when he came home he felt he was coming to a clearing in a tangled wood, a place that was open, light and safe. After a few days each of the almost bare rooms acquired its own qualities, which had less to do with their size and shape than with the moments of his being with Bec that remained when others didn't.

The unpredictable resilience of certain moments puzzled him. The wonder was not in the remembering, but in the way forgotten things tumbled away into oblivion and sacrificed themselves to give remembered things their shape.

Bec's optimism that she and Alex would succeed in conceiving where he and Maria had fallen short was so firm and unthought-through that it hardly seemed like optimism. Without speaking of it they conspired to push their doubts out of reach.

There was a phone booth-sized lock-up at garden level at the back of the house, accessed from an outside door, where Harry had kept the bric-a-brac of the reluctant suburban gardener – clipping shears, a strimmer, various bottles of chemicals. Matthew had, Alex assumed, cleared it out, then locked it. As spring came on and weeds began to appear in the garden Alex found the fat old key and went to see if there were tools inside. The shelves and hooks were bare. On the floor were a pair of gumboots and four pairs of men's shoes. Alex recognised some two-tone brogues that Harry had worn in his last months. A feeling of dread came over him as he looked at the shoes. Their openings seemed to gape and squeal at him like the maws of a brood of little blind creatures who would never understand that the man whose feet they were expecting to fill them up would never come again. They had been waiting in the darkness all this time, screaming for Harry.

Alex wondered why Matthew had left them there, and remembered that there were things of his still at Maria's; or rather things that in a sense were their joint property but for which she had no use. A box full of all the papers generated by the bureaucratic-medical process of trying to get pregnant when it wouldn't come naturally. A box on the bottom shelf of an upstairs cupboard, if he wasn't mistaken, on one side of which Maria had written, without intending to be sentimental, without imagining it would ever be anything other than the most sensible label to identify the box, *BABY*.

Dougie had told Alex once that people like him and Maria, middle-class people who wanted children and didn't have any, romanticised parenthood out of all proportion. That was how Alex remembered it, unconsciously translating. What Dougie had actually said was, 'You shouldn't get too up your own arse about being a dad. You get a wee man or a wee lassie to play with for a bit and the next thing you know there's this superfluous person knocking about who doesn't seem to know much about you, but it's all your fault.'

That summer, when Rose was seventeen, she left home. Nobody told Alex and Bec the whole or the same story, but from the overlaps between what Matthew said on the phone, what he said in his great anguish when he came to London to look for her, what Alex's parents told them and what Rose herself said when she came round one Sunday in her slightly altered headgear, accompanied by a chaperone from the Islamic seminary in Whitechapel where Rose was now studying, Rose's departure from the family house had been intended more as

377

a declaration of independence than a complete rupture, and only became final as a result of a despairing, futile act of force on Matthew's part. As far as Alex could understand Matthew hadn't hit her. He'd accepted that under the law he was powerless to stop her leaving. It seemed that on the threshold of the house he'd wrapped his arms around his daughter and refused to let her go, squeezing her so tightly that she'd cried out in panic that she couldn't breathe. Matthew flinched and Rose wriggled free, passing her hand frantically around her neck on the way out.

Rose seemed relaxed and sure of herself when she turned up unannounced at the house and asked if she could use their landline to talk to her family. Conversing with the chaperone, a second-generation London Bangladeshi, Alex got the impression that rather than the seminarians going out of their way to recruit Rose, let alone indoctrinate her, Rose had found them and to their embarrassment demanded admission.

Rose and Bec had a separate talk. Bec promised Rose to keep her secret, that she had tried to move in with her boyfriend's family, but that his parents had refused, appalled that their son should consider marrying *an English girl*.

Matthew and Lettie accused Alex and Bec of encouraging Rose's apostasy. Dougie's presence in the Islington house; its strikingly bare appearance, which seemed to Matthew to offer a subversive and unstable example to an impressionable girl; Alex's inability to see the difference between Islam and the love of Christ; and Bec's suggestion that Rose's actions might not be about faith, but about adventure, added to their sense of persecution.

Alex went with Matthew to the seminary and they kept up a long vigil. Rose wouldn't come out to meet them. She sent down a note to tell her father that she was well, that she would call them regularly, that she would visit them when her studies were finished, and that they shouldn't worry.

When Matthew left Alex and Bec stood on the threshold of the house and told him that Rose would be all right.

'I don't understand you,' said Matthew. 'You believe this life on Earth is all we ever have, and you treat it so lightly.'

That evening Alex got a call from a TV producer who made shows for the BBC's science unit. He'd seen Alex talking about his work and wanted to chat about him fronting a film project on the science of ageing. He wondered if they could have lunch.

53

In late summer, when preparations for the new season of *Teen Makeover* were far advanced and filming of the first set of auditions was about to start, Lazz checked himself into rehab. Midge called Ritchie to tell him one Friday night, a few hours after Lazz had vanished behind the high walls of the clinic with his overnight bag, an album of whale songs and a six-pack of French mineral water in the boot of his Mercedes. Midge emailed Ritchie the statement Lazz had released to the media, without consulting anyone, detailing his *long battle with drug abuse* and confessing he'd taken cocaine in his dressing room immediately before and after refereeing a showdown between a schoolgirl big band and a quintet of fifteen-year-olds channelling Motown. The statement would be public before morning. Ritchie was on the phone through the hours of darkness, persuading Riggsy to stay away from the clinic, calming Lazz's parents, telling reporters that Lazz had made a *brave decision to confront his demons.* Ritchie said *it came as a great shock to discover* that Lawrence Jones, 29, known to millions as Lazz, had been taking cocaine in the Rika Films studio while children were close by. It was too early to talk about the future of *Teen Makeover*, he said. He emailed his staff telling them to be strong and stand together. He found a driver, an ex-Para who wouldn't flinch from driving a car at high speed into a crowd of paparazzi.

At dawn a cool drizzle soaked the foliage. The car arrived and Ritchie got in the back, thinking he would sleep. The clinic was in Suffolk, two hours away, the car's seats were deep and soft, and the sound the machine made as it flew through the rain was muffled to a faint hiss. Yet Ritchie couldn't close his eyes.

He looked back at his house to watch the automatic gate slide shut and promised himself that he would never allow reporters and lawyers through those gates to molest his children. Savouring the nervous excitement of an unexpected trip after the fear that had tormented him for ten months, he opened the window and let the wind and spray sting his cheeks and beat his hair back. How green and solid England looked in the morning rain, he saw, how eternal. It would look the same, he was sure, whatever made the pack yelp.

I'm glad it wasn't me, he thought, closed the window, and wondered: *Am I a bad man, to think that?* The notion that he was good was hard to prove, but it was intuitively true. The contrary was incredible. If he were wicked, Ritchie reasoned, he would be angry that the chance to save his reputation by shopping Lazz to the Moral Foundation had been knocked away, and he wasn't angry. He was glad to be dashing across England to comfort a fundamentally decent man whose weaknesses had brought him low.

There were only two photographers at the entrance to the clinic grounds when they arrived, which Ritchie took as a sign of disrespect towards Lazz, and by association, towards himself. He wasn't allowed up to the main building, but was directed to a lodge half a mile away where patients could be brought by golf cart. Ritchie was searched in the lobby by a security guard and shown into a bleak meeting area of grey carpet tiles and armchairs with tough hessian upholstery. Midge was there, working his BlackBerry in spasms, as if it were cattle-prodding him.

'Pretty soft search,' said Ritchie. 'I could've had half a kilo of coke up my arse for all they know.'

'Is that what you've got up there?' said Midge. He pointed at the corner of the ceiling, where there was a shiny black bubble. 'They're watching us.'

Ritchie stared at the CCTV eye. 'Listening?'

'Who knows?' said Midge. 'They're in control here.' He rubbed the fabric of his seat viciously. 'Look, even the fucking chairs are done in sackcloth.'

'Why did he do it?' said Ritchie.

'You can ask him,' said Midge. 'They're sending him down in a buggy.'

'I want you to tell me.'

'I don't know why the why matters. That's the least of it for you. The BBC's on its way. They're sending somebody I've never heard of.' Midge closed his eyes and leaned back. 'You know how the jackals are always talking about these bureaucrats, these *penpushers* at the Beeb who get paid shitloads and don't have anything to do? What they do is the most important thing and they don't often have to do it. They're the antibodies. They only come in when it's the organism's life and death.'

'You remind me of my sister.'

'Why did you wince then?'

'I didn't.'

'You did. You said "You remind me of my sister," and you sort of grimaced, as if your sister was bad medicine. I thought she was good medicine, if you spend too much time around mosquitoes.' Midge swallowed as if trying to force down a surge of his own vomit. 'Scenario. Lazz does penance. He cleans himself up. He takes himself off the scene for a bit but lets it be seen that he's doing healthy things, wholesome things. He does older-and-wiser interviews. He gets back together with his wife.'

'His wife!'

'It could happen. You know how much he loves his career.'

'Why did he do it? Why did he go public? Was it because he got the call?'

'What call?'

'You know what I mean. The MF.'

'Ask him.'

'Did you get the call?' said Ritchie, leaning forward and speaking more softly.

'Did you?' said Midge.

Ritchie didn't answer. Midge stared at him belligerently. Their heads dropped.

There was a gentle knock and the door opened. Its hinges made a drawn-out, enquiring squeak. Lazz stood in the doorway. Ritchie and Midge got up and moved towards him, as if each had the expectation there would be hugging. They stopped short when they saw that Lazz wasn't moving towards them. He recoiled a little. Waiting in the corridor behind him, a few yards back, was an attendant in a white tunic with short sleeves that showed hairy forearms and a fat gold watch. It seemed to Ritchie that Lazz had never looked healthier or more attractive. He brimmed with surplus youth and life. An unfamiliar dishevelment – stubble, untreated hair – contrasted with his naturally smooth dark skin and his clear brown eyes, now looking into Ritchie's with great intensity. Ritchie felt the pulse of a vaguely promised future reward; the same pulse that had made him want to own Lazz at the first audition, and had made him increase the value of his contract by more than he needed to each year, despite Lazz's tantrums, his coldness, selfishness, obsessive-compulsive dressing room behaviour and his lack of ability to do anything exceptionally well. Ritchie felt now as he supposed one of the consuming herd would feel meeting him, as if they were obstructing a marvellous being who only wants to be left alone to commune with the sacred spirit that lives inside the camera.

'I'm sorry, Ritchie,' said Lazz. 'I let the guys down. Thanks for coming over.'

'Don't worry, Lazz,' said Ritchie. He blinked. He felt the tears about to spill and teetered between letting it out and holding it back. He controlled it. 'The most important thing is that you get yourself sorted out.'

'If there was a way I could come back, I'd like to,' said Lazz.

'We'll talk about that when you're better.'

'I'm not ill,' said Lazz. 'It's rehab.'

'I know,' said Ritchie. 'But I didn't come to talk about work. I wanted to tell you I think you're courageous, we're going to get through this, and as soon as the doctors –'

'Counsellors,' said Midge.

What do they do here, anyway? thought Ritchie. 'As soon as the counsellors have done their stuff, we'll sit down and work out where we go next.'

'You're dumping me,' said Lazz.

'Ritchie's right,' said Midge. 'The only thing that matters today is that you get yourself in a good place.'

'Did he tell you?' said Lazz to Ritchie.

'I said he should ask you,' said Midge. He passed his fore-finger quickly along the bottom of his nose, forward and back.

'Midge wanted me to shop a mate,' said Lazz.

'I said you had options,' said Midge, and raised the finger in the air. 'I wouldn't be much of an agent if I didn't tell you you had options.'

'A specific mate?' asked Ritchie.

'My granddad was a prisoner in Korea,' said Lazz. 'The Communists couldn't make him crack.'

The nurse, if it was a nurse, called Lazz away and Lazz turned and followed him out. Ritchie and Midge stood in the doorway and waved him off, telling him that they would be thinking of him, and that they would see him soon.

'He'll never work in children's TV again,' said Ritchie.

Midge put his hands in his pockets and chased a pebble in a circle with the toe of his shoe. 'Everyone will be forgiven one day,' he said.

Ritchie said: 'If you were telling him to shop somebody else, how did you know he wouldn't shop you?'

'I'm not famous like Lazz,' said Midge. He looked at Ritchie and smiled. 'Or you. Besides, I'm a good boy.'

'Not in Chiang Mai.'

'Not sure what you're talking about, mate. You know in Thailand the age of consent is fifteen?'

'Don't get me wrong, Midge. I'd never . . . not to you.'

'I'm sure. And I wouldn't to you. But you'd never tell me if you'd got the MF call. If you got one of those codes.' Midge stopped, as if waiting for Ritchie to speak, and went on. 'Do you know what they offer you if you give them something they can use on somebody else? Twenty years' immunity. They deposit a certificate with a lawyer, in your name, undertaking not to publish material detrimental to your standing in the community for twenty years. They've got us all. Nobody trusts each other. And if somebody's out there, riding high, untainted, pure, nobody in the know's thinking *What a great guy.* They're all thinking *Who did he sell to buy his peace of mind?*'

A woman was walking towards them from the gate with her hands in the pockets of her coat and the hood of the coat over her head. She moved as if she were strolling to pass the time, but she came up to them and introduced herself as Jane from the BBC.

'Corporate affairs,' she said. The whine of the golf cart taking Lazz away had gone and her voice sounded in absolute silence. Ritchie was shocked by how young she was. Was she even thirty-five? She had glasses with thick black frames and a large crusted-over spot in the middle of her cheek. It seemed to Ritchie that her lack of make-up showed disrespect. Somewhere across the park a crow cawed and, as if cold, damp air had gushed from its throat, they each felt the temperature drop and of their own accord went back inside.

Midge started sketching out a path to redemption for Lazz and Jane listened from one of the hessian armchairs until Midge ran out of words under her gaze and stopped talking.

'As far as I understand they make you healthy here,' said Jane. 'They don't make you good. I'm not sure where you go these days for that kind of rehabilitation.' She turned from one man to another and her glasses caught the light, hiding her eyes behind bright, cold squares. 'The Corporation's very unforgiving about attractive young celebrities taking hard drugs in close proximity to children. Is that unreasonable, Ritchie?'

'Of course not,' said Ritchie.

'Be that as it may,' said Midge.

'It is as it is,' said Jane. 'Lazz is out of *Teen Makeover* for good. There's nothing to be talked about there. The question is about the show itself.'

Ritchie waited for Jane to go on. He wondered if she was a lesbian. He was impressed by her confidence. Could he offer her a job? Yet it would be murder to have her around. She seemed to him like someone who looked down on everyone, not because of what she'd done at university or in adult life, but because she'd passed the entrance exam to some swotty London day school when she was eleven.

'Everybody wants the show to go on,' said Jane. 'Unless you feel the loss of Lazz would knock the heart out of it.'

'We're broken up, of course,' said Ritchie. 'But even the most golden of golden boys is replaceable.'

'I'm off,' said Midge. He got up, but Jane asked him to stay, and he moved to the side of the room and leaned against the wall with his arms folded.

'Good,' said Jane. 'There'll be a meeting later. We'll have to take another look at the format. As long as you understand there's no second chance. If there's another event like this one, it's over.'

Ritchie nodded fiercely.

'At least Lazz wasn't caught fiddling with one of the teenies,' said Midge.

'Have you reason to believe that's been going on?' said Jane. 'Or was that a joke? Do you think the sexual abuse of minors is funny? Do you, Ritchie?'

Ritchie patted the air with his hands and said that they should take it easy.

'I suppose this is all about the Moral Foundation,' said Jane.

She leaned forward as she spoke and squeezed her right ankle. It made her seem girlish.

'Please don't stare at my legs while I'm asking you a question,' said Jane. 'Have you ever had a call from the Foundation?'

'No,' said Ritchie.

'Good. We'd like you to tell us if that happens. It is interesting, though, isn't it? It can't last. They only destroy reputations. They rely on old media to make the reputations in the first place.'

'What's so interesting?' said Midge. Ritchie was surprised by his surliness, when he was bound to need this woman's goodwill one day. Yet Midge's resistance energised Jane.

'The Moral Foundation's only a threat to people who've done wrong,' said Jane.

'So now it's a moral police state,' said Midge. 'A camera in everyone's bedroom, but as long as you stick to the missionary position, you've got nothing to worry about. What about the actor they stitched up last week for cheating on his girlfriend? Why is that anyone's business except theirs?'

'He was lying to his girlfriend about being faithful,' said Jane. 'That's why it's called cheating.'

'Every day millions of men and women are cheating on each other in this country and nobody cares.'

'Somebody should care,' said Jane. 'Whether they care or not, it's the same wrong, isn't it?'

Midge's jaw worked. 'I feel as if I'm listening to the future chief matron of the British vice and virtue police,' he said.

'I don't think I'd be very good at that,' said Jane. 'I'd say something out of turn and somebody would report me. Isn't that how it works in police-state countries? It's not all torture and buying people off, as far as I understand. Don't they catch most of the dissidents out by blackmailing the cheaters and druggies and embezzlers to betray their friends? I suppose that's what's interesting about the Moral Foundation. It rewards people who inform on their friends. That doesn't seem very moral, does it? Ritchie, I wouldn't have guessed you were such a good listener.'

Ritchie told them that he had to leave.

54

Early one morning, without telling anyone, Bec went to a literary festival in Cardiff, shaking with nerves. A few miles west of Bristol she dry-heaved into the stinking pan of the train's toilets. O'Donabháin's session was one of the earliest, at eleven a.m. on a weekday. *He's a harmless old murderer poet these days* was what Wales reckoned, by the look of it; his session was three lines lost in the middle of the festival programme, part of a strand called Voices Redeemed. Other redeemed voices were a white South African apartheid-era cop, a reformed heroin dealer with an inside account of the trade and a perjurer MP who'd found Jesus in prison. They'd been given afternoon and evening sessions. O'Donabháin seemed to have been marked down.

The walk from the station to the festival campus in warm wind and strong sunshine lifted Bec's spirits. When she entered the artificial brightness of the conference centre, her soles squeaking on the expanse of corporate carpet, her gorge rose again and her heart hammered. She stood in a toilet cubicle, arms locked against the edge of the cistern, head hanging, drool spilling from her lower lip. She'd chosen a blue jumper, jeans and trainers and left her face alone. She wished now she'd pancaked on a mask of make-up, found haughty shoes and an elegant suit and jewellery, made herself forbidding. At five past eleven she walked across the lobby to the door with the taped sheet of paper reading *11 am – Colum O'Donabháin*.

The room was smaller than she expected, with a dozen or so rows of about ten folding chairs, divided down the middle by an aisle. Half the seats were occupied. At the far end of the room two men wearing clip-on mikes sat behind a table; a tall one in his fifties with tufts of white hair behind his ears and round, thick-framed glasses, turning his head from side to side like a lawn sprinkler, and an older man, bulky and uncomfortable, eyes downcast.

O'Donabháin had aged since his poet's picture was taken. The collar of his white shirt was crumpled. *He is only a man,* thought Bec, and took a seat in the back row near the door. It was as if the one she'd dreaded meeting was still to appear. Yet this was him. Instead of the necessary visceral connection between the man at the table and the man who'd executed her father, time had confused the trail. He'd got away.

'Shall we get started?' said the man with glasses. O'Donabháin looked at him as if surprised to find he wasn't alone and began riffling through the pages of his book with his thumb.

'I'm Dale Luthbridge,' said O'Donabháin's interlocutor, 'and it's my great pleasure to introduce to you the poet Colum O'Donabháin, who's visiting Wales for the first time, I think? Colum will be reading today from his new collection *Back Road*, which was awarded the McGarragle Prize for the best book of poetry by a former prisoner living in Ireland.'

'Mine was the only one that qualified,' said O'Donabháin.

The audience laughed and Bec got up and left the room. They'd laughed with him; there'd been a feeling of warmth.

There was a table in the lobby covered in a white cloth and

small piles of O'Donabháin's slim volumes. Bec picked up a copy of *Back Road* and began to walk away when the girl minding the stock called her back and told her there was £9.95 to pay.

'For this? Does some of it go to the poet?'

'About a pound, I suppose,' said the girl. 'I don't know. It's poetry. There's not much money in it.'

Bec paid. The cover had an etching of a country road winding over hills, between hedgerows. She looked closely at the hedgerows. There were no people in them. Her damp fingertips left faint marks on the porous cream-coloured paper. The fact that she had heard O'Donabháin's voice struck her as horrifying. She hesitated at the door to the room. There was a burst of clapping and she grabbed the handle, slipped in and went back to her seat as O'Donabháin began to read his poems.

Again he seemed to Bec too bland and quiet to be the man who'd tortured and killed her father. He read out his verses quietly and monotonously, hunched over his book, speaking into the table. He lyricised birds of various kinds, driftwood, a non-specific regret. He read a comedy poem about being the only one in a group who couldn't speak Gaelic. The audience laughed along. Bec's cheeks burned.

The time came for questions. A woman in her fifties with cropped white hair, a purple vest and earrings three inches wide asked O'Donabháin why he hadn't read the poem 'The Riddle of One Small Soldier'.

'I wondered about that,' said Luthbridge to O'Donabháin. 'It's different in style to your other work.'

'Yeah, it's an old-fashioned English style,' said O'Donabháin. 'Pastiche, almost. There was a time when I started listening to a lot of the old English folk songs about recruiters, about the press gangs. Why do I not read it? Cause I don't much like it, that's why. It's got that word "anthropomorphise" in it. That's quite a mouthful for an old man who never went to uni. Five syllables. I bought the car and it wouldn't fit in the garage.'

Again they laugh! thought Bec. *They're so cosy with him!*

A tall man in a blue blazer, red trousers and a yellow shirt, with a cravat tucked in under his florid chops, stood up and said in a loud drawl, 'I'd like to know what a convicted murderer and torturer' – he seemed to enjoy saying the word *torturer*, as if he were taking the first bite of a hot, crispy treat – 'is doing on the British mainland after his savage treatment of an honourable British officer.' There were intakes of breath and a cry of 'Read the programme!' The man looked round and raised his voice. 'Your presence is an insult to the family of Captain Shepherd, to whom you have never apologised for your cowardly and monstrous behaviour.'

O'Donabháin said: 'The question was, what am I doing here? It's a question I've asked myself every day, wherever I am. People make a lot of assumptions about crime and punishment. They think they always come in that order. They don't, that's all I have to say.'

After the session O'Donabháin left the room with Luthbridge and sat behind the book table in the lobby. Bec watched while he signed books for four people. The man in red trousers left. Bec went to the table and held out the book to O'Donabháin as he was swigging from a bottle of water. He put the bottle down, wiped his mouth with his sleeve and opened the book at the title page. He held his pen over it and cocked his head enquiringly.

'Make it out to Bec Shepherd,' said Bec.

O'Donabháin had bent to the job before she gave her name

and she could see the bald spot on the top of his head. It hung there over the book for some seconds. The pen didn't move. O'Donabháin looked up slowly and stared at her. He seemed anxious. It made the idea of the killer in him emerge to Bec and she dug in to hold her ground and keep her voice steady.

'Do you know who I am?' she said.

O'Donabháin nodded. Now he didn't look so much anxious as curious.

'I have some things to say to you,' she said. 'Come outside with me.'

She led him out of the lobby, down the stairs and out into the daylight. She walked ahead and didn't look back, confident, for some reason, that he was behind her. Near the conference centre was a square edged on two sides by steps where festival-goers and summer school students ate sandwiches and skateboarders did tricks. Bec sat on the steps and O'Donabháin lowered himself with difficulty onto a place a few feet away. He had her copy of his book in one hand and the water bottle in the other.

'My brother thinks I should forgive you, and I've been thinking about it,' said Bec. 'It seems very important to him, and I'd like to do what he wants, because I feel bad about not letting him make his film with you. It's just that I'm not sure what forgiving you means. It's not as if you've asked me to forgive you.'

O'Donabháin shook his head, not taking his eyes off her.

'And I'm not going to tell you that it was all right, what you did. That it was understandable. The only reason I can sit here is that what you did was so cruel I can't bring myself to imagine it.' Unconsciously she scratched the scars on her wrist and O'Donabháin looked away.

'Forgiveness is different for me and Ritchie,' said Bec. 'He thought about you a lot. I think for him forgiveness means not wanting any more revenge. I never thought about you after the trial, only when he brought it up. For me forgiveness means thinking about you at all. It means accepting that you were punished and there's no need to punish you any more. Is that any use to you?'

O'Donabháin nodded.

'I don't want your remorse,' said Bec. 'I don't want your atonement. I want you to know that your being free doesn't bother me. Is that forgiveness? If so, you can have it.'

O'Donabháin shrugged.

'Say something, then,' said Bec, suddenly irritated by his silence.

'I'll take that,' he said.

'Read me that poem of yours,' said Bec. 'The one you wouldn't read before.'

'That's not a good idea.'

'Read it.'

O'Donabháin took a swig from the bottle, found the place in the book and began to read.

The Riddle of One Small Soldier

'That's the title,' he said.

'Go on.'

O'Donabháin cleared his throat and read:

> *I took an oath from paradise*
> *To serve within your blood*
> *You racked my race in vats of ice*

And set me on the flood
To fight against an enemy
Of my own weight and size
I fought it hard and carelessly
I sacrificed your eyes.

For how I sail on human seas
For how I guard the veins
For how I sweep the arteries
You honour me by name.

No one small soldier's life in you
Redeems old soldiers' lives
The killers killed and killers who
In killing them survive
The killers who no longer fight
Who try to voice the dead
Anthropomorphise parasites
That have no heart or head
That multiply without the parts
To know the wrong and right
Or means to prove the human heart
Is not a parasite.

When he'd finished Bec said: 'Sign the book.' Colum wrote *For Rebecca Shepherd, I will make no film. For Ritchie Shepherd, your sister forgives me. Colum O'Donabháin.*

Bec took his bottle and drank from it and gave it back. She tore the dedication page out of the book and put the book in his hand.

'I don't want your poems,' she said.

He took the book. As he got up, turned and walked away the disappointment on his face sank into her and she realised that she'd hurt him more than she'd intended, or known was in her power.

55

A spectre materialised in Ritchie's mind, a long-bodied crook-kneed ghoul without a face who would one day walk through his gates and through the locked door of his house as if they had no substance, drag him from his sleeping wife's side and throw him down in the road outside his property, then stand guard, preventing him ever returning to claim what was his, his home, his woman and his children. He began to spend less time in London. He tried to be back before Ruby went to bed. Twice after term started he surprised Karin and Milena by taking the children to school. He saturated them with attention and gifts. He worried that they were bored by him, and in Dan's polite closing of the door against him with the excuse of homework, in Ruby's flitting suddenly from him to his mother, Ritchie rediscovered, at the age of forty-one, the same heartache over the quick, bright, fickle attention of children he'd felt when he was a child himself.

He began teaching Ruby to play the guitar. At times she would show a precocious ambition and an eerie grasp of the vocabulary of the trade. 'I only want to do acoustic gigs,' she said once. Or she would lose interest and shout that she didn't want to play.

Ritchie's heart rose when he watched his daughter's fingers

stretch to span the fretboard and hold down the tense nylon strings, with her head nodding and her hair waving over the sound box. Sometimes she would make a small mistake and look at him and smile in comradeship; her eyes would look into his with an understanding that was timeless, as if all the ages that she would be were in her already, waiting to unfold, child, friend, fellow-adventurer, lover, mother, grandmother. Ritchie wished that the instant could be eternal, but he never knew when it was coming, and when it did, his pride and possessiveness would shine out of him too hungrily, and the comfort of that sure, timeless bond would vanish.

Bec and Alex threw a housewarming party. Ritchie thought he could get away with not going, but Alex badgered him with emails and a phone call and he said he'd come with Karin. Two days before the party Karin told him she couldn't go. The What were coming to work with her in the studio for a week. She couldn't leave. Ritchie had thought the band too good and too disrespectful to him to appear on *Makeover*, and to encourage them not to make trouble about it Ritchie had put Karin in touch. She'd seen them play in a small venue in Portsmouth, liked their sound and liked that they treated her as a national treasure. Ritchie asked if it wasn't going to be bad for her image to work with a bunch of fifteen-year-olds and Karin said that they were sixteen now.

'They're bringing tents,' she said. 'There's a shower in the studio block. I knew you wouldn't want them in the house.'

'They mustn't take drugs,' said Ritchie.

He reached the party at nine. The windows were lit and the door stood open. A girl in a short black dress and a skinny man with a moustache and sideburns were smoking and drinking wine on the steps. They ignored Ritchie when he went between them and into the house.

There were so many people inside, and Bec and Alex had arranged lamps so cleverly, in corners, in fireplaces, lighting ceilings, casting overlapping pools on the floor, that Ritchie didn't notice at first how little furniture there was, or how naked the walls were. On one floor there was dancing; on another, cushions and paper screens and gentler music; in the kitchen, clever-looking men and women were arguing intensely in different groups, and Ritchie felt he was observing the proceedings of a chic parliament. The guests were better-dressed than he'd expected, with more wit and elegance in their clothes than he'd thought off-duty scientists could show. It hadn't occurred to him that Bec and Alex might have friends who weren't scientists. The wine was superb; they must have spent a fortune on it, he thought. In each room, the first impression that came to Ritchie, before he began picking out individuals, was of a mass of people who were sure of them-selves, thoughtful and open. He'd never been in a group quite like it, and the jealousy that was so quick to rise in him surged up. The luck of it, he thought, for Bec and Alex to fall into this town house and find themselves running a salon, without trying! While he'd ended up a family man out in the sticks! How did it happen? He was the rich one. He was the celebrity. Who were these people? Who was the extremely pretty young girl, and why was she wearing a Muslim headscarf, when she was plainly white? Who was the big sunburned chap with the shoulder-length fair hair and the uncanny eyes?

He saw Alex and Bec from the far side of the room, standing next to each other as if they'd just married, Alex with his arm around Bec's waist. They were laughing with somebody; they looked full of an endless joy. Bec wore a low-cut halter-neck dress, and the light glinted on a silver necklace and silver chains in her ears that swung as she moved her head. Alex had on a plain white shirt and it seemed to Ritchie that the room inclined towards them, like photographers behind the ropes at the red carpet.

A woman beside him asked if he'd like a refill. She was holding a bottle in her hand and Ritchie's glass was empty. She poured him a full measure. She seemed tipsy.

'I'm driving,' said Ritchie.

'So am I,' said the woman, laughed and touched his forearm. 'God, doesn't she look gorgeous? I hate her.'

'Who?'

'Bec,' said the woman, staring across the room with her eyes narrowed. She turned back to Ritchie and smiled. 'I love her. We used to be best friends at school. You know, BFF. It never is for ever, is it? We were out of touch for a long time.'

Ritchie looked at the woman, wondering if he'd met her. He liked to be unrecognised and then to reveal his true identity.

'Did you ever spend the holidays with her?' he said.

'No,' said the woman. 'Oh well, we went to London for the weekend once. Her brother was a pop star. He was in a band called The Lazygods. I don't know if you remember them.'

'Vaguely.'

'We went to see them at the Hammersmith Palais. They were OK. I mean the woman was good, but her brother was a bit . . .' She looked round, touched Ritchie's arm and leaned forward. 'It was quite funny. She made me promise never to tell anyone but it was such a long time ago. She had a backstage pass, and she went looking for her brother, and she walked into this dressing room, and there was David Bowie and Bono! They'd been on as well, it was some kind of benefit gig. And she heard one of them, I think it was Bowie, say: "That Ritchie Shepherd, he sings like a dog trying to get back inside the house." And Bono laughed.'

Ritchie looked back towards Bec. She saw him and waved and he walked towards her stiffly, blood roaring in his ears. Alex clapped him on the shoulder and Bec kissed him on both cheeks. He smelled her perfume and heard her asking if he was OK.

'You look preoccupied,' she said.

'Enjoying myself,' said Ritchie. 'Great party.'

'Wait here,' said Bec. 'I've got a surprise for you.'

'We're keeping an eye on each other,' said Alex to Ritchie, watching Bec go. 'Drunk host syndrome, never good.'

How did it happen that my geeky old drummer is familiar with me about my sister? thought Ritchie. *I am in some other being's new world of punishment now.*

'Do you ever watch science documentaries?' asked Alex. 'They asked me to front one.'

'Why wouldn't they?' said Ritchie, unable to make the effort to part his teeth.

Bec returned with a piece of paper in her hand. She asked Ritchie to come with her and took him to the landing outside.

'I'm sorry, I'm a bit tipsy,' she said. 'I forgot what I was doing. I forgot it was about Dad.' They were standing close together. Bec looked into her brother's eyes. 'Did you know O'Donabháin was reading his poetry in Wales recently?'

'No.'

'I went. I know how important it was to you that I forgive

402

him. I know it means more to you than making your film.' She hesitated. It seemed to her that Ritchie was greatly surprised at what she'd done. 'So I went to see him, and I suppose I have forgiven him, in my way. We had a talk. Here. He wrote this on the title page of his book.'

She gave Ritchie the piece of paper and he read what O'Donabháin had written.

'It's for the best,' said Bec.

'Yes,' said Ritchie with difficulty. He felt as if he were choking.

'It's all settled with him and there won't be any film. It's closure, as you said.'

Ritchie opened and shut his mouth a couple of times.

'I'm sorry,' said Bec, beginning to cry and putting her arms around him. 'I don't know why I brought this up in the middle of a party. I just saw you and thought about it. I don't see you often enough.'

Ritchie went through the motions of returning the embrace and gazed over his sister's shoulder at the dark window opposite and the stairs leading downwards.

'Imagine you going to all that trouble to stop my film,' he said. 'To forgive him, I should say. That was so *good* of you. You really are quite a piece of woman. Well done! I'm feeling a bit the worse for wear, though, my dear. I must go.'

Ritchie went to a nasty bar nearby, drank three double whiskies in quick succession, left and hailed a cab. The driver was sceptical about driving seventy miles to Petersmere until Ritchie showed him a sheaf of red banknotes.

What Ritchie wanted more than anything was to kiss his sleeping children and to get into bed beside his wife. But Milena had taken Dan and Ruby to stay with Karin's parents for the weekend. The taxi dropped Ritchie off at the gates and he walked up the drive. It was well after midnight and the lights were still on in the studio block. He heard music. He went to the window and looked in. Karin was on a stool, wearing headphones, working through a tricky chord sequence, and one of the boys from The What was cross-legged on the floor next to her, writing in a notebook. She looked up, smiled uncertainly as if somebody had said something to her that she thought was probably funny even though she couldn't hear it, and took off her headphones. Ritchie saw her smiling mouth form the word 'What?' and somebody he couldn't see must have repeated it because she laughed, and looked down at the boy and said something to him just as he was taking a swig of Dr Pepper. He laughed and held up the back of his wrist to his face so as not to make a mess.

Ritchie walked to the house. A faint ripple of bass and snare drum sounded behind him in the darkness as if fireworks were bursting far away and out of sight. A sadness greater than he had ever known quivered inside his ribs, terrifying in its weight and apparent permanence, and the thought of suicide returned to him not as a desire to end his life but as a counter-force to that sadness, as if, by going through the motions of ending his life, he might frighten the sadness, make it seem small and trivial. Yet once his intention to take steps was formed, he couldn't help thinking *What if?* All the peaks and troughs around him would be flattened: his own sadness, Bec's joy, Karin's happiness. As for his children, what had his clever son said? 'If you did so well without a father, why is it good for me to have one?' And the sadness reached into him again, like a clawed hand groping through his body for a grip on his heart firm enough to drag him underground.

He went to the scullery, where he knew he'd stowed the old rope swing from the garden after it fell. He found it coiled in the back of a cupboard, slung it over his shoulder and took it upstairs. The lights in his study were indecently harsh and he switched them off except for one small desk lamp. He dropped the heavy coil of rope on the floorboards under the main roof beams and looked up.

For a moment he felt foolishly defeated by the mechanics of the problem before realising that he first had to tie one end of the rope to a fixed object at floor level. He lashed it to a radiator, then set to creating a noose at the other end. *How do they make nooses in the films*, he thought, *with the rope twisted round the loop ten times? That's not something they teach in the Scouts.* He made a loop with a simple slip knot and tried to throw it over the roof beam. The rope was heavy, and his first attempts weren't strong enough to top the beam. On the fifth try it went over and came down on the far side. For a moment he felt pride at a job well done. But the noose didn't hang down far enough for him to be able to get his head inside it.

He fetched a small stepladder and by standing on it was able to pass the loop comfortably over his head and fit it snugly against his throat. The rough strands pressed against his Adam's apple and he saw in horror that the length of rope was exactly right if he really had been intending to kill himself.

He passed his fingers quickly inside the noose to loosen it and pull it off his head, but the tightening of the slip knot had caused it to catch on an imperfection in the rope and it wouldn't come free easily. Ritchie panicked and tugged hard at the sides of the noose with both hands. It loosened slightly and rose to just behind his ears but his violent tugging, and the effect on his balance of the alcohol still in his bloodstream, made him slip. He felt the stepladder sliding away from him and he scrabbled for a better foothold but instead he kicked the stepladder away, it toppled and hit the floor, and Ritchie was left dangling from the roof beam by his jaw. His metabolism responded to terror with power and instinct told him that his life depended on him putting all his strength into his hands, still stuck between the rope and his head, to overcome the slip knot and his own great weight and wrench the noose up over his chin and nose and let him fall to safety. Whimpering with fear and pain, thrashing his legs in space, straining every muscle in his upper body he pulled and pulled at the noose.

He saw quite clearly that his strength was about to run out, and he expended it all on one last effort. He cried out, the rope dragged savagely along his jaw, struck and passed the bump of his chin, hit his nose with such force that it seemed it would be torn off, and he fell onto the floor, where he lay for a long time, crying.

He got up, unfastened the rope from the radiator and coiled it neatly. He washed his face. There was no mirror in the study to examine himself. He couldn't feel any damage, no cut flesh or bleeding, just a sharp stinging around his neck.

Still sniffing and wiping his nose he went to the fridge and took out a chocolate pudding. He ate a couple of puddings with a bottle of beer and went to the shelves where he kept his films. He found the DVD he'd ordered, but never watched, after his first meeting with Colum O'Donabháin. He took another pair of puddings and another bottle and sat down to watch *Army in the Shadows*. After half an hour he came to the scenes showing the Resistance's execution of the traitor Dounat.

Ritchie watched Dounat in the car, realising what was about

to happen to him, swallowing and wiping his thumb over his voluptuous mouth in fear.

The driver drew up on a bleak esplanade, alongside the high Mediterranean surf. Dounat's former comrades Gerbier and Felix walked the traitor up a narrow alley, holding an arm each. Ritchie could feel the cold wind off the sea.

They entered a rented house. Inside was another young man, Claude LeMasque. In a bare shuttered room, LeMasque told Gerbier that he'd prepared everything for the interrogation. He smiled, rocked on his heels and massaged his left hand with his right ingratiatingly, as if he were talking about arrangements for a party: he'd prepared chairs, desk, paper.

But Gerbier said there would be no interrogation. 'This is what it's about,' said Felix, taking out a pistol.

LeMasque said it was his first time. Gerbier swivelled round to face him and said with passion: 'This is our first time too. Can't you see?'

Ritchie swallowed a gulp of beer. He felt such sympathy with these characters: with LeMasque – how could he stand by and watch Dounat, yes, a traitor, but a good-looking, well-dressed young man like himself, be killed? Yet there was Gerbier, who'd seemed so experienced, suddenly revealing that he, too, was writhing with horror inside at what had to be done!

They talked about how to kill the traitor. Felix asked whether they couldn't just smash his head in and the traitor lifted up his hands as if to hold back a crushing weight rolling towards him. Gerbier ordered him gagged and Felix and LeMasque, brave LeMasque, stuffed a handkerchief in his mouth. The traitor began to whimper and they manhandled him face-down onto a mattress.

Gerbier said that they would have to strangle him, using a towel from the kitchen. LeMasque put his hands to his ears, unable to bear the sound of the traitor weeping through the gag. Gerbier told LeMasque that he'd asked for harder assignments, and now he was getting one.

How right they both were, thought Ritchie, a sweet sadness swelling in his chest, his eyes prickling. How tragic that this noble young man should have to take part in this terrible deed, and how right that Gerbier should remind him how necessary it was to be cruel sometimes, for the sake of justice, for the sake of order, so that good people and their families might live in peace! In ordinary times, this traitor wouldn't need to die; but now he would have to be sacrificed for the good of others.

Felix drew the curtains over the shutters and switched on the light. LeMasque stood stiffly, looking down at the sobbing, gagged figure on the mattress. Gerbier planted a chair in the centre of the room. They hauled the traitor upright, sat him down on the chair, and Gerbier said: 'I promise you won't suffer.' LeMasque held his arms and Gerbier held his legs, looking into his face – such courage, thought Ritchie – while Felix looped the towel around the traitor's throat and tightened it by twisting a piece of wood. The traitor died with tears on his cheeks. His head lolled forward. LeMasque started crying. Gerbier stood at the window with his back to the room for a long time before leaving. 'I could not imagine this was possible,' said LeMasque. 'Neither could I,' said Gerbier.

Ritchie shut down the system and stared with eyes that no longer saw the things in front of them. Forgetting that O'Donabháin had used the film to strengthen his resolve before he killed his father, he was inspired by the nobility of men who did cruel but necessary things for the greater good.

I nearly died tonight, he thought. *My wife was almost widowed and my children left fatherless, my company without a navigator.* He barely remembered his affair with Nicole. He could hardly remember what she looked like, and that distant matter seemed unrelated to the business at hand, which was that an evil force had almost destroyed his family. And although technically Bec might not have done anything wrong – technically, scientifically, as if you could measure good by numbers, but that was how they thought! – Ritchie was amazed to realise, the more he thought about it, how close his sister was to the origins of the evil that had nearly ended his life and might yet tear his family apart.

It was Bec who'd provoked Val's anger by breaking up with him so abruptly; it was Bec who'd released into the world, and to him, twenty years later, the information that two of his heroes thought he was a bad artist; it was Bec who'd stopped him making the film that might have rescued his reputation. You could virtually say, if you took the most extreme view, that Bec had almost killed her own brother. And there she was, in her world of beautiful people, reckoned to be the very best of women. *She has no idea*, he thought. *She has no idea of the gap between how good she thinks she is and what she has actually done.* And as if it had been lying there all along and he only had to find it and pick it up, Ritchie saw how fair it would be if the Moral Foundation showed the world that not everything she did was right.

Ritchie had no idea what secrets she might be hiding, and he wouldn't go looking. But it seemed obvious to him now that there would be justice in it, rough justice, yes, like the summary justice of the brave men of the Resistance, but justice none the less, if he should happen to stumble across an awkward secret of Bec's and quietly, in sorrow yet with dignity, pass it on to the MF. There would be a sort of kindness in it, it seemed to Ritchie; it was risky for his sister to live on in the mistaken belief that she was virtuous. By winging her reputation he would only be pulling her back into the mortal realm where it was safe for women who'd nearly killed their brothers to dwell.

56

It was around the change of seasons, when it was no longer a surprise to see a leaf fall but the days were still warm and the trees still green, that Bec and Alex's unspoken pact to keep the house bare began to break down. If in the beginning they hadn't been afraid to throw away each other's ephemeral things or tidy up each other's messes, that same confidence migrated into a contrary regime of being sure that whenever the other brought something into the house there had to be a good reason for it, and it would be aggression to complain. The unwritten rule against superfluous things turned out to have no weight; it was such that any act of enforcement would in itself be a violation.

Neither was conscious of the change when it took place and it was only later, as the evenings grew dark, that they became aware of its effect. Small piles of pieces of paper from the outside world, neither vital nor straightforward to discard, accumulated. Space was found on horizontal surfaces for gifts and photographs. A Tanzanian friend sent a statuette in dark wood for Bec's thirty-fourth birthday, using an expensive international courier service for fear the regular post would let him down. They put it on a mantelpiece, and at once the space around it looked starved and empty. Family photographs appeared on either side. They had people to dinner; they bought more chairs. After coming back from a conference where she'd spent too much time in heels Bec said she wanted to lie on a sofa, and soon afterwards she and Alex were looking at photos in a catalogue, and soon after that, they were wandering through a store. She saw well-made things she liked, and a month later, the sofa arrived. That plump red piece of comfort acted as a portal, and almost of their own accord rugs began to appear, curtains — as winter approached, the house turned out to be draughty — unfurled along the edges of the windows, and nests of cables squirmed like eels out of sockets.

In late October goods arrived that Alex had put in storage when he left Maria. Most disappeared into the room he was using as a study, but a couple of paintings went onto the walls of the living room; the walls became conscious of their naked-ness. A small round coffee table that Alex had grown up with found its way in. It was neither attractive nor ugly but it seemed to Bec that afterwards it became busy with objects and possessions that, though they were only things, diluted the people. A tiny part of her consciousness and Alex's were diverted into the furnishings and away from themselves and each other. It seemed like a defeat, a retreat, and Bec wasn't sure whether it was a retreat from a never-quite-articulated ideal of minimalism, or the first hints of preparations to defend against a future that might not, after all, be with children.

They were citizens of a domain relatively new to the world, a country much younger than America or Liberia but no longer completely fresh, the domain of sexual freedom. They hadn't won it or been present at its birth; they'd been born into it. Neither had been married before, and were not formally married to each other now, but their inheritance was such that both had been in long, intimate experimental marriages before this one, each of which had, at the time, seemed to be, as this one was now, the actual, final version. These experimental marriages were called *relationships*, but they were marriages none the less, with the same assumptions of fidelity and assumptions of, if not permanence, durability, at least. From one experimental marriage to another, it was easy to misinterpret 'different' as 'better', but Alex, who had suffered in the past – and thus made his partners suffer – from familiarity blunting desire could see, when he compared past experimental marriages to this one, that as time went by his familiarity with Bec only intensified his appetite for her. She felt this and it heightened her desire in return and within the secure borders of their ease and confidence anything was permitted. She drank him and he ate her and they licked each other off their fingers and she permitted violations, accepted moments of ruthlessness from him, that she had not taken from anyone else. When Alex was travelling away from her he would rip the sheets off the bed and disarray them round and between his legs before masturbating to better summon up the hours they spent together. At work, at four o'clock one afternoon, the idea of Alex came to Bec with such force that her cheeks burned and it was all she could do to lock the door and close the blinds before sitting down, opening her legs and putting her fingers between them. She called him and asked if there was any chance of him coming home early; and there was, and he did. Yet she was still not pregnant.

In the past Bec had imagined being pregnant and imagined having a baby. She'd never imagined the state of trying to *get* pregnant. In the beginning this and the delirium of sex and the confidence of love seemed braided together, indistinguish-able. As the months passed, and Alex's nonchalance became strained, the strands separated, and the intangibility of the barrier began to irritate her. She was used to working hard to overcome the obstacles she'd set for herself, and here the work was pleasure and there was no overcoming. It was like waiting to begin a journey without knowing whether there was a journey or where it would take her if it began.

The mind prioritises of its own accord, and although Bec tried to maintain the equilibrium between hoping to get preg-nant and taking her research to the next stage, the having of a child would creep ahead. The diagrams and descriptions of the malaria parasites at work contrived to provoke her. The parasites bumped up against a human blood cell and stuck to it, then rolled, swivelled, butted their way inside and started splitting. It was a clever trick, as if a mouse could butt its way through the skin of an inflated party balloon and get inside without bursting it. In one person, a few thousand malaria merozoites could do it a few thousand times. Yet Alex's millions of gametes couldn't butt their heads into Bec's even once. And Bec's eggs were twenty times the size of a blood cell. The medical databases covered human reproductive science as thor-oughly as parasitology; she only had to tweak the search terms to find more scientific papers about human conception than she could read in a dozen lifetimes, and she realised guiltily that over the weeks she had gained more mastery over the mysteries of the human reproductive cycle than the reproduc-tive cycle of the parasites she was supposed to be studying.

Alex's cousin Matthew, Bec knew, didn't believe in evolu-tion. He didn't believe humans and apes were descended from a common ancestor. He thought God had made the world a few thousand years ago. Bec wondered what Matthew would say if she told him that humans and malaria parasites had a common ancestor millions of generations back. That the cousin cells had gone their separate ways, some to be animals, some to be plants, some to be moulds and slime and parasites. 'You just go ahead and evolve,' said the malaria parasite ancestor to Bec's ancestor. 'I'll catch up with you later.' But the parasite had been lazy. It'd gone to some red algae and said: 'I like your genes. Can I have them? Save me all that evolving.' And the red algae said: 'OK.' Bec and the parasites were alienated now. Not really kin. It was her species against theirs.

Bec didn't like it when Alex told her he'd been asked to make a TV documentary about the genetics of ageing, and that he wanted to do it. What about his work, she asked him? Was he going to drop it, when he'd gone so far, and there were still so many pathways to discover? If he had to give up his job as director, they'd have to leave the house; where would they live?

'I won't have to give up the job,' he said. 'The trustees are keen. They think it'll be good PR for the institute. They'll give me three months' unpaid leave.'

'Then you won't be a scientist, you'll be someone who talks about science,' said Bec. 'They already have people for that. It's as if people think the highest form of anything in this country's not doing it, it's going on television and talking about doing it.'

Next day Alex told her that he'd cancelled the project. She was right, he said. It was a distraction, when there was so much work to do.

Now that Alex had done what Bec told him she wanted, she hated herself. Why, she wondered, had she stopped him?

Who was she to bully him out of following his desires? It wasn't as if he would be giving his research up. It hadn't occurred to her that if she asked him to change his mind about something so important he would do it. The realisation that he would do such a thing for her, so lightly and quickly and with such sincerity, made her want to reward him. She told Alex she was sorry.

'I was jealous,' she said.

'You convinced me,' said Alex. 'What you said made sense.'

'It didn't. Really it didn't. Go back and tell them you want to do it. I'd like to see your mug in TV land.'

So Alex went back and looked forward to his film. Bec thought her envy was not about her being office- and lab-bound while he was free; it was envy in advance, of her being pregnant and then a mother with a baby to look after while Alex was less tethered. Her anger towards him for turning his back on his work for the sake of television was anger in advance at her own turning away from the defence of the malarial lands for her selfish, childbearing purposes.

Maddie asked to see her. They had lunch in an Italian place with a bowl of enormous pink meringues in the window and heavy white furniture moulded as single pieces of plastic. Tiny waitresses with porcelain faces served them precise salads of small, brightly coloured elements, like boxes of watercolours.

Maddie began talking to Bec about the fate of her vaccine, now that it had left the realms of research and was in the hands of manufacturers, bureaucrats and politicians. In the director's severe cheekbones, the swing of her bulbous terracotta earrings and the dark shadows of her eyes, which would avoid, avoid, avoid, then suddenly meet hers, Bec felt a great care and purpose. Feet, Maddie said, were being dragged. Heads needed to be knocked together, but nobody wanted to stick their neck out. There was talk of an ambassador, a charismatic, eloquent, knowledgeable figure who could be the go-between to *roll the vaccine out* in Africa.

'Your name's been mentioned,' said Maddie.

'Is it because I haven't come up with a new line of research?'

Maddie put down her cutlery and lifted one corner of her mouth by a couple of millimetres. 'You make it sound as if I'm suggesting a punishment. You're not fastidious about power, are you?'

'I don't know what that means,' said Bec.

Maddie began telling a story of the future in which Bec was the main character. She was flying from city to city, from meeting to meeting. She was making speeches; she was bringing people together. She was the one who was taking the philanthropists inside the huts of the malaria victims, and taking the malaria survivors to the counsels of the wise and coaching them into telling their story. It was Bec who was bringing the scientists together with the politicians, the politicians with the vaccine makers, the African bureaucrats with the European bureaucrats. And all the while, as she was enduring the cocktail parties, the dinners, the small talk, the tedious glamour of fundraisers in Hollywood one night, Hong Kong the next, she was learning how power works, how deals are done, how countries talk to each other, the body language and cryptic signs of the international healthocracy.

Bec tried to think what Maddie had published since she became director. There wasn't much. She had a grown-up daughter and an ex-husband who had taken pride in moving for her career, then become bitter about it.

'Women in London are good at frightening themselves into being pragmatic,' said Maddie. 'It becomes all or nothing. Research or admin. Responsibility or freedom. Work or motherhood.'

'Why do you mention motherhood?'

'You can switch pages on your screen when I come to your office,' said the director. 'But down the side I can see the last half dozen pages you've been reading.'

Bec blushed. 'I have been distracted,' she said.

She began to think that perhaps she could have all she wanted. Still, by November, nine months after she'd come off the pill, she wasn't getting pregnant.

Harry had been of that generation that reckoned one bathroom in a house was enough. One dark frosty morning Bec stood leaning against the wall in her dressing gown, hands behind her back and one bare foot pressed against the cool white plaster, waiting for Alex to finish in the shower. She heard the water lashing the enamel and Alex whistling monotonously and cheerfully. She tried to work out, from the splashes, which part of his body he was working on, and how long it would be before he finished. It seemed to her that he was washing his whole body three times, and still he whistled.

She pushed the door open and stood on the threshold with her arms folded. Alex looked round from behind the shower screen, grinned and went back to washing, as if he thought she'd come to watch.

'Why are you whistling the same four notes over and over again?' she shouted.

Alex switched off the water and asked her to repeat herself. 'It's Philip Glass,' he said. '*Akhnaten*. That's how he writes.' He stood there naked with the water pouring off him, clapped his hands together rhythmically, pedagogically, and began singing the same four rising notes. *La la la la, La la la la, La la la la, La la la la* —

'I want to see the test results from when you were trying to have a baby with Maria,' said Bec.

Alex stopped clapping and singing, stepped out of the shower and took a towel, his shoulders and head slightly hunched, as if she'd struck him and he was bracing himself for her to do it again.

'They couldn't find anything wrong,' he said, tucking the towel in around his waist and looking at her bravely.

'I know, but all the same.'

57

Bec liked having Dougie around. He was a reminder of the early months in the house when they'd lived a less encumbered life. Since he'd tried to kiss her, he'd become a quieter presence. He found a job at the local sorting office and paid Alex two hundred pounds a month in rent, which Bec thought it mean of Alex to accept. He'd go out drinking several evenings a week; he didn't eat with them often. He took on the weeding of the garden and the skimming of the pond. At weekends he would visit one of his daughters, who lived near London, or so Bec thought, till she caught him at five one Saturday morning leaving the house with a backpack and a fishing rod. He sometimes took a bus into the country, he told her. He liked to fish.

'My Dad used to go fishing in the stream at the bottom of our garden,' said Bec. 'But there was a heron that took all the fish.'

She asked Dougie whether he'd ever taken Alex fishing and he said it had never occurred to him. He hadn't thought Alex would like roughing it overnight in a field. Bec told him to try and a few weeks later she was woken up while it was still dark by Alex, fully dressed with a small rucksack on his back, kissing her goodbye.

Alex and Dougie took a bus north into a county that Alex thought had long since been swallowed up by London but which turned out to have hedge-lined lanes, woods and streams in the spaces left between motorways and commuter bungalows. They changed buses and got out in a coldly charming village and walked for half an hour down a lane, along the edge of a field, over a fence, through nettles and hogweed to a meadow by a deep green stream. A slow current engraved an endless curl on the surface under a screen of willow branches.

Dougie asked Alex where his rod was and Alex said he didn't have one and it put Dougie out.

'I asked you to come fishing, not to come talking,' he said.

'I thought you were going to teach me.'

'Aye, that'd be a novelty, me teaching you.'

Alex put up the tent and stowed their gear inside while Dougie boiled water from the stream on a small gas cooker and made tea. Dougie put his rod together, baited his line, cast it and took up his station on a tiny folding stool by the water's edge.

'What now?' said Alex.

Dougie shook his head. Alex put his hands in his pockets. Dougie hunched on the stool, not moving. Alex went into the tent with a book and read thirty pages. He looked out of the tent. His brother was in exactly the same position.

'I'm going for a walk,' Alex said. Dougie looked at him and nodded. Alex walked upstream. Wind stirred the branches of the trees and the dried leaves crept round his feet like insects.

There was a splash behind him. Dougie was lifting a live thing out of the water. Alex went back and asked if he could help. The fish was about the length of his hand, thrashing like an escapologist trying to free itself from a silver sack. Dougie reached out with his left hand, took the fish off the hook and threw it into the water. Alex asked what it was.

'Dace,' said Dougie. He sat down, rebaited the hook, cast it and settled again, climbing back into silence and stillness as if he were climbing back into bed.

'I wonder if it'll live,' said Alex.

'Fishing's no really about the fish,' said Dougie. 'It's about quietness and knowing how to wait.'

Alex didn't say anything for half an hour. He sat on the grass next to Dougie, with the bait and tackle box between them, trying to be patient, trying to lose himself in the circles on the water and the bubbles in the eddies or to follow the floating leaves describing the swirl of the current beneath the willow. But his mind churned. He asked Dougie about his children and when Dougie said that they were fine Alex told him that he and Bec were trying for one and Dougie said: 'Good for you.'

'It's not happening,' said Alex.

'Patience,' said Dougie. 'It hasn't been long.'

'I tried with Maria, and now Bec. It doesn't look good.'

'Patience.'

'You've never had any trouble.'

'You think two wee daughters at opposite ends of the country's no trouble? I never even wanted kids.'

'That doesn't make me feel better.'

'It was no wearing a condom that did it for me.'

'You think I forgot to take the lens cap off?'

'I'm saying I was *totally irresponsible*. Being that thoughtless is a knack, buddy boy. How come I slept with those women if I didn't like them? I gave in to myself. It's no like that with you and Bec. You're in love with her and she loves you. She's one in a million. Remember, there's options.'

Alex did think he was in love with Bec, and yet it still seemed to him that the word 'love' was like a flat heavy stone that people hauled over disarray to keep it hidden in the dark.

'What options?' he said.

'You're the scientists. I don't know. IVF again. Adoption. The old turkey baster.'

'No,' said Alex.

'How d'you mean, no?'

Alex stared into the opaque water. 'I think it's me,' he said. 'Maria and Bec, it's too much of a coincidence.'

'Patience.'

'I don't want somebody else to father my children, I don't want to adopt somebody else's children, I don't want Bec to have her eggs harvested and frozen and be fertilised in a dish. I want to know that me and her belong in nature.'

Dougie looked him up and down. 'Nature?' he said. 'You?'

'The chain of time reaching back to the first things,' said Alex doggedly.

'Too late for nature, buddy boy,' said Dougie. 'Where would you start? Give up your clothes and shoes, your house, your books, the shops, then you can start talking about the natural way. Making sick people better, or making people, what's the difference? What's natural in medicine? What's natural in science? What's natural in anything you do? You can't even catch a fish.'

'What I do in science is try to understand,' said Alex. 'If other people want to use that for medicine, it's up to them.'

'You gave Harry a dose before he went.'

'Oh well, that was Harry,' muttered Alex.

423

'I don't get you, brother.'

'It's not about fairness. It's the way the universe is set up. Every generation there's a sorting out, and there are those who get picked to go forward, and those who don't get picked. And if I'm not picked, fine. I accept it. The universe can go on without me.'

Dougie bent forward on the stool. For a moment Alex thought he was going to topple into the water. He looked at Alex, blinded by tears of laughter. 'Aha. Ahahaha. I get it now. There was me thinking I had a chip on my shoulder, and it turns out it's just a bit of fluff compared to yours. Pride!'

He moved his fishing rod gently from side to side. In the water the line hardly stirred, as if it had caught on something. 'If you sit around all day waiting for evolution to make you a bicycle, you'll end up walking. It's no just you now. You haven't said to Bec what you've just said to me?'

Alex shook his head.

'That's good. Don't. Less thinking and more making love to your beautiful girlfriend. Why not marry her?'

Alex bent his head quickly, frowned and tightened his mouth. 'I'd stay with her whatever happens,' he said. 'But I wouldn't stand in *her* way if she wanted children I couldn't give her.'

'I shouldn't be giving you advice,' said Dougie. 'Don't pay attention to anything I say. Look how far you've got and look at me.'

'That's not the way it is. You have a few setbacks and you make a fake failure personality for yourself.'

'The personality came before the failure. It goes way back. You know what happened when Harry tried to help about that cunt Bridgeman giving me a hard time at school.'

'Bridgie?'

'Aye, Bridgie.'

'I don't remember that.'

'You were off on that school trip to Paris. Bridgie was getting money off us and if I didn't cough up he'd twist my arm behind my back and it hurt like fuck. Harry finds out about it and the next thing is I come home and there's Bridgie sitting at the kitchen table, our kitchen table, trying not to laugh. Harry's set up a peace conference for us. He's made flags for us, cards with our names on, and he gives us this talk about conflict resolution, and starts quoting Noam Chomsky.'

'And you were how old?'

'Eleven. So there's Uncle Harry, he's done all this, he's set up a peace conference, all the trimmings, little flasks of water on the table, gives us an agenda, and we have to go through it, make an agreement, then make a joint statement and shake hands while he takes a picture of us. He was making this huge effort and trying to do the right thing for me and stick to his ideals about humanity, and all I knew was my own uncle had brought my worst enemy into my own house. I threw a glass of water in Bridgie's face and went and hid in my room. I wouldn't come out till he'd gone.'

Dougie's rod bent. An underwater force was pulling on the line and Dougie pulled sideways. The line quivered. Dougie fought, tried to play it, stood up, lifted the rod sharply and turned the reel. The line snapped and rippled free in the air. Alex thought of one of Bec's long hairs that he'd found on his jacket when he was walking through a faraway town and how he'd lifted it off and held it up and watched it drift in the wind, caught in the sun, then let it go.

'There's something big there,' said Dougie. He fixed a new hook to the line, baited it and cast.

He said: 'What do I still owe you?'

'A hundred and nineteen thousand pounds.'

'Pounds, eh,' said Dougie. The rod bent again and Dougie braced his heels against the bank. 'Here,' he said, and passed the rod to Alex. Alex could feel a powerful living energy yanking at the line. He could feel the anger and fear in the muscles of the creature in the stream.

'What should I do?' he said.

'Just hang on,' said Dougie. He took a net and stood over the water.

'How can a fish in a little English stream be this strong?' said Alex.

'It's throwing its weight like punches. It's fighting for its life. Pull, rest, pull. After the next pull start reeling it in.' The line slackened, Dougie leaned over to flip the catch on the reel and Alex began turning it.

'Turn and pull. Fast! That's it! Now pull it out!' Alex swept the line up and across and the fish, so much smaller and brighter than he'd imagined, flew out of the water.

58

Maria sent Alex the documents from their conception files without a covering note and with the papers about herself weeded out. Bec read through them; it was as she'd been told. The doctors couldn't find anything wrong and Bec saw the years change in the dates on the documents and understood how long Alex and Maria had been trying. There were places where the dry language of the doctors softened. *However . . . unfortunately . . . always possible . . .*

Bec said they should be tested again together and Alex said it had only been a few years since he'd sat in the bathroom of Maria's house, trying to produce a sperm sample into a tiny plastic cup with a sharp, abrasive rim while their elderly Polish cleaner was vacuuming the hall outside. So Bec went to the fertility clinic alone. They measured her hormones, scanned her womb and told her that for a woman of thirty-four she was in fine reproductive shape. She waited for Alex to ask how the tests had gone, but he didn't; he told her with strained cheer *We need to be patient.*

One night in February, when she came home from work, Alex was waiting for her in the hall with a pair of African drums. Beating a complex rhythm with his hands, he announced a special dinner on the occasion of the first anniversary of their Tanzanian betrothal. Dougie was out and Alex had cooked ugali and stew with some kind of meat; London bush meat, he swore, a little bit of rat, fox, pigeon. *Look in the bin, the bones are there.* Afterwards they watched a *Daktari* DVD and drank the best part of two bottles of wine before they went to bed and made love in a warm, drunken way. In the small hours of the morning Bec woke up thirsty. She'd gone to sleep glad, and now was full of anxiety that they'd been rehearsing to be a lifelong binary, affectionate, amiable.

It seemed to her that Alex's yearning for children had been the cause of the precious hard-edgedness of their lovemaking, the shadow that had moved between them when Alex was inside her, when she enclosed him, the savage ghost that stripped their tenderness of all that was cloying, when they'd bare and clench their teeth as if possessed by the beast they were fighting to break.

A couple of weeks later, when Alex went to America with a film crew, Bec was strangely joyful, and he noticed this. He asked *why she was in such a good mood* and she didn't tell him she was several days late. She wanted to surprise him with a phone call, perhaps the same day, when he got off the plane in Los Angeles. It would still be Saturday in California, and Bec anticipated she would be in bed, after midnight, telling him everything. Pregnant! Why not? When Alex had gone she went to the chemist's and bought a testing kit. She'd supposed the sales assistant would smile at her or wish her good luck but the young girl scanned the packet and took the money without her expression changing as if Bec were buying a toothbrush.

Bec remembered that the last time she'd bought a test it'd

been more in fear of pregnancy than in hope of it. At home she came out of the bathroom, sat on the bed and watched the display flash. Words appeared. *NOT PREGNANT*, it said. Her heart jumped. She stared at the tester and shook it and wondered if she'd done it wrong.

She looked towards the open doorway. Dougie was there, tapping the door with a single knuckle. She hid the tester in her fist, got up and slammed the door in his face. She shouted at him to leave her alone and mind his own business. She walked trembling around the room. Outside she heard Dougie talking and what sounded like a little girl's voice. She came out and saw Dougie leading one of his daughters downstairs.

'I'm sorry,' she called, and Dougie looked round.

'Come and have lunch with us,' he said.

They went to a pizza restaurant on Upper Street. Kirsty, who was seven, was quiet and shy and wary of Bec, who told her she was sorry for shouting at them. She'd been cross about something, she told Kirsty. She wondered if Dougie had seen what she'd been holding. The deceptive candour of his eyes, which looked so frankly into hers but gave no indication of what they saw, gave their table of three an intimacy and a unity, drawing her closer to Dougie and Kirsty and pushing everyone else in the restaurant further out. She felt she was always looking away from him; each time it was as if at the very moment of her looking away a delicate change came across his face that made her curious, so she looked back.

A woman in her sixties at the next table kept turning to look at Kirsty, smiling and trying to catch the eye of Bec, who smiled back and wished Alex was there. When they brought Kirsty's ham and pineapple pizza the woman said to her that goodness, it was a large pizza, was she really going to eat all of it? And Kirsty said yes, she was, and the woman laughed hard and looked at Bec and Dougie and tried to hook them into joining in, and Bec laughed a little. Kirsty didn't finish the pizza, but she had chocolate cake afterwards, and the woman leaned over and said to Kirsty that the chocolate cake looked absolutely fantastic! She said to Bec: 'Their eyes are so much bigger than their stomachs at that age, aren't they!'

'I don't know,' said Bec. 'I'm not her mother.'

She didn't think she'd been rude, but the woman's face lost its jollity and she turned away and didn't speak to them again.

Later, alone at home, Bec loaded the washing machine in the scullery at the back of the kitchen. In theory there was a common basket for dirty clothes and it was a general chore to do the washing. It seemed to Bec that she did it more often than the brothers. She'd noticed that Dougie scrupulously kept his underwear out of the basket. She imagined him sneaking downstairs in the small hours to perform his secret laundry of intimate things. His shirts and jeans and t-shirts were in with the rest. Their colours and fabrics and patterns were as familiar to Bec as her own and Alex's. The sleeves of Dougie's rose-coloured denim shirt were twisted in a braid with the sleeves of Alex's sky-blue dress shirt and a white blouse of hers. She lifted the tangle out of the basket and carefully unpicked the garments from each other. She put her blouse and Alex's shirt in the machine and put Dougie's on the floor. She went through the basket separating Dougie's clothes from theirs. The closer she got to the bottom of the basket the angrier she became. *I'm not Alex's brother's skivvy*, she thought. When she had the basket empty and Dougie's clothes lay in their heap apart at her feet, older and more worn than Alex's or hers and of strange old fashions, she saw in them only evidence of her own madness. She picked the clothes up and crammed them into the machine with the others and swirled them round with her hands till she was up to her elbows in tangled cotton and polyester and her eyes were hot and wet. She tore her limbs free, went to the kitchen, grabbed a half-full bottle of wine and poured a glass and sat at the table trying to tilt the tears back into her head. According to the kitchen clock Alex's plane would land in LA in an hour.

Dougie came in. Bec stood up and he hesitated on the threshold, each tensed to take steps back as if each had caught the other doing something they shouldn't.

'I was going to get a bit of supper,' said Dougie.

'Have some wine.'

'Not for me. Are you OK?'

'Why?'

'No reason.'

Bec smiled and fetched kitchen paper to blow her nose. Dougie approached and she let him put his arms around her and hold her. She pushed gently on his chest and he released her and stood back.

'I miss Alex,' she said.

'Place feels empty with just the two of us.'

'It was nice to meet your daughter.'

'Aye she liked you.'

'I never asked about your fishing trip.'

'It was fine. We had a rare time. Did he not tell you?'

Dougie stopped to clamber up a small step of courage. 'I'm thinking of leaving, going back up to Scotland.'

'Oh.'

'I shouldn't have stayed so long. I've been imposing.'

'We like having you.'

'Is that right?'

'I like having you around.'

'It's getting hard for me, Bec.'

'What do you mean?'

'Ah, you know what.'

'I don't know. What's getting too hard?'

'You know.'

'You keep saying that. Maybe you should leave.'

'Aye, maybe I should.'

'Do you want to?'

'No.'

'Do you want to stay?'

'I can't. Not like this.'

They stared at each other.

'I don't know what you're offering,' she said.

'What makes you think I'm offering anything?' said Dougie.

'I'd like you to stay for as long as you want and for you not to get crazy ideas about me. And I'd like to be sure, absolutely sure, that the day I tell you to go, you will go, and not come back.'

'Not come back? Why would I not come back? What am I going to do?'

Bec blushed. She left Dougie and went to her room and called Alex and on the twentieth try he answered and said he'd just landed. Speaking to him took the weight out of the day and she only told him that she'd spent time with Dougie's daughter. She went to bed calmer and happier. The next morning her body confirmed what the tester had told her, that she was not pregnant.

59

On Monday morning, forty-eight hours after Alex left, Bec had the first meeting of her new job. At lunch she turned down an invitation from an Indonesian-Austrian WHO official and went by herself to a sandwich bar, dazed by the number of things she had to do and by the knowledge that in the year to come she would have to make speeches at banquets and circle the world. On her way she passed a woman walking in the opposite direction who caught her eye, slowed down and turned her head to follow as they drew level. Bec didn't recognise her. She smiled a quick uncertain smile and went on and into the sandwich bar. She stood in the queue and glanced round when the bell fixed to the door rang. The woman entered and came up to her.

'Are you Rebecca Shepherd?' asked the woman.

'That's my name,' said Bec.

'I recognised you from your picture in the paper. I'm Maria, Alex's ex.'

She had short black hair, chestnut eyes and dark skin, with little constellations of olive freckles on her cheekbones. She was shorter than Bec, a few years older, and prettier than Bec had imagined. Maria's black coat was open over her loose white top and black leggings and Bec could see that she was pregnant.

'Congratulations,' she said.

Maria laughed, thanked her and looked to the side with a quick I'm-not-worthy hunch of her shoulders.

'It's due in March,' she said. 'I don't know why I came in after you. You must think I'm a stalker.'

Bec told her not to be silly and instead of waiting in the queue for a sandwich she led Maria to a table by the window, where a waitress served them. Bec had lost her appetite and felt that she must look miserable. A horrible thought came to her.

'This isn't some sort of delayed IVF thing, is it?' she asked. 'From when you were together?'

'Oh no!' Maria held Bec's arm. Her sympathy and apparently sentimental rather than visceral concern for Alex's wellbeing unsettled Bec. 'We made it the natural way, me and my new partner.' She became grave. 'So he told you about the IVF? Of course he did, of course he did, why wouldn't he?'

Bec wanted to give herself time to think, but her mind didn't come up with the pleasantries, and she stared at Maria with an expression that must have provoked pity in Alex's former lover, because she grasped Bec's hands and wrinkled her forehead and made a long, motherly 'Ooooh' sound. 'I shouldn't have bothered you. My office is just around the corner, though, we were bound to meet. Your institute's near here, isn't it? I have been a bit of a stalker. I didn't see your picture in the paper, I saw it on the Internet. I did a search and found the pictures of you. You're quite a celebrity. I was a bit shocked, to be honest.' She looked at Bec as if she'd swallowed something bitter. 'Of course he went for someone younger.'

'There was nothing going on between us while you were together. And you've obviously found someone you like.'

Maria showed by smiling and looking away that Bec was right. She became serious and said: 'I haven't told Alex I'm pregnant. Are you going to tell him?'

'I don't know.'

'I wouldn't.'

'He'll find out eventually.' *She's showing that she knows him better than me*, thought Bec.

'He won't find out so soon. We're moving to Italy for my partner's job. I don't know how things are between you. It's none of my business. But if he told you about the IVF he must have talked about why we broke up. I'm sure you asked him.'

'Is there ever one reason?'

'He never said but I'm sure he always thought it was my machinery that was broken, not his. He has this crazy pride. Ego.'

'Why shouldn't he find out?'

'It'd be too cruel. It'd seem so final.' Maria drew in breath and put her hand to her mouth. 'My God I'm sorry, I haven't been thinking clearly. I was thinking about him, not about you.'

Bec shrugged.

Maria said: 'The thing I resent him for is never being prepared to countenance artificial insemination. If he's so liberal, why does he have to insist the child's genetically his? What does it matter if the father's some anonymous donor you're never going to meet who wanks into a pot in a kiosk in Doncaster?'

'Why Doncaster?'

'I don't know. I imagine sperm donors coming from places

436

where there's not much else to do on your days off. Have you met his mother? I always thought she was hinting at something. That I should *take matters into my own hands.* I thought about it. I'm sure it happens more often than we know. If there'd been a decent man I liked and he didn't look completely different from Alex, I would've taken the chance, as long as I was sure Alex would never find out.' An absent expression came over Maria's face as if she were remembering an old story and finding new nuances in it. 'I don't see anything wrong with that. Everybody would get what they wanted.'

'What about the other man?' said Bec.

Maria shrugged. 'Having sex with random women, impregnating them and never having to worry about the child? Isn't that what men fantasise about?'

'Not all of them.'

Maria looked at her coolly. She pushed herself back with her hand on the end of the table so that the front two legs of her chair lifted a few inches off the ground.

'If I was in that situation again,' she said, 'if I was sure, I'd do it. I'd do it in a moment.'

60

The time difference made it hard for Bec and Alex to catch each other to talk. She was moving offices, to a government building; a promising young parasitologist, Isobel, would run her research group while she was doing her new job. But these changes didn't distract her as she would have liked.

On the Friday after Alex left, Karin came to town to consult with her label. She met Bec afterwards, looking as if she'd stepped out of *Vogue*. She'd dyed her hair crimson and wore a short tweed dress, red tights, brogues and a jaunty feathered hat. The label gave her a car with a driver. When they arrived at the restaurant Karin chose, two photographers came up to them, took their picture and stepped back without saying anything.

'Is it always like that?' said Bec.

'Maybe it's you they want.'

'Why should they?'

'You and Alex are public figures now.'

'Are we?'

Karin told Bec how the boys of The What – my young men, she called them – were on tour, and how she missed them, and what good work they'd done together in the studio in Petersmere, and how their album would soon be out. 'We did a cover of I Want To See The Bright Lights Tonight. It's so Seventies, I sound like Suzi Quatro doing Devil Gate Drive,' she said. 'My boys started kicking their feet in time.' She laughed and wrinkled her nose.

'I'd love to meet them,' said Bec, touched that Karin thought she'd know who Suzi Quatro was, and she wished she'd been there in summer in her brother's garden, making daisy chains and dreamily fending off the boys' paws, listening to them sing. 'Do you need somebody to stand on stage with a tambourine?'

In the past, Karin's terror of being contaminated by scientific knowledge had been an obstacle between them. Now that Bec was able to talk about her immediate future of foreign trips, banquets and escorting film stars on tours of malarial Africa there were no barriers. After a couple of glasses of wine Bec told Karin that trying to conceive had changed her sense of time.

'It used to be that there was work-world and there was not-work-world, and they stretched in and out together,' she said. 'If something big was happening in work-world, like malaria, not-work-world would shrink to make space for it, and if something big was happening in not-work-world, like . . .'

'Love?'

'Exactly like love. Then work-world would shrink for that. It was like one breath passing from lung to lung.' She held up her hands and stretched one open and closed the other into a fist, then opened the fist and closed the other.

'You look as if you're showing somebody how to milk a goat,' said Karin, and some wine went the wrong way up Bec's nose. Even while she laughed she was annoyed that Karin wasn't taking her seriously.

'But you know what I mean.'

'Of course.'

'Now there's a third world. It's not work, although it would *be* a lot of work, and it's not exactly love, although it would be all *about* love, I suppose. Anyway, it isn't happening.'

'It's too soon to worry. It hasn't even been a year.'

'You mustn't tell Alex this, but I saw his ex, Maria. She's pregnant. The old-fashioned way.'

Karin said something quiet, but Bec didn't take it in as fully as she took in the tilt of Karin's face and the sorrowful, slightly pitying compression of the tiny wrinkles at the corners of her eyes and mouth.

'Why wouldn't you tell him?' said Karin. 'If the two of you want to have children he needs to know he's probably the one with the problem.'

Bec smiled, feeling less close to Karin than a minute earlier. 'It's not a scientific standard of proof. I don't know what he would do if I told him. He might leave me.'

Karin rolled her head and lifted her eyes upwards. 'Then what kind of a lover is he? What kind of a man? You make him sound like a terrible mix of martyr and coward, and vain with it.'

'What if it was you? If you wanted to have a child, the doctors couldn't find anything wrong with you, and the one who breaks it to you that it's your problem is the person you say you love the most, the one you've been trying to have a child with?'

'He needs to know. He needs to be brave and face up to it. There are other ways. What does he need to populate the world with a whole lot of mini-Alexes for?'

'Why does anyone need their own children?' said Bec. 'He's

proud.' She was looking down at the surface of the table. 'Maria said I should sleep with someone else to get pregnant and not tell Alex.'

Karin put her hands down flat on the table and leaned sharply forward into Bec's face. 'What? Would you *do* that?' Her grin was wide and her eyes shone. Bec felt she had never held another woman's attention so completely. She went red.

'I told her I couldn't.'

'I'm sure it happens,' said Karin.

'Do you know anyone who . . .'

'No, but I'm sure it happens.' Karin laughed in wonder and shook her head, staring at Bec as if she'd thought for years that she was dealing with an entirely different person, and only now saw the actual her. Bec watched her sister-in-law's beautiful famous face and felt the warmth of her affection. Wonder from an artist, wonder from a beautiful woman and a mother who had seen, no doubt, so many sexually transgressive wonders in and around the playgrounds of the great, seemed like approval.

Ridiculous, she thought, and wondered what was ridiculous, Maria's suggestion or assuming that it was impossible. She wanted a child with Alex, and she wanted Alex to be happy, and there was ridiculousness in the obstacle that stood in the way of such a good outcome. *This is not the old world*, she thought. *Sex can't ruin us now. Not in London, not in our time.*

61

Bec avoided Dougie. Perhaps, she thought, he was avoiding her. How else could two people alone in a house not cross paths more often? Their hours were different. They seldom ate in. They kept to their rooms. Bec would hear the boards creak as Dougie passed her door, keys in locks when he went in and out and his whistling from the bathroom. When they did see each other they nodded and said hello. He was like a lodger, except that he would try to hold Bec's eyes and she avoided his. At these moments he seemed to her to become very large and still and she felt herself to be a scurrying creature scampering for cover from a storm-laden sky.

Once she went into the living room with her laptop and sat down on the sofa not realising until she'd began pecking at the keys that Dougie was already there, cross-legged in a dim corner, reading. Bec's heart galloped and she blushed.

'I didn't know you were here,' she said.

Dougie stood up.

'I like to be by myself when I'm working,' she said.

Dougie went out of the room and Bec sat still with her face on fire.

Late on Friday evening, a week before Alex's return, Dougie came to Bec in the living room. She was watching a film.

Dougie stood on the threshold and apologised for bothering her. He wanted to let her know that he was leaving the next day.

'Going fishing?' said Bec. She stopped the film.

'I'm heading back up north. For good.'

'Oh. I'm sorry to hear that. Any particular reason?' She was cold and polite. She sounded what foreigners would call *English*.

Dougie looked at her without speaking for a moment and said: 'I came to let you know. I'll try and take as much as I can. I'll come back for the rest later.'

Bec stood up and hooked the loop of her top over her shoulder where it had slipped down. 'I'm sorry I was a bitch yesterday. I don't know why I lost my temper.'

'I know why.'

'You haven't done anything wrong.'

'You just don't like us, Bec, it's normal. I'm not the kind of guy you want to have around the place.'

'I thought you said you weren't going fishing?'

'See that's funny, Bec, that's the old Bec, and if me leaving's what it takes to bring her back, I'm better just getting the hell out of Dodge, eh.'

He turned to go and Bec called him back and asked if he wanted a drink. Dougie said that it was all right, he wouldn't, and Bec asked if he'd sit with her for a while. Dougie came and sat down at the far end of the sofa. He sat on the edge, leading forward, looking down at his hands.

'What were you thinking when you tried to kiss me?' said Bec.

'I told you, I wasn't thinking.'

'I can't hear you very well.'

'That's you and Alex's way, working everything out in advance,' said Dougie. He hunched his shoulders and made a mime with his fingers of a mean, sneaky animal.

'And if I said that there was nothing wrong with thinking ahead, you'd say, "Oh, I know, I just haven't got the brains for it."'

'You can't do my accent.'

'I can do you, can't I?'

'Go on, then.'

Bec met his eyes and swallowed. 'You thought, "I want her, and maybe if I kiss her, she'll like it, like me and like being wanted by me, and like my boldness in taking what I want, and I'll fuck her, and maybe she'll like that."'

Dougie tilted his head and blinked, like a horse bothered by a fly.

'"And maybe she'll fall in love with me."' Bec waited for Dougie to speak. He stared at her. She went on. '"And if not at least I'll have got a fuck out of it."' She paused. Still silence. '"I've got nothing to lose."'

'When you say "I've got nothing to lose", is that you or me?'

'You. I've got plenty to lose. But maybe I have something to gain.' Bec was beginning to tremble.

'Something to gain,' repeated Dougie. Bec searched his face for a sign of mockery, greed or triumph, but she could see none.

'For me and Alex,' she said.

'Is that really what you want?'

'Of course not. I mean yes, maybe. A way.'

'What about me?'

'You get what you want.'

444

She thought he might disagree, but he only said: 'I am in debt to Alex.'

Bec heard 'indebted'. She meant to say 'There are terms', but her mouth was so dry that the only word that came out was 'terms'.

'Terms?' said Dougie.

'Yes.'

'OK.'

'No light. No light at all.' Dougie nodded. 'No kissing. No touching.'

'No touching?'

'You know what I mean. And no words. You mustn't say a single word.'

Dougie nodded.

'Once.' Bec held up an index finger. 'Once. And then you get up and leave and we don't see you again for a long time.'

'Once?' Dougie looked away. 'Are you . . .'

'I counted days.'

'Aye, but once! I'm a gambler, but that's staking a lot on one roll, and the odds aren't good.'

'I'm going upstairs to my room,' said Bec. Her voice was cracked and shaking. 'I'll be in bed. I'll be on the bed. Remember what I said.'

She went upstairs and into her room, leaving the door open and the lights off. She was trembling so much that it was hard to take off her clothes. She stripped and by touch in one of her drawers she found a thick old hoodie. She put it on, pulled the quilt off the bed and lay down on the cold sheet on her back. She lay still. All she could hear was the sound of her heart and a roaring of blood in her ears. Her eyes were open but it was dark and she felt as if she were alone in the universe, floating through grainy space. Her mouth was dry. She got up and went to the bathroom and drank a glass of water, avoiding looking at herself in the mirror. She took off the hoodie and showered and dried herself quickly and took out her contacts and put the hoodie back on and lay on the bed. *What if he doesn't come?* she thought. *What if he didn't understand? Would it be better?*

She heard Dougie pass her door and go to his room and invocations rose in her for him to come and not to come. *Why do I trust him to do what I ask?* she wondered.

She heard him come back and approach the bed. She closed her eyes. She sensed him standing at the side of the bed. Could she hear him breathing? Could she smell him? She felt threatened and excited. *I should tell him I've changed my mind*, she thought, and opened her legs a little. Her skin moving across the sheet sounded loud to her. She opened her eyes just as he moved onto the bed, resting one knee on the edge and swinging over to straddle her left leg, barely touching it. He was naked. She closed her eyes. She felt Dougie shift and the mattress creaked slightly as he lifted his knee over. He was kneeling between her legs. She parted her thighs a little more widely. She felt the back of Dougie's hand, the little hairs on the back of his hand and the knuckles, stroke her inner thigh as he held his cock, then she felt it butt softy against her as Dougie sought the entry. *He'll hurt me*, she thought, and *How can he be hard when I've been unkind to him?* It did hurt for a moment when Dougie pushed in, and then he slid into her easily, and Bec felt ashamed that it slid in easily.

It was quick and Dougie did his best to do as she'd asked him, keeping his body supported on his arms and just his belly moving against hers. She didn't come close to coming; a

446

moment of distraction was the nearest thing to pleasure and she half-spoke a word involuntarily, she didn't know what, before she remembered what she was doing. When just before the end Dougie put one hand over the base of her spine and pulled her more fiercely onto him she didn't resist.

Dougie gasped and croaked in finishing and pulled out of her. He rolled away and sat on the edge of the bed. Bec opened her eyes and saw his dark form there. She lay still for what seemed a long time, wondering if she should try to stop it leaking out.

'Why are you still here?' she asked Dougie.

He didn't answer and she asked again. She rolled over and pushed him in the back. 'Hey,' she said. 'Get out.'

'No,' said Dougie.

'You promised.'

'Did I?'

'I'd like you to leave.'

'Too bad,' said Dougie. He turned round and laid his hand on her calf. She snatched it away. 'I think you enjoyed it.'

'You're wrong. I didn't.'

'You were wet.'

'You don't know anything about women.'

'It's no a science, Dr Bec, is it?' said Dougie. His voice was strange. He made a hop and he sat astride her, holding down her wrists. He was very heavy.

'I'm going to stay,' said Dougie.

'No you aren't. Get off me.'

'I'm going to fuck you again.'

'That would be rape.'

Dougie's hands tightened on Bec's wrists and his body tensed and Bec got ready to fight.

Dougie shuddered and she flinched as a warm drop fell on her chest. Another one fell. They were tears. Dougie's shoulders shook and he began to sob. He rolled off her and fell off the edge of the bed with a thud and lay on the floor, heaving up sounds from his chest. Bec got up and switched on the light and looked down at the great pale slab of man shaking at her feet, his face scarlet, his mouth open as if in pain, his eyes screwed shut and heart-tearing sounds coming from him, like a newborn. Bec put her hand on his shoulder and he pulled it away as if her palm burned him. She kneeled down and tried to pull him up, telling him it was all right, and got him up with his back against the bed, still weeping.

'I'm sorry,' he whispered.

'It's all right.' Bec sat next to him with her arms round his shoulders.

'You shouldn't touch me.'

'It's all right. Everything's all right.'

'Nothing's right.' Dougie's voice came high and thin through sobs. 'You know I love you, and you tried to let me show you by letting me do one simple wee thing for you and Alex, just one nice, simple, wee thing, just one wee fuck in the dark, and I can't bear it, Bec, it just makes me want. It just makes me want. It just makes me want so much.' He bent his head and was overcome by crying.

'It's all right,' said Bec.

'No,' whimpered Dougie.

'I'm sorry.'

'No.'

'I've treated you badly.'

'It's fine.' Dougie got up and went to his room. Bec followed him and saw him start to get dressed, sniffing, avoiding her eyes.

'Don't go,' said Bec. 'There's no need to go. I thought you'd like it. I thought it was what you wanted.'

Dougie was dressed. He gave her a single look and put some things into a rucksack. At eleven o'clock that night he left the house.

62

Bec woke up at seven the next morning and remembered what she'd done. She didn't understand how she'd slept so long and deeply and with such gentle dreams. It was as if another self worked inside her at night to smother her conscience. Daylight made it merciless. She put on a coat and walked out into the bright grey morning. Every sound was angry – the thunder of an aircraft, the cry of a braking bus, the snarl of a scooter – or seemed to reproach her behind her back: the ticking of bicycle wheels, the breathless laughter of girls, the tapping of heels. And this was only the rustle of the world, a world incorporated against her. It watched severely, the severity an authority waits in when it has asked a question you cannot avoid answering yet cannot answer without lying or incriminating yourself.

Bec walked down Upper Street, down City Road and east towards Shoreditch. There was a rupture between the Bec of this day and the Bec of other days preceding. She saw bars and clubs she'd been in and it didn't seem to her that she could go into them as Bec again. She forgot she'd acted for Alex's sake. All she could think of was that she'd lived without betraying anyone, and now she lived a traitor's life.

Once all a woman had to do to pick up a poisonous secret

was to have sex without being married. There were girls in London who still lived that life. Muslim girls. Rose, perhaps. For Bec's caste, the liberals, all the post-religious girls, sexual freedom was old. Bec's mother had boyfriends before her father. Her grandmother had lost her virginity to a soldier when the Germans were bombing London. Sexual freedom took the poison of infidelity, the lies and the secrets, the cruelty of abandonment, and distilled it into a single drop, sufficient for two or three doses. Before it was a matter for the world: now the world didn't care. Only Alex would care, and Bec and Dougie, and it was still poison. Sexual freedom was old and it wasn't really freedom. It was just the domestication of disgrace.

It was as if there were two separate worlds for which hypocrisy was too simple a term: the world of names and the world of deeds, and life was less a matter of concealment than of keeping deeds and their names from touching. An unnamed deed was harmless, and a name was just a name. Put together they were toxic. And if you named your deed to yourself? Then you were carrying a poisonous secret.

The first betrayal, before Alex, had been of herself. She'd put up with Dougie's kiss but avoided naming it. And the name was *Alex's brother is in love with me.* The night before, she'd done it again. *I deceived Alex.*

If she didn't name her deed to Alex, the secret would poison her and spread to him. Her friends would advise her not to tell. *They're wrong,* she thought. *They think what's done is done and can't be undone and you have to live with it but they're wrong, they're wrong, the confessed deed is a different action to the secret deed. You can pull out the thorn and it will hurt terribly and it may kill you but the thorn won't be inside you any more, it will be out.*

She leaned over the wall of London Bridge and whispered 'I cheated on Alex' to the choppy black Thames.

A middle-aged man with a kind face and silver-rimmed glasses passed her on the pavement and Bec said to him: 'I slept with my boyfriend's brother.' The man hurried on, frightened.

For many minutes Bec stared at her phone, thinking that she should call Ritchie and ask him what he thought she should do. Her finger hovered over the button so close that she might have called him by accident, but she didn't call him.

63

When the aircraft carrying Alex to California pirouetted over Los Angeles and he looked out at the squares of the city stretching to the horizon in every directon, as if it covered the entire planet, Alex felt like a conqueror. He forgot London for a while. He was busy, learning the arts of the popular science documentary.

His first disappointment was the amount of transparent fakery in the documentary. He was filmed moving through San Francisco in a tram, as if he were on his way somewhere, when they actually got around in taxis and rental cars. He'd knock on a scientist's door and the scientist would get up and say 'Hello' and they had to pretend they were meeting for the first time when really they'd been talking for two hours, working out what they were going to say, and the scientist had been prepped by a production assistant in half a dozen phone calls over three months. The documentary would be fifty minutes long; how much substance would be left, Alex wondered, once the sham shots of him gazing at the sunset or walking along the beach were included, along with panoramas of snowy mountain ranges, horses in the desert haze and helicopter shots of the Golden Gate Bridge? The crew and the producer were friendly, but there was a level of warmth beyond which they wouldn't go. Once he overheard them refer to him sarcastically as *the talent*.

They shot him in dusty hills, kneeling by clumps of tough, gnarled bushes, and he looked into the camera and said that the plants were more than ten thousand years old, that they had been growing in this place when Britain had only just been released from the ice age, when humans were learning how to farm. He said it five times before he got it right. He tripped over his words and put the emphasis in the wrong places. He didn't like the script. It was too respectful towards the mean patch of scrub that had lived so long without learning how to die. Speaking into the camera he composed a different set of lines in his head. *Look at this gnarled, bitter old survivor. It doesn't have the dignity to step aside and let green shoots take its place. It can't bear to be replaced. It won't let go.*

The love of knowledge in the scientists he interviewed had been spoiled by their quest to lengthen human life. Each had experienced a moment of fame for one discovery, then been sought out ever since by visitors asking the same questions about the same discovery, and even while they grew bitter because their new work was being ignored in favour of the old, their desire to recapture their earlier glory had driven them to travel further down the same dead-end road towards immortality; and that journey had made their own ageing, their own failing powers, so much harder to bear. As the days in California went by Alex thought about Harry, how ungraciously he'd treated Matthew, and how his desire to be literally immortal had poisoned the alternative immortalities he might have claimed in the lives of those he left behind.

After two weeks, as the trip neared its end, he was longing to be home. He wished he'd taken Bec's first advice and not left the institute to make the film. He wanted to show her that he'd stay with her until the end, whether he could father children or not. He would marry her if she liked. When they spoke on Skype he was preoccupied with this and didn't notice how quiet she was and how she did all she could to get him to talk and tell her about his time there while telling him as little as possible about herself.

She told him that Dougie had left without giving a reason. Alex told her that it was time for his brother to move on and he saw her smile quickly on the screen. He asked if she was relieved, too, and she nodded and said she was.

Alex's flight got in to Gatwick in the middle of a workday morning and there were people Bec had promised to meet so it wasn't until six in the evening that she got home. Alex had been there since the early afternoon. He'd slept for an hour, washed and fidgeted about the house nervously, checking the time every few minutes, changing his shirt twice, eager and anxious, going over what he wanted to say.

Bec had been deciding whether to tell Alex what she'd done. She'd already sent Dougie a message, which he hadn't replied to, saying that she was going to tell him. But as she opened the front door of the house and called Alex's name she still hadn't made up her mind. She was beginning to get used to the mental barrier that stood between knowing she should tell him and actually speaking the words out loud. The barrier between knowing the right thing to do and doing it became a shelter for her to crouch behind.

She heard Alex coming downstairs and hesitated, feeling she should have taken more care about how she looked. She rubbed her hands together – they were a little damp – and not knowing what else to do ran them down over her blouse and skirt. When Alex appeared she moved her hands away from her body and rubbed the fingertips against her palms. She smiled, and in her acutely self-conscious state it seemed to her like a guilty smile. He was bound to ask, she thought. He was tanned. It made him attractive.

Bec wasn't as Alex remembered. Her colour was high and he felt he could hear her heart beating. He'd just travelled here from the far side of the world, and she'd walked in off the street, and yet he felt as if he'd been nowhere and she'd come from far away, from a place he'd never been to where she would, if he wasn't bold, go again without him. She looked as if she'd been breathing different air and been under another sun. If it was possible for her to run away from him and surrender to him abjectly with the same gesture, he thought, she would do it. Panic swept through him and he thought that all along she'd been on a journey past him to a greater destiny and that he hadn't risen to her. In the wake of fear came a thick hormonal cloud of aggressive lust and as it drove him towards her the only thing resembling a thought in his head was that to hold and keep Bec was more to him than life or death.

For a moment she followed the path of greeting and tried to kiss him. She meant to speak. Their lips touched and Alex grasped the hem of her narrow skirt with both hands and pulled it up round her waist and she drew her head back and looked in his eyes. She unbuckled his belt as his fingers found her.

Lying on the floor of the hall, when they began to feel the cold on their bare skin, Alex said: 'We could get married.'

'What about children?' said Bec.

'I'm going to be less proud about it. I'm going to be less

selfish. I'm not going to care if they don't have my genes. Why are you crying?'

'You can't just change your mind like that.'

'It's a good thing, isn't it?'

'I don't know.'

Bec felt his unhappiness swell. He said: 'You don't want to get married.'

Bec pressed her face into the dark of his chest. 'Of course I do,' she said.

Fourteen days later Bec went back to the chemist. This time there was a single word in the window of the tester. *PREGNANT*, it said.

64

It was mid-morning. Alex had left the house to do voiceovers and Bec was by herself in the kitchen, looking at the items on the table next to her hand: a pen with the logo of a drugs company down the side, a block of Post-it notes with the corners fluffed up and a pregnancy testing kit. In a way, nothing had changed. There were still two possible futures, one with children, one without. But the appearance of a word on a pregnancy tester spoiled one future. Childlessness was something she'd probably have to go out and get if she wanted it now. It wasn't that motherhood had instantaneously become more desirable; childlessness had become less. And yet she felt pleased, as if, in this, the relative and the absolute were one and the same.

She left the house and walked to Angel station. *The doctor,* she thought, *clothes, space, work, belly, diet, feed the beast.* She imagined telling Alex that she was pregnant, letting him be happy, and telling him that the child might be his brother's. She imagined telling him that she'd slept with Dougie first, letting him react – and how would he take it? Would he run away? She would chase him.

Or she would keep it a secret. That was easy to imagine. Nobody would find out; how could they? Years would pass and the secret would be overgrown and covered by new events. The child would grow, and it would be a Comrie-Shepherd child.

Bec passed through the station entrance and caught sight of herself in the CCTV monitor over the ticket barriers. *How ordinary and anonymous I look*, she thought. *Like pictures on the news, like the last pictures of someone before something terrible happens to them, before they're murdered or raped.* She didn't look, she felt, like a mother; but how was a mother supposed to look?

A long time seemed to have passed since Dougie lay on top of her, and the pregnancy gave her confidence. It belonged to her in a way it could never belong to the father. It was easier for her now to talk to Ritchie. She called him and asked if he could see her. He answered on the second ring and sounded pleased to hear from her. She told him that she needed his advice about something important and he told her that he could see her that morning, if she would come to the studio.

65

No one outside Ritchie's household knew that he'd almost hung himself. He wore scarves and polo necks in public and was mocked for it in paparazzi picture spreads. Karin told him she'd found him lying asleep on the floor of his study, surrounded by beer bottles and empty cartons of chocolate pudding, with a noose on the floor and a rope burn scarlet round his neck. In the weeks that followed he told her so many truths about his deep fears that the truths he didn't mention – that he'd exchanged his celebrity, his time, his attention and about thirty thousand pounds' worth of gifts for flattery and sex from a fifteen-year-old girl, and that this information was about to be made public – didn't seem to him to be great omissions.

He told Karin that Bowie and Bono were right; he was a poor singer. He'd been a fool to imagine he could be treated as an equal by artists like them. Karin was the talented one. Everyone said so. It had always been his destiny to end up running a show that championed mediocrity. Bec's high moral principles had destroyed his last chance to do something great by stopping him making the O'Donabháin film. When he was away Ruby and Dan didn't miss him as they would have missed a better man. He'd always been surrounded by more extraordinary people; his brave father, his brilliant friend Alex, his wife Karin, who wrote wise, tender songs with the clever boys from The What, and, most extraordinary of all, Bec. How could he compete with his sister? No wonder she'd been their father's favourite. She was kind, clever, hard-working, good, humble and beautiful. She didn't cheat or lie. Everybody loved her. Why wouldn't they? She'd found a cure for malaria. She deserved her wonderful life, the fame, the beautiful house, the ideal boyfriend, the glorious future. She deserved success in a way that Ritchie, coarse, fat, trashy old Ritchie never would.

Karin didn't let him down. She picked up Ritchie's broken hopes, carefully, one by one, like toys he'd thrown to the ground and smashed, and gave them back to him mended and wrapped, transformed into building blocks of confidence. He was a wonderful father, she said. He was a creator and an artist with a great love of music. Without him, she said, there would have been no band and no songs. Was David Bowie so perfect – was Bono? Wasn't it possible they'd been jealous of a rival? Couldn't it be that for Bowie it was a compliment to compare someone to a dog howling? Wasn't Hound Dog Taylor one of Ritchie's favourites? She mentioned the musicians who'd praised Ritchie behind his back and he was glad to hear her recite those names again. And did he suppose, she said, that the millions of people who watched *Teen Makeover* every week were stupid, were ignorant? Some of them were, no doubt, but wasn't that the wonderful thing about popularity, that among the vast mass there were bound to be some of the best people in the world, who loved the show for its special magic? Life was hard. Life was full of pain, Karin said – and here Ritchie could tell she was making a great effort of logic – imagine, she said, if there was no malaria, and people in Africa lived as long as Europeans, and had the same amount of time and money? Wouldn't they be just as bored and depressed as Europeans were, and need popular talent shows to fill the emptiness in their lives?

Ritchie nodded and said he supposed they would, but Karin's reasoning didn't entirely satisfy him, and without noticing how often he was doing it he began to say out loud, whenever he felt low and in response to the softest of cues, how base he was compared to his sister. A mood of fatalism crept over him.

66

The Rika Films studio was in far east London, where it shaded into Essex, where the city's builders and fixers and deliverers lived in estuary light, where dense layers of mean-windowed, low-ceilinged homes rose between roads, canals and railway lines. It was a world of pylons and bridges and cranes, of container trucks barrelling to and from the eastern ports, of drive-ins and lock-ups and lay-bys. Bec's taxi dropped her at the security booth at the entrance to the studio car park and Ritchie came out to meet her in a black sheepskin coat, flapping open over his belly.

'Let's go to the caff for a change,' he said. He looked exhausted and an extra pouch seemed to have been added to the bags under his eyes. He was no fatter, but there was a slackness to him, as if his weight had somehow hollowed from within. Smiling was an effort for him today, Bec thought, and it seemed to her that his face bore traces of an attempt to apply make-up. *I take my troubles to him and get none back*, she thought.

The café was around the corner in a remnant row of shops, set in red brick like old teeth in gums; a boarded-up chippy, a place offering Export Services, a fatal-looking pub and Wilson's Refreshments, the name hung in fat scarlet plastic letters fixed to a wooden strip painted yellow. The other buildings around were newer. Like the outer shell of Ritchie's studio they were not really buildings, more giant sheds that could be struck like tents when their owners moved on.

In Wilson's they sat at a trestle table and a Polish girl with a ponytail and an apron took their order.

'The chocolate's good here,' said Ritchie.

'I'll just have a tea, thanks,' said Bec.

'A tea, a hot chocolate and a bacon roll,' said Ritchie to the waitress. Most of the men in the café wore hi-viz waistcoats and steel-toecapped boots. There was English shouting and Slav murmuring.

'It's busy,' said Bec.

'Do you mind?'

'It doesn't matter. Is everything all right with you? You look tired.'

Ritchie grinned. 'People have been saying that to me all my life. It's just the way I look. Sleepy old Ritchie. I'm a coper. Whatever they throw at me I'll catch it.'

He was jiggling his knee up and down, a new tic that distracted Bec. 'Tell me what's on your mind.'

'Your crazy sister has excelled herself this time,' she said. 'I've done something extreme and I'm not sure what to do. Why are you looking at me like that? I haven't told you what it is yet.'

'Like what? Sorry. You know how I worry about you.' The jiggling of his knee was faster. He was unaware that he was doing it. Some slithering worm seemed to coil and uncoil in his belly. He was filled with terror and hope and had an urge to shriek *Don't tell me!* at his sister. As Bec told him what she'd

464

done with Dougie, and that she was pregnant, he stopped jiggling and a great peace spread through him.

'I would never have thought such a thing was possible,' he said gently, full of tenderness and pity towards his sister. *How terribly she has fucked up*, he thought. A violent indignation rose in him towards her for pushing him to act as he would rather not. He jiggled his knee again.

'Whatever you do,' said Ritchie, 'don't tell Alex.'

'But what if it comes out later?'

'Just don't tell him,' said Ritchie. He lifted the cocoa to his mouth to hide the impulse that came on him to let rip with a snorting guffaw. His hand shook slightly and this fact had an almost unbearable pathos for him. His eyes filmed with tears. His heart was beating very fast. He wanted to get out in the open air. Bec wouldn't let him go.

'You think I should just bury it? Let it become one of those family secrets?'

'Exactly,' said Ritchie. 'Alex was desperate for a child and now he'll have one. Congratulations.' As he spoke these words he became powerfully conscious of his own good sense. He smiled warmly at Bec and she smiled back. *He's not wearing make-up*, she thought. *The daylight made him look rough.*

For the rest of the day, and on into the evening at home, Ritchie was distracted. When he should have been listening to someone else, or carrying out a task, he found he was looking at an object, or a texture, a knot in the varnished wood of the kitchen table, fascinated by its detail, as if he were high.

'Why are you staring at the bread?' asked Dan. Ritchie was wondering how many holes the slice of bread in front of him had; how they'd got there; whether there was more air than solid matter in the slice; what it would look like if he could be shrunk to microscopic size and clambered over the bread's surface. Did the holes have holes?

He stood up. 'There's something I forgot to do in the study,' he said. 'I'll be back in a minute.' Karin looked at him in surprise. He climbed the stairs. It was hard for him to believe that the wooden steps always made so much noise, that their creaks always sounded as loudly in the silence of the upper floors of the house, or that the stairs always took as long to climb. He went into his study, which was, he knew, exactly as he'd left it; yet it seemed to him he was entering a space that he'd prepared specially for this moment. There was a high-pitched singing in his ears and the skin over his cheekbones prickled unpleasantly. He felt it was not him who went over to the desk but his limbs and trunk, moving of their own accord, and that his consciousness was observing it. It seemed that the arms of his will were folded while his physical fingers flipped through a notebook.

He began thinking *It's done now, it's out of my hands, there's no way to make it un-done.* And yet he still had not done it.

He called the Moral Foundation, and heard a digital voice message.

'If you have a code,' the voice said, 'please enter it now.'

67

Next morning, in the lobby of the building where Bec had her new office, she saw her happiness reflected in the faces of the man and woman security guards, sitting behind their counter like a couple in uniform.

'Hello, love,' said the woman guard.

Bec's assistant had taken the day off. Bec was too energised to sit down and she walked around her office, trailing her fingertips along the wall. The room had seemed too big and too low-ceilinged when she got it and yet now the most ordinary objects, the yucca plant in the corner, the photograph of her father and mother with her and Ritchie, the year planner busy with marks and stickers, taped slightly squint to the wall, seemed to express an equal amount of an obscure quality, the sense of a world gone right.

The night before she'd taken Ritchie's advice and told Alex that she was expecting, without confessing that she'd been with Dougie and without telling him Maria was pregnant. The news had shocked Alex pale before he stood on chairs and jumped off them, drummed with cutlery on the draining board and spoke wildly about setting out, at last, on the great migration. He shook his head, clapped his hands to his temples, ran his fingers through his hair and hyperventilated. He was struck with panic about the child's future, about all the things that could go wrong. He called his parents; he wished Harry was alive; he called Dougie, but Dougie didn't pick up. The whole joyful, ridiculous evening seemed to Bec to have heaped new structures of reality over the secret on which they were built.

She picked off the tape holding the year planner to the wall, meaning to fix it straight, and found herself looking nine months ahead to a point where she would be obliged to clear her diary. She found that this didn't worry her at all.

Her office phone rang and she let the year planner fall to the floor and went to answer it.

'Am I speaking to Dr Rebecca Shepherd?' said a woman's voice.

'Who is this?'

'Are you Rebecca Shepherd?'

'Yes. Who is this?'

'I'm calling from the Moral Foundation.'

'Is that Val Oatman's website?'

There was a pause, and the woman said: 'I'm not authorised to discuss Mr Oatman. Do you have a pen and paper handy?'

'I don't have time for anything now, I'm afraid. What's this about?'

'Are you aware of the Foundation's work, Dr Shepherd?'

'I know there's a sleazy website that does celebrity scandals.'

'We're a not-for-profit organisation, set up to make the public aware of immoral behaviour by prominent people. I'd like you to write down a date.'

'I haven't got time.'

'You've got to make time, Dr Shepherd. On the

468

twenty-eighth of February, at six a.m., we shall be publishing, on our website, information about immoral behaviour, concerning you or someone close to you. It will concern one or the other, but not both.'

'I don't know what you're talking about. I have to go.'

'You can't go, Dr Shepherd. You have to listen. The recording starts now. Please pay attention.'

Bec heard a beep, then a click and a rustle, and her brother said 'Hello.'

'Hello,' said Bec.

'Welcome to the Moral Foundation,' said another voice.

'Hello, it's Ritchie Shepherd,' said her brother, and Bec realised that she was listening to a recorded conversation. Ritchie's words overlapped with the other voice, which was saying: 'We're currently experiencing a high number of calls to our tip-off hotline, and all our operators are busy. Your call is important to you, so please stay on the line.'

'Oh, for God's sake,' Bec heard Ritchie say.

'If you're a lawyer, please press two on your telephone keypad now. Otherwise, please hold,' said the voice.

Bec could hear Ritchie breathing.

'Thank you. To report criminal activity, press one. To pass on a rumour, press two. To report immoral behaviour, press three.'

Bec heard the beep as Ritchie made a choice.

'Thank you. If you have an authorisation code, please enter it now.' Bec heard a series of six or seven beeps. 'Please hold.'

'Ritchie!' Val was on the line. 'How nice to hear from you. What have you got for us?'

Ritchie cursed Val with a roughness Bec had never heard him use. He sounded afraid. 'Do you want this or not?' he said.

'I don't know what you've got.'

'I've got to be protected.'

'You know how we work, don't you? I hope you're doing this because it upsets you to see people do wrong, not because you imagine we've got some dirt on you. I like to think you're concerned about the moral fabric of the nation, and that's why you're going to tell me what you're going to tell me, not because you're looking out for yourself. That kind of virtue needs to be rewarded. Of course if you tell us what you know we won't tell what we know about you, if we do know anything about you, and I'm not saying we do.'

A few seconds of silence passed.

'I'm waiting,' said Val.

Bec heard Ritchie say: 'It's my sister.'

'What's her name?'

'You know her name!'

'But I want to hear you say it.'

'Bec. My sister Bec. She slept with her boyfriend's brother while her boyfriend was in America and now she's pregnant. Are you satisfied?'

Bec crumpled into a sitting position on the floor, her back against the desk. She no longer knew how to breathe.

'Is that enough?' said Ritchie.

'What's the brother's name?'

'Douglas. Dougie.'

'Surname?'

'Comrie.'

'Got a number for him?'

'No.'

'Got pictures?'

'For God's sake!'

'We could pull something together, I suppose. She's still not as famous as you are. It'll have to be something like "Exposed: Science's Not-So-Good-As-Golden Girl."'

'Don't you have feelings? Doesn't Bec mean anything to you?'

'Does it mean anything to you that you're betraying your sister? Or did you give her up because your sense of decency was outraged by her whoring around?'

'You tortured me,' said Ritchie.

'I only torture the people who've forgotten how to torture themselves,' said Val.

'You made me do it.'

'It's sad to see how weak a good British family can become in just one generation. Don't cry, Ritchie. Be a man about it. Crying only makes you more despicable.'

Bec heard the distant small yelps of Ritchie sobbing.

68

When Bec typed messages to the people she was due to meet, saying that she was unwell and would have to go home, her fingers no longer seemed part of her; they were like wooden pegs tacked to the ends of her arms. In the bathroom she couldn't wash the look of being hunted off her face. She left the building, near Victoria, and got into a cab. Her phone rang. The number didn't come up. A woman's voice said: 'I have Mr Oatman on the line for you,' and Bec heard Val say 'Why do you think he did that?'

'He said you tortured him,' said Bec.

'He did say that, didn't he. I wonder what he meant. You should ask him why he thought I had the wherewithal to torture him.'

'And now you're torturing me.'

'I'm just the man who's looking after your conscience. I'm what happens if you do something wrong and keep it a secret and don't believe God is watching.'

'You don't know anything about my conscience. You don't know why I slept with Alex's brother.'

'But you didn't tell Alex.'

'I was going to.'

'And now you *have* to.'

'I was going to tell him of my own accord.'

'But you didn't.'

'You didn't give me time to do the right thing on my own. Who are you to set yourself up as the judge of other people's lives?'

'There was a need. If people don't attend to their consciences where do their consciences go? The Moral Foundation gives them a shelter.'

'Are you going to write about me on your website?'

'Why shouldn't I? So you can keep your dirty secret secret?'

'I'm going to tell Alex whatever happens. You told me you loved me once.'

'The Moral Foundation can't let personal relations get in the way of the truth and goodness.'

'You keep talking about goodness. What about mercy? What about kindness?'

'You didn't show me any, you hedonistic bitch,' said Val. 'Now you know what you are. Now you know what you do, when you know everyone's going to know. Ritchie betrayed you, and you betrayed Alex Comrie. I wonder what your father would say.'

'But you're betraying Ritchie,' said Bec. 'You said you'd protect him, and now you're betraying him to me.'

Val's voice was quiet again. 'You and your brother should have a nice family chat about all that. You'll have plenty to talk about.'

'You've got too much malice in you to be a good man,' said Bec.

'Now you're confusing goodness with likeability.'

'If you're offering yourself as a God substitute, I hope I never meet God,' said Bec. 'As for conscience, I've got one,

473

and it works, and I don't need you or God or my brother or the people who read your filthy website to tell me that I did a stupid thing, and that I have to deal with it. Now leave me alone.'

Alex had switched off his phone while he was in the recording studio and when he came out he saw he'd missed calls from Bec. She'd sent him a text message: *When are you coming home? Come soon. Love love love.* He texted back to say he would be home in an hour, at five.

A strip of sunlight stretched into the hallway when he opened the front door of the house in Citron Square. He called Bec's name and was about to go upstairs when he heard her voice from below, from the kitchen. He found her sitting behind the kitchen table in a plain black long-sleeved top. She had her arms tightly crossed in front of her as if they needed to be there to prop her up. She watched him and she blinked rapidly. On the table was an open bottle of red wine and two glasses. She smiled at him without joy. She watched his face sink and his shoulders slump. He looked at the bottle and the glasses and at her.

'Are you leaving me?' he said.

'No,' she said. 'I have something to tell you.'

She patted the table in front of her and told him to sit down. It took an effort for her to talk normally, but Alex couldn't see this.

He sat down opposite her, sitting sideways, only his face to her directly. Bec folded her arms more tightly, squeezing and hunching her shoulders and pressing her knees together. It looked to Alex as if she was trying to make herself as small as possible, when she was actually trying not to shake.

'What is it?' said Alex. 'Are you still pregnant?'

'Yes,' said Bec, and her heart beat hard. Time passed and Alex started to say again 'What is it?' but Bec interrupted him, raising her voice and imploring 'Wait. Please.' A tear rolled down her cheek and Alex, without thinking, gave up his sideways sitting and leaned across the table towards her with his open palms outstretched. She put her hands in his and his hands closed around hers. She dropped her head and rested her forehead on their clasped hands. She drew a deep breath and lifted her head. She looked him in the eye and said: 'It's very difficult. Will you let me finish before you say anything?'

Alex nodded.

She gripped his fingers more tightly and said: 'Whatever happens, you're the one I love, you're the one I want to be with, and you're the one I want to be the father of my child.'

Alex frowned and opened his mouth and Bec squeezed his fingers and went on: 'I have to confess to you and I have to ask you to forgive me. I did wrong. I thought I had a good reason, but I shouldn't have done it, and I don't know whether it's worse that I did it, or that I thought I could keep it a secret from you. I knew how badly you wanted children, and I knew you wanted them to be *your* children, and I was afraid if that couldn't happen, you'd leave me. While you were in America I met Maria by accident. She's pregnant. I knew Dougie liked me – oh your face, please don't look like that, it's so terrible! – and I had sex with your brother once while you were away. And now I'm pregnant. I'm going to have a child, and I want it to be ours, yours and mine, whoever did the . . . act of fathering.' She stopped. Alex had turned his head to one side and was staring at the floor with his lips slightly parted.

'You can speak now,' she said.

'Speak?' said Alex, looking at her as if he'd never seen her before. 'How can I speak? Is that everything?'

'No,' said Bec, and she told him about Ritchie and Val. Alex pulled his hands away and fastened them to his skull.

'I'm sure I was going to tell you when I didn't have to, I'm sure I was going to, but now I'll never know,' said Bec.

'Why would he——' Alex was blindly following what Bec had said. He couldn't process. The very spars of thought had melted. There was no framework and no feeling. He was nothing except consciousness in a body. He got up and looked around.

'What are you doing?' said Bec, coming round the table towards him.

'I need something to hold on to,' said Alex.

'Hold on to me,' said Bec. She tried to take him in her arms, but he shook her off and stepped back.

'I can't,' said Alex, and the first sense he could recognise coalesced in him. 'I'm ashamed.' He backed into the corner of the kitchen, slid down onto the floor, hugged his knees and hid the lower part of his face behind them.

'Talk to me,' said Bec, kneeling down beside him and putting one hand on his shoulder. 'How can you be ashamed?'

'I'm ashamed not to feel angry,' said Alex.

'Remember you're going to be a father,' said Bec.

'Am I?' said Alex. 'You should go with my brother. He needs a wife.'

'I don't have those feelings for him,' she said. 'There was no love in it.'

'How could you——' Alex stopped, and lowered his head again. 'I should be angry with you. I should be angry with him. But I don't feel angry.' He looked at her in surprise. 'If

I was a man I'd be angry, wouldn't I? I'd be violent, hysterical.' He got up. 'Look, there it is. It's too easy for me to forgive you. I've got no teeth. No claws.' He held up his hand in front of his face. 'I'm not fit to survive. I'm not fit to reproduce. Men like me are bound to step aside. I'm weak. I'm the superfluous product of a soft civilisation. You were right to doubt me. I don't feel anything except shame that you felt forced to do this. Shame, and shame in the shame, and shame in the shame in the shame.'

'Do you think I want you to be angry?'

'I don't feel anything.'

'Feeling nothing is what hurt feels like.'

'What you did made sense.'

'But it wasn't the right thing to do.'

'I don't see why not.'

'Because you're the one I want, not somebody else.'

'People don't always know what they want. Hormones have the last word.'

'You're the one, not somebody else, and there's a promise in that, and once I start breaking that promise, everything I say or do is tainted. If it makes so much sense, I should have talked to you about it.'

How did they do it? he thought. *In our bed?* And it seemed to him that there was something wrong with him for being more curious than enraged by imagining his brother naked between Bec's legs; the shame came on again.

'Maybe he thought he was paying me back,' he said, before remembering he hadn't told her about the loan. 'He owed me some money.'

'I know,' said Bec, frowning and looking at the floor. She turned back to Alex. 'How much was it?'

477

'A hundred and twenty thousand pounds.'

'So when your brother agreed to do what I asked him to do, he thought he was returning a debt?'

'In his mind, maybe.'

'Why didn't you tell me he owed you so much?'

'I didn't want you to think I cared about money.'

'So you preferred me thinking you were mean? How could you let me share a house with him and not tell me he was carrying that huge obligation?'

'Nobody knows. My family doesn't know.'

Bec shuddered. 'Did you make a deal with him?'

'No.'

'Perhaps you did without realising it.'

'No.' He remembered the riverbank, and decided that he would keep that conversation secret.

Bec's phone chimed with a message. It was Dougie.

'He's on his way to London,' she said. 'I don't think he knows you know. What should we do?'

'What should we do about Ritchie?' said Alex.

'We? Are we still we?' said Bec. Neither could touch the other any more, and neither knew what to say.

69

That afternoon Dougie had faced an acquaintance and his associate over a small round table in a pub in Shettleston. Between them were Dougie's half-drunk pint, Smith's black coffee, McGilveray's glass of sparkling water, a stack of printed out pages stapled at one corner and a silver ballpoint pen. It was three in the afternoon in Glasgow and there wasn't much daylight coming in.

'I'm more of a standing at the bar man,' said Dougie. 'The smoking ban had me scunnered. Guy at the bar with a fag, he's occupied. Got a project.'

'Nobody ever got paid to smoke in a pub,' said Smith. 'Are you going to sign?'

Dougie looked over to where the solitary silhouette of a man moved to and fro across the flashing lights of a bank of bandits. Occasionally he'd stab one of the buttons, never managing to stop the machines' couthie chatter of grunts and whistles. The only other soul in the place was the girl behind the bar, barely old enough to buy her own drinks, polishing glasses with baffling energy.

'What happens if I don't?' he said.

'You don't get the readies,' said Smith. He reached inside

his jacket, took out a white envelope and placed it next to the contract. 'And I still get your flat in the end.'

Dougie opened the envelope and zipped through the red paper edges with his thumb.

'How much is here?' he said.

'Eight grand.'

'We talked about ten.'

'You talked about ten. Folk these days want their lassies skinny and their white envelopes morbidly obese. It's no my fault the times make it the other way round.' Smith leaned comfortably back in his chair and clasped his hands over his belly. He and the lawyer were wearing North Face ski jackets, open over their suits and ties.

'You're a real lawyer, eh?' said Dougie to McGilveray, picking up the pen.

'Yes, I am.'

'Got a nice house, wife, kids?'

'I do. And I work hard to take care of them.'

Dougie began skimming the contract again. The phrase 'shall be forfeit' stood out, though it was in the same type as the rest.

'If you're a real lawyer how come you're working for this deep cunt?' he said.

Smith leaned towards him. 'You get nothing, and you always will get nothing, from playing the hard man in this town. You're no even from here. You're the son of a country doctor, for fuck's sake. I'm doing you a favour. Eight thousand in cash and thirty K of debt wiped out for a tatty ex-local that's not worth forty.'

'It was worth seventy-five when I bought it.'

'That place was never worth seventy-five. Here.' Smith

pulled out a ten-pound note, crumpled into a ball, and some loose change and dropped them on the table. 'I'll throw that in for your buyer's remorse.'

McGilveray said: 'If you make the payments according to the schedule, there'll be no problem. You keep your property.'

'And you get your thirty per cent,' said Dougie.

'Your brother'll bail you out again,' said Smith.

'That's not going to happen,' said Dougie. He bent over the contract and scribbled his signature with furious speed.

'And initial here,' said the lawyer, flipping pages. 'And here.'

'There you go,' said Smith, handing him the money. 'Got a tip for Newmarket?'

Dougie folded the envelope in two and put it in his jeans pocket. He scooped up the ten-pound note and the change Smith had dropped on the table.

'If I don't pay you back, couldn't you just break my legs?' he said.

'That's never been my style,' said Smith. 'I don't want to break your legs. That's no good to me. I don't want your nasty little flat. I'm just like the bank. All I want is for you to pay me a monthly sum for the rest of your life for the privilege of being allowed to exist.'

Dougie went home, put on a clean white dress shirt and his suit, took the bus to Glasgow Central and bought a one-way ticket to London. Just before the train crossed the border he began texting Bec. *It's love*, he wrote, and *I'm coming to get you. I know what we can do* and *Believe in us, babe. I haven't stopped thinking about you* and *There's places in Glasgow I've tried so hard to see your face it's left marks* and *Trust me. I'll make it all right.* He told her where to meet him and to bring her passport.

For four hours, he texted different versions of the same messages, and Bec didn't answer.

He reached London just before nine p.m., bought a bunch of red roses and took a cab to a casino in Mayfair. He tipped the driver five pounds, checked his collar in a wing mirror and went inside. The girl at the counter asked if he was a member. She had long blonde hot-tonged hair and a tight silver sleeveless dress. The tips of her fingers were crossed on the counter as if hiding some tiny treasure.

Dougie took out a black plastic card. 'I haven't used it for a while,' he said.

'It's fine. Can I put those roses in some water for you?'

'Thanks, love,' said Dougie, giving her the flowers. He fished out a fiver for her.

'Tip me on the way out,' said the girl.

'What if I come back in just my pants?'

'You look lucky,' she said. 'Double or quits.'

Dougie knew the way. He climbed the translucent steps, lit from within by lights that raced on and off from side to side, and swapped the remainder of Smith's loan, £7,800, for chips. He took fifteen black 500 chips and three pink-and-green hundreds, dropped them in his jacket pockets and headed for the Punto Banco table.

Dougie took three of his black chips and staked them on Punto. He lost. He repeated the process and lost another £1,500. He reached into his pocket, fished out the remaining black chips and placed them in a single stack of nine on the blue baize in front of him. He lifted three chips off the pile and placed them in the Punto box. The dealer dealt the cards, an ace and a three for Punto, a five and a king for Banco. Punto's third card was a nine.

'Banco wins, five over three,' said the dealer, scooping up Dougie's three chips. 'Place your bets, please.'

In three minutes Dougie had lost £4,500. The other players were looking at him; a middle-aged white guy in a cerise polo shirt with hyperthyroid eyes and a watch the size of a jam-jar lid and a Chinese couple wearing matching satin-effect bomber jackets with *The Venetian, Macau* embroidered on the back. This wasn't a night for rollers. They'd been betting tens and twenties and the dealer kept his hands on the shoe.

Dougie closed his fingers round his remaining pile and moved all three thousand pounds' worth into the Punto box. None of the others made a bet. They seemed frozen. The dealer pulled four cards from the shoe, a nine and a jack for Punto, a ten and a six for Banco.

'Player wins with a natural nine,' said the dealer, and pushed six thousand pounds' worth of chips towards Dougie.

Dougie's luck turned. He kept betting on Punto, sitting out games after a win. In half an hour he'd amassed fifty thousand pounds. He went to the restaurant, ordered a steak and a fifty-pound bottle of wine, and read through the contract he'd signed with Smith. He could liquidate the loan the next day and there was nothing Smith could do; he could start paying Alex back. He texted Bec. *Come on babe. I'm winning. I need you now. It's going to be OK.* He finished his meal, drank a glass of wine, left the rest of the bottle and went back to the Punto Banco table.

There were more players, and some bystanders. All the seats were full, yet Dougie's return was like a wind cleaving a channel through the reeds. The Chinese man offered him his seat. Dougie sat down, watched Banco win twice and put

£10,000 on Punto. Punto won and Dougie got back double his stake. He now had sixty thousand pounds.

He waited for a run of Banco wins and after three in a row he bet £10,000 on Punto again. He lost. He staked another £10,000, and lost. Twice more he staked £10,000 on Punto and lost each time. In a few minutes he'd lost £40,000.

Phones weren't allowed at the table. Dougie gave his a covert keek. No one had called or texted.

The dealer was a youngster in a black waistcoat and bow tie with a pale, bloated jaw that was misaligned a fraction with the rest of his head. He'd shown no emotion in the one and a half hours since Dougie first sat down. He looked at him now without interest or excitement, only a smooth, inexhaustible patience, as if the shoe and the eight decks of cards it contained had existed before the planets formed, and would exist long after the sun had gone cold.

'Any more bets?' he said.

Dougie looked across the room. He saw Alex. His brother was searching in the crowd by the blackjack tables. The players and onlookers around Dougie sensed something lurch in him, like a climber when his rope goes slack. His hands pressed the sides of his Manhattan of remaining chips, his £20,000.

'I'd like to put twenty thou on this hand,' said Dougie.

'The floor limit is ten, sir,' said the dealer.

'I'd like to go to twenty.'

The dealer picked up a handset under the table. After a few murmured words he replaced the handset and nodded. Dougie pushed £20,000 of chips into the Punto box.

'No more bets,' said the dealer. He pulled four cards from the shoe and placed them in the boxes. The edges lined up perfectly each time. Punto's first card was an eight, Banco's a six. Punto's second was a Queen. The dealer didn't slow down, yet those watching had long enough to understand, before they saw the fourth card, that the odds were in Dougie's favour. A two would be égalité, but only a three would beat Punto, and what were the chances of Punto losing eight deals in a row?

The dealer laid Banco's second card face-up on the baize, exquisitely aligned. Everyone counted that which could be counted with a single glance, one, two, three; three red hearts in a column in the centre of the card, inexorable, and the numeral three in two corners.

'Banco wins, nine over eight,' said the dealer, and took Dougie's £20,000 away.

Without hesitating, Dougie took out the two 100 chips from his jacket – he'd spent one on the meal – and placed them on Punto. The dealer dealt. The hand went to Banco, and Dougie lost the last of his money.

Alex found him as the dealer swept it away.

'What did you just do?' said Alex.

'I just lost two hundred pounds on Punto Banco,' said Dougie.

'Two hundred pounds?' Alex kneaded his forehead. 'You just threw away two hundred pounds?'

'I didn't throw it away. He took it.' He nodded at the dealer. 'I've still got – hang on.' His wallet was empty. He searched his pockets and found the ten-pound note Smith had given him, still crumpled in a ball.

'Here,' he said. 'They should make a law says folk like me are only allowed one pocket, stop us hoping. I—' Alex put his hand over his brother's mouth and told him to come outside.

Dougie followed him. At the cashier Dougie slowed down, smoothing the tenner between his palms. 'Might as well get a tenner's worth, Alex, I could still come out ahead on the night,' he said.

Alex took him by the lapel and dragged him to the stairs. As they passed the counter Dougie slapped the ten-pound note in front of the girl.

'I said you'd be lucky,' she said. 'What about the roses?'

'Keep them!' shouted Dougie as he followed Alex outside.

Alex led Dougie away from the casino till they were out of earshot of the bouncer in the doorway. He faced his brother. It was one of those mild nights in early winter when the paving slabs and asphalt have a sheen of wetness without ever seeming to have been rained on and shoe soles scrape the pavement with a sound like striking matches. Around them stood the town houses and mansion blocks of the transnational super-rich, groomed and desolate. Cabs puttered between the lines of parked German cars.

'Did you think she would come?' said Alex.

'Aye.' Dougie made a movement of his shoulders that could have been a shrug or a nervous twitch.

'She told me what happened,' said Alex. 'Just before your messages started coming in. It's going to be on the Moral Foundation on Sunday.'

'I don't know what that is.'

'Everyone's going to know what you did. You thought you were going to win some money and the two of you'd run off to a desert island?'

'Thought didn't come into it,' said Dougie.

'How can you do it? How can you do the things you do?

You borrow a hundred and twenty thousand pounds from your brother and instead of paying him back you have sex with his partner. You have two little daughters whose mothers are struggling to get by and you throw away two hundred quid in the casino. How? Isn't there ever a voice in your head that says "no"?'

'I just . . .' Dougie looked around, opening and closing his mouth. He was like a child who suddenly remembers that the ruins through which he is happily wandering are the ruins of the man he would become. 'Yeah, I've got one of those wee guys who says "no". He's a nice guy, like a lawyer or a professor or a politician. It's not like I don't have him in my head. But he seems too much of an achiever for me.'

Alex sat on the steps leading to somebody's front door and rested his head in his hands. Dougie sat next to him and lit a cigarette.

'I'd like to be angry with you or Bec,' said Alex. 'It'd be interesting to punch you in the face and see how the blood came out. Give you a nice black eye.'

'I wish you would.'

Alex shrugged, took the cigarette from his brother, drew on it and gave it back. 'I know you do. Bec's the same. The two of you are more like each other than either of you are like me. There's the idea you want forgiveness and love and really you're feeling *How weak he is.*'

'Don't feel bad about not giving me a kicking,' said Dougie. 'Look at me. I'm like some new product that comes with its own punishment included. Just add sex and money.'

'That's not a new product,' said Alex.

He took Dougie to a hotel and paid for a room. He gave him a hundred pounds and Dougie said he'd pay him back.

'I'm not lending it to you,' said Alex. 'I'm giving it to you.'

In the room Dougie kicked off his shoes and took a beer from the mini-bar. He offered Alex one and Alex took it and they sat facing each other on the edges of the twin beds.

'Bec's pregnant,' said Alex.

Dougie lay back on the pillow. He bit his lip and swallowed. 'There's a turn-up,' he said. 'Can they tell whose it is?'

'It's harder with brothers. But they can do a test.'

After a while Dougie said: 'Don't do a test. You want to be a father? Be one.'

Alex listened for noise from the street, or other parts of the hotel; there was none. They were lucky to have found a quiet room. He stared at the light shining down on the curtain from a sort of horizontal box. What was it called, that box? He could spend as long as he liked staring at the curtain now. The folds pleased him and he didn't have to talk. *Catastrophes are holidays*, he thought. *Not part of normal time.*

'This is like Scout camp,' said Dougie. He'd rolled over on his side and his eyes were bright and boylike. 'I hated that.'

'What you did,' said Alex. 'You didn't think you were paying me back in some fucked up way, did you?'

Dougie lay back and didn't speak for so long that Alex thought he'd gone to sleep. Then he said: 'Hey maths boy. In a bullshit card game that looks complicated but is just like tossing a coin, what are the odds of getting the same result nine times in a row?'

'Five hundred to one,' said Alex.

'Seriously? I never would've put it that low. If it was you

you'd know the odds,' said Dougie. 'You'd know the house always has an edge and if you were a gambler you'd know when to quit.'

'You didn't answer my question.'

'Bank your winnings, brother. Quit while you're ahead.'

70

The day after calling the Moral Foundation to betray his sister Ritchie started telling people that he was running again, as if he'd been a great runner, when he'd only ever trotted a few miles a couple of times a week. His assertion that he was running again was taken as a euphemism for the intention to live a materially and spiritually purer life, to drink less, to work harder and to be kinder to others, and he did, indeed, make the pronouncement in exactly that spirit. But having declared he was running again he had no choice except to run. He got up in the dark, before Karin and the children, put on trainers and a tracksuit and a hi-viz vest and jogged out into the cold, heavy silence of the English countryside in winter. All he could hear was the sound of his own breath, the soles of his trainers striking the grit at the edge of the road and the occasional sinister rustle from the hedgerows or gurgling from an invisible watercourse.

He ran for half a mile, then walked, sometimes stopping altogether to rest. He stood panting with his hands on his sides, breathing in the smell of rotting leaves. Cars announced themselves by the glow and fade of their headlights far away on bends and rises, like miniature moons rolling up and down the crooked lanes, giving Ritchie enough time to start running so that when they passed they would see him moving powerfully and confidently along through the dark. By the time he reached the first village east of Petersmere it was light. Old people waved to him from their gardens and he waved back. He didn't know them and he wondered if they recognised him from TV or whether, driven from sleep in the early hours by the mysterious conditions of the old, they had a lonely yearning for community.

Ritchie didn't know if Karin had noticed the restoration of his contentment, but he wanted her to be unsure what drove him. He didn't like the amount of time she was spending with The What; he didn't like the thirty-date tour they'd lined up for spring. His love of the music they were making didn't seem to him to contradict the hostility he felt towards his wife over her leaving home for the best part of two months. He didn't notice that as soon as he'd betrayed his sister his love for Karin reverted to the wary, questioning, competitive condition that had prevailed before Val Oatman first threatened him.

It was on Ritchie's mind, when he trotted homewards on Saturday morning, that the next day his sister, who had no idea she'd been exposed, would be the victim of Val's revenge. It hurt him but the pain was outside, not inside as it had been before. Ritchie had found it so easy to absolve himself of treachery that he was no longer conscious of the absolution. It seemed to him to be chance that he'd become the bridge between Val's desire for vengeance and what he now thought of as Bec's promiscuity. He'd hated having to nominate a lawyer but when the lawyer called to tell him he'd read through the certificate of immunity from the Moral Foundation and as far as he could tell it offered a watertight guarantee that the MF wouldn't make public anything they'd found or might in future find out about his private life, he felt safe.

Louise and Nicole could still tell what they knew but one and a half years had passed since he'd seen or spoken to either of them. Ritchie decided that next day, when Bec woke up to the harshness of the world, when she was introduced to the reality that the media only ever canonises you in order to damn you harder later, he'd help her. She'd call him in a panic, asking him what she should do, and he'd calm her down and tell her it wasn't the end, that people would forget.

Back at the house he was making himself a fry-up when a text message came from Bec. Unaccountably she was at the cemetery where their father was buried.

At Brakesborne. Dad's memory pulled down. Horrible. Come now.

Ritchie didn't want to meet his sister on the eve of her downfall. He called her and she didn't answer. Surely, he thought, she could deal with the vandalism of a gravestone herself? But Karin insisted that he go.

The cemetery was in Dorset. The last time he visited had been with Karin and the children. He remembered Karin swooping on Ruby at the graveside, lifting her up and carrying her off to a line of trees at a run so the infant wouldn't pee on hallowed ground. He remembered watching his daughter's little bare legs swinging from side to side as Karin ran away from him and Dan, thinking that if his daughter was being stolen it would look like this, and feeling foolish (he'd called himself an agnostic then) because his father's name on the gravestone and the presence of a box with his father's bones underneath it made him feel that his father was watching him. As he remembered, he remembered more. Karin and he had fought in front of the children, exchanged bitter words, so bitter that Dan had walked away, not wanting to hear, and in Karin's snatching up of Ruby, besides bodily necessity, there *had* been a kind of taking away, an anger against him; and he'd been there by the gravestone, alone with his dead father, looking at his son stumbling off in tears in one direction, his wife and daughter running into the distance in the other, and had felt alone, cut off in a fragment of the present while the future fled from him and the past went dark.

There was a car in the parking bay in front of the church-yard when Ritchie arrived. The ground rose in a gradual slope from the road towards the church at the far side and when Ritchie passed through the lich-gate, beyond the screen of yew trees, he could see the graves paraded in ragged tiers, but couldn't see Bec. He wasn't getting a signal on his phone. He walked up the gravel path towards the church, remembering how hot it had been on the day of the funeral. There were sweat patches under the armpits of the Marines carrying the coffin. He'd watched Bec's pale, serious, wondering face and felt a need to protect her and his mother. He held her hand, even though he thought the Marines would reckon it weak and sentimental, and she'd looked at him in surprise. *Yes*, he thought, *you never imagined I'd do that, did you.* His poor little sister! Not so much older then than Ruby now.

Bec stood in the shadows in the church porch, shivering. She watched Ritchie's big silver car pull in next to her little red rental, heard the slam of the door and saw Ritchie lumber through the gate in a heavy black coat and red scarf.

Ritchie couldn't see her. She watched him leave the path and walk slowly across the grass to their father's grave, turning his head from side to side. He stopped in front of the tomb-stone, squatted down and took his right hand out of his pocket to stroke the white marble tablet and run his fingertips across the heads of the flowers Bec had left there. He looked over his shoulder, stood up and took a step towards the church. Bec came out and he stopped and she walked towards him. She kept her hands in her pockets.

He reached out to hold her shoulder and moved to kiss her and she stepped back. An unfamiliar hardness in Bec's eyes made Ritchie hesitate to ask about the undamaged memorial stone.

'I can't see anything wrong with it,' he said. He gestured back at the grave and pressed his hands together. He tried to speak cheerfully. It came to Bec as a frightened smile and she wondered if some instinct was prepping him to beg for mercy even before he knew what she was going to say.

'Do you remember who's buried there?' she said.

Perhaps, Ritchie thought, *she's had a nervous breakdown?* He asked her if she was all right.

'You didn't answer the question,' said Bec.

'You're being silly,' said Ritchie, trying to touch her again. She twisted away but kept her eyes on him.

He said wearily: 'Dad's buried there.'

Just before Bec spoke, it seemed to her that she had an array of words to use against her brother that were both cruel and just. The moment she opened her mouth, she was reaching blindly for anything. She said: 'You have no honour.'

She thought she'd found a weak word to attack him, an obscure, old-fashioned word. In twenty-first-century England honour was not in play. But the four words darkened Ritchie's vision and pressed a fistful of cold needles into his heart. The words of the poem by their father's executioner came to him and he understood them. *The clapper jings the sky.*

'Tell me what you mean,' he said. The coldness of his voice and eyes reminded Bec of Val's transformation on the night they had broken up.

'You betrayed me to Val,' said Bec.

'I don't know what you're talking about,' said Ritchie.

'You told the Moral Foundation that I slept with Alex's brother.'

'Listen,' said Ritchie slowly, exaggeratedly enunciating his words and pointing his finger at Bec, 'I did not denounce you to the Moral Foundation. I'd never, ever do that to my own sister, it's outrageous to suggest I would, and I want to know who slandered me by telling you so.'

'How can you lie to my face?' said Bec. 'Were you born a liar, or did you become one?'

'What gives you the right to talk to me like that? Didn't you hear what I just said? I did not snitch on you. Why do you have to be such a sanctimonious, patronising bitch?'

Bec took a step back, as if she'd been struck.

'Well?' said Ritchie, trying to hide his surprise that he'd called his sister a bitch and wondering how it could be erased from the record. 'Who's been telling these lies about me?'

'You never called me that before,' said Bec. She pointed at the gravestone behind Ritchie and he followed her finger. 'I can see Dad's name, right there, while you call me that.'

'I won't have you spreading this slander.'

'Please stop,' said Bec, resting her aching forehead on her hand. The tears trickled between her fingers. 'I know you're lying. I know what you did.' She looked up at him. 'I heard you. I heard every word. Val played me the tape. I heard you dial the number, and key in the code, and tell Val that I slept with Dougie, and tell Val that you didn't have any pictures. I heard you telling Val that he'd tortured you. I heard you crying.'

Ritchie stared at his sister till her outline burned and jumped. 'Val,' he whispered. How he would love to kill him! He saw how he would hurt Val if he were in front of him now, how he would grab his ears and yank his face down onto his uprushing knee, breaking his nose, then hook his fingers into his eyes and fling him across the graveyard before charging down on the blinded, whimpering demon to kick, kick, kick his soft body with his boots, breaking through bone, tearing flesh and organs, making blood gush.

Hands were pulling his coat. Why couldn't they let him kick, kick, kick?

'That's someone else's grave,' Bec was saying. 'You're going to kick it over.'

Ritchie collapsed onto the ground. His right foot hurt. He sat on the grass and pulled up his knees. He had kicked a hole in the toe of his right boot, kicking some dead fucker's gravestone. He started unlacing the boot.

'He tortured me,' he said, without looking up. 'He's evil.'

'What do you mean, he tortured you?' said Bec. 'How? Why didn't you tell him that I slept with Dougie to get pregnant?'

'Have you told other people?' said Ritchie.

'Alex and Dougie, so far.'

'Not Mum?'

'Not Mum, yet.'

Ritchie pulled off his damaged boot and bloody sock and regarded his mangled big toe. A fresh dose of rage swilled into him and he beat his fists on the grass, clenched his teeth together and growled like a dog.

'Why did you betray me?' said Bec. 'What do you mean,

he tortured you? Did he tie you to a chair and hit you? Was he going to kill you?'

'Worse,' said Ritchie.

'Worse than having to choose between giving up an informer and being killed?'

'Dad's got nothing to do with this. That was a war.'

'All life's a war if you make it one.'

'You don't understand.'

'You're such a coward.'

'I nearly died!' shouted Ritchie. 'I hung myself. I only just managed to get my head out of the noose. It was your fault. You made me feel worthless. You made me feel that I wasn't a good man.'

Bec squatted down close to Ritchie and said softly: 'Maybe you're not a good man. Maybe you're a bad man. Have you considered that?'

'I am a good man!' said Ritchie. 'I'm a good man, I'm a family man, I love my wife, I love my children, and I'm not letting you or Val or any police or lawyers tear us apart.' He stared at Bec. A brilliant idea came to him. *I'm always brilliant under pressure*, he thought. 'This is what he wants!' he said. 'What we're doing now, this is what Val wants. It's his revenge, on you, for what you did to him. He wants to destroy you and me and everyone around us. He wants us to fight and break up and hate each other. He's evil, pure evil.'

'This isn't about Val,' said Bec. 'It's about you. You haven't told me. Why did you betray me? Your sister? And Alex, your friend?'

'I didn't betray him. You did. You slept with his brother. I didn't make you do that. I had nothing to do with it. If you hadn't slept with him none of this would have happened.'

'Why did you betray me?'

'I'm a good man,' said Ritchie. 'Look, I think my toe is broken.'

'I'll have to ask Karin,' said Bec, getting up and striding off down the hill. Ritchie tried to go after her, telling her to wait. Atrocious pain shot up his leg from his foot and he fell over. 'You can't tell Karin,' he shouted. He clutched his leg and screwed up his eyes against the pain, which had spread to his side when he fell.

An idea came to him. Relief bloomed and he realised he was strong and safe.

Bec came back. He could see her legs, dimly. He couldn't bear to raise his eyes any further.

'You can't tell Karin,' he said.

'Why not?'

'Because then she'd leave me and take the children with her, and I'd lose the show, and maybe . . .' he winced. 'I think now I've cracked a rib as well.'

'Maybe what?'

'Go to prison.'

'For what?'

'You know how the Moral Foundation works. They get people to stitch each other up by trading in secrets.'

'What have you done?'

'You know that in Thailand, the age of consent is fifteen?'

The expression of pleading and cunning on Ritchie's face, the hope in his eyes recognisable as hope but hope choked in the grasping fist of a bully who wouldn't let it go, almost made Bec retch. 'What have you done?' she whispered.

'You had sex when you were fourteen.'

'Not with a forty-year-old married man!'

I must be dignified, thought Ritchie. He said: 'Since you insist, I'll tell you. There was a girl who appeared on the show, pretty and clever but not very musical. She wasn't quite sixteen, but she was extremely mature for her age, and a *very* experienced flirt. I knew it was wrong but she was persistent. It was stupid of me to give her my phone number. She wouldn't stop calling. She took advantage of me.'

'She took advantage of you?' said Bec.

'Yes. Repeatedly. Of course I ended it, but by that time . . .'

'She was a child.'

'She was no child. I wasn't the first.'

'What happened to her?'

'I don't know.'

'You just dropped her?'

'She went off with a footballer.'

'So she left you.'

'Yes.'

'Is she all right?'

'What do you mean?'

'Were you in love with her?'

'Of course not.'

'So what you wanted was to have sex with a fifteen-year-old girl.'

'You don't understand. It's not that simple. It's not like that.'

'So Val found out, and blackmailed you.'

'He was clever. He made it seem like it wasn't blackmail.'

'You betrayed me to save yourself.'

'Bec, Bec!' Ritchie reached out to grab his sister's legs and she stepped back. The movement caused him to yelp with

499

pain. 'I do love you but there are priorities in love. I love Karin and my children first.'

'So you sleep with under-age girls and lie to your wife about it.'

'Are you so much better? You talk about how good Dad was, but when I try to forgive the man who killed him, you stop me.'

'I didn't stop you forgiving him. I stopped you boasting in public about it.'

'You put your own children ahead of Alex's brother when you slept with him and you don't even have any.'

'What does Karin think about what you've done?'

'She doesn't know.'

'She doesn't know anything?'

'No.'

'I'm going to tell her.'

'You can't.'

'She needs to know what kind of man you really are.'

'If you tell her about the girl, and about me telling the Moral Foundation about you, she'll leave me. We'll get divorced, the house will be sold and your niece and nephew's parents will live apart.'

Bec marvelled at the earnestness with which he spoke.

'If you tell Karin, it'll get out, and I'll be charged and tried and go to prison. *Teen Makeover* will be cancelled and the company will go bankrupt. If you want revenge, that's it.'

'That's not revenge. It's justice.'

'You can have your justice. You can have a cruel, terrible justice that destroys families and livelihoods if you want. But that's not the Bec I know.'

'I think your family should be broken up. Karin and Dan

and Ruby would be better off without you if you're going to lie and cheat behind their backs.'

'You don't mean that. I don't do that any more. That was the last time.'

'How can I believe anything you say?'

Good point, thought Ritchie. He said quickly: 'I know you think I've not behaved as a brother should.'

'Do *you* think you have?'

'You think I'm nasty and worthless. Doesn't that make me exactly like the scumbag Dad was protecting when they killed him? Dad didn't betray that worthless man, even when they tortured him. I'm asking you to do the same. Don't betray me. And I know that because you're a good person, a better person than me, because you love Dad, you won't tell Karin, or Mum, or anyone.'

Bec folded her arms and looked down at the grass, awed by the vast, alien moral landscape Ritchie had taken her to the edge of. 'You did me wrong, and I'm going to suffer for it, and you're not?' she said. She frowned. 'It seems unfair.'

She was sad and tired, and the world was a heavy burden. To walk, she felt, to lift her feet, even to breathe, would be to struggle against the power of gravity and the crushing weight of the sky in an existence that was designed to do nothing but press people like olives till the last drop of joy was squeezed out of them.

'I don't understand,' she said. 'What's the point? Why are we alive if we treat each other as badly as you treated me? What does love mean if my own brother betrays me? We should be better than this.'

'We are!' said Ritchie eagerly. '*You're* better. You can rise above it. You'll never get a better chance to show me how people aren't just out for ourselves. I'm giving you the chance to show how real human goodness is by forgiving me.'

He felt a sharp sting on the side of his cheek. Bec had slapped him.

'Why does everyone feel they have the right to hit me?' he roared.

Bec, who'd struck Ritchie instinctively in the way she'd try to make broken machinery work by striking it with the flat of her hand, said: 'If I keep quiet you'll never be punished.'

'Don't you think this proof of how morally superior you are will make me suffer for the rest of my life?'

'No.'

'I know you better than you know me. You won't tell anyone. You can't help yourself. You're too kind.'

'You're contemptible,' said Bec. 'I put so much trust in you, for all my life.'

'If you had children of your own, you'd understand,' said Ritchie.

'I will,' said Bec. She began walking off down the hill.

'Wait,' said Ritchie, raising his voice as his sister moved further away. 'I can't walk.'

Bec didn't turn round or slow down. Ritchie began to crawl after her on his hands and knees. Using one of the gravestones he propped himself upright.

'Which one's the father?' he shouted.

'I don't know!' His sister's voice rose from the road. She was getting into her car. 'Both!'

71

Alex was at home in the evening when Bec got back. They reported on their brothers. Alex had bought some cooked chicken and made a salad and they ate quietly together. Bec was surprised at how easily the conversation slid away at a tangent from the things they needed to talk about and how cheerfully they spoke of the steps to childbirth, maternity leave and whether it was time for Alex to write a book. They were gentle and patient with each other. There were none of the usual interruptions from her or driftings-off from him. And yet when they were filling the dishwasher together he touched her wrist with the side of his hand and said 'Sorry', and blushed, as if they were strangers.

They were afraid of the night. They feared what the Moral Foundation would say next day and they feared the bedroom, the renegotiation of the terms of intimacy.

After supper Alex went to his study and Bec tried to watch a film. She felt alone. In the past she would have called Ritchie. She didn't want to talk to her friends, let alone her mother, until she knew what the MF would say.

Pressed into the corner of the sofa, staring at the blur of faces on the screen and mashing the soundtrack into white noise, Bec could think of nothing except Alex in the kitchen the previous day, shrinking away from her onto the floor. He was wrong, she thought: she hadn't wanted him to be angry with her and he shouldn't have been. She did what she did for him. She took the pain on herself, for his sake, yet his greatest concern wasn't about her, or about their family; it was about himself, and whether he was fit to be a member of the human race. What was it about the Comries? She thought of Alex's father, looking out of his attic window and seeing his wife and Harry together and blacking out the skylight instead of going outside and breaking them up. Dougie, too, was filled with a selfish self-loathing, and couldn't be trusted, but he wouldn't have left her alone like this, hidden himself in a study or an attic.

Bec went to bed with a book, assuming she would be awake when Alex came. But although he wasn't late – in fact, he went around the house looking for her, and feared she'd left – she was asleep when he checked the bedroom.

He brushed his teeth, took off his clothes and stood next to the bed, looking at Bec's face on the pillow. *Here in the shared bed*, he thought, *this is where it all changes, or doesn't change.* The sex was the least of it, as far as sharing was concerned. These days even kings and billionaires lived like the purest Communists where the bed was concerned. You shared the sheet, the quilt, the mattress, the air. You cooperated or bickered over lighting. You woke each other with your thrashing, your snoring, your nightmares, your needy bladder. If one spoke, the other had to answer. You were naked. You were vulnerable. But if you were frightened, there was someone to hold.

And the worst of it was, the two of you were never alone. Even before the children turned up and even after the children left there was someone else in the room — an entity. You never knew. It might be Excitement, capering all over the bed in a spangled leotard, it might be the corpse of Love lying on the floor in a pool of blood, it might be the matronly Domesticity clacking her knitting needles in the corner, it might be the pale clerk of Boredom examining his nails by the window. Tonight Love, shabby and bruised, was pushing him towards Bec, but in order to lie down beside her, he had to get into bed with Infidelity.

Alex lifted the quilt and slid in next to Bec, who stirred but didn't wake up. He lay straight, not touching her, feeling her warmth but feeling too the almost corporeal presence between them. While he was wondering what that presence was — his own construct, some hormonal taboo, a prejudice of social conditioning — Bec rolled over and wrapped herself around him, and he yielded to her embrace, her human heat and fullness, gratefully.

They woke up at five and at six sat in front of Bec's laptop, looking at the home page of the Moral Foundation. It was still showing the previous week's exposé. Bec pressed refresh on the browser and the page changed to show a new story.

It read:

'FOUNTAIN OF YOUTH' SCIENTIST IN FAMILY DEATH RIDDLE

Top scientist gives uncle illegal shot of mutant cells just WEEKS before he dies – then gets his house

One of Britain's best known medical researchers broke the rules of the institute he runs to give a relative who later died a shot of highly experimental 'fountain of youth' cells, the MF can reveal.

Dr Alexander Comrie, 42, became head of London's prestigious Belford Institute for Cancer Research last year after the previous director, his uncle, Professor Harold Comrie, retired through ill health.

Harold Comrie, 64, had terminal cancer – but not one of the cancers that the so-called 'fountain of youth' cells, also known as 'expert cells', can cure.

Under the terms of his uncle's will Alexander Comrie, rather than Harold Comrie's son Matthew, effectively inherits the dead man's luxury London home.

Sources at the Belford Institute say that Alexander Comrie used his privileged access, bypassing normal procedures, to take the cells out of the freezers where they were stored.

An agency nurse who cared for Harold Comrie in his final weeks, Judith Tembo, said that Alexander Comrie brought the cells to his uncle's house in an orange Sainsbury's bag and that she helped him infuse them. She said: 'I did not think at the time that I was doing anything wrong.'

Matthew Comrie told the MF that he gave verbal permission for his father to be given the cells, but that the implications were never properly explained.

'My cousin mentioned the cells to me, but I assumed what he was doing was above board,' said Matthew Comrie. 'Now I want answers.'

Perk

It had been assumed that Harold Comrie would leave the house to Matthew, his only child, when he died.

But in a highly unusual move, Harold Comrie bequeathed the

house to the institute as a free perk for its director.

'I know my cousin knew about the will when he administered the cells. I don't know whether the cells had anything to do with the speed of my father's death,' said Matthew Comrie, who is one of Lancashire's assistant education directors.

'But now I know that he should never have been given them. It's all very troubling.'

Alexander Comrie shot to fame last year with a paper in the journal *Nature* claiming that expert cells, which his uncle first discovered, could make humans immortal.

The claim has attracted increasing controversy. Sources say there was already concern that appointing Alexander Comrie as his uncle's successor could expose the institute to accusations of nepotism.

Breach

Soon after Harold Comrie died Alexander Comrie and his girlfriend, Rebecca Shepherd, moved into the late director's house, a £1.5 million terraced property on Islington's exclusive Citron Square.

Dr Ben Norridge, a specialist in medical ethics at Oswestry University, said: 'Expert cell therapy is a highly experimental treatment that should only be administered to patients under strict protocols and only when the patient is suffering from a very specific kind of cancer.

'What the junior Comrie did is an astonishing breach of elementary medical ethics. It breaks all the rules. I expect they'll throw the book at him.'

Alexander Comrie's actions put the BBC in a dilemma over his role as presenter of the organisation's soon to be released documentary about ageing, *Why Not Live Forever?*

Drunken

Last year Shepherd and Alexander Comrie were hailed in the media as 'science's golden couple'.k

Before becoming the head of a global malaria prevention campaign recently, Shepherd, daughter of murdered Special Boat Service hero Captain Gregory Shepherd, led a successful effort to develop a vaccine for the disease.

She is the sister of *Teen Makeover* producer and ex-Lazygods front man Ritchie Shepherd.

Since moving into his late uncle's house Alexander Comrie and Shepherd are understood to have

made inroads into the former director's extensive cellar of vintage
wines, which he bequeathed to them
personally.

Neighbours describe a series of
late, noisy parties at the house.
Comrie and Shepherd are reported
to have been seen cycling round the
square late at night singing drunkenly in the company of Alexander
Comrie's brother Douglas, a postal
worker.

72

For the rest of the day it seemed to Alex that everyone – Bec, his colleagues, his parents, friends from different continents, people who knew him and who had known Harry – was on his side. On Monday lawyers got involved. In them Alex perceived the power to enter a room and without any obvious effort make everyone in it move apart until nobody was within touching distance. He was interviewed by the police, who were annoyed to be obliged to do it by the Moral Foundation, and took their annoyance out on Alex in the form of a stern-ness that every attempt by him to lighten made colder.

The trustees interviewed him in the board room. In the larger-than-life full-length portrait behind their heads Belford was looking off into the distance and as the interrogation went on Alex kept glancing at the founder's baggy blue suit, white moustache and watery blue eyes. It seemed to him that the giant Belford knew what was happening and was pretending not to see or hear what was going on beneath him.

Why, the deputy chairman of the trustees asked Alex, had he not followed proper procedures, when he'd been a working scientist for twenty years?

'If I'd followed proper procedures, I wouldn't have been able to give him the cells,' said Alex.

'Then you shouldn't have.'

'I knew it wouldn't help him. I think he did, too. But we knew it wouldn't hurt him. He was infused with cells from exactly the same line when we ran safety tests a while back. They were his own cells.'

'If you didn't think it would help him why did you administer the cells?' All five men and two women facing him had printouts of the MF story in front of them. They had other papers but it was the article they kept referring to, shuffling the two pages over and over.

'He asked me to. I wanted him to be happy. He was about to die and he wanted hope.'

'You're not a qualified medical doctor. You had no business carrying out an untried, invasive procedure on such a sick man.'

'A nurse was present. I was carrying out a dying man's last wishes.'

'You have no way of knowing that you didn't shorten his life.'

'I have no way of knowing that I didn't lengthen his life.'

'I find that an extraordinarily cavalier attitude,' said the deputy chairman.

One of the lawyers leaned forward and spoke. He was turning a pen in his hands as if he was rolling a long black cigarette. 'The issue that concerns me is one of consent,' he said.

'They were Harry's cells, it was his request, and his son agreed to it.'

'There's no paper trail,' said the lawyer. 'There are no signatures. You didn't sign the cells out, you didn't tell anyone what you were doing, you don't have any forms, you didn't even make notes on the procedure. Now your cousin is saying that he wasn't given enough background to give informed consent.'

Alex was sure this face of coldness was assumed, that his inquisitors had forgotten they could relax and deal with it like the decent human beings they were. He leaned forward, spread out his hands in front of him, smiling and frowning, looking from face to face.

'You knew my uncle,' he said. 'He was a great man. He didn't want to die, and he was afraid of not having done enough to be remembered after he died. It didn't seem wrong to give him what he wanted when nobody would be hurt by it. I didn't want to live in his house. I didn't ask for his wine. I didn't want to give him the cells. I didn't want to talk about the cells' potential to inhibit human ageing in the *Nature* paper. I did it for him.'

He thought of Harry not long before he kicked the bucket, petulantly demanding to be taken upstairs when he thought it might be the end. 'I don't want to die in the living room,' he'd said, and a mellow, staccato croak had come from him, the last warm laugh of a dying man.

'Don't you remember how funny he was?' said Alex.

'I'm not sure laughter is appropriate here,' said the deputy chairman.

One of the trustees said: 'Are you telling us that you altered the conclusion of a scientific report to please a superior?'

'That's not what I said, and that's not what I did,' said Alex. His mouth had gone dry. He didn't understand the change that had come over people who'd been so fawning towards him the last time they'd met.

'It sounded to me as if that's just what you did,' said the trustee.

'We're all on the same side here,' said the lawyer.

Alex cleared his throat. 'I don't know what you want me to do,' he said. 'You know what happened. I'll talk to Matthew and if you want me to say sorry to anyone I will.'

The deputy chairman pressed his fingertips together. *How old was he when he first did that?* thought Alex. *Does it comfort him?*

'There's been some serendipity here,' said the deputy chairman. 'Because you're on leave of absence while you make your film, we're spared the awkwardness of suspending you during our investigation.'

Alex's lips parted. The sound of 'ending' persisted in his ears.

'We may need to postpone your return for longer.'

'I have work to do,' said Alex. 'People are still falling ill.'

One of the trustees said: 'Some of us questioned your commitment to the institute when you went off to get your face on the box.'

'You encouraged me to go,' said Alex. 'I sat here in this room a few months ago and you told me that it would be good for the institute's image. Why am I having to defend myself? This isn't a court.'

'The last time we saw you we thought you were a sober, responsible scientist.'

'Nobody told me I wouldn't be able to have a glass of wine if I became director.'

'So it is true about the drunken episodes?'

'You're treating a report in an online scandal sheet, from a vindictive man, as if that's the truth, and I have to prove otherwise,' said Alex.

'You're saying your cousin is being vindictive?' said one of the trustees.

'Not Matthew. Val Oatman.'

'What do you mean, vindictive?' said the deputy chairman.

'That's a personal matter,' said Alex.

The trustee cleared her throat and looked down at her papers. The deputy chairman looked at the others. The lawyer said: 'It would help if we could be sure you were disclosing all the relevant information.'

'I've told you everything you need to know,' said Alex. He got up. 'I take it you want me to vacate the house.'

'It's an awkward issue,' said the deputy chairman. Alex walked out. He heard someone calling after him. It seemed to him that he was watching people he knew tearing at each other's flesh with teeth and talons in a battle between good and evil in the last days of man.

As the week went on, his heart withered. It began to appear that Harry's decomposed body might actually be dug up. He acquired a lawyer of his own, who said it was unlikely that he would face criminal proceedings. A woman named Jane from the BBC called to tell Alex that in the circumstances the broadcast of the film would be put back by at least a year.

The consequence of Alex's mid-life introduction to injustice was a yearning for the world to be rebalanced and he began to look forward to the moment when Bec would expose Ritchie. He couldn't see a way to punish Val or Matthew or to get them to admit they were wrong. He'd forgiven Bec and Dougie. The only possibility of redress was in the punishment of his old friend, and his desire to see him hurt encouraged him. It made him feel that he was a part of the human story after all. Were he able to choose between the ability to want revenge and the ability to dance, he would take the dancefloor over a longing to see Ritchie in the stocks, but thirsting for revenge was something. He couldn't understand why Bec didn't speak about her brother.

On a dark March afternoon they were together in the living room of the Citron Square house, waiting for the removals van to take them to Bec's old flat. Ragged flakes of snow the size of postage stamps were falling and settling in patches on the roofs opposite, cold enough for the snow to cling to like white moss at the overlap lines of the slates. They'd packed and had nothing more to do. Bec was sitting on the sofa, staring into the fireplace. They'd turned off the boiler and the residual warmth in the radiators was fading. Alex was standing by the door with his hands in his pockets. He went to the window that looked out on the street to see whether the van had come. Bec lifted up the coat lying next to her on the sofa and put it on.

'When are you going to tell Karin what Ritchie did?' said Alex.

Bec shivered and rubbed her hands together between her knees. 'Val was too proud to publish the story about me. He thought he could be cruel to me like a gentleman, by attacking you. That's what he seems to think he is: an old-fashioned English gentleman. Because they could be cruel, couldn't they, old-fashioned English gentlemen? They challenged people to duels they knew they'd win. If a woman offended them they'd kill the woman's lover or her husband and shame the woman's brother, but they wouldn't touch her, just leave her crying there with corpses of men around her.'

Alex sat on the sofa beside her. 'When are you going to tell Karin?' he said again.

'I'm not going to.'

'You're going to keep your brother's secret.'

'Yes.'

'He betrayed you, and betrayed his wife with a fifteen-year-old girl in his care, and he's not going to be punished for it.'

'Not by me.'

'And we've been through hell without having done anything wrong.'

'I did something wrong. I shouldn't have had sex with Dougie. You didn't do anything wrong but what Matthew did has nothing to do with Ritchie.'

'It's not fair.'

'I don't want to give him away. I don't want to break up his family. I don't want him to go to prison because of me. Just because he betrayed me doesn't mean I have to betray him.'

'What about the girl?'

Bec bent forward and reached into her bag. She took out a folded page ripped from a celebrity magazine, unfolded it and gave it to Alex. It was a page covered in small photos of people with heavily styled hair, white teeth and shiny skin in various tones of orange, yellow, terracotta, chocolate and flashbulb white. A circle had been drawn in black pen round one of the faces and a line drawn from the circle to the edge of the page, where the words *the 'victim'!!!* were written. The marked face was of a thin young girl with pronounced cheekbones and lots of eyeliner. She was wearing a tight, strapless black dress and a silver necklace and was grinning into the camera. A boy with a shaved head and an earring, looking shy and eager in a suit and tie whose knot was too big, had his arm around her. The caption read *Craig Arbutnot with girlfriend Nicole*

Culhame. Alex recognised Arbutnot's name; he was a footballer.

'Ritchie sent me that,' said Bec.

'This is him showing you he hasn't done her any harm.'

'He wants to show me he did her nothing but good, I think. She's seventeen now. I looked her up. She looks older in the pictures, doesn't she? It must be the make-up.'

'Or the life. Or Ritchie taking away her childhood. This picture doesn't tell you anything. There's a reason it's against the law to have sex with people younger than sixteen. We don't know how fucked up she is. She might be an alcoholic. She might be on cocaine. She might be on Prozac.'

'She might be. She might have been that without Ritchie. It might fuck her up more to have to testify against Ritchie in court.'

'People like us are always rolling over,' said Alex. 'We never fight back.'

'I don't want to be people like us,' said Bec. 'I want to decide what's right and wrong. I want to be able to do things that don't make sense if you're selfish like Ritchie.'

'That's weakness.'

'Now you sound like the Old Testament.' Tears formed in Bec's eyes. She pressed her hands to her belly. 'I did this for you. I never wanted a child before, and I want one now, because of you, and there's still so much I have to do. And instead of us talking about how the three of us are going to get through this all you can think about is persuading me to take revenge on my brother. That's not how I want to live.'

PART FOUR

73

One day the Moral Foundation collapsed. Its last act was to publish a complete list of sources for the dozens of exposés it had run in its short existence. Scores of people were revealed to have betrayed their friends and colleagues. Since Ritchie's treachery had not resulted in a published story, his name wasn't on the list. Midge's was. When the people on the list contacted their lawyers, asking what had happened to their certificate of immunity, they got various answers. Some lawyers said that the certificates were cunningly worded; they guaranteed immunity from exposure of past misdeeds in return for the denunciation of others, but they didn't guarantee immunity from exposure of the denunciations. Others reckoned their clients had a case. But when they began issuing writs against the Foundation, they found it had melted away. Its offices had been shut down a month earlier and its staff paid off. Its servers in Chile were paid up a year in advance, and no one seemed to know how the data could be accessed. Val disappeared, leaving his children in the care of the sister who had looked after them ever since Val had his breakdown and left the newspaper.

The question of what happened to Val became a perennial mystery. He became more mythic in his disappearance than he had been as the unseen genius of the MF. Each report and sighting was picked apart and rewoven into a set of stories, superficially different, that were in fact the same myth of the zealot doomed to be trapped within the shrinking walls of his own zealotry. He'd grown a beard, converted to Islam, learned Arabic and lived in a compound in Riyadh, where he kept four wives and consorted with Wahhabis. He'd grown a beard, converted to Greek Orthodoxy and lived in a cell on Mount Athos. He'd grown a beard, joined a strict Calvinist sect and lived on a croft in the Hebrides. He was a Mormon in Utah, a Jesuit in Manila, a rabbi in Jerusalem. As for his dovecot of orphaned consciences, the consciences, abandoned by their new keeper, presumably starved to death. Despite the social upheaval caused by the Moral Foundation's last act, their original owners didn't seem to want them back.

It seemed to Ritchie that the end of the MF marked a rejuvenation, a sharpening of senses that had been dull and pinched for too long. He would have felt pity for Midge had his former friend not lashed out at him so bitterly. 'Typical of you to rat on somebody so lame they weren't worth humiliating in public,' Midge said.

Midge had no more idea than anyone that Ritchie had given his sister up to the moral authorities; the right reaction to the absence of Ritchie's name on the MF's valedictory traitor list, Ritchie felt, would have been to assume that Ritchie had never betrayed anyone, and Midge's claim of general astonishment among mutual acquaintances that Ritchie hadn't been fingered was surely wrong.

More than anything in those strange times he took pleasure in Ruby's guitar lessons. He taught her to play Sisters of Mercy one day while Karin was off touring. They sat in Karin's room at one corner of the house, with windows on two sides.

'This is a lovely chord sequence,' said Ritchie. 'Shall we try it? D. That's right. *Brought me . . .* D's the mother chord, she's mellow, she's bright, steers clear of the low strings. You've got to love D. Now A . . . *their comfort . . .* A's like D's husband, absolutely straight, strong, reliable, holding it all together. Then we've got G . . . *and later . . .* G's the son, the one they've been waiting for, he spans all six strings, he's low and he's high at the same time, G's kind of magnificent. D, A, G — that's all you need, you can change the world with those chords. And now what comes along? F sharp minor! . . . *they brought me . . .* it's the difficult daughter, sad, complicated, in a different place altogether. That's right, it's a bar chord. Press all the strings down with that finger. I know, it's hard. And then E . . . *their song.* E for end.'

'Am I a difficult daughter?' said Ruby.

'Of course not,' said Ritchie.

'I'm not sad and complicated.'

'I never said you were, darling.'

'You said you were going to put me on television.'

'I'm sorry, darling. It just didn't work out. Sometimes entertainment's like that.'

Big tears splashed onto Ruby's guitar and her shoulders shook. She began to bawl. Ritchie put his guitar down and tried to take Ruby's from her so he could clasp her in his arms but she clutched the soundbox and twisted away from him and went on crying.

'You said you would put me on TV if I didn't tell Mum about the phone and I didn't tell her about the phone and you didn't put me on TV.'

'Oh darling,' said Ritchie. 'I do lots of nice things for you.'

'I want to be on television,' said Ruby, snivelling and letting Ritchie take the guitar away from her. He lifted her up and put her on his lap. She was getting big. He reached for a bunch of paper hankies and carefully wiped her nose.

'I'm going to tell Mum about the phone,' said Ruby.

'OK,' said Ritchie. 'Let's have a talk about this, shall we? Because Mummy's not coming back till tomorrow.'

'I'll tell her then.'

'Fine. So, let's see where we are, shall we? You want me to put you on TV, and if I don't, you're going to tell Mummy about the phone.'

'Yes.'

'You know something about me that I don't want Mummy to know and you're using that to try to get what you want.'

Ruby thought about this for a moment and nodded.

'You're very clever,' said Ritchie. 'This is something grown-ups do. It's called blackmail.'

'Why's it called blackmail?'

'I've no idea,' said Ritchie. 'There's email, and there's Gmail. Why shouldn't there be blackmail?'

'They should call it Bmail!' she said.

'You really are a clever girl, aren't you? Now the thing about blackmail is, it's like F sharp minor. It's tricky. Do you want to learn a bit about it?'

'OK.'

'Well, the first thing is that if you're going to blackmail somebody, you have to make sure that you're not going to hurt yourself even more than the person you're blackmailing.'

'What does that mean?' said Ruby. She sounded a little bored.

'Well, here's an example,' said Ritchie. 'I haven't kept my promise to you about putting you on television yet, so you want to tell Mummy about the phone. But if you tell Mummy about the phone, then Daddy will have to go away.'

'Where?'

'Just away. Far away.'

'For how long?'

'I don't know. For ever, perhaps. You don't want that, do you?'

Ruby looked down and played with her fingers and began to cry again, silently this time.

'You love Daddy, don't you?'

Ruby nodded.

'You don't want to be on television so much that you want me to go away for ever, do you?'

Ruby shook her head.

'Well, you'll have to keep the phone thing secret. I know it's unfair but that's one of these things you have to learn in life. Blackmail doesn't always work.'

'Why's the phone secret?' said Ruby in a small voice.

'The thing about families,' said Ritchie, 'is that no one has to know everything about everyone. You don't know all the things I've said to Dan and he doesn't know all the things I've talked about with you.'

'Can I have some ice cream?' said Ruby.

'Of course, let's get some,' said Ritchie. He took his daughter's hand and they went to the kitchen together. 'It was the same with me and Auntie Bec and your grandfather,' he said. 'We had our secrets from each other. The daddy you see is like Dan's daddy but there's the dad only you see, your own special secret daddy, that nobody else knows about. And when you grow up and have children you won't show all your children everything, either. Each of your children will have their own special secret mummy. That's the way people are. Now, what have we got? Pistachio!'

74

Two years later Ritchie drove east out of London to a pub in a garrison town he visited every few months. The traffic was jammed on the A12, but Ritchie's serenity was indestructible. He'd break out smiling at how well everything was going. He was living in the world's greatest city again. It seemed to him that the BBC had done him a great favour by cancelling *Teen Makeover* far enough in advance for him to get his next project into planning and slim Rika Films down to a manageable core of half a dozen essential talents. The high of the last-season finale was still there for him to savour and nobody was smart enough to twig what a smash the new show was going to be. When he explained the format of *Sing For Your Supper*, everyone asked the same question: 'How does the cooking tie in with the music?' *When it breaks through the upper range of its ratings target*, he thought, *you'll work it out.*

The first therapists Ritchie tried had expected him to do the work. They wanted him to interrogate himself, to compose the questions and answers while they sat back and rang up the bill. He was passed from hand to hand and in the end found a man he liked, not a mere therapist but a proper doctor, a psychiatrist, a down-to-earth Scot who wore a shirt, tie and cardigan under his tweed jacket and had gone to Ritchie's school. The first time they met, Ritchie, who'd been trained by this time, began to talk about his father. The steady, patient gaze of the psychiatrist made him falter and stop.

'Sorry, but you're not prejudiced against drugs, are you?' said the shrink. 'Some of my patients think gabbing away about their problems is going to stop them being unhappy without them ever having to dip into the old chocolate box.'

Ritchie's mouth wettened at the word 'chocolate'. He watched the psychiatrist take a box out of a drawer. It *was* a box of chocolates, a cheap mass-produced brand, but when the psychiatrist lifted off the lid, there was only one chocolate in it. The other dimples in the black plastic tray held pills of different shapes and colours. The shrink took out a prescription pad, took off his jacket and pulled up his cuffs. 'Now,' he said, 'do you feel bad here –' he touched his forehead '– here –' he patted his stomach '– or both?'

'It's everywhere inside,' said Ritchie. 'Not just at night. Even in the middle of the day I get these feelings of –'

'Hup!' interrupted the psychiatrist. 'I try to steer clear of the whole area of "feelings of". It takes up so much time and one never seems to get anywhere. I prefer to be more concrete. Let's start with your tummy. Do you feel a sense of emptiness inside?'

'Hollowness. Not filled in properly.'

'Good. Is it an absent hollowness, or a gnawing hollowness, or a tingling hollowness?'

Half an hour later Ritchie left the psychiatrist's office with a prescription in his pocket. What a modern marvel! Everything that was hollow was filled in, everything sharp was rounded, sleep was deep and worries were muffled, leaving his true self free to flourish.

More than the pills, more than moving back to London or gearing up for a new show, it was being able to share his life with a woman he loved that made Ritchie happy. 'If I have one regret,' Ritchie would say, 'it's that I couldn't bring Karin and the kids with me.'

A few months after Val's disappearance he found out about the old false rumour that he'd been having an affair with Lina Riggs. He was flattered and began to wish it had been true. And it became true, long after it had died, just when everyone, including himself, decided he really had become a loyal husband. It seemed to him that his love for Riggsy was both finer and more intense, more majestic and profound, than his teenage falling for Karin or his infatuations since then. He liked its simplicity. Riggsy was exceptional, and he loved her, and she loved him, and the fifteen-year age gap meant nothing.

Ritchie told friends he was a happy man, and their surprised reaction to this, he felt, reflected an increasing cynicism he had observed in society. Under questioning – and to Ritchie's annoyance, some did question – he explained that yes, his one regret did unfold into a series of sub-regrets. He was sorry about the way it had ended. It had been his firm intention to tell Karin the moment he and Riggsy decided they were meant to be together, and the only reason he didn't was that both of them were busy. Karin was away with her gigs half the time. Still, he would have told her, and it was terrible that she should have found out in the way she did. Ritchie had assumed that after the Moral Foundation debacle journalists would've acquired a sense of decency and a greater respect for privacy. He agreed that the closing of the gates of the big house, with him on the outside and – thanks to the firm of Sigurdsson, Godwinson and Weinberg – Dan and Ruby on the

inside, had been difficult. He agreed that this was a consider-
able sub-regret of that one regret of his, and he supposed you
could say the sub-regrets had sub-regrets. He agreed that it
had been extremely – he faltered, held his happiness in front
of him and sheltered behind it – the main thing was, he said,
that he saw the kids once a week. They loved Riggsy, he said;
they really got on. It was a beautiful thing to see. Everything
had worked out for the best. Once, when he and Midge were
still on speaking terms, he confided that he'd tried to get Ruby
to stay with him instead of Karin. He'd found her answer
sinister for a nine-year-old. Sinister; a horrible word to use
about your own daughter, but what else could you call it when
she said she'd rather stay with Karin because 'it'd be better
for my career'? Where did they pick up phrases like that? How
did they learn to be so cruel?

Ritchie found a parking space in a steep, narrow street of
terraced houses close to the pub. He dressed carefully for
these evenings: black suit, white shirt buttoned to the top, no
tie, black patent leather shoes, hair freshly cut with a little oil
on it. With the same care, he dosed himself. He swallowed
one of the big boys, the chestnut-coloured 150-milligram
Effexors with the W on the side that looked as if they should
be dropped from bombers, emptied a packet of Cadbury's
Chocolate Buttons down his throat, went into the pub and
ordered a double whisky, which he swallowed in one. He
bought another and waited at the bar. He was twice as likely
to be recognised here, it seemed to him, since he was famous,
and had been three times before, but none of the patrons gave
any sign, presumably because they were too cool to. A couple
was still playing darts on the pub's raised level but next to
them was an old man in checked shirt and fisherman's

waistcoat, bent over his equipment like a boatwright smoothing a keel. The place was filling up. There was a group of lesbians with a corporate look of short hair, khaki jacket and jeans, a set of cross-dressing men with pantomime-thick make-up and tired, fussy frocks, a short middle-aged woman who for no clear reason was got up as some kind of member of the undead and a trio of girls with long curled hair, short tight dresses and high heels. A man Ritchie knew was called Tom, who had no job at the pub, or anywhere, but loved to work, who had a dried ketchup stain on his t-shirt and was three-quarters shaved, began rushing around, panting like a puppy and handing out scraps of paper. Ritchie greeted him by name and Tom grinned wider but didn't seem to know who he was.

Ritchie wrote *Robbie Williams – Angels* on the piece of paper and gave it back to Tom. The background music went off and the karaoke began. One of the cross-dressers went first; he did a decent, husky version of Charlene's I've Never Been To Me. The three girls went together and massacred a number by a TV-fabricated fivesome from the previous decade; Tom performed a superb rendition of a Roy Orbison standard; and the undead woman went up. Ritchie knew what she was going to sing after two notes of the intro. He wanted to leave, and he wanted to stay and listen. He stayed, and the undead woman's version of Karin and The What's hit You Lead Me On was stale and flat.

It'd never occurred to Ritchie that his unconditional love of music was a redeeming quality. A few weeks after their separation Karin's voice was everywhere, singing that song. People who knew Ritchie couldn't understand his eagerness to hear it over and over again, to explain to them how it worked musically, to declare that the boys from The What knew what they were doing, to demand acceptance of his claim that Karin was one of the great balladeers of her time. He loved the song, and he was glad that Karin had given him something new from that never-quite-attainable part of herself that he had always wanted to reach. And now a woman made up like a corpse was murdering it. Ritchie turned away from the performance and said to the girl behind the bar: 'She doesn't get it, does she?'

'Sorry?' said the girl, who was shooting Coke into tall glasses from a hose.

'I said she doesn't get it, the song.'

'Sounded all right to me.'

Tom tapped Ritchie on the shoulder and told him he was on. Ritchie buttoned his jacket, checked his collar and walked up. The yeoman of the karaoke machine ran his finger down his handwritten list.

'Angels,' he said. He looked into Ritchie's eyes, wise and kind. 'Sure you can handle it?'

The old Ritchie, thought the new Ritchie, could have lost his temper. Instead he thought about it. Could he manage that jump in pitch from verse to chorus tonight? *And through it ALL* . . . it was the sort of abrupt jump from comfortable baritone to the high tenor reaches that might leave him hanging out to dry if his vocals weren't in perfect nick, and the yeoman of karaoke knew this well, bless him. 'Is it too late to change my mind?' he asked.

'Try me.'

'Do you have Fountain, by The Lazygods?'

Ritchie stepped away and faced the few dozen people in the pub. He had the mike in his right hand and as the first muffled D chords of the intro sounded he groped with his left hand in the air for a mike lead that the wireless age had made obsolete. D moved to G, then to A, and as the drums, bass and synth blazed out in a golden splendour of sound it seemed to Ritchie that the walls and roof of the pub flew off and tens of thousands of faces rippled like a field of human flowers below him. He could feel Karin close to him, his brilliant, beautiful girl, bringing her pick down on the strings and sweeping them all down the foaming river of electric music to glorious paradisiacal damnation. He sang

> *Sunrise*
> *Is only an hour away*
> *And your eyes*
> *Are brighter than any day*
> *And the path is leading on*
> *In the blue light of dawn*
> *To the forest*
> *And the ocean*
> *And the life-love in our veins*

They were with him, the crowd, all twenty thousand of them, the crowd and the band, Karin, Johnny P and The Bat, climbing up to the chorus, building, soaring, with the best always yet to come.

> *Let's all go to the fountain*
> *And drink the years away*
> *Cold water*
> *Clear water*
> *To keep the night at bay*
> *Let's all go to the fountain*

And you and I will be
Forever young!

Ritchie had the mesh of the mike up against his lips, roaring the words, eyes tight shut, tears oozing out of them, twisting his body in all his old stage moves, feeling the resistance of his forty-four-year-old bulk and stiffness as a momentary affliction like a hangover he'd sing on through.

Heartstrings
Are what you most like to play
And some things
Are easier to dream than say
But the road will take us there
Where the words are in the air
To the forest
And the ocean
And the life-love in our veins

If you and I get older, baby
Love gets older too
The world needs one immortal love
Dying ain't for you

'Listen to me now!' yelled Ritchie.

Let's all go to the fountain
And drink the years away
Cold water
Clear water
To keep the night at bay

Let's all go to the fountain
And you and I will be
Forever young!

Ritchie opened his eyes and looked round, confused to be in a small pub next to an old man with a karaoke machine. Karin wasn't there. The audience loved him. They clapped, stamped, whistled and whooped. Ritchie welled up again, bowed to the right and left and ran his sleeve across his eyes. He sniffed and said to the yeoman of karaoke: 'Code of Shame next.'

The old man shook his head. 'One song. There's ten people waiting.'

'Don't give me that shit,' said Ritchie with a raffish smile. 'Did you hear them? We've got to give them an encore.'

'One song,' said the old man. 'That's the rules.'

A young man with tattooed forearms and shoulders twice as wide as his hips came up to Ritchie.

'I'm Ritchie Shepherd,' said Ritchie. 'I'm Ritchie Shepherd, lead singer of The Lazygods. These are my songs.'

'One singer, one song,' said the old man. He nodded at the youngster. 'You're up, mate.' The young man grasped the microphone and tried to take it from Ritchie. Ritchie resisted.

'I've got to do an encore,' said Ritchie.

'No encores,' said the old man.

At the edge of his vision Ritchie saw two dark shapes pass swiftly through the audience towards him. They jumped up, two packages of muscle in black overcoats, and tore the mike from his fingers. They dragged him fighting and shouting to the door, cast him out into the night and returned to their station, brushing their gloves. They watched him pick himself up and walk away without looking back, stumbling once.

'That was Ritchie Shepherd,' said one. 'The *Teen Makeover* bloke.'

'Nah,' said the other.

'What was he saying?'

'He said, "I didn't tell her about the heron."'

'I thought he said "heroin".'

'Heron it was, mate. Totally wasted.'

75

One September Rose packed a rucksack and with the money she'd saved to go to Mecca boarded a flight that took her south. She flew all night. In the morning, when it was light but the sun hadn't come up, she lifted the plastic shutter over the aircraft window and saw a bruise-coloured cloud rising like a rock pillar into the sky. The cloud stretched from the ground to far above the plane, higher than the highest mountain. It was not a European cloud. She was in the tropics. She was twenty. It wasn't her first foreign journey. But when she left the plane and damp, warm air closed around her and she smelled a louche odour like distant sewers, and within it another scent, harder to catch, as if fierce sunlight had heated walls made of aromatic wood, she felt she'd travelled.

Bec was waiting for her just past customs, holding the hand of a small white boy and with a tall African man by her side. The boy turned and seemed to pick Rose out. Bec followed his eyes. For a moment Rose saw her through the screen of what she remembered and imagined. The actual Bec was older, heavier, less tanned and more tired than the remembered-imagined Bec. She recognised Rose and smiled and began to walk with the boy towards her. The glad Bec, hurrying forward, now seemed younger and lighter in contrast to the exaggeratedly aged image of a second before. When Bec smiled three tiny crinkles appeared in the corners of her eyes and Rose wanted to congratulate her on them as if they were a tattoo that she too could buy.

'This is Leo,' said Bec, and they looked down at her son. They tried to get him to say hello, but he twisted away shyly, honouring Rose with a quick doubtful glance when she squatted down to his height. 'And this is Ajali. Ajali, Rose.'

'Pleased to meet you,' said Ajali, grinning and bowing forward a couple of inches.

Leo had light brown hair and brown eyes like Alex, and Alex was who Rose said he looked like, and Bec laughed and said, 'Do you think so?'

Ajali turned out to be the driver. He got behind the wheel, Bec strapped Leo into a child seat and they set off. Dar es Salaam was grimy and covered in cracks and mould, which didn't surprise Rose, but she hadn't expected to see people so busy and purposeful, charging around on mopeds and yakking into their phones. Everywhere they were selling cans of fizzy drink and sweets. Limes and green bananas and fruit whose names she didn't know lay in bright mounds by the roadside.

'No headscarf,' said Bec. She looked at her and Rose knew she was considering her bare arms. 'What happened to your pilgrimage to Mecca?'

'I couldn't get a visa,' said Rose. 'They said I was too young and I had to be accompanied by a husband or a male relative.'

'I'm sure Alex would have gone with you.'

'A Muslim male relative!' said Rose, and the thought of Alex standing keenly among the pilgrims and hurling his pebbles at the jamarat made her double up. Leo laughed with her and bounced up and down.

They stopped off at Bec's office on the way home. Rose was disappointed. It was an ordinary set of offices and labs, with people in suits and white coats, such as you could find in a British city. The only difference was that so many of the people in suits and white coats were black. Rose knew that what Bec did concerned malaria. She'd imagined her aunt in villages of grass huts in the forest, helping dying children with swollen bellies and big eyes. This was like visiting her dad's work, being introduced to a succession of people who bobbed up from behind computers, whose names and jobs she forgot instantly. But Bec was proud, to the point of tears, of having helped bring this kind of boringness to Tanzania, and Rose pretended to be impressed.

They drove down a broad highway and turned off into a grid of streets lined by well-kept walls painted cream and pink. Bec's house was inside one of these compounds. From the outside it was forbidding, with a high gate and shuttered windows peeping over the wall. The building inside the walls had a humbler, more amiable look. In the middle of the lawn was an old tree with a thick black trunk, spreading branches and vivid red flowers that seemed to glow in the sunshine with their own light.

Bec picked up Leo and walked through the house, putting her head round doors, searching, trying to hold back a smile, as if there were something she felt awkward to be looking forward to. She found what she was hunting in a small room at the back of the house. It was lined with bookshelves and had a window looking out on the garden. In it were a small old desk, an elderly laptop with the letters on the keys half worn away, papers clumped in disorderly heaps and, on a couch, Alex, asleep, fully dressed, shoes and all.

'Look who's here,' said Bec. Alex opened his eyes, saw the women and swung upright. He got up and kissed Rose on both cheeks. He was tanned and had more silver on his temples than Rose remembered and like Bec had a deep tiredness. Somebody put their head round the door and murmured a question to Bec and Bec introduced her to Rose as Zuri, the housekeeper.

'Wow, you've got all these servants,' said Rose when Zuri had gone. 'So retro.'

Bec and Alex looked at each other. 'If we stay here much longer we'll turn into real old ex-pats,' said Bec.

Alex grinned. 'So let's go,' he said.

'Alex wouldn't have had time to write if we hadn't had this life,' said Bec, and turned to him. 'Would you? We're not exiles.'

It seemed to Rose that in that moment Alex looked at Bec like someone fascinated by a quirky stranger, wondering how to strike up a conversation, and she looked back at him in the same way. Rose had the sense that four years after they got together they hadn't completely understood each other, and that instead of this making them turn aside, it brought them closer. She thought of how it would be if you had to step over all the things you *did* know about somebody just so you could get to where the things you didn't know began, and then go on, into the unknown. She didn't think she'd have the patience for it. Still, they were scientists. She didn't have much time for science, but she liked watching this.

Alex took Leo from Bec, set him down and asked him if

they should get Rose some breakfast and Leo agreed that they should.

'Rose thinks Leo looks like you,' said Bec. She stared intently at Alex as if, Rose thought, her comment was conclusive proof in an argument they'd been having; and judging by the way Alex turned his eyes away, straightened some papers and didn't speak, he knew he'd lost; and judging by the way Bec bit her lip, she hadn't wanted to win.

Bec took Rose to her room. 'Alex tries to do too much,' she said. 'He's writing a book, and lecturing at the university, and hanging out with Leo, and when I tell him not to work so hard, he says: "But we've got servants."'

'You both look tired.'

'Do we? Are we haggard?'

'Not haggard,' said Rose, blushing. Her heart speeded up; a thought she'd meant to keep to herself rushed to her mouth. 'It's nice of you to have me after what my parents did.'

Bec looked at her shyly. 'It's harder to forgive when it's family. But Alex isn't bitter.'

'That's what Dougie said.'

'Oh, you saw him. Here's a towel for you.'

'I wanted to ask him if he thought it'd be all right to get in touch with you and he said I should. He sends his love.'

'I'll tell Alex.'

'He always calls me English Rose. I asked him why he'd never been to visit you. He said you had enough parasites in your life.'

Bec didn't seem to be interested in hearing about Dougie, and Rose sensed that she should pretend to be tired and let her host go. She showered and changed and afterwards found

Alex and Leo on the verandah at the back of the house. The sunlight on the grass looked painfully bright but in the shade it was cool and peaceful. Alex was trying to get Leo to eat yogurt.

'Help yourself to coffee,' he said. He didn't look at her, and Rose tried to guess whether he resented her, or was just concentrating on his son.

'I didn't tell Mum and Dad I was coming,' she said. 'I don't talk to them much these days.'

She'd said the wrong thing. 'You should talk to them,' said Alex. 'You've seen what a family feud looks like.'

She blushed and swallowed and said: 'It's great that you're writing a book. What's it about?'

'I don't want to bore you,' said Alex. 'It's a science book.'

'I want to know.'

'Well,' said Alex, and in between exhorting Leo and controlling his regurgitations and distributions of yogurt, he explained his book. He was right; to Rose, it was boring. Anyway, she didn't understand it. For thirty seconds or so she tried hard to follow what he was saying. She caught the odd word: 'pathways' kept coming up, and 'cells' and 'proteins' and 'meta-analysis'. Her eyes were pushing themselves shut with almost unbearable force. She drank her coffee and poured another cup and couldn't help yawning.

'I warned you,' said Alex.

'It sounds really interesting,' said Rose. 'But you should write a book about the things you say. You know, when it's late at night and you get that expression on your face and you start getting excited about . . .'

'About what?'

'Like when you came to visit us a few years ago. When I

542

came to empty to the dishwasher, and you were sitting by yourself, and we started talking.'

'I don't remember.'

'You were going around the table pretending to be a big bird. I always think about what you said then. I'm always telling people about how we're on a great migration, and we're born on the wing, born flying through time.'

Alex said again that he didn't remember. And yet he looked happy, as if she'd told him something he'd longed to hear. He frowned, and smiled, and opened his mouth, as if he was about to contradict her; as if, being Alex, he was about to contradict himself.

Alex supposed that Bec loved him, although her sudden bouts of temper, over as soon as they began, seemed to him more frequent. He wondered if she was running a diet of anger for him, like a daily dose of vitamins, to keep him alert. The cell was becoming harder for him to visualise: he relied more on diagrams. *I can't concentrate*, he thought, and realised that it wasn't that he couldn't concentrate on the cell in his head but that he couldn't be distracted into his inner world as easily as he'd been when he knew Maria was giving him all her attention. Bec didn't give him all her attention. She kept some back to regard the mysteries that pestered her, just as he did. It seemed to Alex that love thrived in this uncertainty as it had withered in his absolute confidence Maria was his.

He found that once Leo was born his mania for a natural child came to seem like madness. But he'd been right that he wanted to meet his son, rather than *have* him. The superstructure of paternal love was not quite the actual thing that touched his heart when the boy was in his arms. The love for their children that people talked about seemed like some quaint, reliable old bureaucracy that existed in order for the father to cheat the system and rig up something that actually worked, a contraption held together by luck and instinct that got them through the dangers and occasionally delivered something like joy.

It'd become impossible for Alex to stay on as head of the Belford Institute after Harry's body was exhumed. The post-mortem was inconclusive, as Alex and his supporters warned it would be, and the possibility of criminal charges faded, but by that time the media had taken Alex's reputation to pieces. He was reprimanded by the board; he resigned and found that legal fees and an unforeseen tax bill for the benefit in kind of a free house in the most expensive part of Islington had left him broke.

Matthew and Lettie were challenging the will in the courts, and in the meantime Harry's old house would have stood empty, if it hadn't been occupied by a group of squatters protesting at social inequality in London. The squatters, young, radical and exhaustively educated, became notorious for all-night parties where they danced, drank, took drugs, screwed and argued over art, religion and philosophy. The phrase *Citron Square* became synonymous with a male social type, with bearded, priestly young atheists in v-necks and ties and skinny jeans.

Citron Square was one of two phrases the Comrie-Shepherds bequeathed the culture in those days, the other being *BabyBjörned*. Around the world, wherever two members of the global healthocracy gathered together, one was likely to ask the other 'Have you been BabyBjörned?' – describing the experience of Dr Rebecca Shepherd marching into their office with her infant strapped to her belly to demand funding, support, votes or training for an international malaria vaccine complex to be built in Dar es Salaam. They agreed Shepherd was naïve, shameless, vexatiously persistent; yet she got her way, and they shook their heads and laughed, wondering how the boy would turn out. Bec moved back to Dar with Alex, who was grateful, at first, to escape the northern hemisphere.

Stephanie came to visit them, and was disappointed to discover that there was no fountain-of-youth therapy trial for her to get her name on the waiting list of. *I'll settle for half*, she said, *like Bec's vaccine. Fifty per cent immortality.* Maureen came, having *left Lewis in the attic*, and got sunstroke planting roses in the heat of the afternoon, as the regular gardener clutched his hair and begged her to put down the spade.

Sometimes Batini would drop her daughter off on her way to college, where she was studying to be a legal secretary, and Leo and the little girl would play on the verandah under Zuri's eye. *When are you going to have more children?* Zuri would ask, and Alex realised that he looked forward in time less and less. He felt homesick for the north, for the four European seasons, frosts and long summer evenings. But he wasn't homesick; he was past-sick, the regret that comes to everyone. If Bec was the obstacle to his going home, if Leo was the future, they were, together, his family, the only medicine against the loss of past days.

The notion that the chronase complex might be the gateway to immortality was an easy target for Alex's scientific critics to take down, but it was his speculation that the molecular clock didn't stop counting from generation to generation, for which he had no proof, that came in for most ridicule. Gradually, the chronase theory itself gained traction, and the first signs appeared that, applied in medicine, it would allow a few people to live a little longer. Alex found his reputation hadn't been destroyed, it had been changed; that his journey to the edge of disgrace, together with the fact that he actually had made a discovery, made him what he could not otherwise have been in his time, a famous scientist. He found that what the consumers of news wanted more than the story of a man's rise and fall was a continuous rising and falling, to see him returning from the depths each time with more scars, more grotesque burdens.

The day after Rose arrived they took the ferry to Zanzibar, Bec, Rose, Leo and Alex, and made camp on a quiet beach where the water was shallow far out to sea. Alex went to fetch drinks from a kiosk. Rose lay in her bikini on a towel, propping herself up on her elbows. Leo sat under an umbrella, digging a hole in the sand with a plastic spade under Bec's supervision. In a moment, Rose decided, she'd run down to the water.

'I like it here,' she said. 'You must be happy.'

'I try not to think about it,' said Bec. 'It sometimes seems you're only enjoying the present because you're looking forward to the nostalgia you'll feel for it later.'

'Don't think about it, then!' said Rose. She jumped up and ran off towards the sea and Bec watched her go, thinking how the world threw off young girl after young girl, like flames in the air.

Bec reached out with her fingers and moved the hair away from Leo's eyes, even though it would fall straight back, even though he didn't want her to. She just wanted to touch him. She hated to think she might miss a touch that could never be made again. He moaned in protest and shook his head and dug more fiercely. He was only two, and already she was having to work around his autonomy.

'What do you think's down there?' she said. 'Silver? Gold? Uranium?' She began shaping his workings into neat cones of sand. The story of BabyBjörning had worked in her favour, but it had never happened as often as the legend had it. Carrying an infant around was one thing; lobbying with one was another. It was hard to work a baby into a presentation. They screamed, they shat, they puked, they demanded the nipple. What you gained in drama you lost in coherence. She'd come to rely more on Zuri and Alex. She'd begun to think about a full-time nanny.

The haemoproteus vaccine was still crawling towards production, along with the other malaria vaccines that didn't quite do the job but in combination might. Now that she had a child of her own in Tanzania it wasn't so obvious to her that a live parasite would be his best protection. She remembered what Ritchie had said: *They're not going to thank you in Africa if you cure malaria and all the kids are wearing bottle-bottom glasses and bumping into trees.*

She hadn't spoken to her brother since the day in the cemetery almost three years before. Her mother had been angry with her for not seeming to care enough when Ritchie split up with Karin. Ritchie had called and emailed her for a while, asking for forgiveness, and Bec hadn't replied. His last message had been to tell her of the death of O'Donabháin, of heart failure, in his sleep.

In Northern Ireland her father operated, she'd been told once, at the margin of military control, with his own network, and it had never been possible to fix, from the notes he left behind, the identity of the informer whose life he'd saved by keeping silent under torture. At his trial O'Donabháin claimed to have later found out who the traitor was from another source, and to have ordered his murder soon after her father was killed. There was a body; there was a name. Her father's silence had given the informer a few extra weeks of life.

After he'd visited O'Donabháin in Dublin, when he was still trying to persuade her to let him make his film, Ritchie told Bec about what the old fighter had said, and Bec had been surprised and moved by O'Donabháin's angry tribute to her father's courage. *Having to play the fucking hero*, that's what he'd said.

It seemed to Bec that she'd tried to be something like a heroine, to be something like her father, to draw from the same certainties he stood by. She'd looked hard for the roots of goodness holding up the world. She'd been ready to be supported and limited. She'd been ready for a moral foundation, but she hadn't found one.

Had it been after Leo was born that doubts had set in, or had it been earlier, when she'd fallen in love with Alex? And had her doubts about whether O'Donabháin had told Ritchie the truth come of their own accord, or was it that she wanted to invent a different version of what happened when she realised there was a limit after all, and that she was constrained not by some universal structure of good and evil, but by the needs of the ones she loved?

She'd believed so strongly in her father the hero, who'd sacrificed his life so that another man might live. And now she found herself wanting to believe something else. She imagined him sitting bleeding and bruised in the chair in the farmhouse, looking up at the masked O'Donabháin yelling at him, with the two other masked Republicans watching and pointing their weapons. She imagined him having recognised O'Donabháin's voice at the beginning, and she wanted to believe that he realised eventually O'Donabháin was not, as he thought, going to find a way to help him.

She wanted to believe that at that moment her father decided he would name the traitor, not because he was a coward, but because he had a wife and children. She wanted to believe he thought of her, Bec, and that she was more important to him than saving the informer. She wanted to believe that O'Donabháin shouted again: 'Who is it?' and that her father began to form, with his swollen mouth, the beginning of the letter 'Y'. And she wanted to believe that, at that moment and for that reason, O'Donabháin had shot him, before he could pronounce the word *You*, because the traitor was O'Donabháin.

Bec saw Alex coming towards them with a fistful of cold bottles, hopeful, distracted, loving, as he'd been in the village with the vaccines. Later Rose would look after Leo for the night and she and Alex would have a hotel room to themselves. Nothing could have been less like making love than the evening in Citron Square when Dougie, cumbersome, restrained, damp with fear, had impregnated her in the dark. And yet a strange turning-on lingered; in those moments when Alex seemed to forget her, when their family became all form and process and procedure, the memory of her transgression gave her heart a kick and her desire a dose she could use.

Bec would rather have been sure that she'd transgressed purely for Alex and for their happiness, for the idea that became Leo. But she didn't think it wrong that her love for them was made more sound by the memory of a few minutes with Alex's brother, a moment of choice and freedom and danger and being herself that had its own needle-like purpose, beyond its aim. The memory of the tiny dose of selfish, raw desire contained in an unselfish act of will protected her now that she'd yielded so much to fate. After all, had her father fought his way back to her, she wouldn't have begrudged him the longing for his own freedom, the longing to feel the wind and sun on his own skin again, if only it had helped him get home.

Thanks to

Ghaith Abdul Ahad, Safa Al Ahmad, Laurel Baker, Francis Bickmore, Jamie Byng, John Byrne, George Christophides*, Lina Christopoulou*, Victoria Clark, Natasha Fairweather, Tad Floridis, Caroline Gillet, Courtney Hodell, Max Houghton, Andrea Hoyer, Brigid Hughes, Sandro Kopp, Duncan McLean, Rob Meek, Russell Meek, Susan Meek, Jeanet Pfizer, Linda Shaughnessy, Tara Bray Smith, Tilda Swinton, Tom Whitehouse & Donald Winchester.

Who is not to blame for any science mistakes or implausibilities herein